KINGS OF ALBION

KINGS OF ALBION

JULIAN RATHBONE

WELCOME RAIN PUBLISHERS
NEW YORK

For Alayne, Arthur and Nina

AUTHOR'S NOTE

Kings of Albion is a work of fiction that purports to be set in the fifteenth century. Readers bothered by anachronisms and inaccuracies are asked first of all to consider whether or not these may have been intentional. If they are still bothered then I must ask them to accept that the whole thing could have happened in an alternative solar system on the other side of the universe.

Nevertheless, I did read around a bit.

Once the conceit of placing a small group of oriental characters in darkest England had occurred to me I had to decide where they might have come from. Originally I thought Burma. Seeking information about medieval Burma I got in touch with Richard Blurton of the Department of Oriental Antiquities at the British Museum and told him my problem. 'Not Burma,' he said, 'Vijayanagara.'

Where?

In common, I imagine, with most people who have read this book, I had no idea where he was talking about. He told me, and directed me to the available sources. The Empire of Vijayanagara was the result of the unification of the states of southern India which took place in the late thirteenth century and survived as a unity until 1565. When it was finally conquered by a coalition of Bahmani Sultans it was completely obliterated in an uncharacteristically thorough way: the libraries were destroyed, the massive buildings and cities stripped of almost all their ornaments both sculpted and painted; the surviving population and its civilisation degraded to the status of peasant serfs. For centuries almost the only sources of knowledge about what had been lost were the chronicles and records of sixteenth-century Portuguese traders and explorers, particularly those who penetrated the empire after their annexation of Goa. It is only in the last few decades that archaeologists have begun to work on the huge sites and piece together a new conception of what this lost civilisation must have been like.

Vijayanagara was just what I wanted: a civilisation very probably more civilised than Europe in the fifteenth century, and one about which still comparatively little is known so I could allow my imagination to roam freely. No doubt true students of Vijayanagara will condemn the results on every possible ground and I apologise to Richard Blurton for dragging him into this farrago. Nevertheless I owe him a real debt of gratitude.

I also made copious use of *Indian Art* by Vidya Dehejia, published by Phaidon.

I first discovered the Brothers of the Free Spirit in *Lipstick Traces* by Greil Marcus, published by Picador, and followed them up in Norman Cohn's *The Pursuit of the Millennium: Revolutionary Millennarians and Mystical Anarchists in the Middle Ages* published by Mercury, both classics which were a joy to have to read. I first read of Hassan Ibn Sabbah in the works of William S. Burroughs (whose Family of Johnsons I've also borrowed), though the Assassins figured in many schoolboy romances I read when I was a boy, while, not much later, Eric Linklater's *Mr Byculla* was my first introduction to Thuggee.

Among other borrowings there are short but more or less direct quotations from the *The Heart of Darkness* by Joseph Conrad and an adapted paragraph from Sir James Frazier's *The Golden Bough*. The peroration of Brother Peter's sermon is taken from *Eros and Civilisation* by Herbert Marcuse at a point where he himself quotes from Friedrich Nietzsche and Sean O'Casey. And finally Ali ben Quatar Mayeen and Prince Harihara Kurteishi each owe just a little to Alan Quatermain and Sir Henry Curtis in H. Rider Haggard's *King Solomon's Mines*.

As will always be the case with a writer who is tolerably well read and arguably elderly there may be other borrowings I am not aware of.

No doubt my fifteenth-century England is as out of kilter as my Vijayanagara. I made no use of primary sources. I did, however, read all the popular histories of the period that are in print or could be found in public libraries, and the social histories too. In the end I kept Alison

Weir's *Lancaster and York – The Wars of the Roses* (Pimlico) beside me as the most lucid and in many ways most detailed blow-by-blow account I had found, and I should like to acknowledge my debt to that title. The modern versions of medieval verse which appear are by Brian Stone and are taken from *Medieval English Verse*, published by Penguin Classics.

However, my main source, for all aspects of *Kings of Albion*, the one to which I always turned first and where I usually found as much as I wanted, was the 1911 Eleventh Edition of the *Encyclopædia Britannica* which I inherited from my father: it sits in its case a yard to my right and in all the time I have spent on this book I doubt if half an hour has passed when I have not pulled out one or other of its volumes.

J R
December, 1999

PART I

CHAPTER

ONE

Ali ben Quatar Mayeen ('Call me Ismail, if you must, but I prefer Ali') was a retired trader – or, rather, a rep for a trader, a sort of latter-day Sinbad. Never made a fortune out of it, not until that last trip he took so long telling me about, and even that was not a real, serious fortune. It was enough, though, to see his son Haroun – Ali called him Haree – through medical school in Misr-al-Kahira, which Christians call Cairo, keep a rainproof roof over his head, and buy all the bhang he needed until the day he died. And I mean needed. After two winters in Ultima, or almost Ultima, Thule, Ali's joints played up like hell, especially his knees and knuckles, and especially when it rained, and bhang is the only thing that eases that sort of pain when you're seventy years old. Seventy? That's a guess. Ali himself was capable of putting his age at anything between sixty and seventy-five.

Rain? Yes. For a couple of months a year it rains very seriously in Mangalore, rain, Ali would say, as he'd never experienced it before, not even in Manchester, and even though it's warm rain it got into his joints, made his knuckles swell, and they hurt as if a skilled torturer were sliding red-hot needles into the cartilage between the bones. Knees too. But it doesn't last long, and the bhang helps. In fact, look at it this way, for two months a year he was as high as one of those dragon kites you Chinese fly during your festivities and, yes, the pain was still there but as if it belonged to someone else. And, apart from the rainy season, the Malabar coast of

India, in the empire of Vijayanagara, seemed to Ali like paradise
on earth.

He had a couple of wives, sisters, not yet in their twenties, he
reckoned, who cooked the native food to perfection, saw that the
servants kept the place clean, bathed him, fed him, put him outside
on the patio where the fountain played and the lotus and the roses
bloomed, and encouraged a couple of friends, traders like him, to come
in and swap yarns about old times and old adventures. If he was feeling
particularly well, and it was not too hot, he'd potter down to the port,
drink some lemonade in one of the Arab-owned establishments, and
watch the big dhows with their huge triangular sails coming in over
the harbour bar from all four imagined corners of the rounded world.
There was an Arab girl down there too, who sang like an angel while
she played on a guitarra, nostalgic songs about Granada where she was
born. It was there, of course, that I first made his acquaintance.

When dusk came, his wives took him back to bed and put him
between them so his old bones seemed almost to suck the warmth
and life from their soft bodies and he slept, so he told me, like a
new-born babe.

Not bad, eh?

Who am I? What is my history? Didn't they tell you? I'm sorry. My
name is Mah-Lo, I was born in Mandalay, moved down to Rangoon
when I was a nipper, went to sea on a Malay Arab's boat as ship's
boy . . . but this is Ali's story not mine. Suffice it to say, when I'd
learnt all there was to know about sailing from the archipelagos to Port
Suez in the west and back, I called myself an Arab and a Muslim and got
myself made master of a trading dhow owned by a Malay sultan. Trade
took me up to Nanking on the Yangtze. There the local governor and
mandarin told me I could sell information as well as copra and he sent
me up here to Cambaluk. Which some call Peking.

Back to Ali.

It's not a problem being an Arab and nominally a Muslim in Mangalore.
It's a port and therefore cosmopolitan: they've had Christians there almost
since there were Christians, going back to a guy called Thomas Didymus
who actually knew Jesus and made some converts; Jews who didn't know
Jesus and stayed Jews; and of course the Indians themselves come in all
sizes and shapes – pale Aryans and Hindus, copper-coloured Dravidians,

like Ali's wives, and dark-skinned Tamils. Most of the seamen are Arab and now they're getting Europeans, who come through the Mediterranean, down the Red Sea and across the Arab Ocean. But, of course, they have to transfer to Arab boats for the last leg. I know the Portuguese reckon some day they'll bypass the Arab Ocean by sailing right round Africa and use their own ships for the whole trip . . . I'm wandering. Old men do. Something you'll have to get used to. And, of course, there are Chinese. Like yourselves.

Being a Muslim isn't, as I say, a problem, although Vijayanagara has been at war with them for a hundred years, that is with the Bahmani sultans. A couple of hundred miles north, up beyond Gové, Goa the Portuguese call it, you get into their territory. The war is territorial, not ethnic or religious. None of that stupid *jihad* stuff. Indeed, many commanders and some regiments in His Imperial Majesty's army are Muslim mercenaries. Ali was more likely to get into trouble for being a merchant than for being an Arab. Merchants are noted for being spies, double spies, and for taking remuneration from two opposing sides. There is some justification in this for what trader will deny that the summit of his ambition is to buy and sell in the same market? Trust me. I'm a merchant. I know.

Ali and his fortune. As a result of the adventures I am going to recount, he acquired land, good farmland in the spice-growing foothills of the Western Ghats, with a couple of villages to go with it. He sent what he could to his son Haree and enjoyed the rest.

Once we had started our routine I used to arrive in his enclosed garden three or four times a week. A regular thousand and one afternoons it felt like, though of course it was nothing like as many as that – I doubt if Scheherezade's were either. He said he did it because he enjoyed talking about his life, because he would retain thereby a sort of life beyond the grave. According to Ali, this life is it. There is no life after death, neither as the proverbial fly or bug as certain high-caste Hindus, Brahmins they call themselves, would have us believe, nor in a Muslim paradise feasting off ambrosia and nectar, waited upon by *houris*, entertained by damsels with dulcimers. That, Ali already had.

It was fun, he said, to live again the ecstasies and agonies of a long life from the safety of a wicker chair, well padded with cushions, in the shade of a fragrant cardamon tree, drinking lemonade, nibbling a bhang cake as a *digestif*, and letting his lunch, the main dish of which might have been mutton braised in butter with coconut, turmeric, coriander, cumin and ginger, go down. The rest of the household were taking their afternoon naps; even the enamelled fish in the pool hardly shifted.

'I don't take a nap in the afternoon,' he told me, the first time I took my place beside him. 'Sleep does not come easily when you're old. My girls won't come to bed with me while it's still hot – that's what they say, anyway – too sweaty and I tend to fart a lot after a meal. Actually they're probably copulating with their current lovers . . . If they're not, they should be. At their age I would have been. Where shall I begin?'

'At the beginning?'

Ali ben Quatar Mayeen was born in a small village in the hills near Damascus. When he was eight years old and had just been inducted into the first circle of the mysteries of the Islamic sect his tribe belonged to, a form of Shiism, known as the Ismailites, the local caliph, a Sunnite, took it into his head to have the lot exterminated. In a trice it seemed Ali was robbed of a happy if frugal childhood by circumstances that would be almost too horrific to contemplate now, had I not seen them repeated countless times since, right across the known world, in almost every place I have been to. Only Vijayanagara itself proved free of such horrors. Everywhere one goes it is the same. In the name of God men dismember each other, torture, use ever more vile and yet cunning ways of inflicting pain and death. In a way Ali's family and their friends had been lucky – they were raped and beaten, yes, and cut literally into pieces, but all quite quickly. Nothing compared to the sufferings the Christians inflict on each other when one sect gets the members of another within its power.

On the day that changed his life, that day on which he was born again, he saw his father, his mother, his step-mothers, his brothers and sisters and half-brothers and half-sisters decapitated in front of his eyes, having first been mutilated in unspeakable ways. Well, he would have, had it not been the case that while all this was going on he kept his eyes closed.

'How did you escape?' I asked him.

'I was only six years old and I ran and hid.'

'Just now you said you were eight.'

'I said eight? Just now? You're quite wrong. Six. I should know. Naturally I fled to the safest place I knew . . . my grandmother's skirts. I would hardly have done that if I had been as old as eight . . .'

Well, he's by no means the first unreliable narrator I've listened to.

According to Ali, a Sunni warrior decapitated her neatly with a horizontal swipe of his razor-edged scimitar and as she fell, or rather collapsed, fountaining blood from the stump that had been her neck a moment before, into the cloud or cushion of her apparel that billowed out around her as she sank to the floor with her head in her lap, he aimed a second cut at Ali, who now stood revealed behind her. He would have been cut diagonally in half had he not swayed back at precisely the right moment. Instead of taking the edge, the blade of the scimitar, he was merely scratched with the point. Scratched? The cut was an inch deep running from the outer corner of his right eye, taking off his right nostril, passing across his mouth leaving him with a peculiarly nasty hare-lip, crossing the right collar-bone, which it broke, the breast-bone, which it nicked, finally slicing four of his left ribs and laying open the flesh to the left of his belly. Quite a scratch.

He continued his backward fall and passed out. Now, it appears that the trauma caused by this wound was so severe that he went into a catatonic trance, much like those assumed on purpose by Hindu godmen, so that all his bodily functions slowed almost to a complete halt, but did not cease. And because his heart was beating, but possibly as little as once a minute, there was no force in the bleeding after the initial rush of blood, and what did leak out clotted before he bled to death or, indeed, before he had lost more than a couple of jugsful.

It was winter and cold at nights, the village was in the mountains, and his trance continued unbroken until the following morning. The murderers, no doubt wishing to render the village and land uninhabitable for ever, sowed the fields with salt and, having first stripped the bodies, dragged them all, Ali's family and neighbours, to the wells and tipped them in, hoping thereby to poison them. The wells, that is.

Should he have offered thanks to Allah that he was left to last and was thus at the top of the heap? Perhaps. But, then, it was in the name of Allah that all this had been done.

He came to when the sun reached his exposed posterior and warmed it. Caked with blood, not all of it his own, and racked with pain – most of it actually a deep-rooted stiffness – he struggled down off the pile of corpses at the top of the well, took a brief look round. Apart from the flies that gathered with the sun, and the rats, he was now the only living creature there. The sheep and goats had been taken, and the dogs as ruthlessly dispatched as their masters. He ran. Pausing only to wrap himself in some sacking he found still hanging from the arms of a scarecrow, and plucking a bean-pole from a villager's allotment for a staff, Ali ran.

Not too far or too fast at first, but once his wound was healed he ran a long way. Perhaps he has been running ever since, or at any rate until he fetched up in Mangalore. He slept occasionally, but in those first years not much, and anyway he continued to run even in his dreams. He ran to Baghdad, then Tabriz, and finally Kabul. From then on, for the most part, he walked, rode or sailed.

He assumed the role of beggar, found his way on to the Golden Road to Samarkand, joined a passing caravan in which the ostlers, camel-men, bearers and so forth had kept in mind the injunctions of the Prophet regarding a Believer's responsibilities to the poor more clearly than their masters had, and begged his way with them right up the Silk Road as far as Karakoum and the Roof of the World. He did the trip again and again, and discovered a certain skill at bargaining, at detecting the ruses of cheating vendors and, when the caravan was ready to return for the fifth time with animals laden with silk, lapis-lazuli and gold, he had become the trusted employee of one of the merchants, a Parsee whose leanings were also towards Shiism, and who looked on him favourably.

It would be wrong to say that thereafter he prospered, but at least he survived. For ten years or so he worked for the Parsee as a general amanuensis, dogsbody, factotum. He learnt to read and write, to add and subtract, to keep accounts. Later, as the Parsee aged and became increasingly attached to his godown and counting-house, he employed Ali as his agent, his traveller. He discovered a gift for languages born of the earlier necessity to beg from and live with people who had no cause to learn his own. He also found time in which to study the inner secret teachings of the deeper Shia and took a year or two away from trading to dwell with wise men in a community who live among the mountains that lie to the north of the Hindu Kush.

He returned to the service of his Parsee, who eventually reached the sort of age Ali is now. Ali expected to be made his partner with a loan to enable him to continue trading in the Parsee's name. However, the Parsee preferred a more complete retirement and, urged on by his daughters who wanted to make good marriages into the gentry of the land, liquidated his assets, dug up his gold reserves, and bought

plantations of pistachio and apricot trees, thus raising his status to that of
landowner. Ali continued to act as his salesman abroad and did tolerably
well, selling his ex-master's sun-dried Hunza apricots and green nuts, but
basically he was now a freelance, without the capital to set up as a proper
merchant.

His son Haree? The disfigurement Ali had suffered at the hands of
the Sunni fanatic taken with the fact that he was never a rich man
virtually precluded the possibility of marriage or indeed any sexual
relationship other than the transitory sort that can be bought. He was
not a pretty sight, and as he aged he became less pretty. His left side
slowly collapsed, and his left arm, possibly because a vital nerve had been
severed, withered, though he was left with the use of the thumb, index
and middle fingers. His face was like an apple that has begun to rot: fine
on one side but dark brown and spongily shapeless on the other, and at
almost all times when he was in any sort of public situation he covered
it with the edge or hem of his scarecrow cape, leaving only the left side
and left eye visible.

However, not long after his Parsee withdrew from trading, Ali was
doing business on his own behalf with an Egyptian cotton-grower whose
crop had failed as a result of an attack of weevils, leaving him substantially
in debt to Ali. Now, there is an endemic disease amongst those who live
along the banks of the Nile and the canals that irrigate the surrounding
flatlands that causes blindness, and this cotton-grower had a daughter
who was blind but in other ways attractive and apparently healthy. Ali
married her, having first bestowed on her impoverished father all the
worldly wealth he then had about him. They settled in Iskenderia where
he set up as an agent in the port. Haroun, Haree, was the only fruit of that
union since the cotton-grower's daughter died of puerperal fever shortly
after he was born. Ali put him in the care of his dead mother's cousin
and set off again on his travels but he has paid for his keep ever since.
He never really got to know Haree properly, passing as he did through
the area once every two years or so, but he now has the satisfaction of
knowing that Haree will learn an honourable profession and hopefully
make a reasonable living with less trouble than his father has had.

Enough. I am wandering. A tedious recital of a thousand and one
adventures on the road was not Ali's purpose, but rather an account of
the one big adventure that came at the end. And that is what you want
to hear now. It far surpasses all the others in length and interest, in horror,

tragedy, passion and even, occasionally, in the happiness it brought. And hopefully you will take from it the insights you desire into other nations and empires, insights for which you have paid.

It all began, as it ended, in Ingerlond, but that part of Ingerlond which is on the mainland of Europe, namely Calais, a small enclave whose importance lies in its role as the gateway to the island – indeed, almost all the trade with the island is now conducted through this port. I have heard it said that Ingerlond is the arsehole of Christendom and Calais is the arsehole of Ingerlond. Ali didn't find anything to quarrel with in that.

The main exports through Calais are wool and woollen cloth. Indeed there is very little else the Inglysshe, or Anglish as they are sometimes called after one of the savage tribes that settled there, produce in surplus that anyone could conceivably wish to buy, except possibly tin and lead. Calais is the only town where foreigners are allowed to buy Ingerlonder wool, which makes its export easy to tax, and is therefore known in the jargon of their traders as the Staple. The quality is high, though not as good as that of Kashmere, and much in demand in climates too cold for cotton or silk. The Inglysshe have the art of spinning their wool to a fineness that almost equals silk and of dyeing it too, and of weaving it in artful ways. This fine wool is called worsted, and it was in the hopes of picking up some bales of the stuff in exchange for some sable furs Ali had brought from Muscovy that he was in Calais.

He was staying in a tavern or lodging-house in the quarter that lies between the harbour and the main cloth market, and suffering, as almost everyone does in those climes, from what seemed to be an everlasting cold – his nose leaked like the bladder of an incontinent octogenarian, his chest churned and rattled as if it were a bucket filled with unset mortar, and he had gone early to bed. It was a big bed and, following the custom of those uncivilised regions, he had been constrained the night before to share it with two mariconic tinkers who buggered each other off and on, and a squire, his lady and two children on their way to join the Duke of Burgundy's court. The two infants whined and whimpered until their mother prevailed on Ali to expose his face to them. She told them that he was the devil and would carry them off to hell if they didn't shut up. They did.

However, on this second night, because of the ague from which he was suffering, he had gone to bed while the rest were still at supper and was alone in what the landlord was cheat enough to call his best 'guestroom' when there was a knock at the door.

I remember that at this point Ali ben Quatar Mayeen shifted a little in his chair, then moved the chair so the wickerwork creaked a little, took his head out of the dipping sunlight and glanced across the table at me. 'Shall I go on? I'm not boring you?'

'No, no. Not in the least.'

'You yawned.'

'A moment or two ago, perhaps, when you were describing the status of Calais. But now I am caught in the net of your tale as surely as the Sultan Schahriah was in the web Scheherazade spun. But if you, Ali, are tired, I can come back tomorrow and hear who your visitor was in that dreadful lodging-house.'

'Perhaps that would be better. The house is stirring again, and presently, no doubt, my wives will want to attend me as they usually do when the afternoon gets cooler . . .'

CHAPTER

TWO

·

*T*he following afternoon, when I returned to that delightful patio with its pool of iridescent fish and cages of singing birds and its scent of cardamom, Ali took up his tale. He spoke slowly, with difficulty even after the lifetime that had passed since the scimitar sliced his mouth, but making expansive gestures with his good hand.

Loosening my stiletto in its scabbard beneath the covers, I called out that the door was unlocked.

On account of the grey habit and hood worn by my visitor, I took the figure that came in to be a friar, or mendicant preaching monk, of the Franciscan order. He was carrying a greasy tallow candle that gave off more black smoke than light and, to my fevered brain, made the wooden plank walls of that cubbyhole sway back and forth like the sail on a luffing dhow. I noticed that his robe had been patched with a tiny heart-shaped piece of red felt just above the waist – but I was, at that time, unaware of its significance. He squeezed between the bed and the wall and thus sidled up to where my head lay propped on a dirty bolster filled with unwashed fleece trimmings and set the candle on the shelf above me. I gripped the silver-wired hilt of my stiletto and wished that my palm were not so slippery with sweat. He must have sensed my unease.

'I wish you no harm,' he said, and sat on the edge of the bed, pushing back his cowl as he did so. His face was lean, grey, clean-shaven, apart from a slight stubble, and marked by two deep creases that ran from the corners of his nose, which was large but bony, past the corners of his mouth and gave him a look that combined asceticism with melancholy. His eyes were dark, but in that light piercing.

'You are, I believe,' he continued, 'Ali ben Quatar Mayeen, a traveller and merchant from the east.'

I conceded that this was so.

'But I understand, too, that you belong to a secret brotherhood under which you also carry the name—'

But now I was alarmed and I let him see the stiletto. 'Pray do not utter the word on your lips, or it may be your last,' I said.

'Very well,' but I could see how his thin mouth lengthened into a smile that held both delight and mockery, 'names are power and should be respected. However, I should like you to believe that I come to you as a member of a similar society that shares many of your beliefs. I am putting my life at risk by admitting as much, but hope thereby to gain your trust. I have a favour to ask that may or may not be in your power to grant, but will be easier for you to perform than anyone else I am ever likely to meet.'

I waited to see what would be forthcoming.

'My fellow sectarians have a secret house in the north-west of Ingerlond. Amongst our number is a man, who, like you, came from the distant east many years ago. He is the younger brother of a prince of an eastern country who sent him abroad on a particular mission. He now wishes to return. However, due partly to the fact that both his legs have been cut off through the knee joints and also to certain vows he has taken, he is unable to travel. He instructed me to find a traveller who came from his part of the world and give him this . . .'

He held up a packet. It was as long as the span of a stretched hand, from little fingertip to thumbnail, its width a little less, its depth half the thickness of a large thumb. It was wrapped in black oiled cloth, and tied with rust-coloured leather thongs.

'What is it?' I managed to croak. Much of my success as an agent for traders has arisen from a gift of insatiable curiosity, which I share with cats. Curiosity, you may say, killed the cat, but then you will recall Allah mitigated that threat with the gift of nine lives. At least eight of which I have used.

'I am not permitted to say,' my visitor answered. 'It should only be opened by the man to whom it is addressed or by his direct heir. Indeed,

for what it is worth, my friend, whom we know as Brother John, since
that is the nearest our tongue can get to his real name, added a curse of
some viciousness on anyone else who might even attempt to undo these
thongs. But judging by its weight and shape I would hazard a guess that
it contains pages of parchment, and is therefore some sort of message,
testament or whatever. Will you take it?'

By now, for all I was suffering from a fever and all the other symptoms
I have described, to which were added severely aching knees, that near
fatal curiosity was stirring like a waking lion. Or cat.

'First,' I said, 'tell me to whom this packet must be delivered.'

The stranger's eyes gleamed yet more brightly, and his tongue touched
the corner of his thin mouth. Clearly he believed I was hooked.
Indeed, I was.

'The prince you must take it to is called Harihara Raya Kurteishi.'

Even by then, after such a short acquaintance, I was not able to quarrel
with that 'must', though immediately I suspected that I was likely to be
committing myself to a journey longer than the one I had envisaged.
I cleared my throat and swallowed the evil-tasting phlegm that filled
my mouth.

'And where does he live?'

'In Vijayanagara, an empire which is ruled by John's cousin, a great
emperor who is known as Mallikārjuna Deva Raya.'

I sighed and let my aching head fall back on that noisome bolster. I
swear it smelt of dog-shit.

'Vijayanagara is almost on the other side of the world. Only Cathay lies
beyond it,' I croaked. 'If I travel for half a year I will come to the lands
I was born in, which you call the Holy Land. To get to Vijayanagara I
will have to travel as far as that again.'

'There was a Venetian who went the whole way to Cathay, and others
have followed since. I believe he even called in at Vijayanagara on his
way home.'

'Marco,' I scoffed. 'He went with his father, Niccoló, when he was
twelve and came back a middle-aged man. I am already as old as he was
when he returned, probably older.'

But at that moment there was uproar below, filling the narrow street,
and indeed we could see the glimmer of torches flickering through the
cracks in the shutters of the one dormer window of that tiny room. I
was not then as fluent in the Inglysshe tongue as I have later become,

but the gist of the shouts, bellowed commands, was clear enough. The commander of the men-at-arms who had burst in on our landlord had reason to believe that a foul miscreant, a counterfeit friar, a most evil heretic, was sheltering beneath his roof.

My visitor's visage went paler even than it had been before and with one swift movement he thrust the black packet beneath the bolster and headed for the window. However, before he could pull back the shutters, which had probably not been opened since summer and were jammed, three men-at-arms, clad in chain-mail and steel helmets with rims like those on a barber's bowl, burst in and apprehended him. At least I must presume they did, for I had buried myself beneath the stinking covers of the huge bed. Even cats curb their curiosity at times. And survive.

My stay in Calais was longer than I had expected. First I had to recover from the Influence of the Stars, or Influenza, as the Venetians call it; then, when I came to trade my Muscovite sables I found that they had been ravaged by moths. It took me some time before I was able to find what I took to be a more than averagely stupid Ingerlonder whom I could persuade that these holes were the fashion in Moskova and conveyed a greater value upon the furs. In truth he had the last word. The bales of worsted he gave me in return were similarly damaged: 'Broderie anglaise, my old china,' he said, and slapped me on the back.

All in all it was getting on for a month later before I was able to set off on my travels again, and, though I had no intention at all of going to the southern extremity of the Indian peninsula, I had almost inadvertently slipped that oiled black packet into one of the deeper recesses of my baggage.

My destination was Bruges, and to get to the eastern postern I had to pass through the central square. A burning was about to begin. I do not like to witness such barbarities but the press was such that I had to wait until it was over. It was, need I say it, my quasi-Franciscan friar who was tied to the stake, high above the crowd, high enough for me to be able to see that his thumbs (his hands were bound in front of him) had been crushed and his body broken on the wheel. He was, however, still alive and aware enough of what was going on to spit on the crucifix that a Dominican was waving under his nose, conjuring him to repent as he did so. There was a plaque attached to his neck by a noose so it rested on his chest and it bore the words: 'Self-confessed but Unrepentant Brother of the Free Spirit'.

The flames caught, the smoke rose, and as they did it was my impression that somehow his mysterious eyes, still gleaming with intelligence and possibly knowledge, found mine and for a moment I felt he was communicating to me both a sense of collusion and trust. Then his eyeballs rolled upwards and his whole body seemed to relax as he breathed in the smoke that was billowing about his head. I recognised the symptoms of ecstasy, that most sublime ecstasy of all, the ecstasy of a death embraced, of union with the god within.

The smell of burning flesh remained in my nostrils for a week.

CHAPTER

THREE

For the next three days Mangalore was the scene of a prolonged festival in which the Goddess, in her role as Queen of the Sea, was wooed and bedded by Vishnu to the accompaniment of dancing, music, fireworks and the rest. On the fourth day I returned to Ali's large bungalow and rejoined him in his garden where he resumed his tale as if there had been no interruption at all.

The next two years saw me inexorably drawn eastward as if my soul were a sliver of magnetised steel, mounted on a pin and dragged by a lodestone. No doubt this was in part a response to the trader in me for commerce recognises that a promise given has the strength of a contract, but also there was a more spiritual bond which my Franciscan had evoked. The Brothers of the Free Spirit, whose innermost councils have renounced God as well as the Devil, have their Islamic equivalent to which I belong. Having studied at the feet of the successors of the Old Man of the Mountain, Hassan Ibn Sabbah, I count myself an adept, and it is my duty to do all I can for all who share our disbeliefs, whether they come from Muslim, Christian, or Hindu beginnings.

At this point Ali must have noticed the shift in my expression for he paused with the eyebrow above his good eye raised like an inverted black crescent moon. I took the plunge. 'You are, then,' I stated, somewhat uneasily, 'an Assassin.'

He cracked a walnut between the thumb and forefinger of his good hand and used the digits of the other to pick over the white flesh he had exposed.

'You may say so, so long as you do not attribute to me the practices the vulgar ascribe to us. As you know, I take hashish a great deal, and the word assassin derives from the word hashish. And occasionally I have had good cause to bestow on mortals the supreme ecstasy of death. But I don't make a habit of it.'

This was a relief, and I allowed him to return to his narrative.

My first visit to the Malabar coast arose out of business I had in southern Arabia, at the south end of the Red Sea, in a small port called Mokha, where I was trading silver ingots for woven camel-hair carpets with certain Bedu chieftains. Once we had concluded the deal they sealed it with a beverage I had not come across before, which they called *k'hāwah*. It is an infusion made from the ground-up pits or bean-like stones of a small cherry-like fruit of a low bush, which is grown on the sea-facing slopes of the mountains that border the Red Sea. I was impressed by its beneficial effects: it enlivens the spirit without intoxication, removes headaches, and stimulates mental activity. Moreover, taken with sugar crystallised from the sap of the cane that grows on the plain below the hills, it is remarkably palatable.

So impressed was I with this concoction that I immediately bought half a dozen sacks of these beans and took them to Venice, where I sold them at a very considerable profit. The enterprise was aided by the cunning of a Venetian alchemist I knew who had invented a way of improving the infusion by expressing steam through the grounds of the *k'hāwah* inside a sealed retort. This improved its potency and flavour. He sold the resulting drink in tiny cups for enormous prices in the Piazza di San Marco.

Thinking I was now about to make a proper fortune at last I returned to Mokha only to find that during my absence the local imams had declared *k'hāwah* to be an intoxicating liquor and therefore proscribed by the Kor'ān and it underwent a brief spell of prohibition.

I do not easily give up and enquiring amongst fellow traders learnt that the nearest habitat they knew of that resembled that of the south-west-facing slopes of the Yemeni mountains was that of the Western Ghats lying behind the Malabar coast of southern India, particularly that part served by the port of Mangalore. I bought four dozen potted *k'hāwah* bushes for almost nothing since they were now of no commercial value and booked a passage for them and myself on a dhow bound for Mangalore and its palm-green shore. Once there, I arranged for a landowner who grew cinnamon, cardamom and ginger on his estates in the mountains to set aside a quarter of an acre of his poorer, higher land where the earth did indeed resemble that of the south Yemeni hills. My forty-eight bushes were taken from their pots and planted there. He was happy to gain rent however small from this unlikely patch with a promise of a share of the profits if any accrued.

Since any profit that there was to be made from this venture would be at least a couple of years or so in the future I returned to Arabia, but not before I had ascertained what commodity the Vijayanagarans were most in need of and would pay for most handsomely.

Horses.

The Vijayanagarans' only mounted arm at the time was a regiment of elephant, which, in the well-ordered and virtually harmless form of warfare practised between Hindus, performed a merely formal function. When a phalanx of elephants advanced on infantry it was understood that the infantry would retreat.

The sultans, however, took warfare more seriously; elephants do not like horses and, when faced with a cavalry charge, run amok trampling the infantry behind them and often unseating their mahouts. Indeed, so serious had the situation become, the sultans would surely have overrun the Vijayanagaran empire decades before I got there, had they ever been able to agree amongst themselves. However, they tended to fight each other with yet more vehemence than they fought their neighbours. Meanwhile the Vijayanagarans were beginning to build up a horse cavalry of their own, retaining elephants for ceremonial parades only. But the process was still in its infancy, and at that time, for a prime, partially broken, three-year-old stallion, strong enough to carry a man in armour or service a mare, they would pay its weight in coriander seed or dried ginger.

And in Moskova or Stadholmen they pay for those spices, weight for weight, in silver or amber.

For what – the tenth time in my life?, I thought my fortune was made. However, I did not have the wherewithal to buy horses in any great numbers and had to borrow heavily from the Yemeni Jews in Aden. Nevertheless I got together a string of eighteen horses including six brood mares in foal and, heedless of the warnings of those who know best, put them on ship for Mangalore. Even the ship's captain, who was also in debt and in a hurry to make money, told me to wait a few weeks, but I would have none of it. We were duly caught in the north-east monsoon and shipwrecked on one of the Laccadive coral islands where we remained for five weeks, eating horseflesh, before we were picked up by pearl fishers and taken on to Mangalore.

I was now penniless and return to the Yemen was not an option – the Jews there would have had me impaled as a warning to reneging borrowers and indeed it seemed the only asset I had left was the black packet my Brother of the Free Spirit had given me two years earlier and a handful of gold coin I had managed to keep about my person. I called at the godown of the agent of a Cairo-based trader I had done business with in the past, though not in Mangalore. However, his chief clerk here had heard of me and was able to advise me that Prince Harihara Raya Kurteishi was part of the Emperor's household with a senior position in the military establishment and, of course, resided in the City of Victory itself. In the course of the next few days a large caravan was due to leave Mangalore, headed by the governor, or *nayak*, and I should be able to buy myself a place in it.

A day or so later I joined the caravan, which was indeed substantial, and set off for the hinterland beyond the Ghats. At the front went priests and monks, some wearing jewelled vestments, others in simpler robes the colour of burnt earth, blowing their gilded trumpets, striking their gongs and chiming their finger cymbals, scenting the air around them with frankincense, and bearing on a shoulder-high litter a bronze but gilded and polychrome statue of the dancing, four-armed Shiva, ringed as usual with fire, draped with silk and decorated with jewels and garlands. Behind him came the governor, who was returning to the City of Victory for the great festival of Mahanavami, which marks the end of the monsoon season, the same monsoon that had shipwrecked me and my horses.

He rode on the first of six elephants, caparisoned in velvet with gold bullion tassels and edgings. Next came a score of mounted soldiers carrying burnished spears and shields inlaid with gold, silver, copper and mother-of-pearl, all of which flashed sunlight back through the moist haze. They were there for show – war-parties from the sultanates do not come so far south and none of the civil population has any cause to threaten the lives of their rulers. In this happy land even mountain brigandage is unheard of.

Behind this ceremonial bodyguard came twenty or so donkeys on one of the first of which I rode, the rest being used to carry the impedimenta we might require on the way. Westerners despise people who ride donkeys, reserving the animal for purposes of draught, even though their principal goddess rode one on her way from Palestine to Egypt and later her son, the Prophet Jesus, also used one to enter Jerusalem in triumph. I had no such reservations, especially as by then I had reached an age where riding was always preferable to walking. Behind the donkeys came mules and a camel train carrying goods from all over the known world which, once the monsoon was over, had begun again to arrive in Mangalore.

Forgive me for dwelling a little on this journey. I have been constrained at times to make a mendicant's living out of telling tales of travel on street corners or in places where men eat and take their leisure, and old habits die hard.

First, once we had left the bustle and mess of Mangalore (ports, even in the best arranged of places, are always messy, are they not?) there was a narrow plain some thirty or so miles wide, of wetlands, of lagoons filled with wading birds and fishing boats, rafts and floating villages with, where the land rose a few feet, plantations of coconut palms and plantains. The road, a causeway, threaded its way often across a carpet of lotus whose flowers the women and girls of the villages, Tamils, wove into garlands, which they either wore or offered in homage to the god who went before us. Often they sang and danced, and the twanging of their stringed instruments and the wailing of their flutes signalled our arrival or faded into the mists behind us.

As we left the lagoons we crossed land that was still wet but drained, where water levels could be controlled, and here were the paddy-fields of rice, a bluish green at that time of year and like a haze of fur across the greenish blue of the water. The earth beneath the hoofs and feet of our animals became firmer, so they clipped and clopped instead of squelching, and lifted us above the palms, watery lotus plains and rice paddies. We camped for the first night on the outskirts of a village set in fields of coriander, which almost overcame us with the sweet, fruity, spicy fragrance of its flowers and seeds and the more acrid odour of leaves crushed by the passing feet of peasants.

More pungent yet and peppery were the plantations of cardamom trees on the higher slopes above the village, which we passed through on the following morning, leaving the coastal plain behind us under a nacreous blanket of mist. It came to my mind that somewhere nearby was the tiny plantation of *k'hāwah* bushes I had caused to be planted, but I was given no opportunity to leave the caravan and seek out the plot I had leased.

As well as cardamoms there were groves of cinnamon and hedges of peppercorn vines and, near the copious streams that tumbled out of the Ghats, reed-beds of ginger whose bulbous rhizomes were hung along the cane walls of the dwelling-places to dry. Amongst these spice plantations there were also groves of citrus trees, whose fruits hung amongst their star-like flowers, golden lamps in a green night, including the sweeter varieties recently imported from China.

We camped that second night in the foothills of the Ghats and near the entrance to a soaring but narrow gorge through which tumbled one of the many rivers that fed the lagoons we had passed through and would continue to do so, months even after the monsoons had passed. Already the air was cooler, partly on account of the height we had climbed but also because of the continuous and conflicting breezes that funnelled through the gorge or eddied over the rounded foothills. Much of the area remained virgin forest stalked by jaguars, hunted over by eagles and forming not only wonderful groves filled with flowers and honey but shelter, too, for many animals, tiny deer, pigs and even wild elephant.

But I suspect you would prefer me not to describe every stage of that journey. Suffice it to say the next day the climb through the winding gorge became more and more terrifying, the track narrower, the precipitous drops from it to the cataracts below steeper and deeper until we reached a point when looking down we could see the *backs* of soaring eagles and vultures. Then, at last, the sky opened out again and we found ourselves not at the top of a pass with a descent equally horrendous in front of us, but rather in an upland of broken countryside, riven with valleys that opened out into undulating plains albeit crags still soared above them. This vast and varied landscape now tilted towards the east, for the large rivers of the area ran in that direction towards the Eastern Ghats, through which they tumble along the Coromandel coast.

This broken plain, scarred and scored by rivers, was by far the most fertile land I have ever seen, for the areas the rivers could not reach were served by a network of artificial canals and waterways, carved from the virgin rock or built of cunningly interlocked blocks of stone. Every crop flourished in that rich soil, that warm atmosphere, and so plenteous was the supply of food that the lords of that land were able to maintain tracts of untouched forest as hunting reserves without diminishing the welfare of the ordinary people.

After a day or two during which our path meandered with a river we came to its confluence with a larger waterway, one of the two great rivers of that empire, the great Tungabhadra, and the next day the most wonderful sight I had ever seen presented itself to my eyes as we wound with the river round a vast crag and saw beneath us the City of Victory.

It is a city larger, more beautiful, more harmonious in architecture and in the lives of the hundred thousand who live there, than anywhere else in the world. Byzantium and Rome may have monuments to equal those of the City of Victory, but none to surpass them, and by no means so numerous, and both have suffered the ravages of age and numerous conquests while those of Vijayanagara are at the most only a century old; indeed, building even now continues apace in the suburbs and on the summits of the surrounding crags. Cambaluk alone has ornamentation and open spaces as fine – but forbidden, of course, to ordinary mortals.

Religions the world over have tempted us away from the proper purpose of our lives, the pursuit of happiness on Earth, by promising an afterlife in a heavenly city unachievable on earth. Let their prophets and priests look on the City of Victory and admit their error.

CHAPTER

FOUR

'*M*y dear Mah-Lo, you must have been there yourself. Why am I wasting your time with an account of what you already know well?'

'*My dear Ali, clearly you have not been advised of the new laws.*'

'*What new laws are those, Mah-Lo?*'

'*Since the most recent incursions of the Bahmani sultans there has been an interdiction on all aliens and foreigners from leaving the coastal ports. Trade with the interior can now be conducted only through approved intermediaries.*'

'*I did not know that. What a terrible shame for you. You are not bored by an account of our capital city? Well, then, I shall proceed.*'

The City of Victory occupies a natural basin through which the river flows and which is surrounded by wild crags in a crescent that protect it from attack from all quarters of the compass, save the east. These crags are linked with massive walls of wedge-shaped masonry and the gates are so placed in this indomitable combination of natural and man-made defences that caravans, or approaching hostile armies, have to make sharp turns beneath angled battlements from which missiles and boiling pitch can be hurled and tipped. These gateways also serve as customs posts where tribute and taxes, which are a major source of the wealth and splendour inside, are collected: the City of Victory is not merely a consumer, using its own vast wealth deriving from spices, diamonds and gold to buy in luxuries of all sorts, but is also an entrepôt where traders from east and west can meet without having to cross the deserts, mountains and war-lords' domains north of the Himalayas. At least, such was the case when I first made the trip.

It was at the great west-facing gate that the governor of Mangalore and his entourage and guard left us. The rest of us, especially those clearly not citizens of the empire, were subjected to the usual questions, form-filling, payment of entry taxes and the like, which are everywhere the scourge of anyone whose livelihood has depended on trade. I had to state my business, how I had come to bring to Prince Harihara Raya Kurteishi a package addressed to him, that I intended to seek him out in the next day or two and give it to him.

I have to say that at Vijayanagara (for the name serves both the empire and the city) these formalities were conducted with more politeness and genuine condescension than I have experienced anywhere else, the officials courteous and punctilious and, being no less prosperous than any of their fellows in that earthly paradise, quite immune to bribery. Indeed, they showed a humanity I had never previously experienced from such functionaries, to the extent that when I had to let my cloak drop, their attitude to my scarred and mutilated face and body was not of fear or derision as is usually the case, but solicitude and polite curiosity as to how I had been so horribly disfigured. Moreover, they recommended to me a hostel attached to a temple where I would be well received and not charged at all, apart from what I might feel able to give freely, as charity. Admitted at last through that great gate, I began my descent, following their directions, through the Sacred Zone, to the small temple they had indicated.

The great river itself divides the city into two main sectors, which are built on the steep hills above it leaving a wide plain between. This is filled with fields, especially of cotton, orchards, plantations, parks and gardens, terraced on the higher levels and all irrigated with abundant water, channelled into canals that feed tanks and reservoirs. The loftier of these supply large, ornate fountains, set on decorated belvederes, from which the citizens gaze across the valley to the broken mountain ranges, often clad in mist, a hundred miles away.

This Sacred Zone was filled with temples dedicated to the pantheon of what I soon learnt I should *not* call the Hindu religion, of which the most magnificent were dedicated to Shiva and Vishnu and the Goddess

Pampa, who is identified with the river. I cannot do justice to this vast complex of temples with their endless ornamentation, decoration and colour. There was also much fantastic statuary, particularly at gateways or at the bottom of the many flights of stairs. These were representations of tigers and elephants, done to the life so you almost felt nervous of walking where a massive foot might tread on you, or a large cat might sink its claws into your back.

Every wall is pierced with galleries and pillared arcades on which a thousand thousand images in carved and painted stucco present the lives, adventures and loves of their gods and goddesses, and their heroic avatars. Siva rides his bull, or Rama, an avatar of Vishnu, searches for his wife Sita, abducted, according to legend, by Ravana; the tale continues as the monkey general Hanuman leads his hordes against Ravana. And in places where the vast walls were not divided into countless alcoves and shrines they were filled with statues in deep relief, or were richly painted with murals of dancing men and women, princes and princesses, gods and goddesses, often performing with open joy the act of procreation, which seem somehow to express the fecundity of the area and an eagerness to enjoy and share with others the earthly pleasures of this life.

These decorations are all richly coloured in every hue of the rainbow, with scarlets, crimsons and the deep rich blue of lapis–lazuli, speckled with gold, predominating. Indeed I have not mentioned the gold, beaten to airy thinness on every dome, gleaming more solidly on crowns and sword hilts, inlaid in granite, with diamonds from the diamond pipes that are not far off. Everywhere there are flowers, in beds, in hanging baskets, growing in pots, woven into garlands and hung about the images' necks, flowers white, yellow, red and purple that fill the air with a fragrance that mingles with that of the smoke that lazily wreathes the air from a thousand bronze pots that serve as thuribles.

To the south and below this upland area of temples and sacred precincts, and hardly less magnificent, is the Royal Enclave, then east of that, on the far side of the river with its parks and gardens, the township proper. Lacking the natural defences of the higher places it has its own fortifications and includes the multifarious markets, the artisans' shops and factories, the merchant houses and the barracks of the military.

The temple-hostel to which I had been directed was dedicated to Ganesha, the elephant-headed son of the god Shiva and his consort Parvati, or Pampa, who personifies the great river Tungabhadra. I have said that already? Well, I warned you, my mind wanders at times. One of my companions told me that Ganesha is the god to whom one makes supplication at the outset of any great undertaking so it seemed to me therefore an apt place to stay on the first night of my first visit to the City of Victory, a visit that would take me to the end of the world and back. Or, at any rate, as far as Macclesfield.

The temple itself was small, little more than a large kiosk; an intricately carved roof of sandalwood set on eight slender pillars gave the structure an octagonal ground plan. Under the centre of the finely carved pyramidal ceiling, on a raised octagonal platform, sat the god, a charming brick-red figure with a plump male torso, pantalooned legs crossed on a cushion set in a lotus, with his four hands holding a necklace, an axe, an ornamental sickle and a lotus flower. His elephant head, which bore an expression of open welcome, wore a gold crown, rakishly tilted, decorated again with enamelled lotus flowers while various fine bracelets, anklets, armbands and necklaces of gold chain, pearls and sapphires circled his limbs. Offerings of garlanded flowers, food, sweet cakes and incense were arranged neatly on all sides, and as I stood there admiring this homely, pleasant but rich and enriching figure a small family of husband, wife and three lovely children came in with more offerings.

I should say here that the religion of the Dravidians is not congregational: they do not attend their temples in huge masses to listen to or assist in long ceremonies so there are no huge spaces of the sort one finds in Christian cathedrals or the great mosques of Islam. Believers come singly or as families, to make their simple offerings and commune with the saint, avatar, god or goddess of their choice through wordless meditation.

This charming temple was set in an open garden filled with roses, jasmine and many brilliant and huge flowers unnamed in our tongues since they grow only where the air is always warm and where there is abundant water. There was also a pool where the evening breeze caused lotus flowers to tug at their subaquatic moorings above the gold and silver whiskered carp who sought the shade beneath. Birds with brilliant plumage, some so tiny they were no bigger than a child's thumb, others trailing clouds of glorious plumage, flitted, hummed or strutted amongst the bushes and beneath the palms.

One wall was filled with a pavilion in which a dozen or so pallets stuffed with cotton flowers were set out for passing travellers or pilgrims to take their rest, but not before dark-skinned maidens with almond-shaped eyes, clad in rose and emerald silks, had brought us bowls of rice, spiced vegetables, and cakes spiked with bhang, no doubt taken from the day's offerings to Ganesha. They danced sinuously, dramatically and, I have to say, provocatively to a small group of musicians with long-armed rebecs and pottery drums to which the girls added the silvery chime of their finger cymbals. Some of the older of these dancers offered themselves freely to the more prepossessing of our company for conversation, dalliance and, if the mood took them, love beneath the silken sheets that covered our pallets.

CHAPTER

FIVE

I arose with the sun and breakfasted off ripe mangoes and spiced bread, which I found had been left at the end of my bed, and washed myself in a marble basin set in the wall behind the pavilion. Thus refreshed I made my adieux to the temple maidens before strolling down wide, palm-lined boulevards to the Royal Enclave. It soon became clear that I was part of a swelling crowd making its way to a huge square, whose centre was a magnificent platform some thirty feet high and some hundred and more paces square, made out of granite and rock that sparkled with green crystals. It was pavilioned in splendid fabrics and jewels and girded with as yet unlit flambeaux and torches. As we made our way down, I fell in with a young man whose simple garb, shaven head but proud mien suggested that I was in the presence of a neophyte of some priestly order.

In Urdu, the *lingua franca* of those parts, he explained to me why he and the countless others around us were there. Such was the interest I felt in what he had to say, I walked with him right down to the big square with its platform, leaving the Royal Enclave behind me.

'Tonight,' he explained, and his voice was soft and musical, though quite deep, 'is the first of nine that make up the great festival of Mahanavami, which celebrates the end of the wet season. People are already gathering to be sure of getting places in the square around the platform from which they can enjoy the best views of the joyful celebrations that will begin at nightfall . . .' He went on to describe the form the festivities would take – a succession of dances by troupes from each ward of the city – and as he did so I took the opportunity to examine his appearance more carefully.

He was about twenty years old, perhaps a little more, not tall but, as far as his voluminous but simple gown would allow me to guess, well built, with long hands and fingers and long feet. His head was round and shaved to a short furry pelt with a ridge of longer hair, an inch or so long, running from his forehead to the nape of his neck where it ended in a small twisted pigtail. His eyes were dark, large and deep-set beneath a long bushy eyebrow that had no gap in the middle. Often they seemed focused on some distant or perhaps inner reality, but when brought to earth they glowed with humour and an affection too easily bestowed. His voice, as I have indicated, was deep but gentle, not in the least harsh.

I expressed disappointment that I might miss the performances, or at least be left on the outer fringes of the crowd, as I expected to have to spend most of the day tracking down Prince Harihara Raya Kurteishi. But my new friend insisted that first I must go with him and see where he would station himself in the throng so I could join him there later. Once established at a good vantage-point he would give me directions to the palace or the part of the complex of palaces where I would most probably find the Prince. When I suggested that I might have to make an appointment and cope with the formalities and bureaucracy that protect such high dignitaries in most countries, he told me there should be no problem. All the members of the Emperor's family, and indeed most of the senior members of the Royal Household, made themselves available to the general public for long periods every day; while I might be involved in a long wait until my turn came up, I should surely be seen before dusk.

On our way I quizzed my companion about various aspects of the crowd that puzzled me, the two most notable being the way in which the well-to-do mingled freely with the labourers, artisans and peasants, and the absence of any soldiers, armed men, tribunes, constables and the like. This was not the India, surviving under Islam, that I had come to know on my three previous visits to the northern ports. Here was no apparent caste system, no rigid social codification according to occupation or ancestry, no snobbery taken to the level of designating some people as untouchable.

My friend, who said he went by the name of Suryan, explained to me that the river Krishna to the north, of which the Tungabhadra was a tributary, was not only the border between Vijayanagara and the Bahmani sultanates but also marked the southern limit of the Aryan invasions many centuries earlier. It was the Aryans, he said, few in number but warlike and well armed, who had imposed upon the conquered populace of central and northern India laws whereby only Aryans or their descendants could hold land, bear arms or belong to the priesthood. In time these practices had been codified as the Brahminical system, which gave apparently god-ordained legitimacy to a ruthless oppression.

However, he continued, the old practices continued south of the Krishna under the Dravidian Chola dynasties, then later still under the benign rule of the Vijayanagaran Deva Raya dynasty.

'So what is the real Hinduism?' I asked, attempting to conceal my ignorance of what he was talking about, all of which seemed to him self-evident.

He began by asserting that the word itself was Persian and not Dravidian. He went on: 'Naturally, since the Aryans adopted our religion there remains much in common. We honour the same manifestations of godliness, Shiva, Vishnu, their consorts and offspring, but often under different names and very often without any of their harsher characteristics. Indeed there is a gender reversal in their pantheon since the goddess, especially in the form of the beautiful Parvati, is here honoured above the male gods. But we also honour the spirits of place, of trees, springs, seasons and the like, most of whom are also female. I attach myself particularly to the cults of Rati who rides on a swan, her consort Kama, the god of love, Skanda, who rides on a peacock, and Sarasvati, goddess of music and learning.'

'And do you follow the Brahmins in their pursuit of union with the godhead and spiritual perfection through reincarnation?'

'Not at all.' Suryan expressed some disgust at the very idea. 'The goddesses and gods I have spoken of are all human creations, outward manifestations of the goddess within us, and our exercises are devoted to achieving the ecstasies that enable us to become one with that deity.'

This approached very closely the beliefs and practices of the branch of Islam in which I was brought up, until I suffered that cruel sword-stroke and the loss of all those I loved, beliefs I later learnt to understand better in the fastnesses of the Hindu Kush. I was to discover that this Kaula version went to a far deeper level even than that taken by the dervishes who, amongst us, achieve similar if cruder ecstasies in their whirling dances.

By now we had reached a shaded corner of the great square within the portico of one of the buildings that enclosed it. After first promising to return before sunset, I left Suryan there with his back to a less than aniconic *linga*, the phallic symbol of Shiva, and made my way back up into the Royal Enclave. I had no difficulty getting there: casual passers-by were ready with directions and, as I began to move through the Royal Enclave, minor officials and doormen also helped me.

CHAPTER

SIX

My access to the Prince's presence was, indeed, unchallenged
though it did involve a wait of several hours. Meanwhile
messengers, petitioners, mendicants, suppliers of war materials, inventors of new weapons, and who knows what else?, came and
went, singly or in groups, while vendors selling slices of melon or cups
of cold water, coconut milk and *lassi* made their rounds. I asked the
doormen who stood at the various entrances that led into the further
parts of the building if, how, or when I could be granted an audience
with Prince Harihara. My requests were met with polite assurances that
I would be taken to him in no time at all. However, I soon realised that
similar answers were being returned to almost all who approached them,
so, at last I did what I had not done in two years and more: I parted with
my precious bundle. 'Take it,' I insisted to a doorman, an elderly but
kind-looking man who carried an ebony staff with silver mountings,
'and tell the Prince that, if he needs to know more about its provenance,
to send for me before dusk.'

I then sat down with my back to the doorpost and waited.

An hour or so later I saw him picking his way through the crowd
and guessed that it was I he was looking for. Again I presented
myself to him.

'Ah!' he exclaimed, with some relief. 'I was beginning to fear you had
gone. Prince Harihara will see you now.'

His ebony staff was clearly a symbol of some authority for doors opened to him as I followed and door-keepers stood aside. The halls and courtyards he led me through were beautifully proportioned, not grandiose now that we had left the public area but not lacking dignity either, many with slender pillars, intricately carved ceilings and others with small ponds and fountains. Songbirds fluttered at liberty and butterflies cruised low banks of almond-scented purple flowers. Unglazed windows looked out over the lower town and the great valley beyond. It put me in mind of the Alhambra Palace on the hill above Granada but with this advantage: there, following the Kor'ān, the decorations are either abstract or repeat endlessly in fine calligraphy the mantra '*Wa-la ghaliba illah-Llah*' (There is no Conqueror but God), while here wall-paintings and low-relief depicted the joys of an earthly paradise in realistic detail.

We came at last to a loggia set behind a pool with views of the mountains we had crossed the day before framed in its arched windows. Prince Harihara Raya Kurteishi was standing in one of them. He turned to face us as we came into his presence.

He was tall and well-built, his dark skin glowing with the sheen so typical of his race. He wore a rich gown made of fine buttery-yellow cotton, embroidered with silver, which added to the easy grace of his movements. He also wore a necklace of filigree gold and precious stones, which might have been a badge of office but whose function, I later decided, was probably decorative. His hair was long, worn to his shoulders, and thick, a lustrous black, not unlike the mane of the leader of a pride of lions; his hands were large and strong. He carried with him an aura that was almost godlike, the charisma of the anointed. And, for as long as he was more than twenty feet from you, you would swear he was in the prime of life, not more than thirty years old. It was only as he came nearer that you saw the deep lines in his face, particularly on either side of his mouth, giving a sharper delineation to his cheeks and jaw, the crow's feet at the corners of his deep-set eyes, the furrows in his brow, the thinness of his lips. He smiled often, but always with a hint of melancholy. In short, he was fifty years old at least, about ten or fifteen years younger than I was at that time.

He welcomed me with a nod. 'You are Ali ben Quatar Mayeen, a merchant?'

I assented.

'And you brought me this packet?' A slight gesture indicated a small table on which it lay, but now with its thongs of faded red leather unknotted and its outer cover of oiled cloth peeled back to reveal the leaves of parchment it contained. My bowed head signalled agreement.

'Then it is possible we have much to talk about.'

My well-being, and indeed my continued existence, have often depended on an ability to make quick, accurate assessments of the people I am dealing with, and particularly of their weaknesses. Prince Harihara, I decided almost immediately, was vain of his appearance, and had a high regard, perhaps not fully justified, for his own abilities – characteristics I associate with younger brothers of heirs apparent, cousins of royalty, people who owe their position to birth but would prefer to think that they have got where they are through merit. They bask in the light shed by those yet more privileged by birth than they, and presume upon it – yet they resent it.

And what did he see?

The man standing in front of him looked like a scarecrow. He wore a large, greasy turban above a black voluminous sheet, torn in places, faded to rust in others, and grubby with the food that had been spilt on it. A diagonal scar traversed a face that a straggly moustache and goatish beard did nothing to make more prepossessing. Below the sheet his shins were stick-like and the nails on his long sandalled feet were turned down like claws over his toes. In his right hand he held a staff, as tall as himself, ash-white and barkless with age, on which he leant, his body tilted to the left so it made a zigzag against the straightness of the pole. In short, dear Mah-Lo, he had before him what you see now, though perhaps a little less ruined by age and pain-racked joints.

Prince Harihara was, therefore, probably disinclined to believe a word of my story: it would seem to him, on the face of it, an unlikely concoction put together to cover the fact that I had either stolen the package from a traveller or picked it up on the quay of some Levantine port. Yet this magnifico was ready to listen to the vagabond: that surely said something about the package I had brought.

Had he not already perused the parchment leaves I doubt he would have given me the time of day, let alone a full personal audience. However, having established that it was indeed I who had brought the packet, he went on to question me as to how it had come into my possession. Reserving judgement for the time being on my veracity he concluded, 'No doubt you expect some reward for bringing it to me.'

I shrugged and murmured, 'It's a long way from Calais to Vijayanagara. But my main purpose was to fulfil the request of the man who gave it me.'

'He must have made a deep impression on you in what was, after all, a short time.'

I inclined my head but did not elaborate.

'Did you have any knowledge of what this packet contained?'

I glanced at it. 'When I handed it to your major-domo the leather strings were still knotted. It was not I who undid them. I was told that I would be cursed if I did.'

Prince Harihara picked up the bundle of parchment leaves and eased them apart. The cured sheepskin of which they were made creaked repellently and he could not repress a slight shudder of distaste. 'You have travelled much,' he said.

'Just about everywhere, except the southern parts of Africa and the unknown continent of Vinland, which some say lies west of Europe and east of Asia.'

'And you can read?'

'A little of most languages.'

'Inglysshe? Learned men who work in our libraries have already declared that that is the language most of this is written in. However, they were not sufficiently conversant with that language to translate what was in front of them. Can you read Inglysshe?'

'Bills of lading. Regulations regarding import and export, that sort of thing, yes. I can also ask for a room in an inn, order food, get fodder for any beasts I have with me, ask directions and pass the time of day with any travelling companion I might share the road with.'

He handed me the top sheet of the part of the bundle that was written in the tongue we had been discussing. I read it aloud.

> As John the apostel hit syy with syght
> I syye that cyty of gret renoun
> Jerusalem so nwe and ryally dyght
> As hit was lyght fro the heven adoun
> The birgh was al of brende golde bryght

As glemande glas burnist broun
With gentyl gemmes anunder pyght
Wyth banteles twelve of tiche tenoun
Uch tabelment was a serlypes ston—

'Well,' he interrupted, 'what does it all mean?'

'There are many ways of speaking this language, many dialects,' I replied, 'just as there are in your languages. I travelled and traded in the south-east of Ingerlond, and this is written in a dialect which I would guess is spoken in the north-west.'

'But you must have an idea of what it is about.'

'It seems to be describing a city. A city of some wealth, perhaps.'

'Go on.'

'Certainly it says there's gold burning bright, noble gems and, if I've got it right, twelve different sorts of precious stone.'

'How does it go on? What sort of stones? Does it name them?' He handed me the next sheet.

'Jasper, sapphire, chalcedony, emerald . . .'

'Good, good.'

'Sardonyx, ruby . . .'

'Are you sure it says "ruby"?'

'"The sexte the rybé". I'm sure "rybé" must be ruby.'

'I ask because it is generally believed on this side of the world that rubies can only be found in Burmah and Mandalay. But go on.'

My finger tracked down the page as I picked out the words I believed were of interest to him, ignoring the rest. 'Chrysolite . . . beryl . . . topaz . . . chrysoprase . . . jacinth and . . . amethyst,' I concluded.

'Is that all? Is that it?'

I moved on a page or so. 'It goes on about how the streets of the city are golden and the "wones", I think that must mean houses, are all inlaid with precious stones. And the whole place is big, about a mile and a half square.'

He sighed. A sigh of satisfaction, repletion almost. Silence fell. Water tinkled in a fountain, a caged bird sang.

'Where is this city?' he asked at last.

'Jerusalem is mentioned, but I've been there and it was nothing like the place these pages describe.'

'Could it be anywhere in Ingerlond? Perhaps . . . in the north-west, I think you said?' I shrugged, stuck out my more or less scar-free bottom lip. He insisted, 'Have you heard of such a place? Surely, if such a place exists, you would have heard of it.'

'There are stories,' I ventured, 'but it's a part of Ingerlond I have never been in. The north-west, that is.'

He chewed his thumbnail for a moment and thought, clearly trying to decide how to proceed. 'If you wish payment for the service you have done me – indeed,' he added, double-locking, as it were, the stable-door, 'if you wish to receive a permit entitling you to reside here as a merchant for more than twenty-four hours – you will present yourself to my chamberlain tomorrow morning before noon. You may go now. Enjoy the festival.'

And he turned away, picking up the three bits of parchment he had not let me peruse, on which, I presumed, his brother John, or Jehani, to give him his proper name, had written his personal message to him, in the Teluga language, using the script that is the private preserve of the rulers and nobles of that country, and began to read them yet again.

CHAPTER

SEVEN

Back at the great platform, I found that the student, or monk, I had met in the morning had been as good as his word and had kept a small space for me beside him, in spite of the huge press that now filled the square. He had even saved me a piece of unleavened bread smeared with a spicy paste that he had bought from one of the many vendors. With it he had kept for me a half coconut shell filled with soured cow's milk, *ayran*, we call it, *lassi* is their word – a most refreshing beverage.

The festivities that followed were as magnificent as I had expected, and as tedious. These things always are, are they not? Every quarter of the city had its troupe of dancers, its musicians; each vied with all in the splendour of their costumes and the intricacy of their performance – all of which is wonderful, no doubt, if you are a *tiro*, an expert who can distinguish the finer points that raise one troupe above another. And certainly they looked good, in magnificent multi-coloured robes and costumes, mostly in billowing silks with embellishments in gold thread, huge moulded masks crusted with gems, leafed with gold and plumed with the feathers of forest birds. Some wore their nails long or had artificial ones attached, some swung scimitars in ritualised combat. Some stamped their feet and others performed extraordinary contortions to represent their multi-limbed deities. They blew trumpets, banged gongs, tooted on flutes and twanged their long-armed guitars.

After an hour I was bored. After four hours, with the torches and flambeaux at last burning low, I was practically asleep. And then, to my consternation, I saw these replaced with fresh ones, which, I calculated, would take us through to dawn. I yawned, apologised to Suryan, and told him that I had been travelling on the road and before that by boat for many months without a break, that I had had a long and tiring day, that I was not as young as I once was . . .

'Ali, I'm so sorry,' he exclaimed, 'how thoughtless of me! You must come to my lodgings at once where we can have a proper meal and I can lend you a bed. No, no, please, I insist. Like you I have seen enough for one night. The festival runs for a week and we – I – can come again tomorrow. I shall not miss anything of importance.' Already he was leading me downhill, away from the platform, past the huge stables of the imperial elephants, through terraces and parks lit with lamps fuelled with aromatic ghee, towards the river, which we presently crossed on a wide, magnificent stone bridge, guarded by granite lions.

In apology for the spare entertainment he was about to offer me, he explained that he led an ascetic life, although his family were landowners who could have provided him with all the luxuries he denied himself. However, he was not pompous or preachy about all this – he admired showiness in others, and found nothing wrong with worldly pleasures. For, as he had already told me when expounding the Kauli creed, he, like most Vijayanagarans, believed that what happened after death was at best unknowable and that the highest happiness men or women can achieve, through exquisite and passionate sensation, is that unification of mind and body that reveals the godhead within, all achieved in this life.

He also told me that he shared his home with Uma, his twin sister.

Presently he led me to a small suite of rooms in a large, rambling building, which included on the ground floor shops, the offices of traders, public baths and a couple of small enclosed gardens, lit with paper lanterns. Citrus trees grew in tubs above pools filled with small fish that darted about like shards of light.

Suryan's apartment was lined with, or perhaps even constructed from, a silvery aromatic wood. Its ceilings were finely carved with stalactitic formations apeing the structure of stylised flowers and the more exotic crystal formations one can find in certain mountain caves. Below the dado the walls were hung with fine silk rugs and paintings on cloth, mostly representing scenes of pleasure: hunting, feasting, dancing and copulation. There was, after all, little in the way of asceticism that

I could see, but I supposed that in comparison with the luxury and magnificence of his family's palaces, these rooms might have seemed cramped and homely.

And then something strange happened. While I was still admiring the principal room – indeed, as I peered up at the intricacies of the ceiling – he vanished like a wraith, from my blind side, into the shadows.

'Uma, my sister, will take care of you now, I must depart to my studies . . .' and, just like that, he was gone.

A few minutes later a light glowed beyond a gauze hanging, which I now realised masked a long passage. It came nearer and glowed more brightly, and soon I saw the hands that held it, a silver lamp with a tiny wick above a reservoir of ghee, and the face that seemed to float above it.

Uma was a delight. Her skin was the colour of dark honey and she had long, glossy black hair, which yet had hints of fire and copper in it, whether natural or applied I do not know. Her almond eyes were surprisingly light in colour, a golden brown, though occasionally tinged with green. Her forehead was high, her neck long but sturdy; her shoulders gleamed like bronzed butter. Her exposed breasts were like pomegranates, the nipples painted scarlet. Her lips were full, rich and welcoming. On that occasion, being indoors and not expecting visitors, she was naked to her waist apart from jewellery and a tall beehive-shaped headdress, gold and studded with gems. Her waist was circled with an emerald green sarong of fine silk and gold thread, which hugged her hips before swooping in a V-shape below the rounded temple of her belly to a fastening that rested on her pelvic bone. It then swept outwards from the shadowy places beneath to expose her thighs. Her only flaw, if flaw it was, was that her eyebrows met, curiously, like Suryan's, above her nose.

She welcomed me with formal warmth, kissed my hands, made me sit on a low couch. Then, from an alcove she brought a bowl of scented water to wash my feet, and gave me a soothing infusion of fragrant herbs and rice wine to drink. As she knelt in front of me and I saw the way the coils of her hair made spirals in the nape of her neck and down her back, and as her soft breasts briefly caressed my thighs, old longings stirred my ancient loins.

The ablutions completed, she then brought me a simple meal of rice, aromatic with turmeric and other spices, toasted pine-nuts and mushrooms, followed by fruits carefully chosen to make harmony of colour and taste, sharp and sweet, musky and honeyed.

As we began to eat, she raised her eyes to mine and said, in a voice that was deep for a woman but as gentle as fur, 'Ali ben Quatar Mayeen, you have lived many years, travelled to the ends of the world, and seen many strange and wonderful things; Suryan and I, however, are on the very threshold of adult life, our heads stooping below the lintel, our feet upon the step, childhood behind us and the great world ahead. It would be a favour if you told me a little of what you have learnt, and perhaps, too, what has brought you so far from the inland sea, across the ocean, to Vijayanagara.'

I spoke for an hour or so as the night wore on, recounting some of what I have told you, my dear Mah-Lo, over the last week or so. Prompted by her questions, I overcame my reluctance to assume the teacher's role, and intermittently added something of what I have learnt concerning the nature of our brief existence, building on what I had absorbed at my father's knee and later in the mountains of central Asia, of the secret mysteries of the Shiite sect in which are framed my more formal beliefs.

These, as I have already suggested, coincided remarkably with what Suryan had made of the deeper aspects of the Kauli religion, not in formal dogma or in outward representation but at a deeper level of understanding. Uma attempted to put this in words.

'We follow practices known as the *panchamakaras*, which help us to achieve the state we call Kula. Kula occurs when mind and sensation are united, the sense organs lose their differences, and the object perceived becomes one with the senses it stimulates. That is the only true ecstasy, the only goal worth striving for, and thereby and therein is revealed the goddess or god within.'

'And what,' I asked, 'are the means by which this state is reached?'

'They are many,' she replied, stretching out on the cushions that she had scattered to fill a corner of the room, 'and each reveals the goddess not only in different aspects but at different levels of intensity. For instance, the ceremonial dancing and music you witnessed tonight can bring more than a glimmer, as indeed can the contemplation, which we call *rasa*, of the carved and painted images with which our city is filled and which contribute to making we Vijayanagarans the happiest of people. The Brahmins believe that the highest ecstasy comes from *rasa*, from contemplation of the things other people do or have made. But this is perverse and a mere expression of their belief that those who work with their hands and bodies live at a lower level than those who live through their minds. A yet greater revelation comes to those who sing and dance and play their instruments in mystical accord than to those who merely listen and watch, and to the craftsmen who paint and carve and model. At a lesser level are the joys of eating and drinking as we have done tonight . . . Yet,' she added, with a laugh that chimed like temple bells, 'even here the joy I experienced in making the meal surpassed yours when you ate it.'

'And how,' I asked, 'is the greatest ecstasy achieved, the most perfect fulfilment, the ultimate state of unity with the god within?'

For a moment it seemed she withdrew from me into an inner world, then, returned, laughing again. 'Oh, that is a matter of prolonged dispute between the wise men, the *sadhus*. And what it comes down to is that probably no single activity can produce at one moment the perfect resolution of the separateness that keeps each of us from our god. But that some exercises are more likely to bring one nearer than others is self-evident. Some say the divine moment can come in dance and contemplation of dance; others insist that the taking of certain elixirs is an essential – certainly bhang, which you call hashish, and its derivatives are a help. But there are also distillations of certain plants, fruits and flowers whose habitat and preparation only the hill-people know, which may do even more. Others claim they have found the most perfect enlightenment from breathing in the fumes produced by burning the dried gum of the poppy. And, of course, sexual congress performed with proper skill is a favourite route for many.'

I shifted on my cushions, and, following the spicy food, racked with a delicious weariness as I was, released a small fart I would have preferred to keep to myself. Uma smiled . . . like a mother.

'Better out than in,' she said.

An indulgent mother.

'I have been,' I said, partly to cover the mild confusion I felt, 'to places in the Western Lands where enlightenment has been sought not through pleasure but through abstinence and self-mortification. I have seen crowds many thousands in number in which all have beaten each other with many-thonged whips for hours on end until the streets ran with blood. And I have seen others who have taken themselves to caves in the mountains or tiny temples, and there lived on nothing but crusts and water until, with their bodies almost wasted away, their cheeks heightened in colour, their eyes huge and staring, with spittle on their mouths, they have claimed to see good spirits and evil ones and even God himself. I have to say that most of these I speak of are Christian, and as you no doubt have heard, they are the most mad of all. There is positively no rhyme or reason in most of what they get up to.'

Uma nodded. 'There are so-called mystics in India too, who claim enlightenment by similar means: fakirs, for instance, who run across burning coals, sleep on beds of nails, or contort their limbs into absurd and unnatural postures before entering a trance-like state wherein all bodily functions appear to cease for many hours or even days. Perhaps such people do experience the ecstasy we seek, but it seems absurd to resort to such painful means when the same results can be achieved in moments of pure pleasure . . .'

I agreed, for it was indeed the case that the greatest deprivation I had suffered, in spending a day and a night on top of a pile of headless bodies in a well, had not led to spiritual union, ecstatic or otherwise, with the godhead.

And now, while these last few words of Uma were still echoing in my head, I realised that something was happening to me, to my mind and body, which I could not withstand or control. The walls of the room seemed to blow in and out like curtains, I heard a roaring like a wild wind in my ears, and I felt my fingers, my feet, then my lips go numb. A sweat broke out on my brow. Then, as darkness filled the room and the walls with their hangings receded into it, I became aware of a pinprick of white light that slowly increased in size, became red and spun, like a spiral-shaped comet, trailing fragments of light in a tail behind it. It spun faster and faster, and I felt myself falling into it, or perhaps I was sucked into it, until I became part of it, became the ball of fire itself and I heard a voice, perhaps my own, saying, over and over again, 'I am all there is,' accompanied by a feeling of deepest anxiety and deepest exhilaration combined. Then, nothing, for what seemed a long time, just darkness.

Then out of the darkness came a dark figure, a black-skinned woman with four arms, blood-red palms and blood-red eyes. Below a protruding tongue, which also dripped blood, she wore a necklace of skulls. Her crown bore lotus flowers, but they were purple and red. Her robe was as black as night and strewn with stars, and the moon rose behind her head. She was girdled with serpents. Her voice, however, was soft and seductive and she said, or did she sing?, these words: 'Come joyfully into my arms and you will know all there is any need to know.'

I came round to the sound of running water and chiming bells, with the warmth of the sun on my body and a sweet, jasmine-like fragrance in my nostrils. Opening my eyes, which seemed gummed as they are when one wakes from a fever, I found I was lying beneath a low orange tree or bush whose glossy leaves, black against the pearly sky of dawn, shaded my eyes though not my torso and legs. They were lit by the first glow of the sun that had just cleared the crags to the east of the city, bringing with it instant warmth. A deep happiness filled my soul, and without questioning how I had come to be where I was I allowed myself to drift off again into a different sort of sleep, a healing, warming, happy sleep.

Next time I awoke I sat up with a start, and the last shadow of a second or third dream melted like mist. Again it had been of a lady, but as different from the first as could be. This one was pure white, with yellow hair, naked, standing in a cave of ice. Even as I hauled myself into a sitting position (the leaves brushed my old turban and a big round fruit bumped on the top of my head) and re-oriented myself, she vanished. She had left me with a warm, rich glow in my loins and, such was her power, even on an old man, a smear of semen across my stomach.

I plucked an orange from the tree, broke through its rind with my thumb and gorged myself on it. Never had I enjoyed a fruit so much as the juice trickled down my chin and my eyes roved across the domes, *shikharas*, or mountain-like towers, and pinnacles of the city. They were both behind and in front of me, on the far side of the valley, glowing with gold leaf or ceramic mosaic. The great river with its woods, gardens, threaded its way between them before losing itself in the fields and forests that stretched beyond into the mist-enshrouded distances.

Again I wondered how I had got to be where I was. Had the time I had spent with Suryan and Uma been just as little real as the dream of the naked white woman? Perhaps. At all events I had come to no harm, had, for the most part, pleasant recollections to dwell on, but now, if I was to be paid by Prince Harihara, I had an appointment to keep.

CHAPTER

EIGHT

This time, the chamberlain with his silver and ebony wand was waiting for me and eager to conduct me into the Prince's presence. Harihara had chosen to be out of doors, and was sitting in a carved marble chair beneath a palm tree in one of the small, enclosed gardens. Beside him there was an octagonal table, also marble, pierced and fretted to look like one of the more intimate temples. His long fingers picked at a silver dish filled with ripe fresh dates; next to it he had placed the package of parchment leaves I had brought him from across the world, the red thongs loosely tied up again.

He now questioned me far more closely than he had before about my previous journeys to Ingerlond, how well I knew the language and the customs, and whether or not I should be able to find the place where his brother Jehani was hiding. From this I gathered, erroneously it turned out, that what interested him as much as the whereabouts of his brother was the location of the city built of precious stones and gold.

I answered all these questions with as much honesty as I could muster, but as I sensed that an offer of employment was in the air and since I was destitute, following the loss of my shipwrecked horses, I said nothing that might imply a less than complete mastery of the Inglysshe tongue, or a less than extensive knowledge of the country and its customs.

Next he concentrated on the prowess of the Inglysshe in the arts and sciences of war but on this subject I had to confess myself ignorant – at least at first hand. I gave him my impressions: that both gentry and common people fought with foolhardy bravery, were competent in the management of their weaponry, but had been, in recent times, poorly led. In the past their kings, who claimed many cities and much land on the mainland by right of inheritance, had won many great battles against the kings of the Franks, but in the last few years had lost almost all they had gained. This was because their current king was first a babe then a youth and finally an indecisive weakling, some said mad, and partly because the Franks were led by a wild woman, possessed by devils, who inspired her troops to feats of bravery and cunning. How else could a mere woman have won so many victories before the Ingerlonders captured her and burnt her alive as a witch?

'But they are skilled in the most up-to-date improvements in the art of warfare?' Prince Harihara was now insistent, clearly signalling the answer he wanted to hear.

I am a stranger to the courtier's arts but I knew there would be no point in denying something about which he had already reached a conclusion.

'They fight from horses?' Yes. 'They understand the science of building fortifications?' I remembered the towers and battlements that circled Calais. Yes. 'And the art of using fire-powder? Do they have that? I mean not merely as an incendiary but as a propellant.' I recalled that I had seen, on the quay at Calais, monster tubes, known as canes or cannons for their resemblance to the hollow stems of wood children use for simple whistles or pipes, mounted on wheeled carriages. They were used, I had been told, to throw large balls of stone or iron at hostile ships, pirates or Frankish, attempting to cross the harbour bar. So, yes again.

The interrogation continued for a half-hour or more, but, though I could only guess to what it tended, I sensed that I had already said enough and that Prince Harihara's mind was made up. He was merely padding out the process so that it would not appear that he had taken an important decision without due consideration. At last he came to the point, and I confess I was more surprised than I allowed myself to reveal.

He cleared his throat, leant back in his chair so that his face was shaded from direct sunlight. His eyes shone, on account of the reflection from the nearby pool. He laced his long fingers beneath his chin. 'I have a mind,' he said, and his voice was quiet but firm, 'to go to Ingerlond myself, find my brother Jehani and bring him home. I have discussed this possibility with the Emperor and he is agreeable, provided I combine the trip with other objectives that will be of more public value. To this end I shall require the services of a guide who knows the language and the country. In short I expect you to come with me in that capacity.'

Note: not 'I should like . . .' or 'Would you be so good as to . . .', but 'I expect'. The surprise was that he was coming too. That, I had not anticipated − he was of the imperial family, held a senior position in the government, namely Minister for Defence of the Realm. Moreover, considering his age and the pampered ease of his life hitherto, I doubted his capacity to withstand the privations we should undoubtedly encounter.

However, he had arrived at a correct estimate of my circumstances and knew I was in no position to refuse gainful employment. I was not quite sure how I should demonstrate my assent. Had he been a caliph or sultan there would have been no problem: I should have thrown myself on my knees in front of him, grasped his hands, and showered them with kisses and even tears of gratitude, but these Dravidian princes seemed to expect less formal if more subtle appreciation of their rank. They are, however, just as proud as their Arab, Moghul or Brahminical equals, and stand on ceremony too, but a ceremony that is muted, played down, so an illusion is created that discourse with them is conducted as if between equals, near equals anyway. On this occasion I bowed my head, and kept it bowed for a second or two, which appeared to be enough.

'That's settled, then. Chamberlain Anish will take over now and look after you. Through him I want you to make all the preparations you think necessary to get us on our way as soon as possible. I shall require a train commensurate with my position as envoy of the Emperor, but not so magnificent as to inspire envy or suspicion. Anish and you will work out the details.'

He waved his hand, and I found that the chamberlain was already at my elbow, having returned on silent feet. His master popped a date in his mouth, and thus contrived to signal that the audience was over and that he had other business to attend to.

Thus it was that three months later we sailed not from Mangalore but from the more northern port of Gové or Goa, which we Arabs call Sindābur, thereby making the overland journey from the City of Victory shorter by fifty miles or more and the sea voyage to Yemen by as many leagues.

During the in-between time I was put on the Prince's pay-roll and given a room in the compound that served in the Royal Enclave as his private residence, his official offices, and quarters for his servants and staff. The room was small but clean, the worst thing about it being that it was set over a yard on to which the kitchens opened so the air was often heavy with the smell of clarified but rancid butter, garlic and stale spices. The money, however, was good, especially as I had no expenses, and I banked almost all of it with a Jewish diamond-dealer, whom I befriended on the other side of the river, thereby laying the foundations of the minor fortune that now sustains my old age.

I did not, during this time, meet or even see Suryan or Uma. I spent the early afternoon of the day on which I had concluded arrangements with my Jew wandering about the commercial sector looking for the house to which I thought I had been taken. The trouble was that there were, it seemed, literally scores that might have passed for it and none that fitted my recollection exactly, so I gave up. Indeed, by the time we left the city I was more or less ready to accept that the whole experience had been a fantasy brought on by tiredness, the strangeness of my new surroundings, with some wish-fulfilment thrown in too.

However, I did find a temple, a shrine, not in the Sacred Zone but tucked away between the river and the commercial sector the image of whose goddess exactly matched up with my dream, if it had been a dream, of the black woman ornamented with skulls, dripping with blood. The place was deserted, as if ill-omened, though kept clean and properly maintained. No one would tell me who this goddess was, but rushed past when I asked them, some making warning signs much like those we use in Arab countries against the evil eye. However, eventually a small girl, carrying a straw bag filled with flat, plate-like loaves of bread, told me she was Kali, Bhadra-kali, the goddess of death who, in the legend, slays Shiva.

For the rest I continued to enjoy most of what Vijayanagara had to offer. The great buildings, many of them public, whether devoted to government or religion or to utility and pleasure, never ceased to fill me with wonder and delight. Especially I remember the Queen's Bath, the Shiva Temple, with its bewitching wall paintings, the stepped pool with its terraces of stone seats dropping in half pyramids to the cool water where anyone might find refreshment in the afternoon heat, the imperial elephant stables with their wonderful gilded domes and tall entrances. Everyone, it seemed, was a musician or poet, from the Emperor himself, who was considered an avatar of Krishna and who in writing verses in praise of the god thus praised himself, down to the humblest porter in the fruit market.

There was fruit and rice in plenty for all, and so cheap as to be almost free. Milk, butter, cheese, eggs and fish cost a little but not much. Meat eating was discouraged as being both unhealthy and against religion though the nobility hunted deer and wild goat through the mountain forests and served it at family feasts. Everyone was adequately housed for there was timber, brick and stone in abundance. And so, dear Mah-Lo, my three-month stay passed in congenial work preparing for our expedition and in delight at my harmonious and elegant surroundings.

There was just one evil to be feared: the sultans to the north of the river Krishna, their *satraps*, and the envious malevolence of their Brahminical collaborators. For the most part they fought each other rather than the Dravidians, but every now and then a warlord, feeling secure to the north after a brief, successful campaign against his neighbours, crossed the river and penetrated as far as he could, looting, pillaging, raping until the Emperor could gather a force strong enough to drive him back. Then the streets of the city would be filled with the wounded and maimed, temples became hospitals, and the open spaces camping grounds for refugees.

Chamberlain Anish, he who carried the ebony wand, proved a valuable ally, a skilled negotiator and a man of practical sense. About fifty years old, he was short, tubby, had narrow eyes a little like a Chinaman's, and a real understanding of his master's foibles, which yet did not lessen the respect in which he held him. He also had a small silky beard, a fringe about an inch long that ran from ear to ear like a noose: he stroked it with brusque little movements whenever he was pressed to make a difficult decision. Apart from the irritation this habit caused me, we got on well enough.

One day, when time hung heavily as we waited for an official in the treasury to release funds, I asked him what were the real purposes of our journey and indeed of Jehani's before us.

His normally serene expression clouded. 'It is historically inevitable,' he said, 'that Vijayanagara will be overwhelmed, if not by the Bahmani sultans then by the Moghul hordes from further north. It has been the policy of our enlightened emperors to do all they can to postpone that evil day for as long as they can.' He took a turn about the treasury official's anteroom, looked over his shoulder as if fearing eavesdroppers and took me by the elbow to a shady corner. 'The root of the problem is this. Our Mussulman armies will fight their co-religionists only for as long as two conditions are fulfilled. One, that we can pay them more than our enemies can, and, two, that they are assured of winning while suffering only minimal casualties. There is no point in being paid a vast sum if you don't live to enjoy it. This means we must either employ ever larger armies or equip them with the best arms and armour available, then teach them to use them efficiently. The latter course is obviously preferred. We have had indications, by rumour and hearsay, that the Inglysshe, since they are the least civilised and most barbaric people on Earth, are, when well led, unbeatable, not only through their courage and prowess but also because of the equipment they use. It was to establish the truth of this assumption that Jehani travelled west, hoping to bring back with him knowledge of the military technology the Inglysshe possessed, and possibly military men who could teach our armies how to fight.

'There was a personal side to Jehani's mission too. He and Prince Harihara had quarrelled – over a woman, of course. That is all over now. She died shortly after Jehani left, and the Prince is anxious to find him, help him fulfil his original mission and bring him home.'

Thus Anish. Events bore out what he told me then, but with an added dimension. In England Jehani had fallen in with a group of hedonistic atheists who acknowledged no God but the God within, the individual conscience unmediated by holy books or priests – the Brothers of the Free Spirit, who had cells right across Europe and corresponded with like-minded people in the East too. Everywhere they recruited hierophants, mostly from the lower sort, and everywhere they were ruthlessly persecuted. The Brother who had given me Jehani's packet and died at the stake in Calais had been one of their number.

One problem we faced was clothes. Neither the Prince nor Anish could conceive of the effects of cold rain, frost, howling icy gales, the whole panoply of weather those western isles could throw at us. When I described sleet driven by an icy wind they said that they would wear two silk or cotton gowns instead of one. In the end I realised we were approaching the problem from the wrong angle.

'Let us,' I said, 'set aside a certain amount for each member of our expedition, in some easily carried but easily exchanged commodity which we will carry separately from the rest, in sealed packets, and which all will swear not to touch until we need to buy the clothes the locals wear to keep out bad weather.'

Of course they suggested spices, but we were already carrying many sackfuls of many different sorts, and I was afraid that those kept for clothes would be muddled with the rest and exchanged for something of no particular value in Ingerlond, though of substantial value in Vijayanagara. In the end we chose pearls. These, though beautiful, are not rare along the coasts of Vijayanagara or on the many small islands and archipelagos out in the ocean, but in northern climes are highly prized, especially those of any size or of unusual colouring. Each of us, then, took a small bag of pearls, which was only to be sold or exchanged for warm clothing and substantial footwear when these became necessary.

There was another problem too, which I came upon in a small yard behind the stables that had served as an entrepôt for our baggage. It was in the form of a heap of leather cases, tooled, in part gilded and painted, with tasselled straps and handles, varying in length from three feet to ten, and for the most part roughly cylindrical. There were two score or more of them, together with racks and racks of feathered shafts, again of varying lengths and styles. They provided the clue, of course, to what the leather cases contained, though it was Anish who murmured the explanatory word. 'Crossbows,' he said, somewhat drily. 'His lordship collects them.'

'Well, he can't take them with him,' I said firmly. 'What we have here will require six mules and two more muleteers, which means a seventh mule to carry *their* baggage. Moreover, there are enough weapons here to furnish a squad of archers – no one will believe we come in peace as traders when they see this lot.'

'He will insist, I fear.'

'Why?'

'It is not simply the weapons that obsess him but the use to which he puts them. He hunts. It is his passion. He has crossbows and bolts for every sort of quarry he might come across. Tiny ones imported from China, scarcely more than a pound or so in weight, which throw a six-inch dart, for small birds – larks and quail particularly – to machines from Nepal capable of throwing a bolt three hundred paces and bringing down a mountain goat. Finally, this monster,' he kicked a bag big and bulky enough to hold the body of a six-foot wrestler, 'which, when assembled, requires a crew of three, one of whom carries it on his back, another to wind a winch to pull back the string, which is made from plaited water buffalo hide, and a third, his lordship, who aims and shoots.'

'And what does he kill with that? Elephants?'

'Crocodiles.'

I prodded it with my stick. 'It won't do you know. Even apart from the bulk and nuisance of it all, it still won't do.'

'Why not?'

'The Ingerlonder nobility do not hunt with bows and arrows. They hunt from horses with dogs.'

'What animals do they hunt, then, with these dogs?'

'Deer, hares, otters, wolves, foxes.'

'They eat fox?' There was disgust in Anish's voice.

'No. But they like the excuse the foxes give them to ride fast over farmland, regardless of the damage their horses do.'

In spite of my interdiction Prince Harihara smuggled out a large selection of these weapons when we left, almost certainly with Anish's connivance.

So, towards the end of the third month after I had arrived in the City of Victory, we set off for Gové. There were the three of us, plus four cooks, ten muleteers, ten soldiers with all their accoutrements, a couple of secretaries experienced in financial affairs, a fortune-teller, a Buddhist monk, who came along, he told Anish, because he had nothing better to do, four general servants, two of whom were always in attendance on the Prince, carrying huge parasols above him as he rode on a fine mule, a couple of *dhobi wallahs* to keep our clothes clean, a fakir or conjuror, and three musicians: forty-two in all, with enough baggage to need forty mules.

This baggage, apart from an excessive amount of personal belongings, consisted mainly of dried spices: ginger, cardamom, peppercorns, coriander seed, cumin, nutmeg, cinnamon and cloves. Hidden here and

there were more pearls, diamonds and some rubies, including a pair of
kurundams, each as long and thick as your thumb, in perfect crystalline
form, combinations of prisms with hexagonal pyramids, rhombohedrons
and basal pinakoids.

This was all far too much, of course. There were too many unnecessary
people and things. At least I had drawn the line at elephants. The Prince
had not been pleased. 'How will the inhabitants of the countries we pass
through, and the Ingerlonders themselves, know that we are people of
consequence if we do not arrive on elephants?' He only gave in on the
understanding that the subject would be broached again when we arrived
in Cairo where, as he understood it, African elephants would be available
for sale or hire.

On the border with the Bahmani sultanates, Gové is even more
cosmopolitan than Mangalore, and since its traders deal even-handedly
with both empires, although it was at that time governed by the
Dravidians, a wide variety of ships and crews was available for charter,
even including, amongst the latter, some Italian sailors from Venice and
Genoa, Portuguese, Malays and Chinese.

On my advice, we opted for an Arab vessel, a medium-sized dhow
capable of carrying some hundred and fifty tons, manned by an Arab
master and crew. They had just dropped off a cargo of blackamoors
from the Zanzibar slave markets, and the master was looking for a
charter to take him back up the Red Sea. His boat was called the *Moon
of Islam*, and the below-decks cargo space had solid timber bunk beds,
just shelves, really, for the slaves, which made her well equipped to take
all our company and gear. There was also a cane and thatch covered area
in the stern, which Prince Harihara commandeered for himself and his
closest retinue – myself and Anish. There was another similarly roofed
area on the foredeck. The *Moon of Islam* was painted green; she was well
rigged with a newish sail, and her seams were well caulked. These, and
similar matters, are the sorts of things a wise merchant checks when time
and money permit. Otherwise he takes a chance and sometimes comes
to grief, as I had with my shipload of horses.

A hundred and fifty tons? The masters of smaller boats insist on
hopping round the coastline, running for port as soon as a squall
appears on the horizon, even at that time of year when the weather
is generally settled, the winds steady from the north-east. In any
case, with anything smaller we should have had to take two ships

to accommodate us all. As it was, we left the mules behind, planning to hire beasts of burden as soon as we made our landfall in Suways, the port that serves the city of Misr-al-Kahira, Cairo, the capital of Egypt.

CHAPTER

NINE

There is always excitement, even for an old trader like me, in embarcation and departure. Picture us, if you can, towed away from the quay by row-boats, manned by dock-workers, out into the estuary of the Juari river, behind us the gilded *shikharas* of the temple to Shiva, the dome and minarets of the mosque with its black marble portico, and then, as the estuary widens, the customs buildings and the offices of the harbour-master. All seemed to crowd together as we moved away from them. The quay itself was lined with those members of the Prince's household who were not accompanying us, including all the women and his ten elephants. A band played, handkerchiefs and scarves were waved, elephants trumpeted and were rewarded by their mahouts with ripe mangoes.

Across the river, on the other side of the estuary, the forest came down to the water's edge, the sand a white line between green trees and emerald water. Along the edge beyond their beached boats smoke gusted out of the many fishermen's villages from the fires used to cure their catch, and beyond them, above the nodding palms, and far closer than they are at Mangalore, the Western Ghats climbed into the almost perfect blue of the sky. Above them, the north-east trades that would carry us across the Arabian Sea spun angels' hair from the clouds.

While we were still in the estuary but had left the villages behind us we passed a point where dugongs grazed the abundant seaweed that filled a small cove and marvelled at the human way the cows suckled their young. I remarked that it was strange to find a colony so close to human habitation since their meat is highly prized. This prompted Anish to tell me they were protected in this area as servants of the goddess in her manifestation as Queen of the Sea.

On our ship all was bustle: while most of the crew stood by the mast, with the ropes in their hands that would presently hoist the big lateen sail, the rest went about their business making movables fast wherever their passengers would let them; the passengers, apart from those closest to the Prince, moved about the decks seeking places behind gunwales and bulwarks where they might be sheltered from spray and worse, and marking out their territories with their bundled blankets or rattan bags. Few wanted to go below, and in any case much of the space was taken with our larger baggage and spice sacks.

Gulls and other seabirds gathered in our wake, so we carried a comet trail behind us, and the air filled with their angry, pleading mewing. For a moment or two as we passed the harbour bar the ship bucked and shuddered in the swell, and spray flew across the deck; then the sailors in the forepeak cast off the hausers that linked us to the tow-boats, and those in the waist of the vessel hauled up the sail, which filled and bellied like a pregnant woman, pregnant with adventure.

The motion settled now into the steady rhythm of the rollers that slipped beneath us on their way to crash in a line of surf on the already distant Malabar coast. In almost no time at all the uplands of the Western Ghats, beneath their line of mountain cloud, were the only sign of land, they and the birds that followed us until nightfall.

Now the swell was no longer crested and in every direction the sea-acres of deepest indigo-black stretched to the horizon, but this was no watery desert. A shoal of flying fish flashed by, silver shards of razor-edged light, their spiny fins shredding the heaving surface. Behind them, and in ravenous pursuit, came a school of porpoises, tumbling like kittens, snapping like puppies at the fish, their skins the shiny black of carved, polished coal; while further off three whales kept station, venting their lungs in spumy breaths like smoke.

As I said, there is always excitement, a lightening of the spirits at such times. Even though one knows landfall will come, or, if not, then a watery grave, one also knows that for a day or two, a week perhaps, this is a time out of life, a space where anxiety and worry have no place. Meanwhile, there is the brightness of the sky and the rush of the wind to be enjoyed, the smells of tar, hemp and seasoned timber to be relished, and, to be shared, the slow dance of the rise and slip of the deck, the swaying tilt of the horizon, as the ship performs its pavana with the wind and waves.

Thus it was, on that day, for me – but not for Anish who, along with many others, was seasick. I suspect Prince Harihara was too, for he kept to himself in the rush-roofed area in the stern.

For my part, using my old stick to steady myself, and with the hem of my old cape banging against my knees, I took a turn round the deck. Five of our muleteers were already crowded around a cook, who was crouched over a metal bowl of charcoal, slapping slabs of dough on a metal plate above it and flipping them over as the bubbles of air separated the skins of blackening crust. The smell of grilled bread and spices wafted by on the bluish smoke, and the Arab crewmen, properly aware of the dangers of fire at sea, looked on warily, one swinging a canvas bucket ready to scoop the sea-water that rushed by below the lee rail.

Further on I came on our fakir, already with a tiny crowd of seamen, a couple of servants and four of our soldiers around him. Lean, with sinews in his neck strung tight like the strings on a sitar and fingers that flickered in what I imagine he took to be an entrancing way, he wore a baggy loincloth, none too clean, and a turban, so I supposed he was a Mussulman like myself, though of Indian stock.

Our sergeant, the second in command of the soldiers, a big, burly fellow with a scimitar which had a spike protruding from the hilt, grumbled in my ear, 'He won't levitate or do his rope trick on account of the wind. He reckons if he did the ship would go on and leave him suspended above the ocean.'

I could not restrain a laugh. 'Well,' I replied, 'we'll see when the wind drops or when we get to dry land.'

Meanwhile the fakir was contenting himself and his onlookers by discovering long chains of knotted silk scarves in their ears and an abundance of hard-boiled eggs in his own mouth. Considering his entire upper body, apart from his turban, was bare, all this was remarkable enough in its way.

I moved on to the forepeak and found, in the angle of the bow, the Buddhist monk. As I approached he contorted himself into a yogic position beneath his saffron robe and began to repeat, with eyes shut and face lifted to the sky and sun, some meaningless mantra. His head was shaved; the simple accoutrements of his craft – a begging bowl, a pottery drum, finger cymbals and tiny bells – stood on the deck beside him. He was slight of build, had long fingers and feet, and no eyebrows at all, though the skin where they had been was red, raw and flaking. Indeed, apart from a dark haze over his scalp, his skin was smooth and hairless, like a eunuch's. He was darker than most of our party, not African dark but heading that way. Lost in his rapture, meditation, whatever, he paid no attention to me, did not open his eyes or move at all, apart from his lips, which continued to emit their monotonous drone until I passed on. On account of his religion and physical characteristics I took him to be Sinhalese from Sri Lanka.

A sudden commotion in the waist of the ship drew my attention away from him. Our sergeant had the fakir by the throat, had him up against the gunwale the edge of which was in the fakir's back and likely to make an apt fulcrum for levering him over the side. I swung myself past the mast, ducked my head under the corner of the sail and tapped the sergeant on the shoulder with the end of my stick. 'At least,' I said, 'tell me why he deserves drowning before you put him in the sea.'

He twisted his head and brought his big bullish face within inches of mine. His breath smelt of rice beer, garlic, smoked fish.

'He cheats,' he bellowed, 'took a gold ring off of me by sharp practice.'

Distracted by my intervention he relaxed his grip on the sinewy throat of the fakir enough for the mountebank to draw breath and gasp.

'All straight and above board,' he cried. 'He bet me six months in his service against his gold ring he could tell me which hand I had it in. Listen, he can have it back, I'm buggered if I care.' He held out his palm with the ring on it. The sergeant took it – it was a big, chunky affair, a lion's head with tiny ruby eyes – slipped it back on the middle finger of his right hand, then pulled the hand back to his shoulder as if he were drawing a bowstring, and let loose with all his might into the fakir's face. I grabbed his flailing wrist and just saved him from going over. Nevertheless, as he lurched back, he doubled up, spitting blood and a broken tooth.

'There,' shouted the sergeant, and his little eyes roamed over all the bystanders, who now numbered most of those on board, 'that's what I do, and worse, to anybody tries to make a monkey out of me.'

That was not the end of the affair. At least, I am fairly certain it was not. Night came on, the wind dropped, the boat ambled on beneath a moonless sky with just a helmsman, who had the art of steering by the stars, and a lookout in the forepeak on watch. Neither heard anything untoward, though both said that at the darkest time the silence was disturbed by the splash and gurgle of whales or larger dolphins nearby.

And in the morning the sergeant was nowhere to be found. After supper, during which he had continued to drink copiously, he had fallen into a deep slumber with his head cushioned on his arm, in the lee of the ship's side, and when morning came he had gone. Some fingers were pointed at the fakir, but the Buddhist monk swore he had slept beside him all night, below deck, sharing one of the shelves and a thin blanket and neither had stirred until first light. I, myself, had slept on deck, outside the bamboo door of the cabin where Prince Harihara and Chamberlain Anish were bedded and I, too, heard the splashing of dolphin, as I thought. Except that immediately preceding it I had been half woken by the sound of someone pissing long and heavily into the sea. This was followed by a brittle-sounding snap, like a branch being broken over a strong man's knee, a gasp and a splash. The splash a dolphin makes when it leaps out of the water, or that of a small whale's fluke when it smacks the surface? I didn't think so. But there was no point in saying otherwise.

Those with authority on the boat, the master and his mate, exercised the prerogatives laid down by maritime custom and overruled Prince Harihara's desire for a more complete inquiry into the loss of his sergeant. Landlubbers, they said, especially those who get drunk and fail to take the most obvious precautions, have been falling off boats since ocean travel began, and that was that. Questions, of course, remained unanswered, the most weighty being: why did the sergeant not cry out?

The master shrugged with all the disdain of a man who has gone through a long life without touching intoxicating liquor but who has observed the evil effects of drunkenness from Cadiz to Surabaya. Why ask for rational behaviour from a drunk? So the matter was laid to rest, and if any shared my misgivings, they kept them to themselves.

Here is a way of killing a man. You place a long silk scarf round his neck, retaining the ends in your hands at arm's length. You raise your foot and place it on the side or back of the man's head, with your knee bent to a right-angle. Then, very sharply, you straighten the knee. It needs the speed of a falcon's stoop, suppleness, agility, determination and training by an adept. It is the method of ritual slaughter known as *thuggee* and is carried out by devotees of the goddess Kali. So, maybe we had a Thug amongst us. The fakir? Perhaps. But the Thugs are cunning people, usually work in small groups or pairs, at least, and are not above using a likely innocent as a decoy. From then on I always made sure that beneath the folds of my cape and buried in my loincloth my Damascene stiletto was within easy grasp, and at night I slept with its hilt in my hand.

I, too, have my skills.

CHAPTER

TEN

T he voyage unfolded without further incident. We reached the
Strait of Bab el-Mandeb some two weeks later, untroubled by
bad weather apart from an occasional squall, and began the long
haul up the Red Sea, a distance about the same as we had already
travelled. We put into the small port of Mokha where, when I found
that the imams' interdiction against drinking the infusion of *k'hāwah*
beans, which had prevented me making my fortune some four years
previously, had been lifted, I prevailed upon Prince Harihara to lay out
a piece of his gold on a couple of sacks. I assured him they would sell as
well as coriander seed once we got into Europe. We also took on fresh
water and other supplies that had begun to fall low, especially lemons.

Fortunately, at that time of year, the winds were now mostly from
the east and south-east, though frequently falling away, which, with
the presence of much moisture in the air, produced an enervating heat;
nevertheless I took great delight during these calms in swimming in the
warm limpid water of the Red Sea above coral reefs of great beauty,
often plunging my head below the surface and kicking my way down
like a frog so the shoals of rainbow fish darted away ahead of me. I swam
with ease, in spite of my twisted, scrawny and scarred old body, which
filled the rest of the crew and passengers with envy, even awe. It is a
skill few have who do not come from sea or lakeside communities but
one I had been at pains to acquire when it became clear to me that sea
voyages were to take up a significant portion of my life.

Indeed, that early experience of surviving the sabre slash, followed by a night bedded on top of my partially dismembered mother, had left me with not only an inordinate desire to live, but also a willingness to learn how to survive in all foreseeable circumstances. Moreover, it gave me a readiness to grasp the pleasure of each fleeting moment, each sensation, from the tremulous and slight, even the tiny scrabble of a little red spider finding its way through the hairs on the back of my hand, to the mind-blowingly grand, like the glory of a sunset with low-lying cloud at sea.

I also persuaded the Prince to lay out a tiny sum on a sackful of sponges, which were peddled at our ship's side during a calm by a couple of lads who rowed a tiny skiff up to us from the Arabian shore.

The last two hundred miles or so were the worst, as they almost always are on that particular voyage, and took a quarter of the time we spent in the Red Sea. As the banks of the Khalij As Suways, the Gulf of Suez, closed in on us, the winds blew out of the west, carrying on their back the heavy, sharp grit of the desert; the sky became overcast, with a featureless grey haze tinged with ochre, and the master and crew were increasingly bad-tempered as they struggled to keep our head close to the wind without losing forward way. The dolphins and flying fish departed for the south and an evil, grubby spume settled on the decking making it slippery and movement hazardous. As the Gulf narrowed, other shipping, too, became a hazard, those going our way competing with us to find good berths within the roads before nightfall, those leaving scudding by with the wind on their quarters, angry with us for getting in their way, spilling the wind out of our sail when they got too close, so we were likely at times to drift beam-on to that evil breeze.

Still, we made Suways by close on midday on our forty-second day out of Goa, which was about what I had told the Prince to expect. It now fell to me to organise the next stage of our journey: not only was I the only person in the party who had knowledge of Ingerlond, our ultimate goal, but I was, too, the only Arab, with knowledge of that tongue and of the processes and prices, the snares and snags that befall travellers in those parts.

First, I had to find lodging for our party and then camels to carry us and our baggage to Al-Iskenderia, named after the great Iskender who conquered the world some two thousand years ago, or so they say, and this delay bred another. It had been our plan to give Misr-al-Kahira a miss, and pass as inconspicuously as we could across the delta and out of the country — a plan I did not much like as I had hoped to seek Haree, my son, in his place of study, and spend some time with him. However, wandering in the souk Prince Harihara came across a shop which sold the hides of various wild animals including a tawny, ragged affair with a mask still partially intact beneath a tangled halo of coarse black hair. It was, of course, the pelt of a lion.

He called me to his side. 'Ali, is not this the skin of a lion?'

I thought of temporising, of perhaps speaking to the merchant, a lean man in a red gown with a red tarboosh but no turban to go round the rim, and asking him in Arabic to deny the obvious. But, I thought, why not? I could see where this would lead, and I was in no great hurry to get to Ingerlond. It was not my brother we were looking for. Suddenly I realised I was looking through a window of opportunity, that of seeing Haree, after all.

'Yes, Highness.'

'Can lions then be found in Egypt?'

'I believe so, Highness.'

He stood there, in the dusty dusk of the shop, with the bright sunlight beyond its striped awning searing the eyes, and all the noise and bustle of the alley beyond, and quizzed me further. He pushed his glossy black hair back off his shoulder and briefly caressed his marble smooth chin. 'What other large animals live wild?'

'Crocodiles in the Nile, and, upstream, hippopotami, I believe . . . There are large birds too. Pelicans, storks, cranes and herons . . .'

We left the shop in a hurry, with its keeper tugging at my sleeve. 'Will he not buy, then? Does your master not want to buy? I can lower the prices,' he shrilled.

'I think he plans to kill his own,' I replied, tearing myself away.

It took some organising. First, we had to abandon the status of incognito travellers we had adopted. We went to Misr-al-Kahira, after all, and introduced ourselves to the Caliph's court where, as representatives of an empire as rich as any in the world, and having offered suitable gifts from the small treasury we had brought with us, we were made welcome and given lodgings in that part of the palace set aside for honoured guests. There followed a week or so of feasting and such like while a full-scale hunting party in the desert was prepared.

One of the few bitter moments of the whole trip arrived when I went to Haree's lodgings. There I discovered that he had left only a month earlier to study the causes of blindness under a Moorish physician in the university of Karnatta-al-Yahud, which the Christians call Granada.

We were well lodged in a pillared pavilion set in a rose garden with a rectangular pool edged with basalt. Unfortunately there were not enough rooms so we had to share – cooks, soldiers, servants, clerks, fakir and monk all together in a quite small vestibule. Of course, our Prince and his chamberlain had cells to themselves close to the communal baths. So it was that when the day dawned on which the week-long hunting trip was to start, I asked to be excused. My plea was that I am not happy on a horse, hate camels, and that I am too old for such sports. Prince Harihara was reluctant to leave me behind, but some days previously I had discovered that one of the Caliph's musicians had once played his flute in a military band belonging to a Pathan chief and had enough Hindustani vocabulary to manage interpretation at a simple level. Consequently my services as interpreter were not essential. My aim, apart from avoiding the pains and terror of horse-riding, was to rest: I was, after all, and I do not think I have mentioned this, by far and away the oldest in our party and the strains of travel were taking their toll.

I watched the party leave, the grooms lumbered with a variety of crossbows, including the monster engine designed for crocodiles. As soon as the great arched gate had closed behind them, and the dust settled, I made my way back to our quarters.

There are few delights as rich as that which comes from the knowledge that one has a limited but extensive time to oneself, in pleasant surroundings, with adequate comforts and ways to pass the time with satisfaction. I folded my tired old knees on to a pile of cushions near the pool, and sitting thus cross-legged, completed a breakfast of quails' eggs with aubergine mashed in mare's yoghurt, sesame-seeded rolls, followed by almond and honey cakes. It occurred to me that a cup of *k'hāwah* would be the ideal accompaniment, but the effort and time required in preparing it precluded the possibility and I made do with my usual glass of *lassi* aromatised with a pinch of the Moluccan nutmeg we had brought with us.

For a time I watched and listened to the songbirds, many with bright and lovely plumage, who inhabited that walled garden as if it were an aviary, and made friends with a sleek grey cat with a broad flat forehead and large ears which, either from lethargy or experience of repeated failure, made no attempt to menace the birds. The time wore on and the heat built. The sun flashed from the gilded domes and minarets that rose above the nearer roofs, and my eye was caught by a pair of vultures. They were soaring almost without motion on wings white with black tips against the deep azure of the sky – quartering, I reckoned, the execution *maidan* where impalings were scheduled. Since its odours, of charcoal burning and rotten offal, were masked by the fragrance of roses, orange blossom and an almond-scented purple creeper that festooned one of the walls, the birds were the only visible signs of the rapacious hustle and bustle of the great city beyond.

I had thought to begin a letter to Haree, an account of my journey so far, to leave at his lodgings when we left, but already the delightful sloth that comes when one has nothing pressing to do was filling my soul and I decided instead to take a bath.

The main pool was covered by a dome, open to the sky at its centre, and pierced with smaller lights below. These let in direct sunlight, blindingly bright and warm in contrast to the velvety darkness of the rest. The water shimmered blackly except where the light fell, and there it was emerald green and laced with patterns like the veins in marble. A deck of grey granite surrounded it, also rippled but this time with quartz, and beyond were cubicles, or alcoves framed with looped-back curtains of fine cotton gauze. Steps with balustrades led down into the pool and at their head was a pair of life-size sculpted lionesses, which sat on their haunches, heads up and alert, above the taut musculature of their shoulders, round ears pricked.

I stood on the threshold of this circular hall to allow my good eye time to adjust to the dark and light, and for my ears to savour the play of ripples on the sides of the pool and the rhythmical pulses of water dripping on stone and on water. Then I slipped off my sandals, not wanting to soil the floor with dust, and made my way to the nearest but one of the alcoves (who, in such a situation, ever takes the nearest opening that offers?), intending there to divest myself of cape, loincloth and turban. I did not use the alcove out of modesty, for I fully expected to be alone, but because it had a low stone shelf, and the floor by the pool was wet. There I loosened my turban, unwound it, and pulled my cape over my head. Just as it came free I sensed, rather than heard, a presence. My right hand delved into my loincloth, where my stiletto always remains hidden, then relaxed. The new arrival was the Buddhist monk and I foresaw no harm coming from him, though I felt a touch irritated that the solitude I had been relishing was gone.

He pulled off his sandals and his voluminous habit, leaving them on the deck at the water's edge before stepping down between the lions and into the pool.

Most of what light there was was in front of him and, bouncing off the water, as sharp as diamonds, made only a dark silhouette of his figure, yet one sunbeam catching the haze of tiny droplets its heat sucked up, fell between us. A moment or two passed therefore while my mind struggled with the vision my one good eye was feeding it. It is extraordinary, is it not?, how the brain refuses to yield to the evidence of the senses when confronted with stimuli that contradict its expectations. In such circumstances it will swear sour is sweet, and hot cold. And on this occasion that those softly rounded shoulders, the waist that really was a waist above broad dimpled hips and generous buttocks belonged to a man.

It gave up the pretence when she stooped a little and, in a gesture that somehow contained the essence of femininity, scooped water over the breasts I could not yet see before wading into the centre of the pool where the water came up to her armpits. She turned and I could see that her brown body was indeed female and, in a flash, I recognised Uma, the – I was about to say goddess – but the young woman, sister of Suryan, who had given me hospitality on my first night in the City of Victory.

CHAPTER

ELEVEN

'Ali?' How to describe the way she sang those two syllables? Her voice caressed the air and water and yet it was a call, a question. 'Ali ben Quatar Mayeen? Don't be shy. Please come in with me.'

I released the hilt of my stiletto, leaving it wrapped in the folds of my loincloth, limped forward out of the alcove and stood at the top of the steps, between the two lions. With my good hand I gripped the right ear of one. My heart was beating like the wings of a newly caged bird, and I'll tell you why. I had not seen, in the flesh, an entirely naked woman for twenty years, not since the day dear Haree's mother told me she was with child.

Uma was beautiful and whatever she had in the way of what a purist would call flaws, such as a mole or two on her back, gave her the perfection she would have otherwise lacked – they conferred upon her the individuality, the thisness that shields true beauty from the dullness that measures itself against an ideal. In those moles lay mutability and mortality, the twin pillars on which the lintel of life is placed. Ah. Does that surprise you? My way of life and physical limitations, taken with a predilection to speculation, which began with the question 'How can this be?', have led me to read and talk with great minds.

The austerity of her shaven scalp was now mitigated by a thin pelt which lent her head a vulnerability that immediately invited a gentle caress. Her features seemed more marked: her eyes, pools of darkness shot with green, seemed larger, her cheeks less prominent, her red-ochre lips more full. Moreover, when I had seen her before she had been painted, her eyelids green or blue and silvered, her lips carefully outlined and filled in, her arms and neck had been hung with bangles and chains of precious stones and gold, all of which had contributed to an attraction that invited fantasy but precluded tenderness.

She moved towards me through the water, from the deepest part to the shallows, passing through sun-splashes that gilded the darkness of her skin to nightlike shadow and into light again. The water rippled first like blue-black velvet then liquid gold against her rounded breasts, her chest, the gentle mound of her belly, her sex and her thighs. Some drops remained to twinkle like diamonds in the darkness of her hair. 'Come on. Come in.' Her hand unfolded towards me, the paler palm upwards, soliciting nearness.

For a second the water, though warm, struck cold to my ankle as it took my foot in a noose and I allowed myself a short shiver before my feet found the shelving bottom of the pool.

Uma had moved away and backwards as I descended but now she came forward again, the water surged between us, and she folded me into a clinging embrace with her cheek against my chest. I realised that she was shuddering, but I sensed that I was not the cause.

Then she stood back a pace and did something no one had ever done before, not even the whores I frequented in the years before I married Haree's mother, and which she could not do because she was blind and I was loath to prompt her. Uma placed her finger in the hollow between my ribcage and hip, the deep hollow starred with loose skin where the Sunnite's scimitar had finished its work sixty years before. Slowly, so the skin crept beneath her touch, and I shuddered with her, she moved her finger up the jagged line through the valley the steel had carved in my ribs, across my still angled collar-bone, up over my cloven chin and split lips, across my cheek and into the sightless socket of my eye. Then she laughed, the sound like bells reverberating quietly beneath that egg-shaped vault.

She came in closer again and I could smell the cinnamon fragrance of her skin beneath the sharper odours of the water, which rose, warmed by the earth's inner heart, from a deep spring far below, and slipped her hand between my arms and torso, high up almost in my armpits. There was awkwardness now as my twisted left arm got in the way, but she ran her hands down my flanks to my hip-bones and then up again, but on the way she let me feel her nails and provoked a sudden shock of desire. She smiled up at me, put her hands on my shoulders, and I felt the old bald man below thicken at last against her belly and, with a sense of sacrilege almost, trespass anyway, I put my hands – both of them, the withered claw as well – on her sides so that my forearms could feel the swell of her breasts, which were heavy but firm, and then the comfort beyond the comfort of apples as they pressed into my chest.

Her hands slipped up my neck, her fingertips explored its cord-like sinews, plucked teasingly at the loose skin, pulled the pendulous lobes of my ears, ran up the nape of my neck and over the wispy grey hair I keep well hidden beneath my old turban. The laugh came again, hardly more than a breath. 'Ali, how strong are you? Let's see.'

Her caress became a hug as she hung round my neck and launched herself upwards, spilling water from her flanks. Her thighs circled my waist and her ankles locked in the small of my back, and though she was not heavy and the water was buoyant, I was afraid I'd topple forward.

'Hold me, stupid.'

There was only one way I could – by placing my good hand under her buttocks and my bad one round her waist in the small of her back. She wriggled so that my fingers could not help but slip between and find the dark, warm moistness, not of the pool but of her secret places. Her shuddering faded now, and she placed her chin on my shoulder and nibbled my ear, then wriggled so her breasts parted from my chest with a delicious yet comic squelching noise, as when one sucks in one's cheeks through pursed lips.

'Ali, you need a wash, you know? Put me down over there, where the soap is.'

I had not noticed, but now I did, that a ledge ran round the pool just below the projecting rim but above the surface of the water. On it, not far from the steps where the water came only to my knees, there was a small alabaster flask and a sponge, perhaps one of the sponges we had bought from the boat-boy on our way up the Red Sea. I placed her so that she was sitting on the rim and handed her the flask and the sponge. The flask contained a thick, slippery cream, a dollop of which she eased out on to the sponge, which she grasped in the fingers of her right hand.

'Come closer. Between my knees.'

Imperious in the way only a young and beautiful woman can be.

And she dabbed the stuff, which was pearly white and scented with wild lavender, on my shoulders, chest and stomach.

'Closer still, I can't reach.'

Petulant now, she began to spread it over my front, scooping up water, and working up a lather. At first my skin cringed.

'Relax. It's meant to be fun. It's meant to feel nice.'

My heart began to palpitate again and I had to lean forward and put my hands on either side of her on the rim for support – which, of course, brought us closer still and again I could feel her breath in my ear. One hand, and the sponge in the other, slipped down my back, clasped my thin buttocks, wrinkled like walnut shells.

'Put your feet apart. Come on. Don't be shy. Your mother or your nurse did this for you when you were a baby.'

And again the bald man below pressed against her belly, but now he was harder and hot, as were my buttocks as her fingers slid between them. I could feel tears starting in my eyes, of pleasure, yes, but of a gratitude too, so intense that my heart began to swell as if it would burst, and also of a sort of vulnerability rewarded at last by shelter. After sixty years I felt as if I had come home. Her right hand now came round the front and slipped between us. Still pressing the bald man against her belly her fingers began to slide along him, up and down, and the heat became burning. 'He's thin,' she murmured, 'like the horn handle of a knife, and long, and just as hard. Only in sensation are we truly alive,' she continued, 'but, remember, you have five senses.'

I could smell her, a muskiness like hot metal with the cinnamon and the soap; I could feel the water, the vapour around us, the stir of air on my back, the sting of tears, the heat of my body that now centred on a burning rod of fire, the slippery flags beneath the hot soles of my feet, the warmth of her breasts, the ripple of her fingers; I could hear the rustle of her breath, the drip of water and its lolloping gurgle too, the storm of beating blood in my ears; I could taste salt on her skin and panic in my mouth; and through my one blurred eye I could see the whirling sky-shards in the roof, the flashes of diamond off the water. Then all came together in a brief nova of joy.

Down in the water I knelt in adoration and clasped her, buried my face in her. She hoisted her buttocks on to the marble rim, spread her thighs and, with her hands now at the back of my head, made my mouth find her sex. She pushed on over me, and 'Eat me,' she said, 'eat me and drink me.'

I did. And when she arched back her neck and cried I heard through it a rising shout, prolonged like surf, then crashing to a fall. It came from a distance, from a thousand throats, and it was real enough. Again she shuddered, and not from the ecstasy she had just experienced.

We resumed our clothes and returned to the gardens and the pavilion in the noontide heat, where the white stone seared the eye and the black shadows drowned it. The songbirds were still and only white doves cr–cr–crooed in the eaves. Uma sat in a leather-slung chair, legs stretched out, head forward and to one side, resting on the palm and fingers of her right hand. The posture was mannish and revelatory. I suddenly realised that this Buddhist monk was not Uma but Suryan, her brother. Or, rather, that she adopted the disguise as Suryan or as a monk so that she could move about on her own, indeed travel to the ends of the earth, untroubled by the annoyances that crowd in on a lone woman.

'I had,' she was saying, 'just come back from the impaling. I did not stay for the second lot – you heard the crowd shout just now when they were done.'

My blood ran cold to think she had been to the place of execution and seen what she had seen.

She went on, 'They were no good, you know. They wasted it. Such a waste.'

I felt a glimmer of understanding. 'They were cowards?' I volunteered.

'The worst sort. They screamed, they struggled, they shit themselves. They had the chance of the highest ecstasy, the greatest sensation. Through their agony they could have experienced, if they had been prepared to relish it, a moment of immortality. More than a moment. Instead they made it a village shambles.'

I have lived in Misr-al-Kahira and in many other Arab caliphates. I had known what that shout had been: the public impaling of robbers in the execution square. Snake-shaped hooks like those butchers use to hang dead oxen had been slung over the parapet of the gaol. The criminals had been hoisted on to the upturned points, which had thrust up through their backs, their entrails and out through their stomachs, and there they had been left to die. And Uma, driven by her strange theology, had been there to watch, hoping to see souls as well as bodies transfixed with the spikes of ecstatic pain.

Trumpets and drums. A week had passed. The hunting party was back. They came in through the big double gate, trying to look as if they had had the time of their lives – but nothing could disguise the fact that they were caked in desert dust, scratched and bruised from where they had taken tumbles, almost incapable of walking after being mounted on galumphing camels for hours on end, splattered with dried blood, their own as well as that of the animals they had killed, and weary to the point of terminal exhaustion. Behind the hunters came four carts that seemed to be loaded with heaped black flies; they trundled along beneath a buzzing, snarling haze.

Even Prince Harihara, who had been determined that the trip should be judged a success, looked thoughtful as the carcasses – matted, shapeless, bloody lumps of fur and hair – were tipped out beneath spiralling twisters of insects into that peaceful, harmonious courtyard, lined with citrus trees and roses, its long rectangular pool running down the middle. He walked through the black cloud, which glittered in the sun, prodding the bodies with the butt of his hunting spear, his other hand resting on the silver hilt of a Malayan hunting-knife that was stuck in his jewelled belt. His long, normally glossy hair was matted and dirty, his robe was torn, and for once his chin showed signs of stubble. 'Two buffalo, Ali, fine beasts. Six desert foxes. Eight quail, four sand-grouse, three gazelles, a hippopotamus, a crocodile and, best of all, three lions. What do you think?'

He didn't usually turn to me for praise – it is a commodity thought to be debased when offered by the lowly – but no one else was on hand to give it.

Well. The buffalo were white, had spreading horns six feet across and huge dewlaps. I presumed they had not been pulling carts when his crossbow bolts struck home, though I imagine not many hours had passed since they had been. The foxes were dogs which, Anish later told me, had come bounding to greet them from a village they were approaching. The quail had been netted by local bird-trappers and the sand-grouse were poultry, though of a distinctive breed and plumage. Hippo and crocodile were babies, the adults having fled. One of the lions was a cub, the lioness its mother which, while trying to protect her young, had exposed herself to the hunting party's missiles; the male was mangy, old and toothless. The gazelle were genuine, having been shot from horseback with ordinary bows and arrows by an Ahl Bedu chieftain and his sons, in whose tents the party had spent a couple of nights after getting lost in the desert.

'Truly, O Prince, you are a second Nimrod, and before Allah a great hunter.'

'Nimrod, eh, Ali? Who was Nimrod?'

'A great hunter, Prince,' I answered, risking a hint of impatience in my voice.

'Ah.'

And he and the whole troupe headed for the baths, leaving them muddy, bloody and spoiled for a full twenty-four hours until the flow of water cleansed them.

Later I stood with Anish, supervising the cleaning and repacking of the crossbows and the somewhat diminished supply of bolts. 'That,' he murmured, 'was about the worst experience of my life. Truly we have passed beyond the bounds of civilisation.'

I thought about what he had been through and what was to come.

'Anish-bey,' I said, giving him the Arab title since I am an Arab and we were in Arab country, 'I don't think we have passed the boundary. We are close to it, but I would say we are still in a country that may properly be called civilised.'

'With public executions? Impaling? To say nothing of this hunting business.'

'Believe me. You have not seen anything yet.'

CHAPTER

TWELVE

That evening over supper, taken outside the pavilion with silver lamps hanging from its arches and in the trees, the song of crickets and a great orange moon above the minarets beyond, pretending to eat sand-grouse and gazelle meat (the rotten carcasses had been buried and what we had were chicken and goat from the market) the three of us discussed which route we should take to Ingerlond. I favoured running along the coast to Sebta, crossing the straits to the great rock called Jebel Tariq and making our way to Karnatta-al-Yahud which, I argued, would prolong our stay in civilisation longer than any other route. Of course, I had in mind that that way I would be able to see Haree, though I kept that consideration to myself. However, Anish had done some homework on his own through an Indian merchant from Bombay he had hunted out, and had discovered that all commerce between the centres of civilisation and the western barbarians was done through the city-states of Venice and Genoa, that although there was always the danger of piracy the Venetians voyaged in convoys; moreover they used galleys with oars as well as sails, which precluded the delays that might attend calm weather or adverse winds. Consequently, I was commissioned next day to leave for Iskenderia, find a ship-broker and charter a galley to take us to Venice. My familiarity with the port stood me in good stead and I had no difficulty in finding what we needed.

It was then that Uma took me to one side and asked me if I would teach her the Inglysshe language. I proceeded to do so, whenever the opportunity arose, and found her an apt pupil – more so than the Prince and Anish, who occasionally joined us and made a class of these lessons.

Our induction into barbarity remained gradual. Venice, of course, looks to the east and has borrowed much of our glory in its own architecture, along with the treasures it has plundered from us. St Mark's not only looks like a mosque with a minaret, many of its stones were taken from Arab and Ottoman lands. The city-republic boasts painters of remarkable skill some of whom, had they not been fixated either on the infancy of their god and his mother or his ugly death, equalled – so Prince Harihara asserted – those of Vijayanagara. They seemed, too, to have a fair appreciation of the joys of what it is like to be truly human that we found only rarely the further we journeyed west and north.

While we were there I went in search of the alchemist who had discovered such a signal way of making an infusion out of k'hāwah beans. He was still alive, though in straitened circumstances, and delighted to find we had brought two heavy sacks with us. We took a sample along to a Jew who traded in money from a house on the Giudecca. He sampled the drink and lent a considerable sum to my alchemist, who was able thereby to set up a k'hāwah house once more in the Piazza di San Marco. The money we raised defrayed all the expenses of our expedition's stay in that watery city. This Jew, Shillem by name, had an interesting history: he had been forced to convert following a nit-picking judgement made against him by the supreme court of the city. However, he had got over this and had been back in business as a banker for a decade or more. I have to say he treated us fairly.

In miles we were now well over half-way to our destination but not in time; in fact, it took us as long again as we had already taken, and more, to find our way to Calais. The adventures and difficulties we went through are not germane to the main thread of my story so I will cut short the telling of them.

Having hired mules and asses in Mestre, we followed the valley of the river Po across the north of Italy through Vicenza, Verona and Milano to Torino.

There was much to admire in all these places but they were spoiled by the continuous state of warfare between them and even between rival parties within them. Often these fatal feuds were between families of merchants who, instead of competing in the marketplace by improving the quality of their goods or selling cheaper, resorted to swords, daggers and poison. The situation was particularly bad in Verona, which we passed through as quickly as we could after losing one of our cooks in a brawl between two gangs of unruly youths belonging to rival families. These youths even resorted to despoiling each other's tombs, but that's another story.

It was now late summer, and quite hot, so the change of climate did not much bother us until we began to climb the mountains north-west of Torino. Here, at the top of a pass called Mont Cenis, which offered us majestic views of peaks near and distant the like of which I have only seen in the high Pamirs, we caught sight of distant snow. No one would believe it was other than outcrops of white marble and branded me a liar when I tried to tell them it was crystallised water.

'Like purified sugar or salt?' Anish exclaimed mockingly.

'Like purified salt in appearance,' I replied, 'but very cold.'

Prince Harihara, however, supported me. He had heard of it but had never realised it existed in such vast quantities.

We were to see a lot more before we were through.

My companions felt the cold in the mountains and were glad to descend again into the wide valley of yet another great river, this time the Rhône, where we found the peasants occupied with the harvest of grapes from which they made a fermented alcoholic drink that has a similar effect to bhang or rice wine, but leaves you sick and with a headache. Taken in excess over a long period, it produces fatal internal bleeding and even madness. So much were the people of the area addicted to it that they grew vines in preference to wheat, hemp and other wholesome crops.

It was now that my inexperienced companions began to experience the phenomenon that over the next year and a half was to disturb them almost more than any other: the change of the seasons. In Vijayanagara there are two, warm and wet, and hot and dry, and they follow a pattern so predictable that you can tell to the day in advance when the rains will begin and at what time of day it will rain and for how long. My friends soon discovered that a day might begin warm and bright, but end cold and wet, and that as the months rolled by the leaves fell off most of the trees, that almost all growth failed so the people had to subsist on what they had stored in barns which, by the following spring, was usually rotten. We saw people dying of hunger – a sight to which I was no stranger, but which Prince Harihara and Anish declared was obscene, an offence against nature and the gods, which indeed it is.

While I have a speculative mentality Anish likes to categorise, label, evaluate. Once, as we passed across a high plain where the crop of wheat had been burnt before harvesting rather than the stubble afterwards, where we saw the unburied corpses of women and children who had been raped and impaled, where we passed an open grave-pit filled with the blackened corpses of those who had died of plague, he said, 'Ali, you know if you said our Vijayanagaran commonwealth was the First World, and the Arab states we passed through the Second, then this surely is the Third and worst, a world where the evil hounds of famine, sword and pestilence range at will behind the god of war.'

We made slow progress up the Rhône and then the Saône, across those burnt and ravaged uplands then down the Seine to Paris, passing through lands owned or ruled by the King of the Franks and the Duke of Burgundy, who were rivals for supremacy in the area, and many other fiefdoms, principalities and duchies, seeing many skirmishes on our way. We also saw much repression and persecution of the peasantry, and of anyone who raised a voice against the abuses or irrationality of the Church, this resulted in frequent burnings and worse in public places. As foreigners who were clearly not Christians and, since our skins were dark instead of pale, cold and bloodless, possibly not fully human, we were in constant danger of being arrested and condemned as heretics, spies or aliens. However, these people believed above all in money and wealth, although they were loath to admit it, and we were always able to buy safe-conducts and even armed protection from the nobles whose land we rode across from the store of gold and jewels we had brought with us.

Meanwhile the weather worsened and all were grateful for my foresight in this as in other things. Each person's small cache of pearls was sold in the city of Dijon, the principal residence of the Dukes of Burgundy, and soon every great lady of the court, and many of the men too, were vying with the rest in the splendour of the pearl beads they wore as necklaces, rings and earrings. By creating a fashion we turned what might have been a glut into a shortage, and the consequence was that our whole party left the walled city clad in the richest of furs and woollens, and well shod too.

And so, without too much suffering or discomfort, we came at last, in the very depths of winter, to the shores of the sea again, but this time a cold grey sea, and the port of Calais. It was the month the Ingerlonders call January, approaching the turn of the years they number 1459 to 1460.

PART II

CHAPTER

THIRTEEN

T he following day I arrived at the usual time, and was shown in the usual way through a shady flagstoned passage to the pierced stone screen that separated the vestibule of Ali's house from the garden beyond. As usual the light glowed fiercely through the lacy stonework and I could hear the tinkle of water and the chirp of birds beyond. The cedarwood door creaked a little as his gate-keeper, a huge black Nubian with pantaloons, a turban and scimitar, pushed it open and ushered me through with his usual exaggerated obeisance.

I climbed the two steps of black obsidian, the ferns brushed my shins, and I stood for a moment blinking in the hot sunlight before I realised that Ali was not in his usual place beneath the cardamom tree. I hesitated, but the gatekeeper urged me on. I crossed the flat, square stepping-stones and felt the welcome prick of coldness as drops of water fell on my feet, the furthest flung by the fountain. Ali's grey cat came out from under a bush and pushed herself against my hand as I stooped to tickle her behind her ear. Then I straightened and saw sheets of paper on the table where we normally sat. A jug of lemonade held them down, though indeed no air stirred to shift them. There was only one glass.

The top sheet was pure white rag and seemed to throb in my eye, so bright was the sun on it in spite of the fresh black writing; the rest, and there was quite a stack, were yellowed and curling at the edges. I took the top sheet and read:

My dear Mah-Lo,
Today I am tired and it is too hot. About this time of year, although I know it will bring back my inflamed and swollen joints, I almost long for the

monsoon. The heat brings on a dangerous flux from my bowels, a disease I first contracted in darkest Ingerlond and which recurs every three months or so. However, I would not disappoint you and I have asked Murteza to lay out certain documents for your perusal which will carry the story forward. They are copies, made by Chamberlain Anish, of letters sent by Prince Harihara to his cousin the Emperor. Not all the originals made it to Vijayanagara, but Anish, as his duties demanded, made copies before sending them, and these are what you will read here. If they do nothing else they will corroborate for you the veracity of what I have told you so far, and of what I hope, Inshallah, or anyway if this filthy flux leaves me before killing me, I shall be able to tell you when I am fit enough to take up my tale once more on my own account. Yours and so on . . . Ali ben Quatar Mayeen.

I took my place on the cushioned stone seat, poured myself a glass of lemonade, and began to read.

Dear Cousin

We have arrived in the Pale of Calais and it is time I began the letters I promised you to let you know how we are progressing with the various tasks we set ourselves for this expedition. I shall not take up your time, or indeed mine, with an account of the adventures we had on our way here, fascinating though many of them were, since they are not relevant to the purposes of our coming hither. They can wait for our return when, no doubt over many evenings, they will help pass the time between supper and bed.

Calais is like an onion cut in half by the sea. It has many skins. First there is the Pale, a fortified frontier, enclosing a semi-circle of land, the second skin. The town walls make the third, near what would be, were it a whole onion, its centre. At its greatest distance the Pale is some twenty or more miles from the city walls and the fields and pastures between produce enough to feed the population. The fortifications that make up the Pale include ditches in front of low turf walls surmounted with a paling fence, which gives the name 'pale' to the whole area, two or three large forts built to cover the principal roads in and out, moats, canals, and where the natural rivers run in appropriate directions, they have been turned into obstacles.

Inside the Pale but close to it, on the southern side, is a larger fortress called Guisnes, which lies across the road that links Calais with Paris.

The walls of Calais itself are, we have been told and, no doubt, shortly we shall be able to verify this, substantial and castle-like. Inside are the streets and a keep; and finally there is the harbour itself, two basins one within the other, enclosed and protected by moles from both storms and seaborne incursions.

This whole area is held by the Ingerlonders and indeed is considered by them to be a part of Ingerlond, but is at this time contested by two different factions of Ingerlonders who are at enmity with each other. The first faction has as its base the fortress of Guisnes, built to counter incursions from the Franks, whose king claims Calais. However, the Franks are more occupied at the moment with the Burgundians than the Ingerlonders and are therefore not a threat to Calais. So, this first faction can use Guisnes as a base from which they can mount attacks on the second faction, which holds the town and port of Calais.

This first faction is led by the Duke of Somerset. He is a cousin of the King of Ingerlond. The King of Ingerlond's wife, Queen Margaret, sent him to Calais to wrest it from the Captain of Calais, who is the Earl of Warwick. An earl is a noble of high degree but not as high as a duke. Dukes must have royal blood, I think. The Earl of Warwick is a friend and supporter of the Duke of York, who is also a cousin of the King, but an enemy of the Queen. Somerset has good reason for hating Warwick, who killed Somerset's father in a battle some four years ago. I know this is all very confusing, and I confess I am not confident that I have understood it all myself. Perhaps it will become clearer as time goes on.

Guisnes is some way from the sea and we have to cross the sea to get to Ingerlond. The only harbour from which it is safe to arrive in Ingerlond is the harbour of Calais. Either we must get into Calais, which the Duke of Somerset and his army have been trying to do without success for some months, or go back to a Frankish port to the south-west such as Boulogne or Dieppe and this we cannot really do because it is now dangerous for us to go back into Francia. When we were in Francia we promised the Frank king we would have nothing to do with the Ingerlonders

who are his enemies. And, anyway, the Ingerlonder ports are closed
to ships from Francia. So, you see, we do have problems.

They are not helped by what the people here call 'the weather'.
It is not easy to explain what weather is to someone who has not
experienced it. I will try, though, since I fancy it is going to play
a considerable part in our lives in the months to come. Apparently
the 'weather' is even worse in Ingerlond than Francia. Let me start
with rain.

Here it may rain at any time of day or night, for hours or only
minutes at a time, as heavily as it does at home or very lightly in
what they call a 'drizzle'. And, believe it or not, this changeability is
a feature throughout the year. Which leads me to consider the year
as such and the seasons, two of which we have already experienced
– autumn and winter. But no. This will be altogether too confusing.
Let me stay with weather. I'll return to the seasons later, apart from
saying that this is the cold season, which is not surprising as the
nights are twice as long as the days, while in six months' time it
will be the other way round and the season will be summer. I
suppose that just as the weather is now unbearably cold, compared
with our temperate clime, it will become unbearably hot in the
summer. But just now, as I have said, the days are short, gloomy
and cold.

So much for rain. Now, wind. Wind is as variable as rain. It can
blow from any direction at all, at any time of the day or night, or
there can be no wind at all. It may be barely more than a breath or
it may be a gale, but even when it is a gale it comes in bursts and
gusts, not continuous twisting blasts of wind such as occasionally
fall upon the eastern coasts of our own country.

Although at this time of year the weather is generally cold, it
may vary from intolerably cold, so that the water turns solid, to
fairly cold so that the water that was solid in the morning is wet
again by midday. We have had some snow. You remember about
snow? Travellers from the mountains to the far north of our part
of the world have told us about snow, and Ali ben Quatar Mayeen
warned us that it might be encountered. Well, we have had some
snow, but so far, like the hard water or 'ice', it has melted away
to water before midday, leaving everywhere muddy and dirty.

But what I must emphasise above all else is the unpredictability of all this. It is hardly ever the same weather two days' running. The only thing you can say about it is that it is almost always, one way or another, uncomfortable. And cold.

I can't tell you how messy it all is. I am writing at a desk in front of a tiny window in a tower overlooking the land that stretches between here and the town twenty miles away. The desk is rough-hewn to the extent that the quill I am using, as you see, splatters and bumps over the ridges beneath. The stone walls are undressed too and irregular, the stones just piled on each other with mortar slopped between them. The window is glazed with tiny pieces of glass, none the same as any of the others, held together by strips of lead. The glass is translucent, just, but not fully transparent. It is cloudy and it distorts the view. My desk is lit by a candle, although it is midday, made from animal fat, mutton from the smell of it, and it smokes. There is a small fire of smouldering logs in a large fireplace. All the heat goes up the chimney. There are hangings on the walls, with hunting scenes crudely stitched into them, spoiled by the grubs of moths that live in the interstices.

Opening the window, which I have to do if I want enough light to go on writing, I look out over sodden fields, farmed in strips, copses of leafless, dead-looking trees, a road that angles round the holdings of the peasants towards the distant town, which is a smudge of smoke on the horizon. The road is not a real road but a narrow strip of mud and puddles, the mud a pale brown except where the rock shows through, not really rock but a softish, powdery, white material at present slimy with rain.

There is no living thing in sight at present but there are a couple of dead ones: on a rise near the road there is a gallows where two bodies, hanged by the neck, slowly twist. Earlier a bird, big and black with a heavy grey beak, pecked and tore at their faces, but even it has now gone. The poor souls were accused of spying on behalf of those Ingerlonders who hold Calais under the Earl of Warwick.

You know what it is, cousin, about this place? I'll tell you. It feels unfinished, half made, as if Parvati, the Creatorix, has been called away to more pressing business only shortly after she has started. Or put it this way. Parvati, having started the act of creation on the banks of one of our sacred rivers and brought what she created to an early completion and perfection, moved out in a series of concentric circles, and, after many hundreds, indeed thousands, of years has only just begun her work here.

Enough for now. I have just been called to the council chamber of this Duke of Somerset.

I'm back now from the council chamber. This young Duke of Somerset – he's not more than twenty-five – is a proud man and kept us waiting as other supplicants appeared in front of where he sat, like a king, on a throne. When it was our turn, he expected us to make a deep bow when we were first ushered out to stand in front of him. I must confess I am disappointed. I had expected that the nobility at any rate would have manners, a sense of what is fitting. He knows who I am. He knows that I am cousin to an emperor. He has no cause to give himself airs. As far as I can gather he is as much besieged in this squalid little castle as those in Calais are besieged by him. He has only a thousand men here with him though he says he daily expects reinforcements as soon as the weather is good enough to allow them to land on the beaches.

Anyway, to cut a long story short, Ali has managed things well, as he always does. In return for several pounds' weight each of ginger, nutmeg, coriander, cardamom and cloves, this duke is going to give us a safe-conduct to the gates of Calais, but only if we give an undertaking not to cross the Channel and visit Ingerlond. Instead we have agreed, once we have access to the port, to take a boat up the coast to a Germanic city called Bremen and trade there. Apparently it is an important member of the Hanseatic League, which is a cartel of merchants who rule the ports along the mainland coasts from Bruges to Muscovy and control almost all the trade in the area except that of Ingerlond. Since we have no intention of going there, this is all by the way – Bremen is just Ali's excuse to get us into Ingerlond. I'll let you know how this works out as soon as the situation is clear.

Meanwhile, a quick word about Ali. He really has turned out rather well, for all he remains, in appearance anyway, as uncouth as ever. His mastery of languages is astonishing: he has been able to communicate with the locals in every country we have passed through. This should be no surprise since it is what he promised us, but I confess to being more impressed than I had expected to be. But he has also shown great acumen in dealing with people, getting things organised, trading off the goods we have brought, in what seem to me to be profitable bargains. Like the rest of us he now goes about in furs, in his case a long, shaggy coat, rather mangy and shabby. Shiva knows what sort of animal it came from. Underneath he keeps his old cape with the hole in it for his head, his turban and his loincloth. Yet, as ever, he manages to carry himself with a sort of reserved dignity that usually commands respect.

Anish, too, is turning out well enough, though he suffers from the cold more than most of us . . . A knock at my door. I'll finish this off when I have seen whoever is calling.

Well, it was Anish and Ali, with bad news. Our soldiers are to be sent home. Apparently the healthy darkness of their skins together with arms and accoutrements that appear strange and even devilish to these superstitious people have attracted hostility and, I would guess, envy. In short, Somerset refuses to let them go on with us. Ali thinks Somerset is afraid they will join Warwick and be used against him and that their magical powers may prove decisive. So. We will press on without them. Ali says we should have no difficulty in recruiting hired bodyguards whenever we think we need them. This reduces our little troupe to some ten or so including a Buddhist monk, who has hung around us since we left, and a fakir, who no longer amuses us – we have seen his tricks too often. However, he usually gets a crowd of the gullible in the villages and marketplaces we pass through who give him food and small change, which he shares with our Buddhist.

That really is all for now. The light is fading, this candle is burning low and stinking more than ever.

Our soldiers can take this with them. I almost envy them, despite the long haul they have ahead.

I remain, dear cousin,

Your devoted servant, Harihara

CHAPTER

FOURTEEN

Dear Cousin

Well, here we are in Calais, in the castle or keep, and things are a little better than they were before. At least we are warmer, our accommodation is almost adequate, and the company merrier, though in a rough, buffoonish way. But, first, the last twenty miles that got us here.

The road we took was never less than ankle-deep in mud, and often knee-deep. This Duke of Somerset stole our saddle horses – he called it requisitioning, leaving us only the pack animals, which in effect he confiscated as well but then, on Ali's insistence, agreed to sell them back to us. So, although we had to walk we were able at least to take with us the few precious commodities we still had left for trade and barter.

The rain continued to fall, blowing across the bleak plain like curtains of icy grey silk which yet, perhaps on account of the fineness of the drops, seemed to penetrate our clothes or at any rate seek out the gaps between them and our skin. Our feet squelched in the yellowish-white clay, which contrived to be both sticky and greasy at the same time – that is, it stuck like overcooked unwashed rice to our footwear, yet when impacted presented a surface on which one slid and tumbled. Some of the small rivers we crossed had precarious plank bridges, just wide enough to take a narrow agricultural cart, but three of the lesser ones had no bridges and we had to wade through them, dragging our reluctant asses and mules behind us.

The fields were ploughed but not yet harrowed and water lay in runnels like strips of polished lead in the furrows. When, or if, the land dries out, the soil will be broken up and planted with seed which, in eight months' time, will carry grain, which they call rye and which they will grind for the flour to make the bread that is the staple diet of the ordinary people. We have already had our fill of it. It is heavy, grey, stodgy, sour stuff, which has caused most of us to be severely constipated. However, here in Calais the nobility eat a white bread made from wheat, which is almost palatable.

The leafless trees looked dead though some we were told, those planted in regular lines, were fruit trees and would bear fruit when summer, the warm season, comes. They keep these fruits in the roofs of their barns, wrapped in straw. We have eaten some. They are called apples. The skin is dry, wrinkled and coarse, the white flesh squashy yet dry too. They are a pale brown but, we are told, when fresh they were a yellowish green and so delicious that they call them golden. According to Ali, the apples grown in Ingerlond are better.

There is meat available – beef, which of course we will not touch, pork, which Ali refuses, mutton and domestic fowls – though little is eaten by the common people. Almost all the animals and poultry they rear are taken into the city and sold so they can pay rent and taxes to the landowners, who are Ingerlonder gentry. They either boil it in pots or broil it over open fires. In neither case do they try to improve the flavour apart from smearing it with salt before cooking. It is thus either tasteless or disgusting. They drink milk, but straight from the cow without allowing it to mature or ferment so it is bland, ale, which is a sour strong liquor made from grain that has been allowed to germinate and rot, and wine, also very tart so it seems to take the skin off the inside of one's mouth. They do not drink water, which they say carries disease. Consequently the Ingerlonders are drunk by the end of every meal, including breakfast.

Although it was only twenty miles, this last stage of our journey took two days – partly on account of the shortness of the days but mainly because of the state of the road. We spent the night in a fortified tavern with a courtyard in the middle, stabling on three sides of the ground floor, a communal room on the other, and dormitories above. There was nothing in the way of hygiene. Travellers, male and female, were expected to piss and shit on the edges of a great pile of steaming muck in the middle of the courtyard – a mountain of human ordure and the sweepings from the stables. There were no washing facilities. Apart from those provided by the incessant rain.

This inn marked the border between the land controlled by Warwick, which we were entering, and that of Somerset, which we were leaving. We had been accompanied by a small troop of Somerset's soldiers who stayed at the inn, relieving their comrades who returned on the next day to Guisnes. At the inn there were soldiers in the service of Warwick. We expected them to fight, but though they were well armed they saw no reason to do so, which was the first mark of good sense I have seen amongst these people. They carried swords, bows and arrows, and wore rimmed helmets over chain-mail cowls, and jerkins. They did not carry shields, as these, they said, would interfere with their handling of the bows. Shields, they said, were for the gentry. I allowed them to see the keen interest I felt in their bows and they were kind enough to demonstrate them.

They are fearsome weapons. Each bow is a simple branch, shaped and seasoned, nearly six feet long. The arrows are a yard long and tipped with a slim but barbed steel point. Each soldier normally carries ten or a dozen at a time. They can shoot further than almost any crossbow and pierce armour up to half an inch thick at a hundred yards. But, in contrast to crossbows, they have one enormous disadvantage: they require huge strength on the part of the bowman to be of any real use. Most men in Ingerlond apparently begin training with a smaller version at an early age, and are required by their lords to keep up the practice into late manhoood. The result is that you can tell an Ingerlonder, not one of the gentry but the ordinary countryfolk, by the swollen, overmuscled nature of his shoulders and arms, especially the right one, which pulls the feather flight of the arrow right back to his ear.

Although these two troops of bowmen were serving opposed

masters they expressed no enmity or even dislike for each other through most of the evening, but ate and drank together in perfect amity. Until, that is, they got into a game of dice whereat a quarrel broke out with one man accusing another of cheating. By now, of course, all were drunk. The quarrel became a fight, but not with real weaponry, just fists, table-legs, chairs and so forth. The public rooms were wrecked, many heads were bloodied, and two or three were rendered unconscious. Then suddenly all fell back into friendliness again for no apparent reason, and they continued drinking ale together until all had fallen into a stupor as if nothing untoward had happened at all.

We woke to an almost cloudless dawn and a piercing cold wind that blew out of the eye of the rising sun. For a moment it was all almost beautiful: the sky above sapphire, then, in the east, rose-pink like the tips of lotus petals or wild roses; the ground, the broken furrows, the trees and their branches and twigs were all covered in a dust like diamonds that glittered in the sun. Almost for a moment I believed the verses my brother Jehani had copied out, describing a jewelled city. This dust was a little like snow but finer and is called frost. It is made from the tiny particles of moisture in the air that freeze then fall and collect on everything they land on.

In spite of the cold the brightness seemed to cheer everyone, not just us, but the soldiers, the bowmen, the other travellers and the servants in the inn. All bustled about slapping their sides to keep warm, shouting and even singing at each other, though some quietened down a litttle when a small girl, not more than three years old, was found in a corner of a barn where she had gone in the night to piss and had frozen to death once away from the animals and her parents, who had been drunk.

We breakfasted off the foul bread and milk warm from the udder, though the bowmen pushed slabs of ground-up but barely cooked beef between pieces of bread and drank ale, and we were on the road again within an hour of the sun being fully above the horizon. At first it seemed easier than the day before because, with the frost, all the moisture in the soil had frozen so one no longer had to wade and paddle through mud. However, it was all churned up into clods as hard as rocks and unless one kept one's eye firmly on where one was putting one's feet one might twist an ankle in an

ugly fall. And then, of course, where there had been large pools
or puddles there was now sheeted ice, cloudy like watered milk,
and more slippery even than the most highly polished marble or
basalt, even when wet.

Nevertheless, we got along and soon the walls of Calais took
shape in front of us, a long, curving line of battlements marked off
in sections by rounded towers. Much of the stone they were built
from was pale, almost white, and gleamed in the sun that was now
behind us but much of it too, especially near the top, was blackened
with soot. Indeed, the whole city lay beneath a pall of black, greasy
smoke for in winter they burn coal, a black rock of which there are
many outcrops in the area, and which glows brightly and gives off
great heat. However, it also gives off a foul black smoke, sulphurous
in smell and noxious too: apparently every year a great many people
who huddle too close to their fires in winter or have chimneys that
do not draw properly are asphyxiated by it. They fall asleep, then
into a coma and die.

We were, of course, challenged at the gate, which was not
hinged but suspended above the road on hemp hawsers and
lowered or raised by winches mounted high in the walls above.
It is made out of a grid of heavy studded timbers leaving square
gaps through which the defenders can see and shoot arrows at
hostile visitors. It is called a portcullis, and since the principle of
it might be useful to us, I have had it sketched.

Clearly we were neither Franks nor from Somerset's Ingerlonders, which was the first concern of the captain in charge of
the gate, and we soon persuaded him, by showing some of our
wares and the safe-conducts provided by potentates whose land
we had crossed before entering Francia, that we were indeed what
we said we were: merchants from the Orient. The colour of our
skin bore witness to this for the captain, a knight, claimed his
father had fought Moors and Turks in the eastern Mediterranean
and had told him the men and women in those parts often had
skin as dark as ours.

This led to a raucous discussion in their barbarous tongue, which
Ali later told us turned on whether or not we were Mussulmen
and therefore infidels and pagans. On our behalf he told these
Ingerlonders that we were no such thing but had come from lands

even further to the east than those occupied by the Musselmen and that one of the things we hoped to take back with us, along with the goods we traded, was the true religion of Christ the Saviour, and that anyway we were enemies of the Musselmen who had been trying to conquer our country for seven hundred years.

The upshot was that after an hour or so, during which darkness began to steal slowly over the scene instead of falling quickly as it does in our country, we were told that we were free to find lodgings for the night in the town, and that we must present ourselves to the Earl of Warwick early the next day, or if not Warwick himself then some officer empowered by him to issue us with the necessary passports and permits. At last we entered the town.

The trouble with Calais is that it is too small for what it contains. The problem is wool. Wool is what the Ingerlonder economy depends on and the kings have made it a law that no wool should be traded abroad except through Calais. Of course, a trade so large attracts much commerce in other goods, and industries, too, so the small semi-circle, which if the streets were not so crowded one could walk across in less than fifteen minutes, is packed with warehouses, counting-houses, and then, of course, housing for all employed here: ships' chandlers, ropemakers, sailmakers, ship-repairers and ship-builders, smiths and a hundred and one related trades.

The streets are narrow and dark for the second and third storeys of the buildings overhang each other and almost meet at the top so one can stretch a hand from one house to touch the hand of whoever lives on the other side. They are filthy too. You cannot begin to imagine how filthy. Every street is a midden and it is no rarity to see an alley completely blocked off by a heap as high as six feet of shit, kitchen refuse, broken furniture, old bricks where a house has fallen down . . . whatever.

Ali took us to the inn where he had been staying when the mysterious *sadhu* gave him the parchments from my brother Jehani but I took one look at it and said, 'No!' On our way here we have stayed in some pretty disgusting places as well as palaces, but this was beyond me. I took a second look and struggled not to vomit as the landlord's bitch, a giant mangy hound, shat copiously a foot from where I was standing. I then told Ali that, cost what it might,

I wanted lodgings that were warm and clean and it was up to him to find them. Meanwhile, we took ourselves off to the main square and stationed ourselves round a stone cross that marked its centre, averting our eyes from a gibbet where the thirty-two quarters of eight dismembered criminals had been hung to rot. This, I must suppose, was where Ali's *sadhu* was burnt alive.

It was dark now, but the square was lit by flambeaux made of smoky pitch, which I could see were not likely to last more than an hour. Presently it began to snow. The flambeaux hissed and spluttered and three or four were extinguished. There were, however, many sounds of revelry, raucous music, shouting and singing, and many windows overlooking the square were lit. I surmised that possibly some festival was in progress, and in this, as you will shortly learn, I was right.

I had almost given up on Ali, suspecting that he had been waylaid and murdered by footpads and was reckoning that in the morning the populace would awake to find us frozen statues, when at last he reappeared, swinging himself along on his thin white pole.

'Prince,' he cried, 'we are in luck. I have persuaded the chamberlain of no less a person than the Earl of Warwick himself to welcome us into his hall where there is a feast already started, food, shelter, warmth and entertainment.'

Well, we all pulled ourselves together, shrugged the snow off our cloaks and stamped our feet. The muleteers stirred our draught animals awake, our fakir came out of his trance, and the Buddhist jingled his finger cymbals and started his monotonous chant.

'In fact,' Ali went on, as we began to make our way up a slight incline, 'we are expected. There have even been men out looking for us.'

'How should this be?'

'Tonight is a special feast. It is called Twelfth Night because it falls twelve nights after the birth of Jesus, whom they call God. It seems that on this night three kings from the Far East, from India perhaps, came to his birthplace with special gifts. Now. The captain at the gate, who let us in, apparently reported our arrival to the nobles here and likened us to the three kings, both on account of the darkness of our skins and the wealth we appeared to have with us, whereupon Warwick gave orders that we should be found and brought to the hall. And, of course, when I arrived pleading for shelter I was recognised by the captain of the gate as one of the party he had been describing . . .'

Already we were beneath the walls of the keep or central fortress of the city, close to two of the large temples or churches. The guards let us pass beneath a portcullis, like the one in the city walls, and ushered us into an anteroom or guardroom while they advised our hosts of our arrival. There was a fire and rush-lights, and already things looked better than they had. We could hear music, played on squealing pipes with banging drums, coming across a small courtyard from a hall with high, narrow windows that glowed with the lights within.

Ali went on, 'These three kings,' he said, 'were called Caspar, Melchior and Balthazar, and I think it would please them if we represented them as best we can. You, Prince, should be Caspar because he came first, I can play Melchior, and Anish should be Balthazar, since he is always represented as a blackamoor and of the three of us Anish's colouring is the darkest.'

Anish was annoyed by this, he does not like to be reminded of his Tamil ancestry, but there was no denying what Ali had said so I told Anish to be quiet and to do as he was told. Ali concluded, 'The gifts they brought were gold, incense and myrrh. If we use bdellium from our medicine chest for myrrh, the aroma is similar, and I think we can provide all three. And I shall need something a little richer than my usual garments if I am to be a king . . .'

He never ceases to surprise me, our Ali, for now he bustled about like a child with a new game to play, getting us into our best clothes with gold chains and so forth, pulling my second-best robe on over his usual turban and cape, neither of which he divested himself of, and generally getting us lined up and ready, me with a small gold goblet encrusted with diamonds and rubies, with elephants carved round the rim – I expect you remember it, a nice enough trinket and not at all special – he with a handul of incense sticks, and Anish with a silver box containing a small slab of bdellium, which we had brought with us as a prophylactic against stomach cramps.

CHAPTER

FIFTEEN

First, let me describe the hall. It was quite large, perhaps as much as fifty good paces long and twenty wide, with a high, pitched roof supported on hammer-beams and corbels. We entered at one end through large double doors (hardwood of the sort they call oak which they use for all timber work where strength is required, though it is nothing like as hard or strong as the woods we use), and were confronted at the other end by a raised dais on which the chief nobles sat, facing the main body of the hall.

This was filled by two long parallel tables at which sat forty or more squires and knights, lesser gentry. In the middle of the wall to our left there was a huge fireplace in which numerous logs were blazing, enough to warm the whole room; on the other side, facing the fire, were doors smaller than the one by which we had entered, which we soon discovered gave access to and from a large kitchen. The whole place was lit with many candles, some fixed to cast-iron wheels suspended horizontally from the ceiling, others in fixtures attached to the walls; nevertheless, the higher beams supporting the roof and the corners remained shadowy and in darkness, a gloom exacerbated by the fact that the place was decorated with branches of evergreens called ivy and holly.

As the night wore on many of the candles died a guttering smoky death, and by midnight almost the only light came from the great fire. However, this did not prevent the carousing and horseplay continuing almost to dawn.

Above us, as we entered, there was an overhanging gallery filled with . . . I was going to say musicians, but it was scarcely music they produced from their instruments. These were made from brass as trumpets, hunting horns and sackbuts, wood as flutes and a pipe called the hautboy with a reed, which made a nasty squealing noise, and untuned drums, which either gave off a booming bang or a fierce, grating rattle. Some of the pipes had bladders attached with a second pipe sticking out of them. The bladder was filled with the breath of the piper who then squeezed it forcing air through this second pipe to make a long, monotonous drone.

These musicians welcomed us with a fanfare, and as we walked down the aisle between the two tables all the men stood up and cheered, banging their horn-handled knives on their pewter plates or on the table. Somewhat bemused but sensing that the atmosphere and intentions of all were friendly, I led our procession on towards the dais with as much composure as I could muster and found myself faced with a living picture which I recognised from paintings, stained-glass windows and the like, which we had seen on our way from Venice. It was a presentation, indeed a travesty, of the group they call the holy family – Mary, the mother of Jesus, Joseph, his father, and the newborn Jesus himself, to whom we were to present our gifts.

A travesty indeed. Have I said there were no women at all in this hall? Such was the case, though now I believed for a moment that I was wrong. For, though the figure that portrayed the mother of Jesus was six feet tall and exceedingly well built, he was also dressed in a blue robe with a cowl round whose edge he peeked coyly. Moreover, his fair skin beneath the one lock of auburn hair we could see was smooth and fine, his eyes large, wide and intensely blue; his mouth was painted like a harlot's. Once I realised that this was a man dressed as a woman I could see how two other factors had made the deception momentarily successful: he was young, only seventeen years old, and handsome in a light, winsome way. Behind him stood 'Joseph', an older man, in his thirties, heavily built, strong-looking, and dark in hair, though rubicund in skin colour, but wearing when we first saw him a heavy beard and wig hastily improvised from bits of sheepskin worn woollen side out, with a coarse cloak requisitioned from one of his servants.

Most disturbing of all was the infant Jesus, or rather the creature that stood in for him, carried in the arms of the 'mother'. This was nothing more nor less than a sucking pig, alive, but not struggling, quite content to lie on its back in the crook of the 'mother's' arm, gazing up into the face above it, with every indication of content, save that its snout wrinkled and quested . . . perhaps for milk?

The hall now fell silent and I did not need the whispered prompting of Ali to treat the show with some seriousness. I approached the group, knelt at the booted feet of the Mary, with the humblest obeisance I could muster, and placed the goblet on the floor. Ali and Anish did likewise, and then, as Anish heaved himself to his feet (for all the privations we have suffered he is no thinner), the whole hall burst into an uproar of laughter and cheers. Possibly this frightened the piglet, which now wriggled convulsively and urinated on 'Mary's' lap. The young man playing the part launched himself to his feet with a bellow, set the piglet scurrying across the floor, aimed a kick at it, which missed. 'Damned creature,' he cried. 'Wasn't he meant to be in swaddling clothes?'

The two men then threw off their borrowed robes and led us to sit at their high table beside them.

'Joseph' acted as host as, indeed, was right since this was Richard Neville, the Earl of Warwick and Captain of Calais (pray do not confuse him with the captain of the guard). He is, and he made sure we knew it, a man of great wealth and power, owning great estates throughout the kingdom of Ingerlond through his marriage to a lady who had brought with her dowry the title he bore. He himself is the son and heir of the Earl of Salisbury, an old man, once a great warrior, who also sat at the table. Neville, then and since, showed a certain arrogance in his behaviour, a wilfulness, an unpredictability that we soon learnt was a general characteristic of all the Ingerlonder nobility, though exaggerated in him. His pride was not without justification. We soon learnt that he had distinguished himself militarily, especially at sea, clearing the channel that lies between Ingerlond and Francia of pirates, though he was known to be both impetuous and indecisive as a general on dry land.

The other younger man was introduced to us simply as March. Or Eddie. Eddie March. I understand him to be a person of some consequence, but not a lot, owing his position in the company to his prowess, his good looks and the friendship of Warwick, rather than to any claim to greatness he might have through blood or inherited lands.

Incidentally, and in this as in so much else I am indebted to Ali for tutoring me, the Ingerlonders set enormous store by wealth and parentage, and little to talent or merit. But that is by the way.

Now the charade was over the feasting began. The food was, again, disgusting. There were huge amounts of beef and mutton, too, hacked from a whole sheep that was spitted above the fire. There was a centrepiece of a swan stuffed with a peacock, stuffed with a cockerel, stuffed with larks; many vegetables of the sort we feed only to animals, such as cabbage and various roots; mountains of bread, made from wheat and just about edible, butter, cream and hard, strong cheeses. But there were also preserved or dried fruits, some from warmer lands, such as dates and figs, and nuts, almonds and cobs.

But worst of all was the amount of strong drink, a never-ending supply of ales and wines brought to the table in large ewers by serving-boys, which, of course, soon took their effect. I earlier used the word 'horseplay', which may have puzzled you, but I used it advisedly for it describes accurately a particular sort of foolery almost all now gave themselves up to. When the tables were cleared of most of the feast's debris apart from the goblets and ewers, the younger, lighter men climbed on to the backs of the heavier larger ones who gripped their riders' knees in the crooks of their elbows and carried them in combat against the others, the aim being to 'unhorse' the riders, or bring both riders and mounts crashing to the floor. To this end they used whatever they could find as weapons except real ones. Cushions and pillows were brought into play, ladles and big spoons, even empty and not so empty jugs and big drinking vessels they call tankards, made out of pewter.

Soon there was blood everywhere, and broken furniture and tableware but no serious injuries that I could see. Once a couple fell or were beaten to the ground they retired to the sides, where they continued to contribute to the noise, if nothing else, by cheering on the survivors. The result was that there was more noise when only two couples were left than there had been at the outset. One pair was made up of Richard Neville with Eddie March on his back, and the other by an old man called William Neville, Lord Fauconberg, riding a younger knight (though still in his forties, I would guess) called John Dynham. Fauconberg, we later learnt, was Warwick's uncle. Until now I had thought the survival of Richard Neville and March was due to Neville's seniority as Earl of Warwick and Captain of Calais and that none durst overturn him, but I was wrong. His uncle, who had a grizzled beard and shoulders as broad as an ox's, managed to get his foot between those of his nephew and with one hard push had him over. Yet it was not just brute force that tumbled him but cunning too, for Fauconberg had seen an upturned chair behind Warwick and that was enough to provide the leverage to trip him.

Warwick did not take kindly to this ruse, though young March laughed it off readily enough. Warwick claimed treachery and trickery on his uncle's part and his face darkened with anger, but he was shouted down by the onlookers who declared Fauconberg and Dynham had won fairly. I had the feeling that many of the young men were glad of an excuse to belittle their general.

Well, cousin, as I said, the candles burnt low, most of the men fell by degrees into a drunken stupor though not until they had sung many a maudlin song to the accompaniment of the musicians, mostly about lost loves, or the ladies they worship from afar and long for hopelessly, and one or two about friends slain in battle. But even as night wore towards day we were constantly reminded of the barbarity of the people we had come amongst. The stone floor was strewn with rushes and sawdust and this, they seemed to think, gave them licence to urinate and worse against the walls, and the dogs too, of which there were several and all very large, did their business where they wanted. We kept ourselves to ourselves, huddled in a corner near the fire, and dreamt, wrapped in a more complete darkness, of a home we had never perhaps properly appreciated until then.

We were woken quite suddenly, even roughly, shortly after dawn, first by a servant who came and stirred the great fire back into life, adding some kindling and dry logs, then by the general shift and shuffle of men stirring whilst still suffering from the effects of carousing on alcohol. Into all this came the sudden clatter of horses' hoofs on the cobbles outside, challenges and passwords exchanged, and in came three men wearing chain-mail, conical helmets, with broadswords scabbarded at their sides. Their heavy boots rang on the flagstones. They also had plate armour on their arms and legs, but none on their bodies that we could see, though these were concealed by tabards decorated with a white diagonal cross on red, which we later discovered designated them followers of the Neville family.

They strode up the hall and were shortly in animated conversation with the Earl, who had fallen asleep under the high table to which he had returned to nurse his pride and drown his sorrows after the horseplay tournament.

Meanwhile, the grey light from the tall windows slowly spread and filled the great hall, casting its dull light over the mess and ordure left from the night before. I was glad at least to see that some of the boys who had served had reappeared with brushes and brooms to push the filth and debris into piles which they then carried out before strewing the floor with fresh straw and rushes. The to-ing and fro-ing also meant that various doors were left open, including the big ones through which we had entered and the smells and stuffiness were to some extent lifted by gusts of cold, fresh air. These, by the way, presaged a mighty storm of gales and rain that lasted almost a week. Ali hung around on the fringes of activity and was soon able to report back to Anish and me.

'It seems,' he said, 'that a thousand men have gathered in Ingerlond on the outskirts of a small port called Sandwich, barely twenty miles away, across the sea, where they are led by officers of the King. It is expected that they will cross and join the Duke of Somerset at Guisnes as soon as the tides and winds favour them. Our hosts fear that, with this increase in his forces, the stalemate will be broken and Somerset will be able to attack Calais and either capture Warwick and his men or drive them into the sea.'

'If he succeeds our own position will be compromised,' Anish interjected, with some anxiety. 'Somerset will not be pleased to find us still here since the passport he gave us was on condition that we made our way from here up the coast to Bremen.'

'Ali,' I commanded, 'go and see if you can find out how Neville is planning to cope with this crisis.'

He was back ten minutes later. 'A John Dynham, he who won the contest on the back of Lord Fauconberg, is to lead a small force to Sandwich, where he hopes to do them some delaying mischief such as burn or steal the fleet of ships there. Apparently he knows the town and harbour and believes this knowledge will enable him to do much damage without too much risk, especially as the main body of the thousand men is camped on the outskirts of the town.'

'If that's the best they can think of,' Anish remarked, 'I don't hold out much hope for their success.' And he went on to say that he thought we should try to get out of Calais before we were caught up in a siege or a battle.

I reminded him that our aim was to get to Ingerlond and find my brother, and our only chance of doing that depended on remaining where we were.

Well, once the storm had blown itself out, this Dynham embarked with three hundred soldiers Neville could hardly spare. He returned a few days later, but before I tell you what the outcome of his expedition was, I must fill in two more matters of some importance that we learnt or happened to us in the interim.

First I asked Ali to find out what he could to add to the knowledge he already had concerning this feud or civil war that seemed to be occupying the lives of all the Ingerlonders. Here is what he told us after a day or two spent questioning the acquaintances he made both amongst the knights and the young men who served the nobles.

CHAPTER

SIXTEEN

'It all goes back,' he said, 'eighty years and more. At that time Ingerlond was ruled by a great warrior king called Edward, who conquered much of Francia and won many great battles against the Franks. He had several sons, the eldest of whom was known as the Black Prince because of the colour of the armour he wore and who was as great a warrior as his father. However, this Black Prince died before his father, and when Edward himself died it was the Black Prince's son, Richard, who came to the throne, following the laws that govern such matters in Ingerlond.

'This Richard was a weak and pleasure-loving youth, who fought no wars against the Franks but stayed at home and lived in luxury with his favourites, wasting the kingdom with his extravagance. Many of the nobles began to hate him for this and eventually chose a leader to oust him, even though this was against the law and religion of the land.

'Their rebellion was led by a nephew of Edward called Henry, the son of John, known as John of Gaunt, Duke of Lancaster. This Henry thus became King. But many others of the nobles thought he should not be King and his reign was troubled with civil strife. Moreover, he connived at the murder of the ousted Richard. Henry survived and was succeeded by his son, also a Henry. This second Henry, the fifth King of Ingerlond to bear the name, was another great warrior and returned to Francia where he, too, won many great victories before he died, leaving as his successor a child, hardly more than a baby, to be King in his place.

'This child was also Henry . . .'

Here Anish intervened with a whining complaint. 'Are these people so short of names they have to give the same name to every King they have?'

I reminded him that Your Excellency's three predecessors were all called Deva Raya, and he shut up.

Ali continued, 'This Henry, the sixth to rule Ingerlond, is still alive and is now nearly forty years old. Like the Richard whose vices were the first cause of all this, he is a bad ruler, not a wastrel living in luxury but spending his revenue on colleges, monasteries and places of learning, all built with great magnificence to the glory of the Christian god. He is also a weakling in mind, body and spirit. He suffers periods of madness, is often ill, and lacks the ability to be decisive or firm. He is of poor judgement. He is ruled, and the whole country through him, by his Frankish wife, Margaret of Anjou, who wastes what is left of the royal revenues on less exalted things than churches and puts favourites whose families are of no consequence in high places. Because the royal coffers are often empty and her followers grasping and incompetent, the government performs ill and general lawlessness has become endemic throughout the land. Many nobles take advantage of this state of anarchy to pursue personal feuds over imagined injuries, or disputes arising from contested claims to property and demesnes.'

He paused, took a turn in front of the fireplace, swinging on his pole, hitching his fur over his shoulder. 'Now,' he went on, once he had collected himself again, 'when the King's madness becomes insupportable and of some duration a regency is formed, of three or four magnates, to rule in his name. And when this happens the Queen is usually one of the three, but another is Richard . . .'

Anish sighed.

'. . . Richard, Duke of York. This Richard is descended from a younger brother of John of Gaunt, Duke of Lancaster, and on that account has no claim to the throne. However, he is also descended in the female line from an older brother of Gaunt, which might give him a claim to the throne better than the present King's. But he has never pushed this claim – at least, not publicly. As I have said, though, he has ruled the country with others during the King's madness. You will have noticed how inbred this family is – hence the high incidence, no doubt, of illness and madness.

'The Queen hates him and suspects his motives and intentions. He himself has proclaimed himself Protector as well as Regent. He has said that the country needs strong government to set all to rights, and that he should lead it. The dispute between them led to open conflict and the magnates and nobility of Ingerlond all sided with one or the other. At first this Richard of York gained the upper hand, made the King his prisoner and ruled in his place, but then the Queen won a battle and reversed the situation. At present the Queen rules, with the King by her side, from a city called Coventry in the middle of Ingerlond, not from London where the merchants generally favour Richard of York. York himself is in exile in Ireland, while, as you see, his cousin, friend and ally, Richard Neville, Earl of Warwick, maintains himself here in his support.'

Thus Ali ben Quatar Mayeen. Now I must close, dear cousin, with an account of the two other significant matters that have taken place during the last few days.

One afternoon, just after the storm had blown itself out and Dynham had sailed for Sandwich with his three hundred men, I, Anish and Ali were taking a turn round the courtyard of the keep. We were not alone. In one corner our fakir was entertaining a cloud of urchins with six-ball juggling and in another our monk was passing an hour or so in the lotus position or whatever.

We were conversing about our situation. Were we prisoners or guests? Would Neville and his Yorkists aid or hinder our crossing into Ingerlond? Were our tradeable goods safe or would he simply confiscate them and turn them into commodities he could use for his enterprise of taking one king from the throne and putting another in his place? Certainly it was a constant complaint amongst his affinity that funds were low; none had yet been paid their hire as liveried gentlemen in his service while the best they could hope for, if their enterprise failed, was a life spent wandering the continent and even the Orient, plying for hire as mercenaries . . . for in Ingerlond they were already attainted.

We asked what this meant and certainly it seemed an unpleasant fate for anyone to suffer. First a Bill of Attainder had been passed against them by Act of Parliament (of which more later if it becomes important). This meant that the King had legally seized all their lands, movables and money, disinherited their families and, if they fell into his hands, could have them hanged, drawn and quartered.

This is a most barbarous form of execution and goes far beyond the foulest things even the Arabs have dreamt up – far beyond, for instance, impaling. First, the criminal is hanged by the neck, but not for long enough to kill him. Then he is laid on a table and the executioner draws out of his body his inner organs, particularly his intestine which he holds before his victim's eyes. Finally the heart and liver are plucked out. The poor man will now probably die after a process that will have lasted up to a full half-hour and the executioner will cut off his head and cut his carcass into four quarters. These will then be displayed separately at points some distance from each other, as at the gates of a city or over a bridge, as a warning to whomever might see them.

Now, following a battle they had lost, through treachery, at a town called Ludlow, a couple of months earlier, all the nobles and gentry in Calais and the exiles in Ireland had been attainted by Parliament. Their lands in Ingerlond were confiscated, their families reduced to poverty. So, all we met and talked to during our stay in Calais were impoverished and thus open to temptation to steal from us.

However, this they did not do, but one at least came at us another way. As I say, we were walking round the yard and had just passed the stables when a tall figure who had been grooming a big black stallion came out to us, wiping his hands on a cloth. Now that he was in full daylight (so-called, but still damp and grey) we recognised him as Eddie March. He came straight to the point. 'Prince,' he said, 'you are on your way to Ingerlond, seeking your lost brother.'

Ali translated for me, though I had already picked up the gist. I assented.

'You will need a guide.'

At this Ali bridled somewhat. 'I can find our way around,' he muttered, but March pressed on.

'I should like to present myself to you in that capacity. I have been in most parts of the kingdom and I have friends who will help you in your search and provide us with lodging. Quite often, out of friendship for me, they will not charge you.'

I looked him up and down. He was certainly a well set-up lad, with shoulders definitely broad even though the fashion of padded, fluted upper sleeves exaggerated the effect, with a narrow waist clipped in by a tight belt on which he wore a small dagger. On his lower half he wore tight woollen hose, which revealed well-shaped muscular thighs and when he turned, lean, hard buttocks. His expression was open and pleasing, and his features regular. He smiled often. His voice was mellifluous too, but fittingly strong. I looked at the rest of my entourage: Ali, like a cross between Sinbad and the Old Man of the Sea; Anish, plump and wheezy, and, since we had arrived in Calais, always with a drop of watery phlegm on the end of his pointed, drooping nose. And both of them elderly. With no soldiers we would be in poor shape if attacked by footpads.

'It is kind of you to offer your services,' I said, and made a slight bow. 'We are happy to accept them.'

'There is just one thing,' March now added, with some confusion in his face, a heightening of colour. 'I have no chinks at the moment, dead out of funds.'

His speech, perhaps out of embarrassment, had become clipped and formal.

'I shall pay you, of course.'

'I would not dream of hiring myself out as a paid hand. However, a small loan . . . I do have prospects, you know.'

'Say no more. Anish here will provide you with whatever you think you need.'

And so, with little more ado, we settled on arrangements, and fixed a day, a week from now, for our departure. I looked up at the sky, wishing to bring to an end an interview that I guessed March might find embarrassing if it were continued in front of his companions.

'It looks like rain. Again. Anish does not like to be caught

in the rain. And you will want to finish grooming your master's horse.'

As we went indoors Anish grumbled that March would probably
make the loan to which we had committed ourselves far too large,
while Ali muttered that I had made a silly mistake: the stallion
belonged to March himself. He might lack a servant to look after
it for him, but he owned a horse fit for a king. Both of them
were right.

The second notable event was the return of Sir John Dynham
and his three hundred men. His expedition had been successful.
Knowing the harbour of Sandwich, where the commanders of the
King's or Queen's men would be lodged, and the narrow streets of
fishermen's cottages and ships' suppliers around, he had contrived
to surprise and capture all who were within the town of the King's
people without alerting the main body who were camped in the
fields a quarter of a mile away.

The commanders of the captured men were a certain Richard
Wydville, Lord Rivers, his wife who had been born a princess,
married a duke, and now was married to this Wydville-Rivers,
and their twenty-year-old son, Anthony. Warwick decided to put
on a show to humiliate these people, whose commission had been
his arrest or death and who had been so ignominiously dragged
from their beds and shipped across the Channel. He lit the hall
with a hundred and sixty torches as well as many hundred candles,
celebrating, he said the Feast of Candlemas and the Purification of
Mary, the mother of Jesus. Odd. I thought she was meant to be
pure already. We fought our way through another huge meal,
which was not, this time, quite so awful since there was spit-roast
wild boar, and sweet puddings called syllabubs made from soured
cream and honey which, with a little of our nutmeg, were quite
palatable.

When the tables were cleared Warwick called for these Wydvilles
to be brought before him and, old and dignified though the father
was, began to berate him. Apparently Dynham had reported to him
that Richard Wydville had behaved arrogantly since his humiliating
capture, calling the lords in Calais arrant traitors and worse. But it
was Warwick's father, the Earl of Salisbury, much the same age as
Wydville, who began.

'Just who do you bloody think you are?' he shouted, using the clipped form of speaking which I have already noted is typical of the Ingerlonder nobility when they are crossed. Normally they drawl, in a lazy way, dragging out vowels and dropping consonants. 'Just where do you think you get off calling us traitors? We are the King's men, you know. It's from you people and your pernicious influence that we aim to free the poor man. It will be your lot to end up on the scaffold as traitors . . . mark my words.'

Lord Rivers withstood this onslaught with, as I have said, some dignity, not to say continued arrogance. His son, too, contrived a superior sneer, though he said nothing. This infuriated Salisbury's son Warwick.

'Just recall, my good man, who you are dealing with and where you came from. It may be forty years have gone since you were pushing a plough, caught my lady's eye and grubbed a coronet for yourself out of the ditch, but you still carry the smell of the farmyard with you.'

At this the young Wydville flared up. 'My father is a gentleman, born and bred, and that is all an Inglyssheman need be to command the same respect as a king. And if you give me back my sword I'll prove it so on any in this hall.'

At which our Eddie March joined in. 'I don't think so. When all's said and done there are those here in whose veins runs the blood royal. Such men do not fight with yeomen.'

And there was an end of it. Cousin, I tell this story only to illustrate to you the strange customs of this Inglysshe tribe. All the nobility are descended, sometimes admittedly only in the female line, from the Norman barbarians who conquered the land four hundred years ago and it is a matter of pride in them that their blood is untainted, at least in the male line, with that of the ancient Inglysshe whose land they seized and on whom they look down, considering them boors, churls, uncivilised brutes. But, in truth, these nobles show little in their behaviour that you or I would readily call civilised.

Well, cousin, it is time I brought this letter to an end. All you really need to know is that we are making some progress in the tasks we set ourselves, that we shall be sailing for Ingerlond just as soon as the wind is fair, and that in Eddie March we have a guide who will look after us.

I shall not take up my pen again until we are in Ingerlond and have achieved some of what we are here for.

I remain, dear cousin,

Your devoted servant, Harihara

CHAPTER

SEVENTEEN

*I*t was a relief, you can imagine, to return to Ali's house a day or so later and find him recovered and sitting at his usual place. I had no wish to find another sheaf of papers waiting for me filled with the fustian Prince Harihara had written. I mean, could you follow all that stuff about Edwards, Richards and Henrys? Did you feel the need to?

Yes, Ali was there. But he was not alone. Beside him sat a startlingly beautiful lady, some thirty or thirty-five years old. She was, I suppose, on that cusp of perfection that mature women achieve when they have seen much, done much, have had children, and either out of strength of character alone or character combined with widowhood have achieved control of their own lives.

She was dressed in a bolero and full trousers made from rich embroidered silks, which were yet almost transparent in their fineness. In the gap between these garments her navel, filled with a substantial diamond, was exposed in the centre of a rounded but unblemished belly. A shawl covered her shoulders and head, which she held high, always with pride. Her high broad forehead was framed by rich dark hair, large dark eyes glowed with humour and sometimes malice beneath full eyebrows, her nose was sculpted and slightly aquiline with a smaller diamond in the side of her right nostril; her full lips were painted a deep crimson above a small but strong chin and a long neck. A pair of creases in the latter, just above her collar-bones were the only physical signs of her maturity apart from her dignity, humour and self-possession. She wore a lot of jewellery, gold bangles on her upper arms, rings encrusted with emeralds and rubies, anklets and so forth. An invisible miasma of perfume hung about her and shifted in tone when she moved.

'Mah-Lo, effendi, I should like you to meet the lady Uma. Uma, this is Mah-Lo. I have told you about him.'

My bow expressed, I hope, some of the reverence and wonder I felt. The goddess in front of me placed her palms together in front of her creamy bosom, which her bolero, cut low, scarcely hid at all, and gently inclined her head above her pointed fingertips. The eyes that looked up at me were watchful, calculating and seductive.

I sat beside her with my hands on my knees. She picked up my right hand and placed it on the table between us, keeping it covered with hers, and murmured that it was a pleasure to meet me, or some such greeting.

'Uma, you know, has figured in my history,' Ali continued. 'As a vision, a promise, a sort of consummation – you recall how we bathed together in the Caliph's palace in Misr-al-Kahira – and, of course, disguised as a Buddhist monk. She is also the aunt of my two wives.' He took a date from the silver bowl that stood by the lemonade jug, popped it in his mouth, discreetly removed the stone in his palm, chewed, swallowed and went on. 'Now, there are parts of our story which she can tell better than I since she was present at important times and I was not. In any case what happened to her and the things she caused to happen have their own intrinsic interest. So she has very kindly agreed to share some of her afternoons with us . . .'

He passed his good hand over the empty socket of his missing eye and sighed. 'Uma. You may as well start,' he murmured.

Uma withdrew her hand from mine, sat upright. 'Very well,' she said. She took a sip of lemonade and closed her eyes. For a moment the garden seemed still, almost as if with her it held its breath, though I suppose I fancied this. No doubt the fountain continued to play and the birds sang.

Then she began.

Sea-wrack and spume, sail-crack and whistle, heaving brown water swinging like a mother's soothing hand against the rough, seaweed-festooned stones of the pier. The blow of the wind round my midriff as, head down, I clutch my outer cloak about me – they must not see my rounded breasts, my steepled nipples. Well, that's what they feel like in this wind.

There's quite a gang of us, a caterpillar almost for legs and cohesion, inching along a bent stick towards the tightly moored vessel, held snug against hempen bolsters by hawsers as thick as my arm, in spite of the lash and whip-slash of wind.

Looking back above their heads I see the spires and towers of Calais, the tumbled roofs of thatch and slate, the smoke shredded down the alleyways of air between the chimneys, and the rainclouds bustling across the sky above them. Prince Harihara Raya Kurteishi, a purple velvet cap trimmed with gold braid pulled over his glossy black locks and tied with a red silk scarf below his chin to hold it on, his plump dark face screwed up against the wind which I know he hates, black sable furs as glossy as his hair, and soft leather boots also fur-trimmed; Chamberlain Anish, eyes red-rimmed, moving with exaggerated care lest he slip on the sea-slimed cobbles, his elbow held by Ali ben Quatar Mayeen [here the Lady Uma offered a warm smile to our host] who's in a muddle trying to keep his turban on, hold his stick and support Anish all at the same time, and with one hand not as functional as it should be, yet he finds time to peer around him with his one good eye, ever curious, ever seeking out the strange, the new. Then our fakir, with wild hedgehog hair, muttering arcane spells and mantras into his pointed beard or scolding the ten-year-old lad who carries his box of tricks for him. Last, or rather not last because our baggage train follows him, Eddie March, clanking and jingling with his accoutrements and leading by a bridle trimmed with scalloped purple hessian his high-stepping stallion with its balls like giant plums. This Ingerlonder is the only one of our party I've yet to fuck with, but I shall, I shall, and each of the rest thinks he's the only one who knows my breasts, my buttocks and my crimson quim.

Then there's the mules, only twelve left now, so much of the goods we brought with us have been spent, and six out of our original ten muleteers. Anish sent the *dhobi-wallahs*, the cooks and all but two of the secretaries home with our soldiers. He said they were too expensive to keep.

I turn away and look now across the sweep of the harbour, the forest of masts in front of warehouses, and quays stacked with bales of wool and casks of wine. I breathe in and the sharp air stings my questing nostrils: it's laden with smells, of tar and rope and timber, of fish and vinegar, of sea and all the smells of sea, the rotten sweetness of old fish offal, and salt and seaweed, rats' breath and urine, bleached wood and the bones of drowned sailors, and the cleansing ozone, which seems to carry the tang of semen freshly milked.

And then the farmyard smell, mingled with all the spices and perfumes of India, as the mules clop by and one dumps yellow turds at my feet.

They won't be coming on the ship, we'll have to hire or buy another lot in Dover, but the sacks and bags are all to be humped on board.

I love departures, arrivals too, and today we shall have both, the latter either in Dover where the burghers favour the men of York, or in the bosom of the deep.

Although this is the shortest by far of our sea trips the boat is the largest, a great big three-masted tub, fat within hooped staves, like a barrel on its side. There are several of these freighters in the harbour, carvels they are called, built to carry wool out of Ingerlond, and coal and pig-lead, firewood, ironware and cheap tin trays, then back they come with furs and silks, German armour, French and German wine, and all the precious things merchants like Ali have always traded from east to west, but mainly, the Ingerlonders being as they are, wine.

Because the hull bellies out, the gangway from the quay is eight feet long and quite wide, with roped sides and rungs nailed across the planks to stop us from slipping. First the muleteers unload the mules and carry our baggage below, stowing it in the hold, but now it is the turn of March's stallion, which is called Genêt. Genêt will not cross the gangway. A sweat breaks out on his shoulders, enough to froth in the wind. He arches his neck and rolls his eyes so you can see the whites. He neighs, almost bellows, like a trumpet, rears up then lashes out with his hoofs, whose clattering metal shoes strike sparks from the granite flags. He gives off a hot, ferric smell, like a thunderbolt. It takes two of the muleteers to hold him and even then he contrives to bite one on the shoulder so blood streams down his back.

Eddie March strides forward, his face black with rage, and taking a long whip from the chief muleteer, which he holds so the long thong is looped up against the shaft, he beats the animal about the face and neck until he backs away, head down and cowed, but as soon as they lead him forward towards the gangplank, he rears up again and almost breaks loose. I can see March will beat him again, and since he is a noble animal this distresses me. I move forward. 'Let me,' I say, 'let me.'

'Get back, boy. He'll chew you and spit you out.' Spoken in that lazy drawl these Ingerlonder nobles use when they want to make you feel small, or assert their superiority.

'I think not.'

And I take the bridle, close up to Genêt's cheek, and standing on tiptoe begin to murmur then croon in his flattened ear, which presently he pricks. With my free hand I stroke and soothe his quivering flank. His close-cropped hair is as smooth as silk one way, rough as shark's skin the other. I can feel the dampness of his sweat, smell the fodder on his breath and peer into his flared scarlet nostrils. I sense his power, first shimmering across the surface of his skin, then, as he recognises my kindness, receding like a tide into his innermost organs. His eyes narrow a little, no longer flashing white, and become pools of deepest amber and jet again beneath fringed curtains of eyelashes I might die for. With my free hand I find in a pocket beneath my cloak three sugared almonds I had forgotten I had, and I let his hot, wet lips scoop them from my open palm, and now, it's fair to say, he's mine for ever.

I station myself a little in front of his left shoulder and he turns and bends his neck so his cheek pushes against mine as I let him, with only the slightest prompting of the bridle, lead me across the booming gangplank and down a ramp to the stall that has been prepared for him below.

As I fasten the half-door behind him I hear the clink of Eddie March's ironware. He is not, I think, too pleased: perhaps he has lost a little face. At all events, with a heavy hand and a grip like a blacksmith's tongs, he catches my shoulder, spins me, pushes my stomach up against the gate and hauls up my cloak and robe.

'You spoil a brute to treat him like that,' he growls. 'How will he carry me into battle if he does not fear me more than arrows, gunpowder and shot?'

'He'll carry you to hell and back if he loves you,' I answer.

Coming on deck five minutes later, after his attempted buggery, I find the crew are already hauling and spreading the square mainsail down from its yardarm, against which it was furled, and dragging up the lateen, both of which now belly and swell, pregnant with the future. Whether or not he discovered my sex I am still unsure. Perhaps he did and it was the surprise that made him come prematurely deep in my natal cleft but not actually up my rectum. Though I don't know. I suspect these Ingerlonders take little more account of fucking, both in the time they are prepared to devote to it and in the pleasure they get from it, than they do of pissing. Less, considering how much beer they drink. Well, we shall see.

Soon we are out and briefly we can see white cliffs both in front and behind, lining both horizons, but then the wind shifts and drops a little allowing the racing clouds to slow down enough to sink like a lover upon the sea, grey-green now that we have passed the harbour bar, and shed a driving mist of tiny drops, as cold as ice, that sweep into my face and down my throat. How I love these swift changes in the weather! If they were all we had discovered in the way of new sensations, they would be enough to justify this trip, make all worthwhile. Almost I pull off my cloak, step out of my robe and let the rain sweep over me, cleansing and stinging, caressing and tingling. Certainly, considering what milord has left behind, my buttocks and thighs would benefit from the sluicing. But circumspection is required, if only to ensure the continued stream of sensation I seek, and imagination, anyway, is free and carries no penalties.

The big boat wallows on, heaving and reaching, slipping and dumping, and, right out in the middle, even dipping its prow with the sprit in front of it into the rollers and scooping them over the forecastle and main deck, much in the way an elephant in the Krishna back home will sluice itself with river water. Now I am dizzy with the motion and even my stomach heaves a little, but it is all sensation, sensation that tells you you are alive. Above us the seagulls cry, holding station with barely a shift of their wings above the lateen, and out on the right-hand side we see a school of humpbacks blow then fluke when a pair of black and white masked killers get amongst them.

I want the most, the most I can have at any given moment; indeed, that is why I am here, why I have come on this trip, so I may experience the most powerful sensations the world can offer and thereby discover the goddess within me. I climb the four or five steps on to the foredeck and, clutching rails and ropes, heave myself forward into the pounding spray, take it stinging on my face, plastering my robes against my breasts, my belly and my thighs, while the wind from behind shrieks by beneath the mainsail. Riding thus I begin to see looming up through mist, spray and rain those great white cliffs, so much higher and nobler than the ones we have left behind. Then, nearer still, I can make out the choughs circling their nests and hear above the wave-crash their shrill mewing. And now I feel him again behind me, shielding my back from the wind, the warmth and pressure of his chest against my back and, yes, again his prick above my buttocks, as hard and long, it seems, as that of his stallion stalled below.

His big hands clasp my waist then slide upwards and forwards and close upon my breasts and I hear his sigh in my ear, a sigh of satisfaction, for he knows me now for what I am, a woman.

One word breathes in my ear.

'Albion!'

Although I say nothing he senses the question in the way I lean back into him and raise my head so my temple rests against his neck.

'Albion,' he says again, stooping a little so I can feel his lips in my ear. 'Albion, my new-found land.'

For a moment I think he is talking to me or about me, finding a name for me, but glancing up I can see his young eyes are on the cliffs. 'One day,' he cries, 'I shall be . . . King . . . King of the World.'

And he squeezes my tits so I want to cry out.

At this moment I am saved further pain or embarrassment as the master and crew luff the boat, her sails crack and shake, the timbers creak and the full blast of the rain hits our faces. Then round she comes and the claws of the harbour moles open up before us to welcome us in. To Ingerlond, Engelond, Albion.

CHAPTER

EIGHTEEN

LONDON!

Afte r all we do not properly disembark at Dover, but remain moored on the quay while March talks to the burghers who pronounce themselves friends of the Nevilles and York. However, they fear the King's or, rather, the Queen's wrath if she learns they have given Yorkists hospitality or even allowed them to land. With the Bill of Attainder passed against all who had supported York it would be an act of treason to do so, punishable with death, confiscation of goods and the rest. Why not, they say, go by boat to London where all the important people are Yorkists and who can, if need be, look after themselves? So, it is decided next day, if the wind stays fair, we'll sail round the corner of Albion and up the river to London, and that is what we do, though it takes us a day, a night and a day to make the trip.

Meanwhile the customs and excise officers make a brief examination of our spices, charge us the import tax but, bribed by March with Harihara's gold, ignore the smaller packets of treasure that are secreted amongst the rest. They fix seals to the bags declaring all dues paid, and give us penned receipts as well. Thus we are free to make our way to London with no fear of further molestation by the servants of the Crown.

By river is surely the best way to arrive at an inland port. The long, slow dusk of English winter, which began as soon as the sun had passed its low zenith, marks out with gathering gloom our slow progress on the tide, virtually unassisted save by the lightest of airs out of the north-east. Any coast as it slips by is an enigma. There it is before you, smiling, frowning, inviting, grand, mean, insipid or savage, and always mute, with an air of whispering. Come and find out. This one is almost featureless, as if still in the making, with an aspect of monotonous grimness. Behind us the sea and sky are seamlessly welded together and in the luminous space the tanned sails drifting up with the tide behind us seem to stand still in red clusters of canvas sharply peaked, with gleams of varnished spars. A haze rests on the low shores that run out to sea in vanishing flatness. Ahead the air is dark above Gravesend, and further inland seems condensed into a mournful gloom, brooding over the biggest and the greatest town in Ingerlond.

This time my companion on the forecastle is the ship's boy, a twelve-year-old with a twisted arm caused, so he says, by a break that did not mend properly when he fell from the yardarm of his first ship. Although he has the dark skin of an Arab, he is a Londoner, or near enough, from Deptford, a village on the south bank, and he names for me each place of note as we idle by.

At first we can hardly see the land, which lies low and flat a couple of miles away on either side, but slowly both banks inch in towards us and the great river begins to meander the way rivers do, and the villages we pass become more frequent: Gravesend and Tilbury, Greenhithe and Purfleet, Thamesmead and Creekmouth. The traffic increases too, or seems to, as the space it can move in slowly narrows: carvels like ours, some from distant parts, smaller cogs, flat-bottomed wherries, fishing-boats trailing nets, skiffs and tiny coracles.

Lord Djym – that is his name or nickname for he surely is no real lord – points out to me men and women who swing their way across the mudflats on wooden plates for shoes to gather oysters, scallops, clams and mussels wherever a turn of the river makes a bank of shingle the tide will soon cover, while in the mouths of the smaller streams that empty into the mighty one others cut reeds with billhooks to make roofing thatch. We see slipways, too, and sheds where boats are built, and sawmills powered by the water of the inland streams. Although it is the depths of winter, and we can see snow lying on the hills behind Woolwich and Greenwich, there is bustle and business almost everywhere, except on Bugsby Marsh to our left, an evil, cursed patch caught in a loop of the river where blue flames flicker above outlets of poisonous air.

And then, suddenly, an unnatural darkness falls on us, and the sun, which had shone wanly but low and bright enough to make me want to shade my eyes with my hand, becomes a red disc floating in a pool of blackness.

'What's happened?' I ask, thinking perhaps some sort of eclipse or heavenly intervention is marking our arrival.

Lord Djym is puzzled. 'Nothing.'

'But it's all gone dark, and the sun is almost blotted out.'

'Oh, that's just the smoke from the city. In winter, and especially when it's cold and frosty and there's not much wind, it lies like a blanket over everything. Sometimes it comes down so heavy you can't see your hand in front of your face at midday.'

Slowly, very slowly, we edge round a tongue of land this time on the right bank. It's flat and looks marshy apart from heaps and heaps of smouldering rubbish whose fumes must make up much of the cloud that hangs above and around us. The smell is overpowering, sickening, because amongst it all there is much rotting flesh and much of it is burning.

'The Isle of Dogs,' says Lord Djym, and cups his ear towards it. Indeed now I can hear a monotonous howling and barking, and just make out through the gloom the shapes of diseased, emaciated canines loping along the strand and barking at us, or nosing and digging in the piles of waste and garbage.

The river turns again and now is almost straight for a couple of miles or so with the sun about setting above it. Beneath the swirling fog, the surface runs red, not solidly so but splashed in zigzagging lines where the light catches the crests of the ripples, as if a dagger has been slashed finely but closely across its velvet skin and made it bleed. Soon, looming through the smoke and fog on the right-hand side, we can see four big square towers, capped with pyramids of black slate or lead, heavy against the sky, behind a battlemented curtain wall that snakes round them over a low hill. Behind these towers soars the tall, elegant spire that has been on our horizon but getting ever nearer through most of the day.

'Tower of London,' says Djym. 'And St Paul's.'

And that's as far as we go tonight, for the ship's master lays us alongside a wharf on the southern bank, and March calls us into the waist of the boat around the main mast.

'We stay on board tonight,' he says, his voice loud and firm. 'It's not safe to walk through the city streets at night without a guard, and it is too late to find a proper lodging. We shall be up early in the morning and we'll decide on our next move then.'

The sun dips below what looks like a line of houses upstream of the towers, or Tower, and suddenly all is dark except for the glimmer of a torch one of the crew is holding. Dim lights glow in casements along the riverbank on the other side, more numerous than the few stars that are bright enough to prick the mantle above. The blood has gone from the river, but fills the western sky instead.

The morning is another of those magic mornings like the one we had the day we arrived in Calais. The sky is perfectly clear, a pale azure not the lapis blue of the dawn sky in Vijayanagara, but more like an aquamarine. Smoke, white from wood and black from coal, climbs into it in perfectly straight lines from ten thousand chimneys – it looks like the warp on a weaving frame. Frost glitters on every shingled roof and coats the slates and tiles like ground glass. No thatch: within the walls it's forbidden, Djym tells me, for fear of fire. Shadows long and deep fill the spaces between the houses with purple darkness. Most marvellous of all, every rope and spar on our boat and on all the others moored nearby is coated with tiny sharp crystals.

For a moment there is stillness, then downriver, the sun pushes an edge above the water, fills the sky above with gold, and makes the river, too, run with gold where the night before it ran with blood, and at that moment the city comes to life: church bells ring, cocks crow, a cannon cracks on the battlements of the Tower and a puffball of white smoke hangs like a fist for almost a minute above the water – so still is the air. The river begins to fill with boats that ply as ferries, for the most part carrying goods and people from the south bank to the north. Vendors appear on the quay beside us, selling bread hot from the ovens, filled with melting cheese and the crisp, smoked and salted porkmeat they call bacon, and canteens filled with hot spiced red wine. This is welcomed by the men for, as March says, coming to stand beside me: 'Cold, ain't it? Bloody cold,' then, 'Get brekkers out of the way first, then we'll have to organise some animals here for your baggage. Shouldn't be a problem. There's an inn a couple of streets away called the Tabard where pilgrims heading for Canterbury meet. But the pilgrim season don't get under way until April, so I reckon they'll have spare beasts.'

He throws what is left of his pint of wine down his throat, buys a second lump of bread, and saunters off down an alleyway, whose cave-like shadows quickly swallow him up.

But as he goes a strange thing happens. On the corner of the alley he tosses a copper to a legless beggar whose sawn-off stumps rest on the cobbles. This beggar looks after him, watery eyes narrowed, then blinks the rheum out of them, staring still at March's retreating back, shakes his shaggy head. 'Fuck me,' he says. He grabs his crutches and, with remarkable agility, hoists himself into the air above them and swings himself like a tall bird, a heron or a crane, first one stick then the other, along the quay, upstream.

One by one the others come on deck and I repeat to them what March has said while they, too, buy food and drink, though they refuse the hot wine and take warm milk instead. Then Ali makes our porters bring the baggage up from the hold. The ship's master insists it stay on board until he has been paid and Prince Harihara, not knowing what would be a fair price for our voyage from Calais, agrees to leave it on the deck until March returns. Which he does, about an hour later, by when the sun is higher in the sky, though not much – so low is its trajectory in these climes.

It's all bustle now for twenty minutes or so, getting the mules he has brought with him loaded up, together with two Ingerlonder muleteers, the ship's captain paid, and so on. Then all at last is ready, and I say goodbye to Djym, who surprises me with a kiss. The last to leave is Genêt who, for a horse, is quite intelligent and, perceiving he is to be returned to dry land, gives no trouble. One of March's grooms saddles him up yet March does not mount him, but leads him by the bridle. Perhaps he sees the question on my face.

'Don't do to be conspicuous,' he says. 'Although I have many friends in London, I have enemies too.'

This puts me in mind of the legless beggar, who, I now believe, recognised March and I tell him about it. His face clouds, he pulls his lower lip, then goes to the mule where his own personal baggage is stowed, and, undoing a strap here and a strap there, pulls free a scabbarded broadsword, two-handed, all of four feet long, and buckles it to Genêt's saddle. Then he turns to Ali. 'Ali,' he says, 'if you lose me or lose your way, ask for the house of Alderman Roger Dawtrey off East Cheap, can you remember that?'

Ali nods.

'He's expecting you and will look after you.'

And so at last we set off, March leading Genêt, Ali at his side, and the rest of us following with the mules in the rear. Many of our spice sacks have already been sold so now the Prince's crossbows account for nearly half of them.

A couple of hundred yards and we reach what, the night before, I had taken to be a line of houses marking a bend in the river beyond the Tower, but which now reveals itself to be a bridge, the only bridge for many miles across the Thames. It has big stone gateways at either end, a church in the middle and both sides are lined with houses, with shops on the lower floor opening on to the crossing.

But before we can enter or use this bridge we have to take our turn in a long line of traders, local gardeners and farmers coming to the markets with flocks of sheep, cartloads of cabbages, herds of steers and heifers, pigs and fowl, and now, like it or not, while we wait, we cannot escape the horrors attached to the stone lintel above the gate. For a moment the unwary traveller wonders: why should the sides of several clumsily slaughtered pigs be transfixed with pikes, hoisted and left for the crows and kites, of which there are many, to squabble over? And then it dawns on one that these are not the remains of beasts but of men, and possibly women.

March himself pauses, almost as we pass under these horrors, and looks up, shading his eyes against the glare of the still luminous sky, and I see him shake his head and bite his thumb. He turns to Ali and since I am right behind him I hear most of what he says. 'These are not criminals. The man on the left is Sir John Thin – he changed sides at the battle of Blore Heath and joined my lord of Salisbury.'

At this moment a fork-tailed kite flies off with offal in its beak, is attacked by a black crow, and drops the offal into the crowd. It lands on a costermonger's shoulder. The man brushes it off and, with much laughter from him and his friends around him, kicks it into the gutter. For a moment March eyes his sword, hung from the pommel of his saddle, but restrains himself – which is just as well since one thing I already know about him is that he has a temper. As we pass the offal, a thin cat is already sniffing and dabbing with its paw, and I realise it is a kidney, and quite like a porker's since the build of this Sir John belied his second name.

'What ecstasy these men must have suffered,' I murmur to myself, 'for being men of honour and courage they would not have surrendered to fear or howled with pain . . .'

CHAPTER

NINETEEN

'I have a man here says you are Edward March. Is that so?'
We've come off the bridge which, on account of the forty or so shops on each side, whose stalls and wares spilled out and obstructed easy movement, took all of twenty minutes, and are now to turn left up an alley called Crooked Lane. In front of us is a tall man, dressed in rich crimson velvet, with a black hat and red beard above a heavy gold chain with an enamelled disc on his chest. He's holding a carved stave with a silver ornament on top, and behind him is a small posse of armed men. They wear helmets with the front rim turned up, breastplates, mail, spears, swords, and the three bowmen among them have their bows strung and arrows in place, ready to let loose. At that range one of those could go right through my chest and pin me to Ali who is behind me. I shiver at the thought but feel excited, aroused too. Next to this official is the legless beggar with his crutches.

Eddie looks the official in the eye. 'And what are you that gives you the right to question traders come from the East on lawful business to sell and buy?'

'My staff and badge say who I am. I am Alderman Thomas Gilpin, sheriff of Bridge Ward, and one of my duties is to arrest known miscreants and traitors who come across the bridge. Whatever these people with you might be is no concern of mine, but you, March, are no traveller from the East, but a man attainted by Act of Parliament, and I must ask you to surrender your sword and come with me.'

March looks round him now and behind, so I can see the smile, a grin, really, that is playing on his lips, though his eyes are narrowed in a calculating way. I follow his gaze and see that many of the crowd gathering round us are looking restless, eager. Those who are armed loosen their weapons in their scabbards, and one man is hastily buying eggs from a passing pedlar woman's basket. Eddie raises his voice and shouts, in a strong voice from his deep chest. 'Who here would see a man of York, a loyal subject of King Harry, taken from you and put in gaol?' And with one quick movement he hoists himself into Genêt's saddle and with a flourish draws his sword.

'Not I,' says the man who has been buying eggs and he manages to throw three, two of which hit the sheriff as the rest of the crowd close in round the men before they can draw their weapons. The bowmen, though, loose their arrows into the air above our heads. They mean no harm but to frighten us. However, one hits a woman at an upstairs window in the shoulder. The spurt of her blood and her raucous scream madden the crowd and they surge forward, led by Eddie who makes a pass or two at the armed men, then raises his sword to decapitate one who has slipped on the skin of a black plantain.

'Steady on, milord!' cries the man, looking up from the greasy cobbles. 'I meant your worship no harm, I swear.'

Eddie puts the point of his sword on the man's breastplate and pushes him on to his back. Then urging Genêt on and waving his weapon above his head he charges on up Bridge Street, tipping over a fish stall spilling silver flounders beneath the feet of the crowd.

Led by one of the muleteers, who seems to know where we are going, we dodge into Crooked Lane, take a right up St Michael's and so come on to the western end of East Cheap where we see Eddie, still riding Genêt and waving his sword above his head, coming towards us at a brisk trot, which sends the passers-by scuttling out of his way. No sign now of the sheriff.

He sheathes his sword, grins at us all broadly, high on his little adventure, swings a leg over the pommel and drops to the ground in front of me. He then scandalises all who still believe me to be some sort of eastern monk, and a male at that, by kissing me warmly, in much the way Lord Djym did, firmly on my lips; with one arm round my waist he pulls me close so I can feel the coldness of his iron sleeves.

'That was fun,' he says. 'I enjoyed that.'

I am left with three perceptions. One: I also enjoyed it all; two, this Eddie March, for all his arrogance and fine airs, is still a lad; three, a sense of *déjà vu*, as if I have been here before, will be here again, almost as if, in the previous ten minutes I have been living a cliché. But I push this aside: it is, after all, a feeling to which we can all be subject when disoriented and tired. And then I notice Eddie has not come through his adventure unscathed: the lower part of his left arm, below the armour, is gashed and bleeding quite heavily.

'I am not,' he sighs, many hours later, 'able, I think, to do what I most want to do at this moment. Though the spirit is more than willing, my flesh has been so weakened by this damned cut . . .' and his right hand passes across his bare chest, smooth like marble though rippled with bone and muscle, and almost as free of hair as marble, to touch the swathe of bandages on the other side.

I am lying on my side, supported on my elbow above him. For a moment I allow my free hand to wander slowly over his chest and across his stomach. He flinches and the skin beneath my palm shrinks a little. 'That tickles.'

I reach across him, take hold of his wrist, which is strong, hard, bony, and pull his arm back, slide my hand up to his, lift his fingers, smell his fingertips and suck them gently. They smell of the sea and taste of oysters stewed in honey. I lick his palm, lift my upper thigh a touch and put his hand back where it had been.

'Could be,' I say, 'that you drank and ate too much.'

Indeed, Alderman and Mistress Dawtrey's hospitality had been royally generous, better than anything we had experienced since leaving the Caliph's palace in Misr-al-Kahira. Their house, just a few yards up East Cheap on the corner of St Clement's Lane, was a big three storeyed building, double-roofed and gabled, timber-framed, with red tiles on top. The Alderman and his wife were in the front doorway waiting to welcome us and there I received the third and fourth kisses of the day (there were many more yet to come), full on the lips, which I now understood is the English custom, before taking us through a narrow, wood-panelled vestibule into a hall which fills much of the ground floor though offices, both household and to do with Dawtrey's commercial enterprises, lead off it.

The rest of the day passes in a confusion of eating, entertainment and

business, of much coming and going. A physician is sent for to bind
Eddie's arm and I have to forbear from openly challenging the idiocies
he practises in the name of medicine and offering my own poultices and
herbal remedies, though later on I put together a potion using some of
the spices we have brought and some herbs from the kitchen garden
behind the Dawtreys' house. This will keep his fever down and speed
up the healing process.

The people he saw through the afternoon were, of course, merchants.
What Eddie wants for the Yorkists is money. What they want is lowering
of duties, and a lifting of restrictions once a York is on the throne or,
anyway, the government in the hands of Yorkists rather than a mad,
spendthrift king and a witch of a queen. And, of course, Eddie can't
deliver without the cash, and they daren't be seen to support him until
the Yorkists are in power as to do so might be putting their heads all too
literally on the block. So they proceed with mouse-like caution, while
Eddie makes promises he can't keep.

Then one old man, with a long, flowing white beard and a big red
velvet hat with a long scarf looped round it and round his neck, above
a black velvet gown, comes rumbling in, stamping newly fallen snow
off his boots and refusing to be divested of his cloak until he has drunk
a quart of red wine heated with cloves and cinnamon, our cloves and
cinnamon, with small sour apples bobbing in it, and eaten half a loaf of
hot bread and a plate of rabbit stew. Then he coughs like a whale and
spits a great fistful of phlegm into the fire, whose heat he was keeping
from every one else. He ignores Eddie and turns to Alderman Dawtrey.
'Fucking Hanse,' he says.

'Oh, hear, hear,' say all the rest.

'Over the fucking top this time,' he says.

'Oh, absolutely,' they reply.

'You know what their latest ploy is?'

'No, but you're going to tell us.'

'No Inglysshe cloth north or east of the Weser unless it's in Hanse
ships.'

'You're joking.'

'No. I've a lad works in their kitchens down Steelyard, keeps his ears
and eyes open. They'll be coming up to Guildhall in a day or two with
a proclamation to that effect.'

'Fucking German bastards.'

'What are we going to do? Got to do something. They've already tied up the cloth markets in Antwerp, Bruges and Cologne. We'll be lucky if we make ten per cent.' Dawtrey turned on Eddie. 'You see? If we had a proper king who lived in London, or Westminster anyway, and had some real clout, they wouldn't dare. I mean, if you were king, what would you do?'

Eddie doesn't hesitate.

'I'd tell my Lord High Admiral to get the fleet out and sink the next Hanse convoy that came anywhere near our coasts and then I'd invite the bastards in Steelyard to dinner in the Tower and suggest a compromise might be reached before they go home.'

It's what they want to hear.

At this moment Ali swings himself nearer on that stick of his, takes Eddie by the elbow and they have a few quiet words together. By the way, Prince Harihara and Anish are no longer with us, having retired to a chamber at the back of the house where they're busy filling chamber-pots. I told them not to drink the water unless they had seen it boiled first. Later I'll make sure they eat some plain boiled rice and suck a lemon or two. Then Eddie nods and turns back to these merchants. 'I don't know why I didn't think of it straight away,' he says, 'but my lord of Warwick, over in Calais, has eight carvels – with cannon – and I'm sure, for a fairly large consideration, he could have them mocked up to look like pirates . . .'

And so it goes on, through to about two o'clock when Mistress Dawtrey causes a dinner to be served so all the visitors can eat, and drink of course, before early nightfall. There's roast swan and sturgeon, a barrel of oysters, followed by marzipan made from almonds and crystallised sugar-cane juice bought off a Moorish boat that has just come in from Málaga and a barrel of the sweet wine from the same port. But half-way through Eddie goes a touch pale and begins to sweat, and I suggest he should be in bed. He argues, till I let him know I'll come up and tuck him in.

So here we are now, and his little man is no longer a little man but a very big man, standing up proud like a bowsprit above his stomach, and flicking the way a young man's does when its full of blood and spunk and responds to the heartbeat.

'But I can't lie with you,' he moans. 'My fucking arm, I'll never be able to hold myself on top of you and do it properly.'

'Properly?' I say, marvelling at the innocence of this seventeen-year-old. 'What's properly?'

And I swing my leg, which glows like a ripe peach in the candlelight, across his tummy and kneel above him. I tease the tip of his prick with the lips of my cunt for a moment or two then lower her on to him, swallowing him right up. And, of course, the silly bugger comes straight away and I have to start all over again.

CHAPTER

TWENTY

Not, I promise you, out of our love-play, but taking infection from the filth, damp and cold of the attic they have hidden him in, Eddie's fever worsens. The cut on his arm festers a little, oozes a yellow pus and then a colourless ichor, and he complains of alternating heat and cold, comes out in terrible sweats, and suffers a thirst like torture. It's so bad Mistress Dawtrey wants him out of the place, believing him perhaps to have the plague, but it is winter with frost most nights and sometimes all through the day as well, and the plague never strikes, they say, when the weather is cold. Anyway, he lives thus through three days and nights and no one survives the plague that long. And now it occurs to me that I know why plague absents itself in winter, though no one will believe me. It's carried by fleas. And frost kills fleas. Simple as that.

I find this fever enhances our love-making. Think of the heat of his body almost too hot to touch, after I have stripped off beneath those cobwebby rafters, low, so that short though I am I have to stoop, and the icy draught thrusts like a sword through the gaps round the tiny window. Imagine us on deep straw mattresses, the top one eiderdown from Zeeland, beneath a pile of woollen blankets and furs making a cave filled with the odours of sweat, sperm, my love-juices, the slick sweetness of pus and shit. Then when it's over for a time and I lie with my head on his shoulder, my runny nose peeping above the covers, and our breaths making mist in the dim light above our heads and the pigeons inside the eaves cr-croo, cr-croo, and the mice scuttle between the joists. Runny nose? Yes, I've caught the cold. The cold everyone in this wet, cold island has.

But Mistress Dawtrey has another reason for wanting Eddie out. He is a Yorkist. All right, so most of the City is, but the garrison in the Tower under the command of Lord Scales is the King's. Unpopular though Scales and his garrison are, once he knows where Eddie is a quick sortie with a hundred or so professional soldiers could easily get down the seven or so blocks on East Cheap that separate us from the Tower and snatch him before the City can mobilise its own militia against them. Or so says Mistress Dawtrey, and the Alderman agrees.

And so, outside the attic, the household fidgets and chafes. Anish and his two secretaries, Moplahs from Malabar, lean hard-working youths who are losing their sight through working at their accounts and copying the Prince's letters in light which even at midday is no better than gloomy, work away at the books, pretending there is more to be done than there actually is, yet finding mistakes at the eighth or ninth perusal of their papers. The Prince himself sits in silence at the head of the big table in the hall, which annoys the Alderman since it is where he is accustomed to preside, and there he drums his fingers and stares with what he imagines is dignified melancholy at a future that has become obscure if not pointless. Actually he has chronic indigestion, which I try to alleviate with peppermint cordial I buy at an apothecary's at the Poultry Lane end of Old Jewry. And what an apothecary! What a shop! He has a dead tortoise hanging up, a small crocodile, bladders, musty seeds and it is all filthy. In Vijayanagara he would have been closed down as a health hazard.

And with every hour Mistress Dawtrey, who seemed such a buxom, welcoming person when we first arrived, bumbles about her household tasks, which consist mainly of chivvying the help, muttering beneath her breath about how the Queen will have search parties out by now all up and down Watling Street to the north-west and Ermine Street to the north, as if these are the only thoroughfares out of London to take us to the parts we want to go to. She herself has never left London and has no conception at all of what a place might be like if it be different from London.

Alderman Dawtrey, a vintner specialising in sweet Iberian wines, such as sack and malaga, keeps to his counting-house at the back of the property from where he sends out his apprentices to run errands to the quays, making sure his ships are sailing and welcoming those returning, and generally pretending to be busy. But in truth he is staying indoors because he knows if he goes out their worships the other aldermen and the justices of the City, too, might question him as to our whereabouts and he does not wish to involve them in falsehoods. Clearly the whole household welcomed us on the understanding that we would be there for one night at the most.

Well, there must have been a spy in the household, there usually is, because on the third night they come for us, for Eddie anyway, and know where to go. We hear the tramp of their feet coming up East Cheap, and . . .

'Eddie,' I say, 'that's soldiers, by the clink of their harness and the clatter of their horses' hoofs.'

But this is the first time he's got himself together enough to do it 'properly', that is with my legs spread beneath him, my knees up and splayed, and him lying on top of me supported by his elbows and his arms. And he bangs away in that position, like a pestle in a mortar, pleasuring neither of us as much as we do when I call the tune. But at least she's wet and ready for it, having done it in two of my ways earlier in the evening, so even if there's not much pleasure there's no pain either – though what I am colluding with, had I not been ready to let him do it this way, would have been rape.

However, that we have already been there before is almost our undoing, that and the way I have taught him to hold back, for now he is taking far too long.

'Come on, Eddie,' I cry, as we hear them hammering on the big street door below, 'gerroff will yer.'

See, I am already learning to speak English the way the natives do.

'Damn it, no,' he grunts, 'I'll not be hurried thus,' and he keeps up the same dull rhythm.

Then the quality of the sounds shifts to something nearer and more resonant as they get indoors. There's a crash of pewter and faience and I know that a fine Moorish bowl, freely painted in green and pale yellow patterns, which Mistress Dawtrey prizes, has gone from the big table to the floor. She'll not risk any more breakages and I can imagine the jerk of her head that sends them stamping up the first flight of carved stairs.

It's ladders from now on, two, the first coming through a wide square hole in the first floor, the second propped against the threshold of a low upright plank door that opens into our nest of love.

Thump, thump on the stairs, and thump, thump on my pelvis. Voices, harsh, deep, gruff, with a cleared throat and phlegmy rasp like stones off a shovel.

'He's up there, milord. Up that fucking ladder. Behind that door.'

Silence, then another voice, this time the Norman drawl.

'Come on, Eddie. We know you're there. Be a good chap and come down.'

'Bastard John Clifford,' says Eddie, in my ear. Then, much louder: 'Fuck off, Clifford.' Then quieter again: 'Bastard hates me. He'll have my balls off before he hands me over to the hangman.'

But the thought doesn't stop him fucking me.

Outside: 'Get an axe, old chap, will you?'

Inside: 'His dad got killed at St Alban's, doesn't like Yorkists.' Thump, thump. 'Nearly there.'

Outside: 'Oh, for Christ's sake, try the fireplace in the main hall.'

Lots of running up and down stairs, up the ladders.

'Here, give it to me.' Thump, thump, and the plank door begins splitting not far above my head, and the axe-blade flashes briefly. Then a whoop of pleasure. Two actually.

One outside: 'He-e-e-ere comes Johnny!'

One inside: 'He-e-e-ere comes Eddie!'

Another plank comes loose, Eddie rolls off me, hauls me upright, stark naked as we both are, picks up a chest that's at the end of our makeshift bed and smashes it against the joists. At the second blow he's through and a shower of tiles goes skittering into the gully between the two roof ridges. He's not let go of the chest, though, and now heaves it at the door. 'Aaaargh!' and we hear a great crashing and banging as Clifford, I suppose, takes it on his midriff and falls off the ladder. From the musical, mystical chimes we hear I guess the chest bursts open and showers him with gold pieces.

Eddie's out on the roof, reaching in to get me, grabs a bare arm, hauls me out. Oh, Shiva, it's cold. And I slip down on my bum into the gully, with him slithering behind and almost on top of me. He gets me to my feet and for a brief moment I can take in the night, the stars, the roofs, hundreds of them, the spires, the rising three-quarter moon, the silver ribbon of the river, the rising threads of smoke from still smouldering fires. Then the cold strikes again, like a blow in my lungs, like knives on my feet and hands.

'Come on!'

Two things the Londoners live in mortal fear of: plague and fire. And against the latter the big houses, with yards closed off from the public thoroughfares, have rungs fastened into the walls so people can use the windows, even the highest windows, to get to safety. From where we are the highest, nearest window-sill is five feet below us and the top rung three feet below that. Eddie goes first then, holding the guttering with icy fingers, I lower my feet towards him so he can guide them on to the sill. The insteps of my feet feel ticklish, the rough loam of the wall between its timbers scrape my breasts. There is a brick frame round the window and I get the fingertips of my left hand between two narrow bricks.

It isn't a big drop. The lean-to roof, with a shallower camber than the roofs of the house, is below us. Several things now happen at once.

Ali appears, coming in from the street through the yard door. He looks up at us with his one gleaming eye, waves and disappears into the stable. Clifford, I suppose it is Clifford, appears in the gully above us. Then disappears. I can hear him shouting but not make out what he says as he storms down the inside of the house, calling the soldiers together behind him, or sending them on in front. Ali comes out of the stable, hauling Genêt on the end of a rope halter. Eddie, after a moment's hesitation, launches himself, bare-arsed, on to the stallion's back. Genêt rears like a mad thing but Eddie hangs on round his neck and scoops up the rope halter. Soldiers appear in the gateway behind Ali who steps to one side as, knees and ankles, Eddie drives Gent into their midst. A clatter of weapons and armour, hoofs on cobbles flashing sparks, a neigh like a banshee, and they are gone, with the soldiers making a show of following them.

Ali comes and stands beneath me, looking up with his squinting eye. 'You'll catch your death,' he says.

He helps me down with his good arm, steadying me with his bad one until my toes touch the stones. Then he wriggles out of his smelly old fur and wraps it round me.

'And that, Mah-Lo, is quite enough for one session.'

I drew in breath and let out a long sigh. She was right but I had been so caught up in her telling of this eight-year-old tale that I had quite forgotten where

I was. But Ali's garden was all around me, just as it had been, and Ali himself in the shade of his tree on the other side of the table. He appeared to be asleep, but stirred, emitted a tiny fart, opened his one eye.

Uma turned to him. 'Ali, ask Murteza to fetch the children. I should go now.'

Ali rang a little handbell and presently the Nubian servant appeared, received his instructions and departed.

Uma stood. 'It has been a pleasure,' she said, again dipping her head above her fingers.

I struggled to my feet. 'Wonderful, wonderful, I assure you,' I managed to blurt out. 'Will you . . . when will you . . . ?'

'Oh, I shall be back when Ali reaches a point where my side of the story is needed.'

And she walked away, across the flags, past the little fountain, through the pierced sandalwood door. Briefly I caught a glimpse of two young children in the vestibule, holding Murteza's big black hands. He passed them to their mother and the door swung shut.

There was a long moment of silence before I sighed again.

'She tells a good story, doesn't she?' Ali murmured.

'Yes,' I said. Then I gave it a moment's thought. 'And true, I suppose?'

'As the day is long. Why should you think otherwise?'

Again that brow, lifted like a cobbler's needle.

'Oh, I don't know. These three voices you are giving me. Your own, the Prince's letters, and now Uma's. I suspect art, contrivance.'

'Contrivance? What can you possibly mean?'

CHAPTER

TWENTY-ONE

I glanced up over the low eaves at the fanciful dragons and suchlike that adorned the gables of Ali's house, and shivered. So long, I thought, as he limits himself to three narrators, I'll go along with him. But if a fourth appears, making, forgive me, a set of Chinese boxes out of it . . . I resumed my seat, breathed in. A hint of Uma's perfume still lay on the air.

'What did you do then?' I asked.

Ali sipped lemonade, eyed me across the rim of his gilded cup. 'Dear Mah-Lo,' he murmured, 'this is the tenth consecutive day you have come to hear my tale. And I cannot believe that, following the vigour of Uma's story-telling, you want to hear more from me. I am not so conceited that I cannot recognise that I lack her style, her enthusiasm.'

I could see that my passing doubts had disturbed him and I was at pains to reassure him that truly I was enthralled, and not least by the unassailable veracity of his telling.

'Very well, then.' Ali set down his cup, stretched his legs out into the slanting sunlight and laced his fingers, the good ones and the withered ones, over his hollowed stomach. He cleared his throat. 'I took the poor shivering thing,' he resumed, 'back into the house and sat her down on a settle in front of the fire. I kicked the smouldering logs into life and tossed on another, then went in search of a hot drink for her. At that moment the main hall of Alderman Dawtrey's house was empty, apart from a couple of small long-haired white dogs that he kept, which snuffled about everywhere and rubbed their penises against your shins if you sat down. But by the time I got back from the kitchen

with a mug of mulled wine for Uma, there was quite a gathering, summoned I
suppose by the commotion which had just taken place . . .'

Prince Harihara had taken the big chair with arms at the end of the table,
which, of course, annoyed the Alderman as it always did. The Prince was
wearing a lace-trimmed nightshirt, beneath a velvet stocking cap with a
gold tassle on the 'toe', both purchases made in Venice. His long black
hair and glossy cheeks shone in the lamp- and candle-lights. Next to him
was Anish, shivering despite his coat of beaver. At the other end of the
table Mrs Dawtrey was having hysterics, while the Alderman stood with
his back to the fire and Uma to his side. Although he was angry and
disturbed, I could see how his eyes kept flickering to the flesh she had
left exposed above her breasts in spite of the coat I had given her. I
longed to put the poor fool out of his misery and tell him, yes, you're
quite right, she's a woman and naked underneath it.

The Prince looked up at me as I went past with a cup of hot wine
for Uma. 'Ali, Eddie March has gone, then?'

'It looks like it.'

'And won't be back?'

'I doubt it.'

'March is not coming back here,' Mistress Dawtrey screamed. 'We'll
end up chopped in pieces on Tower Green if he comes back here.'

She had not understood our conversation, of course, but no doubt
had heard the name of March in the middle of it.

The Prince ignored her, went on: 'So, Ali, we no longer have our
guide to show us the way to the north of Ingerlond.'

I assented.

'Master Dawtrey has expressed a desire that we should be gone by
daybreak. The question is, where shall we go? Where is there to go?'

There was an unaccustomed tremor in his voice, a hint of weariness
and anxiety, fear even. It dawned on me that he was at the end of his
tether: thousands of miles from home, divested of almost all the prestige
of rank he was used to; bewildered by everything around him – not just
his dubious position in a strange country of having allied himself to a
rebel, a traitor, but the food, the language, the people, the weather. I
reminded myself that I was the traveller, that I was used to situations
like this, that I had no home, that Vijayanagara was as strange to me as
Ingerlond. It was a consideration I had not given enough attention to,

mainly because until now Prince Harihara and Anish had managed so well. But now I felt nothing would satisfy them but to return to the river, take a boat back across the water and retrace our steps to the warmth, comfort, security, and decency of their homeland.

Uma sneezed.

I turned to Alderman Dawtrey and did the best I could with my limited command of his language. 'Sir,' I said, 'it is unreasonable to expect the Prince and his following to be gone by daybreak. But I think I can find people in London who will help us, if you would give me until the afternoon to organise it.'

After some blustering, largely feigned I believe to satisfy his wife, he agreed, especially when I suggested to him that he might like to take what spices and condiments we still had off our hands for a fair price so we would have money to pay our way on our journey. He offered a fifth of their street value but I got him up to a third – forty-five pounds. I was content to do this: it left us with no large load to carry, fewer mules and muleteers to hire, and we would be far less conspicuous as we travelled through the country. And, when all was said and done, the actual sum remained high: it was enough to keep us all in funds and tolerable comfort for a month or more. And after that we would still have the small bags of gems we had secreted about us.

But I still had to pursue the plan I had in mind and put it into effect – and Uma was still wearing my furs and nothing else. Although almost every man there knew she was a woman, they all believed they were the only ones in the know, so it remained advisable, and might one day turn out to be useful, that we maintained the fiction that she was a man. I murmured in her ear and followed her up the stairs (still strewn with broken ornaments, timber from the chest, and occasional gold pieces that had not yet been collected), and the two ladders to the attic she had shared with March. There, while I looked out through the hole March had made in the roof at the view of the silver river snaking beneath the setting moon in a big loop southwards to the twin towers of Westminster, she took off my furs, and resumed her monkish habit.

'Where do you plan to go?' she asked. 'Who are these allies you have found who will help us?' But she didn't wait for an answer. 'Don't bother. I can guess. I'll come too.'

And, grinning up at me, she pulled the handsome coat of sable that March had neglected to take with him over her monkish gown while

I shrugged myself into my mixture of fox and musk rat, still warm and scented from her skin.

We let ourselves out quietly through the kitchen and kitchen offices, across the yard, through the gate and into East Cheap, turning right up Candlewick, over the crossing and into Budge Row. We could now see the spire of St Paul's at the end of Watling Street ahead of us, a thin needle, with the moon turning orange to the left of the tower it perched on, then we turned right.

'I know where we're going,' Uma said, and squeezed my hand. There was almost a sort of glee in her voice.

'You do?'

'You're following the signs.'

'What signs?'

'The little red hearts.'

She was right. Straight on unless, where there's a corner or a crossing, a small red heart, chalked, painted, or cut from material and fixed high up on a building, tells you to leave the street you're on and take a new turning. You couldn't really see them in the darkness but I had followed them the day before, just as I had in most of the big cities we had passed through since landing at Venice, at least when opportunity arose. Thus we made our way, just as the sky behind us began to lighten, and small birds here or there in the eaves above us stirred and chirruped, and a distant dog barked, into a small warren of alleys, most too narrow to take a cart or even a donkey with two panniers. And, in effect, we moved out of the everyday illusionary world of commerce, politics, law and order, publicly approved religion into that parallel universe where most of us live some of the time, and where, when we do, we are truly human and free, the underworld of the Brothers.

In Needler's Lane a tiny church huddled between taller houses whose eaves spread over it, the church of St Benet Sherehog, and next to it the church of St Pancras. Both were small, not much bigger than the shrine to the elephant-headed god Ganesha in whose precincts I had been welcomed on my first visit to Vijayanagara – but, oh, so very different.

Beneath a semi-circular arch carved with devils and lost souls there was a low double door, with a knocker – a hand clasping a ball, cast in bronze, finely modelled. I struck three sharp blows with it, and then one yet heavier. We waited. A couple of black rats scurried down the alley away from us. Then bolts on the other side of the timbers slipped back, silently because they had been greased, and the circular handle tilted a little. We had heard no footsteps, neither did the hinges creak nor the bottom of the door squeal on the stone floor.

'Nothing is true,' I said.

'Everything is permitted,' the cowled figure on the other side of the opening door murmured. 'Come in, Brother Ismail, and your companion too.'

He was carrying a lamp, which briefly illuminated the almost square nave he led us through, throwing dancing light across the squat pillars with their carved capitals. I had, as I have said, already been there, but in daylight. Now the crudely rendered imps, painted in primary colours, flashing their bums, sucking their genitals, looked even more startling and weird as the shadows cast by the lamp shifted over them. I could not help wondering at these images and comparing them with the sculptures one sees in Vijayanagara. There all is open and happy, here sly and grubby . . . but this is not the place for a dissertation on religious art except to say that the one image that did appeal was of Mary, above the altar in a side-chapel through which our guide now led us. Heavy-lidded, angel-mouthed, she was robed in deep-sea blue and crowned with silver. Her feet rested in the curve of a crescent moon, thin as a sickle-blade. Her smile was knowing – you felt she knew more than she was prepared to acknowledge.

Behind a pulpit there was a staircase that descended to another wooden door. It opened into a crypt or cellar. It was large, serving both churches, and was divided by rows of plain pillars supporting low, vaulted ceilings. It was furnished with plain stone boxes, tombs, about thirty. There was no altar. The air was fresh, a little musty but not noisome. In one corner a family of vagrants, a man, two women, three children and a dog, huddled beneath a pile of rags and scraps of fur and pretended to be warm. Our guide sat on a tomb and set down his lamp beside him.

'This,' I said to Uma, 'is Brother Abraham, a Brother of the Free Spirit.'

'I know,' she said. 'I mean, I know he is a Brother of the Free Spirit.' And offered Abraham a smile of gentle complicity. He pushed back his hood, revealing a lean but pleasant face with smile lines as well as those etched by asceticism. His hair was lank, grey, and tonsured, but by nature rather than a razor.

In spite of the lugubriousness of his expression in repose, he smiled readily enough. He cleared his throat. 'So, what can I do for you, Brother Ismail?'

I explained what I had not told him on my first visit, how we wished to go into the north-west of the country and find Prince Harihara's brother Jehani. Uma took up the tale, of how we had had a guide, Eddie March, but he had fallen foul of the Queen's people and fled arrest by Lord John Clifford and Lord Scales and was nowhere to be found, and how our host and hostess were afraid of the Queen's people and wanted to send us on our way.

Abraham nodded all through this, stroked his bristly upper lip between thumb and forefinger.

'We have a Brother from the north-west,' he said, when we had finished, 'named Enoch. But he's a journeyman-fishmonger and he'll be working down at Fish Wharf at the end of Pudding Lane, next to Billingsgate, until midday. I can send to his house and ask his wife to send him on here as soon as he's finished. Will that do?'

Uma and I looked at each other, shrugged.

'Yes, that will do.'

There did not seem to be anything to be gained by returning to East Cheap until we had met up with this Enoch so we accepted Brother Abraham's invitation to remain in the crypt until our new guide came. We were thus tempted to indulge ourselves with holy conversation, for Abraham was clearly an adept in the science of living. Furthermore, he was curious to learn about Vijayanagara which he quickly realised was as close to a manifestation and incarnation of the Holy City as one could hope for. It was important to him while he had the chance to hear as much as he could of Uma's native city for thus he would be strengthened in the daily struggle to remain true to his refusal of faith in the face of Church and State.

On our side, Uma and I were interested to hear how the refusal was faring in Ingerlond.

'Ali, what is all this?' I interjected.

'My dear Mah-Lo, have we not already discussed three great orders of freemen?'

'I have no idea what you are talking about. What three orders?'

'*The Brothers of the Free Spirit, the Assassins who are the innermost circle of the Ismaelites and Sufis, and the Thugs?*'

'*The last two I had heard of before I came here, and you have said enough to imply that you have sympathies at least with the Assassins. But you make it all sound like a world-wide conspiracy.*'

Ali laughed lightly. '*No such thing is possible. For the supreme tenet of all three orders is that their members should be free, obligated by one principle only: that when you meet a like-minded person in need or difficulties you help him. Conspirators require rules, plans, obedience. Obedience, of all things, is what we most detest.*'

'*I am none the wiser, but you had better continue with your story. You had just asked this Abraham how things were in Ingerlond.*'

'Not well.' He sighed, and shifted a little on the cold stone he was sitting on. 'In almost all places the Refusal lives in hidden places, for too many in the last fifty years have been put to the torture and burned. Yet it is true that many hold to the beliefs of John Wycliffe, even if they do follow the road he signposted for us and even if they do not openly confess their faith as their fathers and mothers did. Yet, generally speaking, a Lollard preacher, in a graveyard, outside a city's gates, even at a market cross, will draw a crowd of sympathisers, who will leave strengthened if not actually prepared to march against the King and bishops as Wat Tyler, John Ball, Jack Straw and John Cade did. And thousands with them.'

'How far, then, will they go down the road of the free spirit?' Uma insisted.

'Oh, not far, and not beyond applying the light of good reason to the doctrines of the Church. They will deny the presence of Jesus in the sacraments, saying it is a strange god that can be lapped by dogs and eaten by mice. They can see how much against Scripture it is that priests should be able to sell forgiveness of sins, and they find the belief in Purgatory whereby the rich can buy their way into heaven through masses said for their souls abominable. They will condemn chastity in priests and monks as leading to unnatural vices, and in nuns as leading to abortion and infanticide. The more extreme declare all war to be evil, it being the murdering and plundering of the poor to win glory for kings, even the making of weapons to be evil . . .'

'But all this is merely nay-saying,' Uma cried. 'Do they not speculate about what can be put in the place of all the evil shit?'

'Some do in the privacy of their homes or in the company of three or four like-minded friends they can trust.' If Abraham was surprised or shocked by her vehemence, he showed it only in the soothing tone he adopted. 'For instance, they will argue that the giving of women in marriage is unjust, not out of lewdness as their enemies proclaim but because women should not be treated as chattels. Some argue that all property should be held in common, that councils where all sit together should decide what laws and customs should be followed rather than the whims of kings, lords and bishops.'

'And what sort of people turn out for the Brothers?'

'All sorts. From ploughmen to gentry, even lords. Eighty years ago, when he ruled the realm as King Richard's regent, John of Gaunt, great-grandfather of our present king, protected John Wycliffe. Lord Cobham, Sir John Oldcastle as he was before he married, continued that tradition and followed the teaching of the Lollards. He, however, was burned at the command of the present King's father, forty-five years ago. Almost worse, thanks to the cunning of the powers that be, he is now reviled as a drunken, whoreson coward, nicknamed Falstaff.'

For a moment his face was clouded with sadness. Then he went on: 'But the main reason why we thrive at present only a little, compared with a few years back, is these present troubles, these wars between the great lords. Since the plague came a hundred years ago, there have been fewer people to farm the land for them so wages have gone up and prices have dropped. Therefore the lords covet each other's land and instead of settling the disputes in courts or Parliament or by the King's command, they fight. And that means any able-bodied man can get a good day's wage wearing the livery of his master with the prospect, if he's on the winning side, of loot, booty, a share of ransom money, even land of his own or a tenancy. If he's on the losing side he just runs away and lives to fight another day. Also, because of these wars, outside London and the big cities law and civil society have broken down. There is nothing to rebel against and every chance of bettering oneself in the crude, brute anarchy that exists. Since anarchy of a sort is already with us there is no point in striving and risking death at the stake for the higher anarchy that might ennoble us all.'

And so we went on through the last heavy dark hours before dawn until the sun rose and with it the less than heavenly city: we could hear the clopping of hoofs, the bleat of sheep driven to the shambles, the squeal of cart-wheels, the shouts and calls of street-sellers, the general hubbub of the great wen, that weeping boil, in whose innermost heart we now were hidden.

It was about then that Brother Abraham told us just how holy was the spot in which we sheltered, dedicated as half of it was to the boy saint St Pancras, a bone of whose finger was kept in a reliquary in the second of the two tiny churches. It was, he said, the first church founded in Albion by St Augustine and the spot chosen for it was the site of a shrine that predated even the great Julius Caesar who built the Tower. This shrine or temple, as old as the henges in the west, belonged, so Abraham's account had it, to King Lud who built the city around it and was indeed no king but a river god.

The family of beggar-folk got themselves up and discreetly, silently, slipped away up the stone stairs. Now we could see them properly, divested of their rags and threadbare blankets, they revealed themselves from the darkness of their skin, darker than mine, almost as dark as Uma's, to be gypsies. I wondered where the rest of their tribe were and why they had separated from them.

The noise came and went in waves as folk opened the doors above and came in to make offerings or prayers to the image we had seen in the side-chapel: the Mother, Mary, Isis, Ishtar, Parvati. Below the stone floor our talk continued as we awaited the arrival of Enoch the fishmonger, and returned to the concept, the vision, of the Perfect Society that dominated our thoughts and longings. Abraham especially dwelt on Ingerlond before the Normans came: it had been, he said, rural and village-based, yet in its way as happy and blessed as the Heavenly City all three of us looked towards and which Vijayanagara represented, in much the same way as its emperor and empress are avatars for the gods Vishnu and Parvati.

We also speculated about the way the same light and knowingness had come to each of us and our fellow hierophants but by such different routes and out of such alien beginnings.

CHAPTER

TWENTY-TWO

In East Cheap a letter awaited me.

Ali

Shortly after your departure early this morning Alderman Dawtrey was honoured with a visit by Lord Scales, Constable of the Tower. He is a forceful old man and came accompanied by a troop of men-at-arms. He was of a mind to grant Anish, the few servants we have left and myself more comfortable rooms than the Alderman can supply, but in the Tower, which apparently is not merely a fortress but a royal palace too.

He is angry that we accepted hospitality from Richard Neville and Edward March in Calais and that we connived in March's escape last night. However, I pointed out to him that Anish and I had had very little to do with any of this, being guided entirely by the only member of our party who knew anything about Ingerlond – namely you. I think he understood.

Things will turn out all right for us – we have money from the sale of our goods, and many gems held hidden in reserve. I have, however, left some of the latter for you under my mattress. I suggest you use these to forward the aims of our expedition as you know them, but advise you to remain amongst the Yorkists as the King's people are now convinced that that is where your sympathies lie.

No doubt we shall be reunited under happier circumstances. Please accept my best wishes, and give my deepest affection [heavily crossed-out] respects to your reverend companion.

Harihara, Prince of Vijayanagara, cousin and accredited plenipotentiary of His Heavenly Eminence the Emperor Mallikārjuna

This was what Chamberlain Anish had written on the back of an old bill of lading the Alderman had found for him in the midst of the scramble that had taken place in the few minutes Lord Scales had allowed before he marched them all off to the Tower.

I turned to Brother Abraham, who had accompanied us back to East Cheap from the churches of Sts Benet Sherehog and Pancras, and did my best to ignore Mistress Dawtrey, who was shouting and squealing in her determination to get us off the premises.

'Can we get them out of the Tower?' I asked.

'No,' he replied, 'No one escapes unless they have the help and collusion of one of the gaolers.'

'Gaolers? It is a prison as well as a palace?'

'Yes. And for traitors most especially.'

'Are the Prince and Anish in mortal danger?'

Abraham thought for a moment, again caressing his top lip. 'Not for as long as their gaolers can be persuaded that there is something to be gained from keeping them alive,' he said at last. 'They have ransom value, no doubt, and they might be exchanged for prisoners the Yorkists hold. They might even be perceived as the means whereby a lucrative trade in spices and gems could be developed. For all these reasons they are probably worth more alive than dead. This being the case it is likely too that they will be kept in tolerable comfort.'

'What should we do, then?'

'You and Uma are in far greater danger. It is you who helped March escape, and as mere servants you have no value if you are captured. The Queen is a merciless enemy and delights in the blood of all who oppose her – Lord Scales will gain merit if he has you publicly dismembered . . .'

I recalled the quartered, eviscerated bodies fixed above the gate to London Bridge and shuddered.

Abraham continued. 'I think it best that you leave the City as quickly as you can and head up Watling Street for those parts of the country where the Yorkists still hold sway. Enoch will guide you. But I think, too, you should go disguised, at least until you are several leagues away.'

'Disguised? How?'

'You could . . . um, white-up.'

Mistress Dawtrey was becoming unbearably importunate, so, blocking my ears to the noise she was making, I got myself upstairs, found my way to the room Prince Harihara and Anish had occupied, burrowed around in and under the mattress and came up with two soft leather drawstring bags, each the size of a fist, which chinked solidly and satisfyingly as if loaded with small pebbles. I fingered one and identified the two large *kurundams*, with their sharp pointed pyramidal ends, and wondered what possible use they could be to us since, with their size and colour, they were fit for a monarch's sceptre and worth far more than we could ever need or, indeed, gain from them. But then, perhaps, I thought, that was precisely what Prince Harihara had had in mind: faced with the greatest magnates in the land and a queen profoundly jealous of her status, he might be forced to part with them, either for nothing or for a sum well below their worth. By leaving them with me he was assured I would keep them secret and not part with them except under the direst necessity.

I stuffed the bags in the deepest recesses of my loincloth beneath my cape and furs, and hurried back downstairs to find Uma undergoing a transformation. Enoch the fishmonger had arrived and was smearing her face with a mixture of pig's lard and chalk dust, converting her physiognomy into that of a clown or juggler. Just as I was about to remonstrate, believing that this would attract attention rather than deflect it, Abraham drew in his breath sharply, moved forward and, with an edge of his robe, smeared the paste into a thinner film revealing the copper-brown skin beneath.

'There,' he cried, 'that's much better. She looks like a leper.'

Enoch nodded enthusiastically and began to alter his handiwork in subtle ways to produce the effect we wanted.

Enoch was a mute. He was a small, round little man, about forty years old, nearly bald, with a thick black moustache and a stubbled chin. He had become mute, Abraham told us, some thirty years earlier when forced to witness the execution in the customary barbaric way of his fishmonger father and his mother too, for sheltering an antinomian priest. All this was part of the Purges that followed the burning of Lord Cobham.

The Worshipful Company of Fishmongers had taken on the orphan and charitably arranged that he should be apprenticed to one of their guild, but for reasons of safety in London, not in the northern fishing village where his parents had worked. He had proved a good pupil, quickly becoming adept at identifying good bargains when the fishing-boats tied up at Fish Wharf, well able to spot spoiled or stale fish, and knowledgeable to the point of erudition in all the species that can be found in the Thames estuary and the North Sea. He was also remarkably adroit with the big, triangular knife the fishmongers use for filleting and trimming the larger of their wares. However, his inability to speak had precluded him from becoming a master and full member of the guild and he was forced to hire himself out. Perhaps he bore a grudge because of this, or had inherited some of his parents' nonconformity, but at all events he was an independent soul, had travelled a lot and worked in most of the larger Inglysshe ports when the fancy took him. Moreover, he was willing to help any he perceived as being, like his parents, outcasts, non-believers, recusants or dissenters.

Wherever he went he took his sharp, shiny knives, the tools of his trade, the second one being a thin blade of grey steel about nine inches long, worn down by constant sharpening to the likeness of a blade of coarse grass.

'He'll go anywhere, so long as he is close to a supply of fresh fish by Ash Wednesday,' Abraham told us.

'Why is that?' I asked.

'For forty days after that day we eat no meat, only fish. It is the busiest time of year for fishmongers. They make a lot of money during Lent. And when is Ash Wednesday? Why, in ten days' time. Through Lent he'll be able to hire himself out for threepence a day, maybe more.'

Such was Enoch, who now worked away with grease and chalk to turn Uma and me into lepers whose white skins had been corrupted with brown patches by the disease.

But first we lacked the necessary adjunct of the trade, wooden clappers, one each, made from a small plank attached loosely to a sounding-box which, when shaken, emitted a loud crack or snap. These we were required by law to use whenever we came close to company as a way of keeping people away from us and infection. We, or rather Enoch, procured them from a tiny shop close to Ludgate, at the bottom of the hill between the gate and the bridge over the river Fleet. It was no more than a hovel but stacked to the rafters with chairs, saucepans, broken kitchenware, broken arms and armour, just about everything you can think of but old and broken – apart from our clappers, which were in working order. A curious place.

Thus equipped it became clear how inspired Abraham's choice of a disguise had been. The moment anyone came near enough to recognise or question us, a brisk clap or two sent them scurrying away. We also found that shelter was frequently available when we needed it in the form of lazar houses along the way: these were built on the outside of many towns and larger villages and consisted of a small barn-like structure large enough to accommodate twelve people sleeping together on the floor. Usually they had a little land attached in which vegetables often still grew, with pens for animals. And graves, for the lepers were often left to bury their own dead.

We were not afraid to use these places for they were almost always empty, and when they were not we moved on, either making shift in other ways or walking until we found one that was. We attempted to question Enoch as to why such provision had been made for so many lepers when there appeared to be remarkably few. He struggled with his affliction in his attempts to tell us, but whether or not he had it right we never found out, because any matter that required more than a basic understanding, anything involving speculation or theorising, was beyond us – he through his muteness, we through our lack of anything beyond basic Inglysshe. Months later I was able to question a learned friar, of whom more later, on the subject but even he was uncertain, so short is the memory of a people when civil disturbance and lawlessness stalk the land: the clear reduction in the numbers suffering from leprosy had begun before he was born and was complete before he grew to manhood. However, he speculated that plague was at the root of the matter: lepers, he guessed, were peculiarly susceptible to it, and while one in three of the population had been wiped out in the plague years, the epidemic had taken almost all the lepers.

Meanwhile, Enoch's first priority was to get us to the western coasts of the island before Lent began so that he could hire himself out to a master fishmonger, practise his trade, and earn enough money to see him and his family through the leaner months of summer when fish goes bad quickly and fish-eaters rely on fish smoked, dried, pickled or salted during the winter months. For this reason we headed more west than north.

It's not my intention, my dear Mah-Lo, to give a minute account of every step of our travels, but I must dwell for a moment on a school or college we passed since it represented the first solid evidence we had of the King's madness. Set outside a large village, in the midst of a water-meadow, at the time partially flooded and frozen, was a pair of large red-brick buildings, each forming a square, the south side, nearest the river, of one of them being a big barn of a church, not yet fully finished.

The road we were on passed between the church and the water-meadow, and was filled at the time with an unpleasant mixture of frozen, dirty snow and hard, churned-up mud. Pollarded willows, their stubby branches like clenched fists against the stone-like sky, edged the river. On the further bank beyond the wide, full, slowly swirling grey stream, there was another small village, but this one was huddled around a castle, quite a large one, with weighty towers that looked like drums. The cawing of rooks floated across the icy spaces between. There was a bridge but whether or not it was in a good state of repair, we did not stay long enough to discover.

The first thing that happened was that our ears were assailed from the interior of the church by a mournful chanting, very high, produced by unbroken voices, a sort of continuous wailing, like the keening of distressed women. We paused to listen to it and were standing thus when a cloud of young boys, about twenty of them, in black velvet gowns, with white collars on their shoulders and velvet caps on their heads came streaming round the far corner behind us.

'I say, chaps, look at this,' a slender but tall fifteen-year-old called. 'Three lepers by the look of it.'

In common with most people we met he had taken Enoch for a leper too, perhaps only in the early stages of the disease and his blemishes not yet significant, for why else would he remain with us and risk infection?

'Look here,' he yelled at us, 'just you clear off, if you know what's good for you. Come on, get a move on, show us your heels.'

Not understanding clearly what he was saying we did not move quickly enough for him. He picked up a handful of grit and snow, compressed it into a ball and hurled it at us. Clearly he had been trained to throw balls accurately for it struck me hard on the side of my face. Involuntarily I raised my staff and moved towards him.

Uma stretched out a hand to restrain me but then she, too, received a snowball in the face, flung by another boy from behind the first. This incensed me further. I snarled, and pressed on.

For a moment I thought he would run, but his friends were all behind him and I could sense that he durst not appear a coward in front of them. Instead he stooped and picked up another ball of snow, hurled it. This one hit me full in the chest, and since I was at that moment crossing a frozen puddle, my feet shot out from under me and I went down on my backside in a fall heavy enough to knock the breath out of me. Now all of these young hooligans followed their leader, picked up snowballs and hurled them at me, and at Uma and Enoch, who would have run had I not been grounded. Some even, wishing to show bravado in front of their companions, found sticks with which to prod me, and, once I was on my feet again, trip me too, so I tumbled back into the snow and mud. And all the time they shouted, 'Dirty old man, take that! Come on, you nasty bag of bones, get a move on. Unless I'm not mistaken he's some sort of darkie, a gypsy perhaps. Filth like that always catch diseases . . .' and so on, mostly in high voices like those that still sang on within the church.

Well, no harm came of it in the end. They chivvied us as if they were dogs and we sheep until we were clear of the buildings then took themselves off back inside, leaving us to examine ourselves to see if we had sustained any real hurt, which we had not, and recover our breaths and tempers.

Now, Mah-Lo, this incident had its interesting side, which Uma and I pieced together later. It was indeed a school, but an odd one. First it was only open to the so-called best in the land, judged by birth. The rest were excluded. Next, the pupils were torn from their families at a tender age and made to live there for the best part of the year, sharing large dormitories, eating together, the young made to serve the older like slaves, and frequently beaten by both older pupils and the adult masters; not only beaten, but often forced to submit to all sorts of cruelty including anal rape. I repeat, this was a school! Not a barbaric prison or a barracks. Finally, the strangest anomaly of all, this place had been founded and funded by none other than the King himself, as a place where the offspring of the best families might learn how to behave properly and assist him and his successors in the governance of his country! This, as I have said, was the first and by no means the last example we came across of his madness, and although we had had no choice in the matter and it was no concern of ours at all, I was glad we had found ourselves allied to the faction dedicated to depriving him, if not of his crown, for these people were superstitious about crowns believing they came from god, then at least of the power and rights that went with it.

The river now took a loop to the north-west at the top of which we came to a small town called Marlow! Just like your own name. No, dear friend, I am not making this up. Here, having seen the name on a signpost, Enoch got it into his head that he wanted to go to Oxenford. He tried to explain why but we could make nothing of his grunts and retchings. However, we were in his hands, and since this meant leaving the river and heading north-west we were happy to comply – at least we would be going more or less in the direction we wanted.

After walking through hills and woodlands for a day the landscape suddenly opened out in front of us below a steep hill, which dropped again into the wide river-plain of the Thames – the same river, but it had apparently taken a wide loop to the south-west before turning back north, making a quarter-circle across whose arc we had walked. And far in the distance, lit by the last shafts of golden sunlight making a fan-spread of beams from behind a low bank of cloud, we could see a city of spires and towers, which seemed to hang like a dream of the lost city of paradise above the mists rising from its river. Then the sun was obscured and all turned to black like the cutouts in a shadow play.

Uma squeezed my less functional hand, which she was in the habit of holding as we walked. 'A place of some ambivalence,' she murmured. I nodded, and the three of us began the long descent into the plain.

CHAPTER

TWENTY-THREE

W e continued down the hills through the rest of that day,
often with the distant city in sight beckoning us on, into
the wide river-plain, and as we walked a thaw set in around
us. Rivulets formed and tinkled as the snow continued to melt, birds
sang, and presently in a copse of thin, elegant trees with patchy silvery
bark we found clumps of tiny white flowers, shaped like bells. The track
we were on became muddy and our feet crackled in what was left of ice
as thin as paper. We saw deer, small and reddish brown with white bellies
and tiny antlers, not unlike those that live in the deepest thickets of our
mountain forests. Indeed, they put me in mind, almost for the first time
since we left London, of Prince Harihara and his penchant for hunting. I
wondered what had happened to his collection of crossbows and bolts,
and for the life of me I could not recall seeing them unloaded from
the donkeys' backs at Alderman Dawtrey's house. I supposed they must
have got there and were stored somewhere – in his cellars, perhaps.

These deer were browsing on holly until they caught our scent when
they melted away from us almost magically and certainly without a sound
and probably before they would have been within easy range of the
Prince's weapons. Once, beneath a grove of bigger, heavier trees, we
saw wild pigs rooting away in the mast that littered the woodland floor.
They would have been easier prey.

As we drew nearer the river, we found small settlements of human
habitation, though to our eyes, mine and Uma's, most of the dwelling-places

seemed less than suitable for domestic animals. They were mostly round, made from woven lengths of willow, the cracks between filled with mud, straw and what was clearly dried dung, with roofs of dried grass or reeds, and high enough in the centres only for a man to stand in. Spirals of bluish-white smoke rose from the centres of these tiny domes, smoke which was aromatic enough and filled the air with a not unpleasant pungent smell, but they must have been hell to live and breathe in. By far the greater part of the Inglysshe people live in huts like these, since those who did not collaborate with their Norman conquerors were enslaved by them.

In the afternoon the track we were on returned to the riverbank, whose serpentine course it followed with an almost continuous line of small, stunted trees, from which the thin branches had been sliced, leaving knobbly lumps like rough boulders at the tops of the trunks. These thin willow branches were used in many ways: woven, they formed the walls of the hovels, or were used in sections called hurdles to make fences. The thinner ones were made into baskets.

Meanwhile, the city of Oxenford loomed nearer through the gathering river mists. Soon we were picking our way through a muddy, wretched shanty-town that huddled around the low walls, which enclosed spires and towers in some numbers, almost as many as there had been in London, but for different reasons. Here they marked the prison- or barrack-like tenements occupied by communities of monks, friars and clerics: Oxenford, it seemed, was not only a prosperous town at the head of the navigable reaches of the Thames, communicating by ancient Roman roads with the middle and northern parts of the country, but also a centre of religious learning and other studies too.

It was not into the city that Enoch led us but to a Franciscan friary outside the city walls, indeed on the southern side of the river and to the west of the main town. We thus passed in front of the main gate, which was protected by a small but ancient castle, and moved on, through a ribbon of tightly packed huts that lay between the wall and the river, until we came to a small ferry station.

Here we divested ourselves of our leprous disguise, smearing the white clay into an even mask and casting aside our clappers, for Enoch managed to make it clear to us that the time had arrived when we should aim to be welcomed rather than rejected by our fellows.

The river was now flowing briskly, brown and with scurrying eddies, and our passage across it was terrifying, bringing us nearer to a watery death than the typhoons I have lived through in the China Sea. Our craft was a tiny round boat like a cockle-shell made of woven willow branches smeared with a black sticky substance, which was meant to render them sound. However, it let in water quicker than a young lad dressed in rags could scoop it out while his father paddled us across.

We were now on a long island called Osney, lying between the main river and one of its tributaries and largely filled by the Franciscan friary. Enoch knew that Oxenford was a good place for us to separate since we wished to head north and he west, and also because we would find here Wycliffites and Lollards, who were in sympathy with the Brothers of the Free Spirit, amongst the Franciscans.

The buildings in which the Franciscans lived and studied were attractive and modern. They were mostly of brick, a recently discovered material amongst these people, two storeys in height with rows of stone-framed windows, built round two squares or quadrangles. The first of these was planted with herbs in formal rows; in the second, there was a fish-pool. From this they took the large black carp that supplemented their Lenten diet. Two larger buildings, whose pitched roofs were a storey higher than the rest, separated the quadrangles. One was a chapel, the other a refectory. On the ground floors to the sides there were also a library, kitchens, stalls for domestic animals, and above, reached by a narrow stone spiral stair, the rooms of the Prior and a council chamber. The rest was made up of the cells where the friars slept and studied, tiny rooms reached by separate staircases.

The Brothers wore coarse brownish-grey gowns, belted with a rope and with hoods or cowls. Often they wore these up, not, we were told, for warmth, but to signify to their brethren that they were deep in thought, meditation or prayer and did not wish to be spoken to. When the hoods lay on their shoulders, their heads were revealed as shaven, not all over like our Buddhist monks, but in a circle leaving a ring of hair above their ears. All priests, and men intending to be priests, monks or friars, wore their hair thus, but the Franciscans' bald patch was larger and more noticeable than that of the rest.

We were given a warm welcome, for it is a part of the duties demanded by the rule of their founder that travellers, especially poor travellers, and we were certainly that, should always be given what they require. Warm, that is, in feeling, though plain and meagre as far as food and lodging went. We were given a broth made from stewed chicken bones, carrots and cabbage, but at least it was hot, served with black rye bread, and a thin beer to drink. Our beds, however, were nothing but sacks filled with straw laid on prickly, if springy, pallets of dried heather in a long, communal dormitory set apart for visitors. At least we had it to ourselves – few poor people travelled by choice at that time of year.

Just as we were preparing for bed, and wondering how we would keep warm through the night, one of the Brothers knocked at the door and told us that the Prior would like to have conversation with us. Leaving Enoch, Uma and I followed our guide across the quadrangle and up to the Prior's rooms, the principal one of which served as his study. In it there were a hundred books or more, a desk to read them on, a large table, several chairs, and a steadily burning fire.

Prior Peter Marcus, the kindest, most considerate man I have ever met, was small, completely and naturally bald, with mysteriously piercing blue eyes beneath bushy eyebrows, a small snub nose and full lips that creased almost too readily into a broad smile. His fingers, too, were extraordinary: short and almost stubby, very pink, but strong with square-cut nails that were almost white. As soon as he saw us he rose from the largest chair, crudely carved (truth to tell almost all the carving we saw north of Venice was crude, whether of stone or wood), and almost rolled round the large table in front of him to take both my hands in his.

'Brother Ali, my poor brother in freedom, Ali, what a state you're in!'

Well, as you know, dear Mah-Lo, at the best of times I cut a sorry figure, but the privations of our journey had taken their toll too. I had, for most of the time since we arrived in that benighted isle, suffered from an almost continuous flux – initially of fecal matter, latterly of blood and black water. The failure to retain fluids had caused a terrible thirst which, of course, I attempted to assuage at any wells we passed and the cleaner-looking rivulets. I had also taken to eating melting snow and ice until the thaw removed their passing solace. No doubt, I looked even more cadaverous than usual.

The cause? Well, of course, the absence of sanitation in London, I suppose, produced a constant presence of pestilential air, coupled with our hosts' readiness to eat and serve meat that had been left to hang for several days, even weeks, before eating it.

Prior Peter asked a few pertinent and succinct questions then rang a small handbell. One of the brethren appeared almost immediately and received from him a short list of herbs, some to be picked fresh from the garden we had crossed in the first quadrangle, others to be found pressed and dried in the friary's herbarium, yet others reduced to tinctures or essences from the apothec. 'However, we shall resort to essences only *in extremis*,' he giggled, 'for such is the advice of one of the greatest of our alumni.'

Weak though I was, I was able to cap his little joke. 'You will, I hope, shave all the ingredients with the sharpest of razors.'

And thus began one of the longest, most rewarding conversations I have ever had, stretching as it did over several months, broken only by sleep and my new friend's administrative duties. These included putting on a show of appropriate devotion at the appropriate times, since disguised emissaries of the Bishop of Winchester, in whose diocese Oxenford is situated, often slipped into monasteries and friaries checking that the daily offices were said or sung in a proper and seemly manner and that no heresies were heard, spoken or taught.

Uma tired quickly of this, both the offices and our conversation, and soon went temporarily out of our lives, practising what we merely preached to one another, and no doubt having an even better time of it for, as Peter was wont to say, quoting Aristotle, 'It is not *gnosis* but *praxis* is the fruit.' Or, knowledge is nothing without action.

However, on this first occasion gnosis went hand in hand with praxis, and within half an hour or so my new friend had prepared, largely with his own hands, an infusion, whose main flavours were peppermint and aniseed, not unpalatable. 'This,' he said, 'will work in two ways. Immediate relief will come in the form of a deep warm sleep, induced by the presence of tincture of opium dissolved in distilled alcohol according to an Arab receipt. We call it laudanum. The opium has the opportune double function of inducing not only the rest you need but a temporary cessation of the peristalsis of the lower bowel. Then there is peppermint oil and oil of aniseed, which, although not as quick acting, will ensure that the cure is prolonged after the effects of the opium have worn off. The mixture was invented by a doctor of medicine here at Oxenford named Collis Browne. Now, look, I cannot send you back to the dormitory, which is cold and uncomfortable. Drink up first, then you must have my couch . . .'

I protested, of course, but willy-nilly he, with Uma's encouragement, led me into a tiny cubicle behind the big fireplace, on the other side of its chimney-piece. Being thus heated it was already comfortably warm. They laid me on Prior Peter's bed, which, though narrow, was mattressed with swan's down, he said, and fragrant with dry lavender.

There followed an interlude as blissful as any I have experienced for first they divested me of my clothes and then, bathed in warm air as I was, they cleansed my tired, soiled body with sponges soaked in perfumed water. It produced a warm glow over my body, which penetrated to my aching bones. Meanwhile, the laudanum had a similar effect on my soul for behind my closed eyes I entered a world hung with crimson drapes and furnished with gilded chairs, a sort of womb-like place where I fancied myself an unborn babe, about to be born into a future of unlimited powers . . .

Ali's voice faded. A deep breath, a sigh, a little bubble of saliva in the corner of his mouth and he was asleep. I tiptoed away.

PART III

CHAPTER

TWENTY-FOUR

I returned three days later, business had kept me away, to find Uma again at the table, sharing a jug of k'hāwah with Ali. I tasted it, found it too bitter without sugar, too sweet with. Once we were settled Uma took up her shuttle and began once more to weave her scarlet thread into the fabric of Ali's tale – a magic carpet which had already transported me to the ends of the earth.

I see Ali, who seems very poorly, his face ever greyer, the sinews in his neck like the thinner branches of holly trees, comfortably established in Prior Peter's cot, with a good fire to warm him, and I decide to move on.

It is less than a week since I embraced Eddie March, and already I miss him: his palms squeezing my buttocks, his fingertips stroking my perineum, his breath hot in the crook of my neck and the thrust of his prick inside me but, of course, I have no idea as to where he might have gone. Without much thought I leave the island of Osney, with its priory and rows of pollarded willows, and head up lanes and byways through the fields and woods in a roughly southerly direction. But presently I sit on a milestone marking the road to Swindon and give the matter some consideration.

Eddie is on the run from the King and Queen who are his enemies. The King and Queen are in the middle of Ingerlond in a town called Coventry. Therefore that is the last place he will be. Until he's caught.

But . . . They, the King and Queen, will have ordered their people to search for him, hunt him out and, if or when they catch him, they will take him to Coventry. At all events news of him, if he is seen and recognised, as he was in London by the legless beggar, will be drawn towards that city like iron filings to a lodestone. Thus, by a pleasing paradox, the one place where I may discover his whereabouts is the one place he would rather not be . . . Having worked this through, I get up from my milestone and head back to Osney and Oxenford, skirt them and continue heading north, sleeping that night in a sheltered ditch.

In the morning I fall in briefly with a pompous young man leading his mule up a hill from which we can still see the spires and towers of the city behind us dreaming in the dawn sunlight. He carries a pouch embroidered with a shield bearing gold lions running across a red ground in two of its corners and silver floral shapes on a blue ground in the others, and as we near the crest of the hill the following conversation takes place.

'Pray tell me sir,' I ask, 'are we on the road for Coventry?'

'Why, yes, indeed,' he replies. 'It lies some fifty miles north at the end of this very road. I am on my way there myself,' he continues, 'being an equerry of Their Majesties, returning from delivering letters to the notables of the city,' and he gestures back over his shoulder.

We are close to the crest of the hill.

'Reverend Brother,' he says, then looks more sharply at me, frowns and looks away, 'you are welcome to ride pillion behind me when the road is flat or downhill. But up the slopes we must walk for my beast is tired after making such good speed with the letters I delivered.'

'I think not,' I say. 'I shall only delay you when I say the Daily Office.'

For that is what monks, friars and so forth are supposed to do, at least six times a day, the Daily Office being prayers and verse directed at the Christian god.

He shrugs, this lean and spotty youth, whose breath smells of bacon and onion and the clove he has chewed to hide them – or perhaps to ease the toothache he must have from his bad teeth. Since we are now at the top of the hill, he mounts his mule and sets it into a trot. I continue behind him and am thus well placed to see what happens next.

At the bottom of the hill, a small group of men in dark cloaks and large floppily brimmed hats, sidle out from behind a ruined sheepcote.

Their leader has a small firearm placed across his shoulder. His mate touches the end that protrudes behind with a smouldering fuse and, pop!, they blow my young equerry's head off. He remains seated for a moment with blood pumping from his neck and then his trunk slips sideways and he tumbles out of the saddle. I wait long enough to see that their interest lies in the pouch, embroidered now with blood as well as silks and precious thread, before leaping the ditch and hiding in a thorny thicket.

The day lengthens, the shadows shorten and the traffic on the road increases. Most travellers are accompanied by armed men. It is, after all, the link between the city in which the King and his court reside, and the one where the wisest men of his realm, known as dunces, carry out their business. Yet, as I have seen, one fraught with danger – hence the fact that all but a few, like my unfortunate acquaintance, travel with bodyguards, sometimes in quite considerable numbers. I reflect on the presence of footpads, murderers and the like hidden in the coverts near the highway, and decide to move off a mile or so to the west and pick my way to Coventry by lanes and byways, even if it means taking four days to get there instead of two or three.

It is a bright day with a gusty wind, and grey clouds roll intermittently across the sky. There are occasional splatters of rain, but it is never bad enough to obscure the position of the sun, and I am able without difficulty to maintain my northerly direction. Occasionally, too, from the top of a hill I can see the main road winding up hill and down dale over to my right, and the chain of villages it threads. With my senses alive and alert to all around me, not out of fear but because I feel they should be for every second of our pilgrimage across this planet, I begin to appreciate, as I could not when distracted by the company of Enoch and Ali, the tiny beauties of this country. With none of the splendours of Vijayanagara, for which I still hanker, none of the awesome crags, the deep forests, the rich plantations and the cities scrubbed and jewelled, the white-sanded shores and emerald seas, my eyes, ears and nose seek out smaller glories.

These include yellow flowers, extended like the grubs of small butterflies, hanging from thin leafless branches. When they catch the wind they dance and tiny puffs of gold powder float from them. In clumps at the roots of these trees or bushes, for they are not big at all, I spy small white stars, not pendulant like the flowers we saw when the snow melted. Then there are elegant trees with drooping black twigs in their crowns whose trunks are covered with a silvery-grey bark which peels off like fringed paper when I pull it. These often have quite large leathery fungi growing on them shaped like the swollen ears of baby elephants. A brilliant green moss, whose foliage is made up of tiny emerald stars, whose points touch each other to form a fine lacework, covers rounded banks where the earth is moist. When I look closely I see that many plants and trees have tiny swollen buds, but none yet show any sign of bursting into leaf. There are birds jewelled with blue and yellow, and one with a red chest and jet-like beak, needle sharp, but all very small. They do not sing but chirp and mew plaintively as they scavenge for particles of food.

All in all I get a sense of life not burgeoning, far from it, but struggling against the cold, the ice and snow, which still linger in patches of shade. It seems it will be a long, hard battle and when a flash of white draws my eye and makes me stoop, I find the fragile skull of what I take to be a rodent from its two sharp incisors: clearly Parvati must wait awhile yet – Kali still rules in these hushed woods.

Towards dusk a winding descent through woodland, with a little brook chattering along beside me, takes me into a wide but meandering valley where the trees have been cleared and a rough sort of cultivation has taken place. In front of me, perhaps a quarter of a mile away, is a village much like those we passed on the way to Oxenford: twenty or thirty hovels, each with a tiny garden and a fruit tree, cluster round a handful of larger buildings – a church with a squat tower and a large barn. But even now and at that distance I am aware that something is going on: I can hear a primitive raucous music emanating from a selection of untuned drums and wailing pipes, punctuated by high screams – whether of pain or pleasure it is impossible to say.

Then, just as I approach the settlement and the sun is dipping behind the hills to the south-west, a crowd of people stream out of the big barn, the music becomes louder, and I can see that amongst them the musicians have come as well, and all are dancing, or at least flinging themselves about in a bizarre way around a large pile of brushwood, holly branches, ivy, broom, brown gorse and prunings. I am now in a small orchard of lichened apple trees, which, in common with most trees I have seen, look dead or nearly so. Since there is a certain wildness in the antics of the people in front of me, which makes me nervous, I hoist myself up into the lower boughs of one, hoping thereby not to be discovered at least until I am satisfied I will be welcomed with friendliness.

A burning brand is poked into the foot of the pile of wood and branches and, despite the soft drizzle that is now falling, the flames take hold and are soon snaking up into the heart of the heap; there is a crackle and snapping as it takes hold, and a plume of white smoke sewn with gold and ruby sparks climbs into the cloud-filled, darkening sky. The next thing that happens is that a life-size human doll, made of straw and dressed in old clothes, is brought out and two men, holding its shoulders and feet, swing it high up on to the fire, which thus becomes a make-believe pyre.

A cry, a shout rises up, and the women who, I can see it now by the light of the fire, are wearing masks or hoods made of coloured cloth with eye-holes, seize burning brands and, still dancing roughly in time to the cacophonous beat of the music, come madly out into the orchard, banging the trunks of the trees with their brands and shouting curses or imprecations such as 'Bear apples, fuck you, Goddamn you, I want pears from you.' Once their brands have broken up, some hoist up their ragged skirts and, holding the lower branches in their hands, grip the trunks with their thighs and knees and rub their private parts against the bark.

Needless to say, in the midst of all this, I am discovered. A tall young woman with red hair flowing from below her hood throws back her head in an ecstasy real or simulated and finds my foot six inches above her forehead. She freezes, then screams: this time there is no doubting the fear and anger.

All those nearest her catch her tone and, still carrying their brands, approach. The effect spreads outwards and soon the whole gathering, maybe forty or more, men, women and children, are gathered around my apple tree, looking up at me. There is no mistaking their hostility, and by now I have enough Inglysshe to glean from the men, who have pushed to the front, a sense of its cause.

''E doos be a fuckin' friar or a monk, no doubt o' that.'

'Arr. But why be 'e 'ere?'

''E be a spy for the Bishop, no doubt o' that neither.'

'Well, what's to be done wi' im?'

'Cut 'is fucking throat, I say, an' bury 'im in the midden.'

'If 'e get out of 'ere alive, then fucking Bishop'll send 'is men to burn our fucking village an' we be well fucked.'

And so on.

'Well, first thing, zummun 'ad better get 'im out o' that there tree.'

Rough hands reach up to me, fasten on my ankles and pull.

'All right, all right,' I cry, 'I'm coming.'

And because I'm a touch frightened I forget to deepen my voice.

''E only be a young un from the sound of it.'

Once on the ground the nearest gets hold of my cowl and pulls it back while two more pinion my elbows to my sides.

'Here's a thing, then. Zumman get a light on 'im, let us see 'im proper.'

They have much to admire and find strange. First there is my head, once shaven but now with an all-over pelt of hennaed black, about half an inch long and no tonsure, then my full but tended eyebrows, also grown back, my straight nose, full lips and rounded chin. My eyes like deep mountain pools. My skin the colour of copper exposed to the air just as it begins to brown and lose its golden look. One of the women seizes my hand and turns it beneath the flickering light. 'This be no man's hand,' she says. 'This be a woman's and a lady's at that.'

'An' this be no friar's mantle,' another says, 'wrong colour and cut, and the material too fine.'

'She got boobies too,' one of the two holding me from behind calls out, after having a quick squeeze with her free hand.

At that, the one holding my hand, who was the first to see me, lets go and pulls up the hem of my gown, all the way, as far as the belt will allow.

'Yers,' she says, 'that's no friar nor monk. That's a hen.'

'Gerroff,' says I, and, looking over her shoulder and seeing curious children as well as men gathering round, one of whom lowers a torch to illuminate my lower half. She does indeed pull down the skirt of my robe. 'Zorree,' she whispers, almost in my ear, and I note a certain female companionship, a sense that I have one quality at least that has provoked a touch of sympathy. I feel better for it.

CHAPTER

TWENTY-FIVE

It is now clear to me that what I have been walking through during the day is the corridor linking winter to spring, the first stirrings of the new season having been beneath my feet and around me in the sights and sounds of the woods. These people, too, were well aware that a threshold had been reached and that the deities that control such things might well need a ritual shove to get us all across. Deities? Not the Christian godling and his mother and his father in heaven but the goddesses and gods who are worshipped here and everywhere, but in many parts are now hidden away like toys we are supposed to have grown out of. Except for these people, and many more across the world, it's not a whipping you get if you're discovered, but the rack, the thumbscrews and a burning. Hence their fear of me when they took me for a friar.

Back home, girls go out into the fields, make heaps of flowers and place on them images of Parvati and Shiva. In play they perform a marriage ceremony between the goddess and the god: it is all done as a childish ritual, a game, but still carries, like the ancient odour one smells when opening a long-closed chest, the survival of something far more powerful from the times when the gods walked among us, something which resembles what I am now caught up in in darkest Ingerlond.

Meanwhile, a debate continues amongst these villagers as to what should be done with me. The older men are all for cutting my throat, though one or two of the younger ones suggest that they should 'give me one' first. However, the women are generally against this for, as an older lady points out, if I am a religious then I must be a Clare, by which she means, I later learn, a member of the sister order of the Franciscans. It seems they are the only females who venture away from their convents, and when they do it is to bring succour and charity to the poor and ill. However, if I am not a Clare, then what am I? It would be foolish to harm me before discovering what the consequences may be.

By now we are all in the large barn, which has an earth floor, piles of dry grass or hay round the sides and heaps of grain. As the elders continue to argue, the rest are clearly preparing for a feast. The musicians, for want of a better word, have gathered at the far end opposite the big double doors, their drums, pipes and stringed instruments around them. There are a few tootles on the pipes and a bagpipe sets up a drone; one of the men rattles a box, filled, I imagine, with dried peas, another begins to beat a primitive drum, a skin pulled tight over a clay pot, with the palms of his hands, and so on. Some trestle tables are set up and a big barrel with a leaky bung is hefted up by six strong men and placed on one. Smoke, laden with the odour of burning meat, drifts in from an adjoining lean-to stable.

I am still held by the arms in a corner furthest from the door and behind the band. The women are close around me and some of the men looking curiously over their shoulders, when at last the one who first found me, whom the others call Erica, cries, 'Only Greasy Joan will know, she's the one, she'll know.'

'You're right,' cries another.

'But who will dare to wake her up?' a third asks. 'She'll give them cramps and stitches for a fortnight.'

'She ought to be here. She never misses a Bride's Day, she never misses the Bridget Feast.'

'But nor 'as she ever slept without food or drink for a month either.'

'Go on, get her up. An' if it kills her, well, good riddance, she's lived long enough, that's for sure.'

And three or four melt away into the smoke that's now swirling more thickly than ever. It smells green, as if they're trying to cook on fresh-cut wood rather than charcoal.

Presently they're back with a very old woman half carried, half supported between them. Because the old crones, the wise old women of Vijayanagara are usually so, I had expected her to be thin, scrawny, a bundle of bones, but this old lady, although, so they say, she has fasted a month, is fat with lolloping breasts beneath her gown, a belly like a barrel, huge thighs, and ankles swollen like puddings packed in the stomachs of sheep. She is also bald and toothless, so only her cheeks look thin. She's grumbling and cursing through her gums, uttering obscenities worse than any I have yet heard, even here in Ingerlond.

They plant her in front of me and she gazes at me from eyes that look left and right at the same time, up and down, and one is misty blue, the other pale green. She has a wart on one cheek with four black hairs growing out of it, and big dewlaps, like a great white water buffalo's, which quiver and shake when she speaks or moves her head. In an ambience already rich with foetid odours, her own stale exhalations, the smells of flesh tired and unwashed, old piss and shit, make a cloud around her.

'Come on, Greasy, tell us who she is,' they call. 'Is she a witch? Takes one to know one . . .' and so forth.

She peers at me, shifts to one side then the other, reaches out a podgy hand, looks more like a long-teated cow's udder than a hand, and touches my wrist. Then she cackles, a hard, rattly sound, and hisses too, like an angry goose, showering us all with spittle and revealing teeth small, yellow and broken. At last the fit leaves her, and she almost shrinks in front of me, seems to sink a little.

'Yer fools, y' know, yer all bloody fools. Can't y' see her skin, how dark it is, can't y' see her beauty, the glow about her? That I should live, live to see this day, this night. Well. I'm blest after all. At the end of me life I'm blest.'

'Oh, come on, Granny Greasy, don't mess about, tell us who she is,' they cry.

'Well, then, I will. This here is none less than Mary Gypsy, Mary of Egypt, Marry Gyp hersel'! Miriam Marina. She'll dance for you, if you ask her nicely, and if she don't like you she'll blast your wombs with warts and fill your cunts with teeth.' Then her voice drops and she speaks to me alone. 'Forgive me, Lady, it's your sister loves me now, your sister and my mother, old Hecate, but truly I loved you once.'

And with that she turns and, tottering like a rotten tree in a storm, she stumps and stumbles her way from us, out through the smoke to whatever bed she's been wakened from.

By Hecate I understand her to mean Kali.

They look at me with wonder.

'Are you really Marry Gyp?' they ask. 'Will you dance for us? Please dance for us.'

I look out beyond them, this small group of women, to where the rest are jigging and stamping to the beat of the drums and the twisting music of the raucous pipes. Every now and then they wave their arms above their heads and holler, 'Hey-ho, silver moonshine,' thus invoking the Queen of Heaven. Over by the tables beer is being drunk from the barrel, most of it direct from the bung, the young men catching the stream, which looks like nothing less than a stream of pee, catching it in their mouths the way a dog will catch milk squirted from a cow's teat. Others are eating slabs of pig-meat wedged into lumps of grey rye bread. Clearly no one's going to watch me dance with any serious attention. I'll look a fool gyrating in a corner while the others stumble about the place locked in their own worlds of booze, food, their own revelry.

'Later,' I promise.

And 'later' comes in an hour or so, but meanwhile I've persuaded my friend Erica to take me to her hut where I make my preparations. Inside there's a small fire of white charcoal, and a baby hangs in a basket from the roof. There's no man about, so either she's a widow or she's been caught out by some other woman's husband. She has no jewellery except for some copper bracelets, which she dips in sour beer to give them a gold-like shine. I prefer copper anyway, it's Parvati's metal, and I have my small bag of pearls hidden away . . . I'm not saying where – no, it's not rude, just that it's good to keep a few secrets, you know?

We scout about and, taking a big risk, she gets us into the church. They only see a priest once a month, but he's left some vestments in a chest. Erica uses flint, stone and a tinder-box to light some candles, and while she goes through the chest I take one and have a look around. There's a damp smell about the place, cold stone sweating the body fluids of the dead. There's Jesus, all taut muscles and corpse pallor skin, stretched on his cross, silly bugger, and his mother too in a side-chapel, holding the baby, a gold-leaf halo round her head. But where's the mother in all her glory? Should be the babe looking at her with adoration, not the other way round.

I return to the vestry and pull my robe over my head. Erica gives a little gasp. I take her hand, rough from washing clothes and field-work, and make her stroke the flat part of my chest above my breasts, then my breasts, my shoulder, my back and my buttocks, and she sighs with wonder at their smooth, gleaming darkness in the candle-light. Then, out of an amice nicely embroidered, with strings and all, we improvise the little skirt or apron temple-dancers wear.

Normally I would matt my hair with ghee and pile it up in a jewelled crown, but now, of course, it is still growing out of its shorn state and is far too short, so we rip up a white and gold chasuble too, and heap that up like a turban. I paint my face with charcoal mixed with butter, shaping my eyes like almonds, thickening my eyebrows and eyelashes, and use red clay and butter for my lips. Finally I draw spiral and dot patterns round my nipples, which I also paint with red.

Thus decked out, in tawdry imitation of the figure I would have been at home, when I would have worn a girdle, necklace, diadem, anklets, ear, toe and finger rings, all made of gold and set with precious stones, I look grand enough, numinous even, for Erica to fall on her knees, clasp my thighs and bury her head in the amice.

'You really are the Marry Gyp,' she moans, 'you really are.'

I put my tiny finger-cymbals on my third fingers and thumbs, bend my elbows in front of me, crook my little fingers, and let her hear the silvery chime.

In the hall things are much quieter now. Only a block-flute from amongst the pipes is playing, and the drummer is using his fingers on the skin instead of beating it with his palms. Five couples sway to his beat, locked in close embrace, the rest are strewn about the earthen floor or giggling in the piles of hay, mostly in couples. There is less smoke and the big barrel on its table is leaking a slow dribble, which an old man, prostrate beneath it on his back, attempts to catch in his mouth. Needless to say, a silence spreads out from where I am until the whole hall is as quiet as a desultory snore here and there will allow, and all open eyes are upon me.

I give the cymbals a ping or two, and head tilted both forwards and to the side, swing one knee up and out before bringing the sole of my foot down with a tiny stamp. Then the other side, the other foot. My arms swing, my fingers straighten and curl. Ping, ping, and the drummer, who is wide-chested, has arms like elephant trunks and a black mat of hair across his chest picks up on my rhythm with his fingers and his friend with the flute, tall and thin with yellow hair, ventures a little run. And round my feet the incense Erica

has brought from the church softens the bite of woodsmoke and
sour beer.

Presently, in the Teluga tongue, I sing.

> Oh, Goddess Minakshi
> whose lovely body has a deep blue sheen
> with long eyes shaped like a carp
> Goddess who provides release from the fetters of life
> who resides in the forest of kadamba trees
> esteemed one
> who conquered Shiva
> grant me bliss.

And later, the drummer adds his ditty:

> Such a one did I meet, good sir,
> such an angelic face
> who like a sprite, like a queen, did appear
> in her gait, in her grace . . .

Prancing and swaying, I swing down the hall and the clouds of incense
part around my thighs, my brown feet raise the dust. Copper and pearls
flash and glow in the embers of a fire and the stir of my passing makes
the flames on the tapers shudder. My naked breasts promise more than
pomegranates, my buttocks are peaches. Eyes turned up at me gleam
and flash and no one moves except to sigh in pleasurable pain. I cannot
dance for ever, and already they know they'll not see my like again.

Flute and drum are getting to know me. Messages flash between us.
The first flutters like breath in a baby's throat, the second quickens in a
lovelorn pulse. I turn on a toe, pummel the floor with my feet, fling
my arms in windmills of desire about my head, and without taking their
eyes from me every he and she there reaches for his or her other. The
sweat glistens on my shoulders, runs between my breasts, my thighs, and
the wind I've raised begins to gust about the corners of the room, the
sacking over the entrances fills like sails, and the gale, a warm wind with
rain on it, rushes in, gathers me in its arms and blows out the lights.

There is plenty of the long night left. In the dark Alan, the drummer, is the first to find me, but he's a noisy brute and his groans and shouts soon lead David and his flute to the corner we're in. The hay is deep and soft and still smells fresh, even of the summer flowers that mingled with the grass when it was mown. They're nice, they take the edge off my hunger, but Eddie they are not. Better, or as good, when they at last fall silent, or almost silent apart from thunderous snores from Alan and sighs and whistles from David, Erica finds me, takes my hand, and leads me to her bower where her boy-child swings from the roof in his cradle and charcoal still glows in the centre of the floor. She sponges me down with rags soaked in warm water, gives me cold spring water, cheese and bread. She makes me lie in her cot with her and rocks me to sleep in her arms with her lips in the crook of my neck, her breasts that leak a little milk against mine, and her strong legs crooked on my waist and lying across my thigh.

Before dawn, but not before cockcrow, she sets me on my way towards Banbury but I'm hardly more than a hundred yards out of the village when running feet make me turn and Alan falls in beside me without a word, his clay drum on his back and a cloak over his leather jerkin and apron.

Ten yards, and it happens again, through the mist and over the sparkling frost comes David – cloaked, too, and no doubt with his flute about him. He gives Alan a look that lacks friendliness and falls in on the other side, also without a word.

This will not do. Both seek to own me, and that I will not have. I whisper a prayer to Parvati and in ten minutes or so it is answered. We are climbing a hill now and once we're over the crest the village will be gone, and nothing will induce them to return. As subtly as I can I reduce the length of my steps. I even pant a little and put my hand on a branch as if I need to rest. And then, at last, they come. First a little girl in a woollen dress, her hair all loose, but she is overtaken by a boy who scampers past her and reaches us first.

'Uncle Alan,' he cries, 'Grandpa Bert has broke the chain on his harrow and none of us will get our fields broken up for sowing if you don't come now.'

Then the little girl is at my side. 'Uncle David, if you don't come now, Uncle Alan will never get his forge up to heat 'cause the bellows has a hole in it.'

I look at them both, first Alan then David.

'So. You are the village smith. And you are the bellows mender. A long goodbye to both of you.'

And humming a little hymn to the goddess I pass on my way, over the crest of the hill and down the other side.

Chapter

Twenty-Six

In Banbury marketplace there is a fair for carnival. An ox is being roasted whole, which, of course, disgusts me, but there is plenty to please the senses too: apples on sticks, dipped in honey and roasted, cubed pork or lamb sizzling on skewers over gridirons, pastry cakes filled with raisins, a local treat, hot spiced wine, nick-nacks and gew-gaws known as fairings are all for sale. And there are sideshows too: jugglers, fire-eaters, tightrope walkers. There are contests of strength, and contests which involve rolling big wooden balls down a long plank to knock over nine club-shaped skittles. And, above all, there is a carnival procession led by a girl of lovely beauty riding on a white horse. She has pale white skin and long yellow hair, and she is wearing a green dress. She has rings on her fingers and bells on her toes and she is followed by a band with the usual pipes, bagpipes and drums. Do the people of Banbury know who she really is, this Carnival Queen? Maybe, but they'll only whisper it.

Best of all, well, best after Her Ladyship, there's a shadow puppet theatre, best because it reminds me of home where such entertainments are common. There's a two-wheeled cart with a very old horse still between the shafts, munching in a nosebag. The tail-gate has been dropped and there's a white cotton or silk screen stretched in a frame just behind it. Then there's a gap in the planks of the floor and up through it, from underneath, and hidden by drapes that brush the cobbles, the puppeteers thrust the two-dimensional dolls and manipulate their limbs and heads in front of a tented bank of oil-lamps and candles. None of it works too well at midday when I arrive, but later as the sky fills with purple clouds and the sun falls behind the big new church and a few flakes of snow drift across the marketplace, it looks better, a little cave of light and pleasure.

There is a notice painted in red and yellow lettering on a semi-circle of wood above the screen: *Geoff Reeve and Family, Shadow Puppets for your Edification and Education, as seen by the Crowned Heads of Europe.*

They are enacting a miracle performed by the Mother of God on the pilgrims' road to Santiago. My initial fascination wears off and I wander through the crowd, sampling some honeyed barley-cakes, which I filch. I hear a cheer from the crowd round the shadow puppets and wander back.

There's another notice up now as well as the first: it reads 'The Last Inglysshe King'. This looks more interesting. I take my place in the crowd next to a peasant who is eating roasted barley, puffed up by a brazier's heat.

A warrior, clearly the hero because he is taller than all the other characters, swears an oath of fealty to a duke. The crowd boos. He has been tricked into it, they shout. An old king with a crown and a beard dies in his bed. The Warrior Hero takes his crown and the crowd cheers. The Warrior Hero fights a battle against two men in winged helmets and defeats them. The crowd cheers again. Ships rock and sway across the screen. The Duke gets out of one. The crowd boos. A second battle takes place. It lasts a long time. Then an arrow hits the Warrior Hero in the eye and the Duke wades in with his sword, kills him and takes his crown. The crowd boo again, but more soberly. Some turn away and I see that one or two look sad indeed.

The show ends with a comedy. It involves an old man with a young wife who climbs a pear tree where she is fucked by a young man. There's more to this than meets the eye. The old man is winter, the pear tree is the tree of love, of the goddess, the young man is spring and the wife is the earth, a good choice for a festival on the cusp of winter and spring. Considering the whole show has been no more than a matter of shadows on a screen it has been well done, and fulfilled the promise of instruction combined with pleasure.

I am about to leave when I hear an irritated sigh from behind me and a smallish man, with thinning grey hair, spectacles and a pleasing, open face, pushes between us, holding a collecting box in one hand and a walking-stick with a crook for a handle in the other. 'Pennies for the puppets,' he says, and my peasant with the inflated barley grain pushes off fast. I put a penny in the box. I picked it, and four more like it, from his purse during the show.

'Generous,' says the new arrival. 'A farthing would have been ample.'

'You asked for a penny.'

'A manner of speaking.' He takes me by the elbow and looks over his shoulder. 'I take it from the way you speak and the darkness of your skin that you are a stranger to these parts, possibly even from some further shore?'

I nod my concurrence.

By now the crowd is drifting away from us. Geoff Reeve, for that is clearly who he is, casts a jaundiced eye over the receding backs.

'I won't get any more out of this lot. Perhaps you'd care for a jar with me?' He ponders a moment. 'At the White Horse, perhaps?'

He shakes his collecting box and I follow him towards his cart and stage. From behind he has a faintly ecclesiastical look: a bald patch at the back of his head suggests the tonsure, his roped robe a monk's habit. Perhaps he was once in minor orders: certainly his erudition and manner are, I have discovered, rare in Ingerlond outside the Church.

'Jenny?' he calls. 'Chap here, awfully nice fellow, but a Johnny Foreigner, so I'm taking him over to the White Horse for a pint. Join us if you've a mind too.'

A handsome woman, younger than him and with blonde hair, who is loading small cushions that had been put out for children in front of the screen into the back of the cart, turns and smiles at me.

'How very nice to meet you,' she says. 'I'll be with you directly.'

Geoff Reeve shakes some coins out of his collecting-box, retains a couple of pennies, and gives the rest to Jenny; then he takes my elbow again and we walk over the cobbled square, past the cross to a tavern called the White Horse, on the side opposite the Fine Lady.

He is known in the tavern. 'Master Reeve, what can I get you?' A cheery girl has singled him out, and is ready to serve him ahead of customers who have been trying to get her attention.

'Two pints of mulled winter ale, Bess, in pewter, if you please, and a couple of dozen oysters from the barrel that arrived today. Get Peter to bring it to the fire for us.' And he pushes me in front of him towards the big fireplace with its large inglenook, a bench and a three-legged table. 'At least we'll be warm here. The cold really gets to me, especially in the hip.' And pulling up his robe to reveal his knees he spreads them towards the fire and his hands above them. His spectacles flash with the flames.

'Where are you from, then?' he asks.

There seems no reason to lie. 'From Bharatavarsha,' I say, giving the Sanskrit name, 'which you generally call India, I believe.'

'Really? Now refresh my memory. Which side of Africa is that?'

'The further side.'

'Ah. And what brings you to this end of the world?'

Not an easy question to answer. To say that I am seeking wisdom when I have left the land that is the fount of all wisdom would invite ridicule from this clearly cultivated gentleman. Fortunately we are interrupted by the arrival of our comestibles.

The oysters are excellent, already opened for us so all we have to do is toss them into our mouths from their glowing nacreous shells, which are thinner and more round than the ones we pick up from the Malabar coast, and more delicately flavoured. The ale is dark, rich, fruity in flavour, and, perhaps because it is served hot, very quick in its intoxicating action. A small wild apple bobs against the rim.

'Your show,' I comment, 'was about the Normans. The people who rule you.'

His glasses flash at me, seriously, knowingly. 'Bastards! No, not really. It's about Harold. Good bloke, but unlucky.'

'The arrow in the eye?'

'Of course . . . he loses. And William becomes king and the Normans take over. Bastards,' he repeats.

'Are they really so different, the Normans and the rest?'

He leans towards me and puts his hand on my knee. 'Yes,' he says. 'They've never fitted in, in spite of marrying Danes and Saxons, which they were bound to do since they brought few women of their own with them. Their kings married into the Frankish Angevins, who call themselves Planta-Genêt after the branch of broom their founder wore in his helmet . . .'

The name stirs up sand from the bottom of my mind, the way a shrimp at the bottom of a rock-pool does, but I couldn't place it. Geoff went on, '. . . and it's only in the last sixty years after nearly four hundred, that they've even bothered to learn Inglysshe. They're not properly English at all, stiff-necked, proud, formal, obsessed with form, order and rank.'

I remembered how, at Calais, Warwick and the rest had treated Wydville with contempt because he was no Norman. Geoff went on: 'They are clannish, and they love sports but the more warlike the better. Those who do not have the inclination or the physique go into the Church and are made bishops. But while their relations with each other may be easy they remain arrogant to outsiders.'

'What about their women?' I ask.

'Obsessed with their men. They serve them like slaves, marry as they are told to, bear children as regularly as cows calve, and are even more concerned than the men with status and the trappings of status.'

'So what are the real Inglysshe like?'

'There are two sorts, those who collaborated and those who did not. Those who did are servile and obedient, content to do anything for a quiet life so long as they are not starving. You see, the Normans had a problem. They had to recruit clerks, officials, sheriffs, constables, customs officers and the like to run the country. And provided they behaved the Normans were happy to let the Saxons do this work.'

He sighs, continues, 'These people, these collaborators, developed a finicky sense of neatness, correctness, to please their masters. They accept the Normans as their lords by right and tradition, and will do anything to please them, showing forelock-tugging deference at all times and aping Norman manners. Usually it was the Saxons who collaborated. The Danes are more independent. But both races shared a way of life, before the Normans came. The Inglysshe way.'

He shifts again, raises his empty lead-coloured tankard to his lips, gives it a shake. I look round and see the boy who brought us our drink and oysters at my shoulder and I order two more pints. This time I pay for them.

When he's ready to go on it is in a tone more speculative than before, as if he were thinking through what he had to say for the first time.

'In the old days both Saxons and Danes governed themselves through village moots or meetings. Even the King was governed by the biggest moot of all, the Witangemot. And although most of these privileges were taken away or driven underground the spirit that lay behind them survived.'

'And imbues the second strand in the Inglysshe?' I guess.

'Yes, indeed. Under our outer robes of conformity we are fiercely independent, and respect each other's individuality. We can work hard when it suits us, but we'd rather drink, dance, and muck about. And there'd be a lot more of that than there is if our Harold had won that damned battle . . .' And he sways a little on the bench, wipes a tear from the corner of his eye. 'Merry Ingerlond,' he says. 'That's what we lost.'

'Geoff. Geoff? Come on, now.' I look up and see his wife Jenny smiling down at us.

'Hello, my dear.' Geoff sits up with a start, suddenly recovered. 'Just telling this young feller about the Inglysshe and so forth. He's from India. Fascinating place. Perhaps we could knock up a shadow-play based on his experiences . . . Call it, let me see, *Far-flung Palaces*? Sit down, dear, have a bite and a drink, see what you think.'

And he gives me a big wink, which I am sure she sees, for she, too, gives me a secret little *moue* before squeezing in next to him.

Coventry. Again I keep to the countryside to avoid the dangers of the road, and it takes me a day and a half to get there. I must confess, too, that I had a bad night sleeping in the stabling of that Banbury tavern. I had to share the straw, pretending to be a man amongst several others in the way of ostlers and grooms. I had drunk a gallon of ale by the time the Reeves departed, which had to be disposed of and it was not easy to maintain the pretence while pissing next to a man similarly engaged. And then the oysters. Never eat shellfish unless you can see the sea is a good rule, and always open them yourself. It only needs one bad one, and one bad one there must have been. No doubt the heat of the fire and the numbness induced by the ale disguised its presence . . .

The result is that I came upon the city at around midday when I might have been there the evening before. The first thing one sees, and that from a considerable distance, is the spire of its cathedral, which soars to a needlepoint out of the smoke and murk that fill the air above the city roofs. Next, and quite clearly seen, since the town is built on a low eminence above the fields and commons around it, is a vast shanty-town outside the city walls. Since London has proved hostile to the royal faction, the King, or rather his Queen, has made this city, in the very centre of the island, her capital and principal seat of government, calling

Parliament to meet here, and bringing in the whole apparatus by which the nation is ruled.

In its train this has brought many thousands of hangers-on, mostly people who have no visible means of support, as out-of-work artisans, entertainers, tinkers, gypsies, prostitutes, unfrocked clerics, unattached professional soldiers, horse-dealers and then the people who would supply this crowd with victuals and drink, especially the strong drink the Inglysshe love so much. Now, in a town the size of London such a crowd can be accommodated, and even employment found for many, but what was a relatively small place of perhaps no more than five thousand souls is swamped, law and order and all the other services break down, and the whole place is enclosed by a human jungle, like a well-formed egg-yolk within a sloppy white.

First, on the outskirts of this shanty-town, there are enormous, steaming middens with heaps of refuse as well as ordure, both animal and human, and up and down these miniature alps old women and children clamber and slither looking for food, such as cabbage stalks, stale loaves, fish-heads, even egg-shells with a trace of egg-meat still in them, and the last of the meat too, pigs' feet and ears, cows' tails and goats' heads – I say the last for we are now into Lent, forty days when no meat will be eaten.

Then come the hovels, crowded about with no discernible streets or lanes, except for the main thoroughfares from each of the cardinal points of the compass, which lead to the gates in the city walls, and which, willy-nilly, every visitor must follow. Here, countless beggars use every art and wile to keep body and soul together. Women, holding screaming babies they have hired from baby-dealers, tug at my sleeve with grubby palms outstretched; there are young men in the prime of life with serviceable limbs tied up to look like amputated stumps, which they claim have been lost in the service of the King or even in the French wars, others have sores painted on their faces and some mimic blindness.

Moving nearer the walls one finds quacks and swindlers selling talismans, pilgrims' medals, amulets and the like guaranteed to give protection against every manner of ill, and street-trading apothecaries offering green dragon's blood, the stones from the heads of poisonous toads, the shrivelled stomachs of sharks, false limbs carved from wood, glass eyes. Others hawk the shrivelled hands and feet of babies said to be the relics of saints, and there is one who claims to have the piss of a witch in a glass vial, which, he says, poured a drop at a time on the nape of a woman's neck will, by its giving off a vapour and a foul stench, reveal her to be a faithless whore.

All seem to do a good trade but he who does best is a tall lean man with straight yellow hair to his shoulders who sells pardons, signed and sealed by the Pope in Rome. He claims these scraps of parchment will get a man or woman time off from Purgatory, a place apparently sinful souls must go to to be purged before progressing to the paradise these superstitious people believe in.

All this, of course, produces a fearful clamour of cries, shouting, screams and singing out, which is like the scraping of slate on slate to my ears, assaulting them just as badly as my vision, sense of smell and touch are lacerated by this wretched throng around me.

Presently the South Gate rises above the thatched and tented roofs, flanked by twin towers and with a lowered portcullis. Fixed to its lintel is the usual ghastly array of skulls and half-eaten heads of those who have displeased the authorities. For a moment I pause, nonplussed, since, yes, it is shut and has a detail of maybe ten soldiers armed with swords and crossbows in front of it. But I hardly have time to consider how I should get in when a trumpet sounds, and from behind I hear the thunderous clatter of iron-shod hoofs on cobbles, the rumble of wheels, the crack of whips and jangle of harness and weaponry.

There is not time or room to get out of the way. What we have is a squad of mounted soldiers, armoured in open helmets, which leave their faces exposed, chain-mail, breastplates, jointed steel casing on their limbs, big swords at their sides, shields attached to their harness, and holding heavy spears. There are perhaps a score, and all riding big horses that sweat beneath their loads but keep up a slow, steady trot, and what makes them take up so much room, so the crowd must press back against the walls of the shanties, some of which cave in bringing down the roofs on the people within, is a big monster of a cannon drawn by a team of mules. A tube made of lengths of cast iron, fused together and bound with brass hoops, followed by a cart filled with stone balls and then another loaded with barrels of gunpowder. It is not as big or grand as the carriage Jagannath is pulled on when he makes his trip from temple to temple in Puri in Orissa, but the effect is similar. However, whereas the pilgrims who are crushed to death beneath Jagannath, which is an avatar for Vishnu, have freely chosen this form of self-immolation, here in Coventry the poor souls who are crushed beneath this monster have not elected this way to die but go screaming to their deaths.

Nevertheless this Juggernaut has timed its arrival precisely at the right moment to get me into the city. Imagine a giant log in a storm-swollen stream — as it passes on its way so it will suck in behind it the turbulent water and all the tumbling flotsam that rides on it. The guards do their best to close in and shut off the flow as the pointed black teeth of the portcullis grind slowly down above us, yet as many as thirty get through, and I am amongst them.

A moment's hesitation then, like the others with me, I choose a side alley and rush off down it between high gabled houses that block out the sunlight and the sky. After a minute or two I slow, stop and look around. The winding dark place I am in is chill, as if the sun never reaches the cobbles and flags beneath my feet, there are few people about, and there is a dank, deep, near perfect silence, quite different from the bedlam I have left. Looking behind me I see no sign of pursuit, yet I feel I am a trespasser, that I have reached a place where those in charge would prefer me not to be. I take a winding course through a warren of similar narrow streets to get away from the gate with its guards. Presently I glimpse the slim spire soaring like a steel poniard into the grey sky, with a flash of gold from the cross or weathercock at its summit, and I bend my steps towards it.

Less than an hour later I am in prison.

CHAPTER

TWENTY-SEVEN

U *ma sighed, her eyes unfocused. Then she shook herself, smiled at me with a tenderness that was inspired not by me but by her memories, and gathered together the small items she always carried with her.*
When she had gone Ali took up his tale – and thus it was for the next few days: turn and turn about they told me their stories to the point where, almost at the end, they merged again into one.

My convalescence was slow, Ali resumed, my body weakened, so Peter Marcus said, not only by the flux, not only by the privations endured over the months of travel compounded by forced reliance on unaccustomed food and drink, but also of course, by a constitution compromised in early childhood by the terrible blow administered by the Sunnite's scimitar. Since I prided myself that, for nearly sixty years, perhaps more, I had maintained through constant privation and travel a lean, wiry fitness in spite of my disadvantaged frame, I took leave to doubt this – indeed, I almost suspected that some of the potions Prior Peter gave me were designed to make me feel weaker and more wearied than I was. The fact was, as he often repeated, he rarely had the chance to meet and converse with someone who had seen as much as I, who had experienced so much, and studied both from books and at the feet of some of the wisest men who have lived during our times. We spent six weeks together, right the way through the period of Lent, never leaving the friary and its gardens, but talking and reading together whenever his duties, which he carried out as I have said with some diligence but not out of devotion, allowed.

'You see, my dear Ali, my situation here places me in an awesome position as the successor and inheritor of the three greatest Inglysshemen who have ever lived and who between them, one after the other, created a tradition of thought, and action, too, which will, I believe, be hailed in time as the greatest gift our nation has bestowed on mankind.'

I knew enough to be sure that the Inglysshemen he referred to were Roger Bacon, William of Occam (to whose apothegm, Occam's razor, concerning entities or essences we had jokingly alluded when Peter was preparing the potion that cured me) and John Wycliffe. I was quite conversant with their teaching and knew of their connections with Oxenford and the Franciscans. All three had made Oxenford their home and their principal place of study, and had been protected from persecution by the university.

It was Brother Peter's aim and ambition to collect, collate and draw together the teaching and praxis of these three men and out of the consensus, the accord and harmony between them, build a unified philosophy of life that would be the foundation stone on which mankind could move towards a millennial perfection. It was a matter of great pride to me, first, that he acknowledged how much of their knowledge represented in turn a growth from the great philosophers of my own Arab nation, particularly Ibn Rushd, known to the Christians as Averroes, and second, that he valued my own insights into and experiences arising from the hermetic teachings of Hassan Ibn Sabbah. Whether he knew I was an initiate because Uma had told him so before she departed, or whether he deduced it from the presence of the thin steel dagger they found in my loincloth when they bathed me, whose scabbard or sheath is marked in Arab calligraphy with the central tenet of our denial of faith, I did not ask.

The snowdrops, which was the apt name Peter gave the tiny white bell-like flowers we had seen in the hills, gave way to daffodils, which we call jonquils, celandines, anemones, love-in-idleness, with, beneath the russet brick walls, gillyflowers, forget-me-nots and even some tulipans. The bulbs of the last named had been a gift from the Ottoman Sufi Grand Imam of the dervishes' mosque in Iconium, who had enjoyed philosophical discourse with some of Peter's brethren. By the middle of March the gut problems I had had, a particularly vicious and persistent form of dysentery, had responded to Peter's potions and we spent much of another warm spell in the gardens, sitting in simple double seats made from dressed planks. The backs of these commemorated in carved lettering the wise men who had meditated so fruitfully in the past in this same garden, amongst them the three who were the subjects of most of our conversation.

All was tidy and orderly here; even the paths were gravelled with small round stones like peas, and behind us on the walls, following the custom of the Arab gardeners in Spain, the espaliered apples, pears, and even a vine began to push out tiny buds. The air was fragrant with the smell of the daffodils and their narcissistic cousins.

Our conversations followed patterns and routes dictated by the logic or fancy of our thoughts, which pursued concepts and conclusions rather than the chronological track dictated by the three lives, the three bodies of work, which we picked at and attempted to unravel. Our aim was to weave all into an intricate but self-sufficient garment of thought that might clothe the bewildered minds and souls of men against the cold winds that blow out of the darkness that surrounds our existence. But, for the sake of clarity and brevity, dear Mah-Lo, I shall now take them in order.

First came Roger Bacon, who flourished some two hundred years ago. Nothing in the world of learning comes from nothing, and Roger based his thought on that of the great Arab thinkers, going back not only to Avicenna and Averroes but to Abū Yūsuf Ya' Qū Ibn Ishāq ul-Kindī and Albumazar. From the former of these last two he learnt much about optics and was thus able to invent, or at any rate vastly improve, spectacles, without which we would all, as scholars, be as helpless as blind mice, and from the latter mathematics and the faith in mathematics that decrees they are as reliable a source of truth as revealed scripture.

But even more important than spectacles were the principles on which Friar Bacon based his study of optics, which were mathematics, of course, but also observation and experimentation.

You ask what I mean by experimentation *[and I have to say that at this point Ali became more animated than I had yet seen him, at any rate when his philosophical fit was upon him]*. You observe a phenomenon – say, the way sunlight may be focused through a lens to a fine point on a surface set in a plane perpendicular to the sun's position in the sky, and you discover that the distance between the lens and the surface on which the point of light appears at its smallest and brightest varies according to the thickness of the lens. From these phenomena you produce a mathematical, algebraic formula that allows you to predict what thickness of lens will require a certain distance between it and the surface for it to achieve perfect focus, or, knowing the thickness of the lens, you will predict the distance. Now. You test the validity of your algebraically expressed formula by using it repeatedly to predict thickness of lens when you know focal length and vice versa. Algebra? A mathematical methodology discovered by Muhommad ben Musa al-Khwarizmi. When an *experiment*, which can be repeated, or controlled observation of phenomena, thus support the mathematically–based hypothesis one can be sure that a truth has been arrived at. Knowledge or *scientia* has been acquired.

Friar Bacon believed that knowledge so attained was the only knowledge worth more than a groat (a small sum of money, dear Mah-Lo, in Ingerlond a skilled manual labourer's daily wage) but, of course, he could not declare this publicly. Why not? Because to do so would be to deny the certain truth of God's laws and will as bequeathed to us in Holy Writ and interpreted by Mother Church. These are jealous gods and would have burnt him alive if he had spoken against them.

He did indeed go as far as he dared in naming four causes of ignorance: one, the example of frail and unsuited authority; two, the influence of custom; three, the opinion of the unlearned crowd; and four, concealment of one's ignorance in a display of apparent wisdom. When you think about it, Peter asserted, three of these four come pretty close to describing the processes by which both scripture and the Church arrive at what they would have us believe . . .

Somewhere at about this point I asked Brother Peter what he thought of the myth of the Brazen Head that Bacon was reputed to have made and which he bade speak forth prophecies, but which produced only the banality of 'Time was, Time is, Time's past' before exploding into atoms, the atoms Democritus took to be the building blocks of matter. My new friend's voice dropped, he glanced about him to be sure no one was near enough to hear what he said, and then he murmured, 'Gunpowder. Gunpowder used as such to fire a gun, to project a cannon-ball. He was the first to do it, and he did it using a huge church bell, made of brass, with a huge bell mouth, and with those very words inscribed around its lip.'

'But why whisper? There is no secret about gunpowder now. It is used in battle and in sieges from Bristol to Bombay.'

Brother Peter kept his voice low. 'Why do you think his brass cannon blew up?'

I thought for a moment. 'Because Friar Bacon's gunpowder was better than he thought it would be?'

'Precisely. Through experiment and mathematics he arrived at the receipt, correct to the last scruple, that produces a powder more powerful and certain in its effect than any other.'

My heart quickened. At last it seemed I might be on the point of achieving one of the aims that made up the purposes of our expedition across the world to this barbarous island, namely to seek out the latest in military technology.

'Do you have the receipt here in Oxenford?

'Here in Osney. But . . . coded. Of course.'

'Why coded?'

'His superiors in the order were not unsympathetic to his enquiring mind; for much of his life he was allowed to speculate and experiment without interference. The condition imposed, though, was that the records of his work should be hidden from the gaze of those who might lack the discipline to treat them with the care and respect they deserve. In other words to prevent their exploitation for personal gain or power, or to subvert the teachings of the Holy Church. So. Code.'

'But you know the key?'

Peter touched the side of his nose with his index finger. 'Trust me,' he said. 'Roger had no inclination to hide his light under a bushel. His code demands little of the cryptologist's art to unravel. He left a thread-end protruding: one good pull and it all falls apart.'

CHAPTER

TWENTY-EIGHT

A penitential Lent I am having of it, and no mistake, most of it spent in this tiny cell, no more than five by three feet across, four feet high, with a vault rising to a foot beyond that. There is a grating of wrought iron for a door, which leads on to a passageway lined with numerous other cells like mine. The walls are rough, undressed stone held together with slapped-on mortar, of which more in a moment. When it rains a sheen, almost a curtain of water, tainted only with the musty stoniness it picks up on the way, runs down them, forms a pool, and trickles away under the bars and into the corridor. There is a heap of straw on the floor, which is changed weekly.

I am of course alone. There was a family of mice, but I have eaten them. This was silly. If I had let the pregnant females come to term, there would have been more. Perhaps I could have husbanded them, and continued for longer to supplement a diet of rye crusts, a handful of which are thrust under the grating on most evenings. The straw, too, has seeds of grain in it, occasionally a whole ear.

The mortar. It was mixed, I would guess, with too much sand, and is further weakened by the presence of flint shards. I managed on the second day to liberate one of these, about an inch long and with a sharp point, and I have been using it and its successors to grind, pick and poke through the mortar. Today, four weeks later, or thereabouts, I achieved daylight, the first I have seen for nearly five weeks, through a hole, a passageway with a slight angle in it, just big enough to take my hand and forearm, up to my shoulder, right through to the outside. Impossible to exaggerate the lift this has given to my spirits: the first two joints of my index finger are in the sun!

I imagine what this must be like from the outside: the blank wall at the back of an annexe to the guild-hall; a sudden trickle of sandy mortar from a point where three corners of stone do not quite meet as they should, a small brown finger poking through and waggling. At what height is this happening? A foot above the floor of the alley? Six feet up? Even higher? Will it be seen? What will happen if it is? I twist and pull and extricate my arm. Knowing these people, I should not be surprised to have my finger bashed with a stone, slashed with a knife, or even bitten off. Instead I put my eye to the hole and, in spite of the bend in my tunnel, I can sense that sunlight. And then, with my ears against it, I can hear a distant bell, the clatter of hoofs on cobbles and, nearer, a hoarse voice, a woman's, insisting that the cabbages she has for sale are spring cabbages, new season, freshly pulled, buy them here.

So. After all, this cell may be a womb rather than a tomb and the naked child within may yet contrive a birth canal. Why not? In the darkness, virtually complete even after my eyes became adjusted to it, I have yet been able to work out the extent of the patch of mortar I have been working at and it is at least as big as the circumference of my head – and, as every magician knows, if your head will go through the rest will follow . . . if you know how. I scrabble about, find the latest of my flint tools, and set about enlarging what I have begun. It is, of course, dull work, scrape, scrape, twist, twist, and then dragging out the dust and grit I have loosened with my lacerated fingertips. Occasionally they bleed, and now I can see the blood. Previously I could only taste it. But it is not work that requires mental concentration and my mind can wander freely.

Or it can, even here and in this situation, do what I like best and dwell, with reverence and relish, on every sensation that racks my body: the ache in my thighs, the cold in the soles of my feet, the stiffness across my shoulders, even the dry, sharp, coarse unpleasantness of hard sand, cement and crumbs of flint beneath my fingers. And hunger. Like a cancer gnawing my entrails. It is only through the senses that we know we are alive, only through the senses that we can make the best of being alive.

However, right now, I muse on the stupidity that brought me to this tomb-womb.

I wandered into an open space. One side was filled with a tall church, perhaps the most elegant I have seen on my travels. Smaller than St Paul's, not as noble as Notre Dame of Paris, it soars perpendicularly with high bridges of flying stone shaped like the bones in the breast of a bird, which balance in equilibrium the forces with which the weight of the roof pushes the walls outwards, walls pierced with windows so it seems there is no wall, but pillars and glass only. It carries the eye, and the people who built it would say the soul too, to the tower and then the steeple and so to the heaven where these people believe their three gods, which they will insist with absurd lack of sense is one god, and his mother too, all dwell.

The big doors at the west end were open and people were wandering in and out, so out of curiosity I joined them. Inside tall thin pillars climbed to galleries stacked on each other, the stones mostly a pale soft grey but some black marble, pillars which branched out into a grand foliation in the roof, like huge fan-shaped leaves, veined with ridges of stone. There are such giant leaves in the forests above our Coromandel coast, but I have never seen anything like them in Ingerlond or Francia. And the wonder of these is that, considering how high they are, they are painted in glowing colour, blues, reds and gold for the most part rather than the greens of the leaves they echo. They are almost as grand as the paintings, tiles, inlays and enamels that adorn our own temples.

The walls of glass beneath and between are all coloured too, some in patterns, others in pictures depicting the lives of their godmen and *sadhus*; but the most glorious windows, the most wonderful, are big round rose windows set high in the end walls where the predominant colour is blue, an awe-inspiring deep, resonant blue, and the subject matter the life and glory of Mary who, no matter what these Christians think, is surely an avatar for Parvati, or, as she is sometimes called, Uma, and for whom I am named as her servant.

But for the most part it is not Parvati but Kali who rules, even if she is never seen, for Death is everywhere: in the man torn and bleeding, nailed to his cross, in the depiction of martyrdoms, or at least in the way the *sadhus* clutch like badges the implements by which they were tortured to death – Catherine with her wheel, Lawrence with his roasting rack, and hundreds more. And finally Kali stalks the arcades and ambulatories below, for here are the tombs of bishops and nobles, with statues of their corpses laid on top, some in armour, some in the vestments of their office. And on one at least is depicted, also in stone, a gruesome skeleton over which the worms still crawl.

So, in one place, we have the ecstasy of godmen and the misery of death, and nowhere in between any love or acknowledgement of the glory that can accompany us on our pilgrimage from darkness through light and back to darkness. What sort of religion is this that carries the mind to a heaven of blue, yet dwells with cadavers?

I have my answer. By these means, splendour and horrid fear combined, the churchmen and princes keep their hold on the souls of the masses who toil for them – for these cathedrals assail the senses with promises of ecstasies always just beyond your reach but ultimately attainable in death, while they terrify with fear of death and everlasting torment. Not only are there colour and light, but there is treasure too, in crosses and croziers, images and vestments. Incense in clouds is released from swung thurifers of polished silver, and music from flutes, fifes, oboes, trumpets, trombones and drums as well as sung. Even that produced by sets of pipes through which air is pumped with a bellows breathes when small slabs of ivory covered wood are pressed, fills the spaces, colouring them with varied sound . . . All this magnificence, appealing to every sense save only that most important one of touch, may induce a euphoria as pronounced as that which comes from over-indulgence in bhang, and fools one into thinking that if one is not in heaven then heaven, when it is achieved, will be much like this.

Heaven is thus the bribe the churchmen and princes promise to their hordes of slaves in return for keeping to the calling God has given them and not seeking or striving to climb above their station or escape the misery they are born to. The bribe – and the threat too: for this benign and forgiving god will also leave the souls of those who rebel against his word to rot in endless torment throughout eternity. That, too, is depicted here and there in the lower levels of this edifice.

And there lies the difference between that religion and ours, exemplified by the difference between our temples and theirs, for while theirs soar and carry one upwards to a perfect heaven and by implication spurn what is terrestrial as corrupt, or dwell on terrors, ours, however tall and magnificent they may be, do not attempt to deny their weight, but sit on the earth and glorify it.

Musing thus I made my circuit of this building, which is dedicated to a demi-god called Michael, a warrior angel who, they say, cast into hell the devil, here depicted as a dragon or serpent with Michael's spear in his throat, and finally came back out into the square.

Opposite me now was another building, almost as grand as the first, with a façade of decorated stone, statues in niches, painted and leafed with gold like those in the church, with many rooms and antechambers off it, and with the prisons and torture chambers I now know too well behind and under it. It is dedicated, in name at least, to the same St Mary, or Parvati, but in fact was built for commerce and trade. It is the new Guild Hall, but right now does not serve the purpose for which it was so recently built: it has been occupied for a year or more by King Henry and Queen Margaret, their court and courtiers and all the senior functionaries of government.

And as I step out of the church and into the square, which has a few market stalls in it and above which jackdaws soar and cackle as they dispute the ledges on which they want to build their nests, there is a brief blast of trumpets and a squad of soldiers comes out of the main doors of the Guild Hall, down the steps and marches into the square to join those already there to make a wall between the people and . . . the cannon in whose wake I came through the city gate.

Following the soldiers comes a small crowd, including the King and Queen, and the seven-year-old boy-child, who is certainly the Queen's but is probably not, I now remember Eddie March telling me, the King's. They pause at the top of the wide flight of steps looking down into the square, facing the cathedral, then descend to look at that awesome tube on wheels in front of which the plumed mules still steam and stamp.

There is not much of a crowd below the steps, just the soldiers who came with the cannon, and no one challenges me as I slip through an arcade of black timbers, sheltering a frontage of shops, to reach the end of the steps which I climb to a point from which I can see and even hear the monarchs . . .

Whoops! Oh, yes, yes, *yes*! A piece of mortar has cracked away in the roof of my tunnel, and with a little manoeuvring and twisting I am able to get it free. It's as big as a coconut and, best of all, the stone above it now shifts a little, like a loose tooth in a giant's mouth. If only I had something bigger than these flakes of flint to use as a lever . . .

Where was I? On the steps of the Guild Hall gawping at the royal party, which is now below and somewhat to the side of where I am standing. The Queen, Margaret, is one of those people at whom, in a crowd, one cannot help looking. Of middling height for a woman, so shorter than most of the grandees and magnates around her, she yet exudes a charisma, a glow. She is thirty years old and in her prime of beauty, physique, intelligence. She stands straight, with her head, supported by a long ivory neck, tilted back a little, which gives prominence to a well-shaped chin. Her nose has a fineness, too, that softens the slight aquiline curve beneath the bridge. Her eyes are small, softly lidded, but piercing and blue, forever alert and seeking to hold and abash the eyes of those who would speak with her. Her fair hair is pulled up and under the velvet cap of a jewelled gold crown. Her purple gown is simple, though pearled and edged with gold, her slippers are cloth of gold too. Her hands are long, with long fingers, rarely still, and with many rings.

The contrast with her husband could not be more marked. He is only ten years older than her but looks twice that. Tall, thin, he wears a brown velvet cap, a brown worsted jerkin, grubby with spilled food, has haunted eyes, red-rimmed and moist, a shambling gait. His thin mouth is a brighter red than one would expect, but not, I think, painted. His only jewellery or sign of rank is a heavy gold chain in which S-shapes alternate with squares in which dull garnets are set and from which hangs a decorated cross with pearls set between the arms.

He is as different from the lords around him as he is from his wife. They all vie with each other like peacocks in slashed and scalloped doublets, jewellery and so forth, or more military accoutrements as half-suits of armour inlaid with gold, jewelled daggers. These are the men we have heard the Yorkists rail against, the favourites of the Queen, who have ransacked the coffers of the realm for coin and taken the King's lands on whose rents the government of the realm depends.

'It's a fine piece,' the Queen calls out, 'my lord Beaumont has brought us.' Her voice is her least attractive feature, being shrill and often petulant. 'Onghrrree, come here and admire this very fine piece.'

Her accent is clearly French for all she has been England's queen for nearly fifteen years. 'Onghrrree' was the closest she chose to get to 'Henry'.

'But what can we do with it?' she went on. 'It is too big and cumbersome, is it not, to take to battle?'

She turned then to a lean, dark man whom I had barely noticed, but now recognised to be a chamberlain of the Duke of Somerset's we had seen in the fortress of Guisnes, outside Calais.

'Mountfort, you know the place, would not my lord Somerset be able to knock a hole in the walls of Calais and get himself in with such a piece?'

'Yes, indeed, ma'am. If one could put it in his hands . . .'

But the King was now stammering and clearly wished to speak. For all they did so with a bad grace, in the way the young humour the elderly or even a precocious child, the small throng fell silent.

'Would not,' he managed at last, 'the French take advantage of such a hole or breach and follow my lord Somerset through it?'

Some of the lords nodded wisely at this, but the Queen was having none of it.

'Onghrrree, you're such a child in such matters. Run along and catch up on your reading, why don't you? Chaucer's translation of Boethius it is just now, is it not? "The Consolations of Philosophy"? So rewarding, I'm sure.'

And, following a sign from her fluttering fingertips, a couple of stewards took the shambling man by the elbows and led him away. One of these was tall and pale and wore a black hat, the other was fat, short and greasy. I got to know them later – the tall one was John Clegger, the fat one Will Bent.

Meanwhile, the Queen, much like a child with a new toy, took her son's hand and trotted down the steps to the cannon. One of her lords picked up the boy and sat him astride the barrel, while the Queen fell into earnest conversation with another, no doubt discussing the deployment of this new weapon. The cold breeze smoothed her fine dress against her breasts so the nipples showed, and the lord, caressing the gun with one hand, grew red about the neck. At this point I felt a presence at my shoulder, followed by a heavy hand.

★   ★   ★

It is loose, really loose, my giant's tooth, give me another ten minutes and I think I'll be able to get it out.

There's someone at my shoulder. Mountfort. Bastard.

'I've seen you before somewhere, haven't I? Weren't you with those oriental chappies who came to Guisnes?'

CHAPTER

TWENTY-NINE

A week or so after our talk about Roger Bacon – we were perhaps into April by then, for I remember it was raining sweetly, gently, but enough to keep us indoors – our conversation moved on to the second of Brother Peter's great Inglysshemen. In his upper room with his cased books around us and comfortable chairs to sit in, he began with an apologetic attack on Avicenna whose version of Aristotle was based on the neo-Platonist Porphyry's interpretation of the Stagyrite. Following William of Occam, and referring to his writings and occasionally to Aristotle's *Organon*, he demonstrated how Aristotle's speculations regarding entities, essences or universals had been corrupted by the neo-Platonists. For the latter, essences existed in the mind of God, and were presented corporeally, materially, on earth, in a corrupted, degraded way. Thus the *idea* of 'cat', for instance, and here my friend fondled the tabby beauty called Winnie, who often slept and purred on his lap, existed in the mind of God as a perfection of cats before cats were created, and no cat that had ever existed was a perfect cat, since corporeality always falls short of the perfection of the idea.

'But this,' he went on, fondling Winnie's throat and forehead, which was marked with a W, 'is to deny what is so markedly the most important feature of Winnie, her haecceity, the fact that she is individual, uniquely herself, unlike every other cat who has ever lived. And she has her own perfection – whether or not she is perfect cat is not for me to say, but certainly she is perfect Winnie.'

'Oh, come,' I replied, 'all cats have many features in common. Quite apart from their appearance and their anatomy, they follow patterns of behaviour which are identical. All wash in the same way. All eat and drink alike. They all use the same techniques when hunting. I could go on and on, but you know what I mean. You cannot deny there exists an idea we can call 'catness' which includes all these qualities.'

A silence lengthened between us. Then: 'You have never been owned by a cat, have you?'

There was a coolness in his voice that irritated me almost as much as the stupid way in which he had framed the question. I was, perhaps, at that time more than usually easily annoyed — as convalescents often are.

'No,' I replied. 'I like them, be sure of that, but they do not travel well, and I have never remained in the same place for more than six months since I was eight years old. Apart from when I was in the Mountain where I learnt what wisdom I have.'

'Then allow me to speak with more certainty of being right concerning the nature of cats.'

'There you are,' I cried, and leant forward to tap his knee, at which Winnie leapt down to the floor and went to mew at the door. 'You speak of the nature of cats. By that you surely mean the essence, the idea that informs them all.'

'No. I simply mean the characteristics we light upon to distinguish them from other animals of a similar size and familiarity. But what I am asking you to consider is this. It is in the nature of cats to be different from each other. Believe me. And not through the corruption of matter by the fall of man or any other such cant but because that is the way cats are.'

It was clear that if a falling-out was to be avoided, we should remove the conversation to a higher plane.

'And you would apply this to everything, every phenomenon in the perceivable world?'

'I, Aristotle, and William of Occam, yes, we agree.'

A sunbeam pierced the rainclouds and fell briefly on the table between us.

'Even to two motes of dust?'

'Observe,' said Brother Peter, 'no two motes of dust occupy the same space at the same time. In that at the very least they are different. And I believe if we could grind lenses sufficiently fine and line them up to study even the most μικρο of particles we would find differences between them – μικρο is the Greek word for very small.'

'I know very well what μικρο means. What I am trying to say is we use words to define types. The word "cat" is meaningful. Do not such words indicate ideas, essences?'

'Types, yes. Essences, no. Though I would prefer to use the words "species" for "types" and "universals" for "essences".'

'I am still confused. You are simply swapping terms, but you prove nothing.'

'That is because you give too great a power to words. Words are tools. Useful, but in themselves they do not contain truth. It is useful to say that beer is beer, by which we indicate a certain species of drink. It is useful because I can say, 'Would you like some beer?' and you will know thereby the sort of experience you are being offered. But this is not to say that there is an essence of beer, a perfect beer in the mind of God. Indeed not. Looked at another way, the word implies quite the opposite, for it allows us to say that this beer is different from that beer, this beer is better than that beer. Do you like this beer?'

We both drank. I allowed myself beer at the priory because Peter said it was weak and because the water was river water, there being no well on the islet.

'Yes,' I said. 'And it is different. You are right.'

'That is because this beer is made with hops of a particular species. Some of our Hussite brothers from Pils in Bohemia sent us a sack. But we must return now to William of Occam. Let me sum up what he had to say about words. There are terms of first intention, which is what we call words that are the names of individual things and which, in Inglysshe anyway, we qualify with an article: the cat at the door. This cat at that door. There is a cat at the door. And there are words used as terms of second intention, as universals, genera, or species. Cats like fish. Cats wash behind their ears when there is rain about. A universal is thus a sign of many things, in this case the many things that make up a cat. Universals do not exist. The only existence they have is as qualities of individual cats.'

'Hum,' said I.

'Words used thus are merely tools,' he repeated, 'which we resort to for convenience' sake: they do not describe something that has a reality of its own. Only individual things have that reality. That is what Aristotle, properly understood, thought. That is what Occam meant when he said: "*Essentia non sunt multiplicanda praeter necessitatem.*" A sharp dictum that slices through a lot of cant. Essences, universals should not be multiplied except out of necessity, and ultimately the only Necessary Universal is God, the Prime Mover. And,' here he lowered his voice for what he was about to utter was a burning matter, 'and he, or it, goes back a long, long way. Maybe all it was was a bang, a big bang like the bang of the Brazen Head, but with the motto "Time is, Time will be, Time might just as well go on for ever".'

He had gone beyond me now, as sometimes he did when a sort of divine afflatus, an ability to prophesy, fell on him. I tried to bring him back to earth. 'Is it not the case that your Friar Bacon was kept mute in the cells of the Franciscan order in Paris for many years, that Occam was imprisoned as a heretic, that even John Wycliffe might have been burnt but escaped?'

'But, my dear Ali . . . one moment while I let Winnie out. See? Like many cats once disturbed she will not resume her former comfort, but not all cats reach with their front paws to rattle the latch to signify they want to go out. There. They were . . . gunpowder. They threatened to blow apart the whole structure of our society. They undermined the very foundations on which the authority of Church and king can be said to stand for they privileged, as inevitable consequences of their thought, individual observation, individual judgement; they revealed ways to the truth that did not depend on the authority of Mother Church nor the divine right of kings, but on knowledge obtained by practical everyday experience, as it was said those doctors of antiquity who relied on experience and observation did, the ones known as *empirici*. What gives a pope or emperor the right to rule? Why, if you take away frail and unsuited authority, custom, the opinion of the unlearned crowd, the display of apparent wisdom, if you take away the idea that a pope or king embodies, albeit corporeally and with earthly corruption, the essence or entity of priesthood and royalty as conceived in the mind of God, you are left with two things, two justifications for investing certain individuals and institutions with authority over the rest of us.'

'And they are?'

'The power to unleash force, death, torture and deprivation on those who would gainsay you.'

'That I understand. But brute force is scarcely justification.'

'Quite so. Nor, really, is the other.'

'And that is?'

'The willing consent of the ruled.'

'But,' said I, 'that does seem a justification. Better, anyway, than brute force.'

Brother Peter again became animated.

'It depends,' he said, and the words tumbled out like nuts from a sack, 'how that willing consent is obtained. If lies are fed to the people for generation after generation and never questioned, they become part of the unconsidered background to their mental lives, never truly looked at or examined, hardly even thought of, but controlling everything in the foreground of their thoughts. By these means, as powerful, as all-pervading but as unnoticed as those that cause an object released in air to drop, is the consent of the people contrived and maintained. And anything that threatens to undermine this invisible wall of belief, the way gunpowder can blow down a castle wall, must be treated as anathema, a burning matter.' He sighed, looked around, then up and out of the cloudy glazing of the window. 'It's stopped raining. Wycliffe, the last of our three, was feeling towards all this. But that is enough for now. Let us walk through our garden, admire the raindrops on the cherry-blossom, then perhaps feed our fish.'

As we walked between the low cropped hedges, and breathed in the fragrances released by rain and a sun suddenly warm, I attempted a summary.

'Without this . . .' I searched for a word and made one up '. . . *intro-jection* of belief, on what grounds would a person offer his consent to be ruled?'

'He, or she, would use observation and analysis as nearly math-ematical as may be, to work out who or what system would best suit his own interests and those of his fellow men. By fellow men I mean the men and women he works with. Clearly the people he works for are a different class of person altogether and will think in a dialectically opposed way. He and his fellows would employ a hedonistic calculus. And he would eschew any pre-given ideas about the commonwealth of men said to be based on the essences that exist in God's head.'

I savoured the subtle sharpness of a needle of rosemary, pinched between my teeth. 'Just now you brought in John Wycliffe, the last of your three Inglysshe Franciscans. There must be more to be said about him.'

But Brother Peter had had enough. Scattering some breadcrumbs on the surface of the first of his ponds (the fish recognised his shadow as it fell on the water and came to the poolside before he threw them), he said, 'You may not have noticed, dear Ali, that we are now approaching the end of Lent. Yesterday was the day of the Crucifixion of Jesus, which we call Good Friday, three days of fasting that last through till the first meal after Holy Communion tomorrow when we celebrate his apparent return from the grave. At that celebration I shall give a talk based on the teachings of Father John Wycliffe, which, if you'll forgive me, I shall now set about preparing. You will be very welcome in our church tomorrow at eleven in the morning.'

CHAPTER

THIRTY

I'll get the fucker out if it's the last thing I do. If I don't then trying
to may well be the last thing I do. I've torn a nail and it's bleeding.
Hurts like snake-bite too.

Oh dear, oh me, they piled up so much against me at my trial. Trial is
hardly the word but it is what they called it. Many wise judges heard
the case, even the King and the Queen, whose shrill voice I got to
know well. First, I had disobeyed my lord of Somerset by taking a
boat from Calais to Ingerlond. Next my skin is what they call black
so I am a pagan heathen and possibly not a person at all but a monkey.
It seems that, unlike us, they feel no kinship or respect for monkeys.
Next it was known from Lord Scales in London that I had consorted
concupiscently with my lord of March. They must have meant Eddie
– lust for whom I admit was the reason I had come to Coventry. But
lord? I didn't know he was a lord.

At this, some of my judges realised that I might not be a boy. None
of us is perfect, I pleaded. And I am indeed a woman. None had doubted
that Eddie might go in for buggery with boys, but best to be sure. Just
for the record. They soon made sure I was female, by the usual method.
I was therefore a witch, as well as everything else.

The Queen especially now went berserk with fury. She screamed
at me, circled me in that cellar that had been made to store wine –
it stank of it as if a couple of barrels had burst there – and came at

me with long scarlet nails, which she dragged down my cheeks. 'You bewitched young Eddie,' she screamed. 'No Inglysshe nor Frankysshe man, either and Eddie is both, could look on your dusky skin without revulsion. Confess you consort with the devil, who has given you charms to ensnare young men.'

Yet above all I was a Yorkist and possibly privy to that faction's plans. It was known Warwick was in Ireland with York. Was he planning to return to Calais? What were York's intentions? And where was March? And so on and so forth. They applied various means to extract from me what they thought I knew, mostly involving hot irons, pincers, and some stretching, especially of the spaces between my legs, but since I could not tell them what I did not know they soon gave up. The John Clegger and Will Bent I named earlier as the Queen's stewards took their turn in all this, though most of the examination was carried out by the city's executioner, a foul man, a blacksmith by trade, with a deep scar down his right cheek, and always the hot smell of burning metal about him. He and his apprentices did unspeakable things to me. Unspeakable? So why speak of them.

All that remained was to decide how I should die. They could not decide. The Bishop wanted me burnt for a witch, the Lord Chief Justice wavered between beheaded as a traitor, or hanged and drawn. And that's how matters stand. Executed I must be. Only the means remain to be decided.

Ouch! Fuck, shit and bugger it all. It came out, but dropped on my toe. Not so much a giant's tooth as a cannon-ball or, anyway, a melon. But, you know, I really think I might be out by nightfall. My rock has brought down a shower of rubble inside the wall, it all seems loose and all I have to do is scoop it out. But minding where it falls.

Standing in the moonlight, in a litter of cabbage leaves, I find I am bothered by my nakedness. Not because it is cold – it is no colder in the alley than it was in my cell. Nor do I feel shame at being naked as these Christians are said to. But because I am a mess. My body is slimed with my own excrement and that of the slugs I have shared my tiny tomb with. It is also scabbed and ill-looking, though a month has passed since it was seriously abused. Worst of all, it is now thin. Well, I might not have got out so easily had it been rounded, glossy and full, though not what you would call fat, in short a worthy temple for the goddess within me. But all the same I do not like to think I might be seen so scrawny and poorly looking. So I head for where I know I shall find clothes.

But first, on the corner of the alley where it feeds back into the square, there is a pump, a public supply of water. I crank the lever a few times and get a great gobbet of water followed by a steadier rhythmic flow, and I contrive to get most of me beneath it while still cranking with my right hand. Then I take turn about and do the other side. Finally I sluice the sheets of water off each arm in turn, my thighs and hips, my stomach, or rather the hollow where my stomach once was, and my shrivelled breasts. The water flashes silver in the moonlight. It is very, very cold, but that makes it feel all the more cleansing. Then walking briskly and trying to control the convulsive shuddering that has seized me, I make it down the arcades by the shops and into the church.

Yes, there are people about. A very large number, filling the wide central nave, many kneeling, some standing, some praying with their eyes shut passing the foolish beads they use to pray with through their fingers, almost all with bowed heads, and those who keep their heads upright have their eyes fixed forward on the high altar beyond the choir, where all is a blaze of light from a thousand candles, some very big indeed. Clouds of incense fill the air, choirs chant that wretched rising and falling wail, bells chime, the chains on thurifers clank, jewelled vestments flash back the lights, and, happy Easter, no one has eyes for the naked wench who strides down one of the side naves, past the chancel and choir and so to the ambulatory and, at its apex, the lady chapel. I suppose if anyone does see me they put me down to hallucination produced in a dirty mind by the devil.

Here, behind the rood-screen, all is almost dark, and certainly deserted. I climb on the small altar and reaching up take her ladyship in my arms and, with a muttered apology, I hoick her down to the floor. She has a gold crown with a sunburst behind it which is not gold at all but leafed wood. She is a wooden doll, quite well carved and painted where her face and hands are visible to her worshippers, but left rough and unfinished where the cloth of her robes covers her. Her face and hands are polished oak, a little darkened with age, and not far off the colour of my own complexion. Her robes are a woollen blue mantle with a hood, a long black dress, and an underskirt of white linen trimmed with lace, which turns out not to be a skirt at all but merely an apron. I prop her against a pillar and climb into these clothes. They are not a bad fit, though I think I would have more than filled them had I not been starved for so long.

I tuck my wet hair up under the hood. The shudders recede. Almost I feel warm. And, of course, hungry too. Well, I have learnt enough of the rites of this strange cult to know what lies in the little walled box behind its glowing oil lamp, and I make a very brief and inadequate snack of the dried white biscuit and the small silver cup of wine I find there. It's not a lot, but certainly I feel better for it. Time to go. I pause. Then, why not? I turn back, pick up the gold crown and place it on my head, over the hood, and then the jewellery – her rings, her ear-rings, and so forth.

Still clutching the bunched-up apron in my hand, I head for the transept doors that will take me back to the square and, in one of the darkest corners of all, find myself faced with none other than old Scar-face himself, my evil-minded torturer, of whom my last memory before I fainted, was of him bringing himself off with one hand while poking a stick up my cunt with the other. A stick with thorns, a pruning from a rose perhaps.

I recognise him, he recognises me. 'By Our Lady . . .' he begins, and 'Yes, indeed,' I reply. For all I have been weakened old skills remain and I have surprise on my side. Furthermore the old fool drops to his knees, crossing himself as he does so. Quickly I wind the lacy apron round his neck once and still holding both ends of the scarf I have made of it, brace the sole of my right foot on his forehead, and . . . Snap!

Unwrapping the scarf and murmuring a Thuggee prayer to Kali, I run out into the square. There I stop, and look around. My breath returns to normal, my heartbeat steadies, the glow that took fire in my womb and spread to my furthest extremities when I straightened my knee, begins to fade, and I look about me with a curse on my lips for all that this wretched city has done to me.

'Burn,' I say. 'Burn.'

And I know one day it will.

CHAPTER

THIRTY-ONE

Interlude

Brother Peter Marcus preaches in the church of St Francis, Osney, on Easter Morning, 1460

'Everywhere on your road preach and say, "The kingdom of God is at hand". Cure the sick, raise the dead, cleanse the lepers, drive out devils. Freely have you received, freely give. Carry neither gold nor silver nor money in your girdles, nor bag, nor two coats, nor sandals, nor staff, for the workman is worthy of his hire.' The seventh to tenth verses of the tenth chapter of the Gospel according to Saint Matthew.

'Dear children of God, my sermon this Easter morning will be a very simple one. All I aim to do is remind you of the teachings of Father John Wycliffe, the kernel of his thought at any rate, and suggest how his teaching points down paths we should try to follow.

'First, at the centre of his thought was poverty. In this he followed in the footsteps of Francis, our founder, who heard the words of the Gospel I have just read to you at the moment of his conversion. From this came the certainty that righteousness has nothing to do with power or dominion or possessions or property. To own something is to take it from someone else. He who has a penny more has caused another to have a penny less. Nor does true righteousness confer power or the right to power, dominion or the right to dominion. John believed that dominion and power were the prerogatives of the civil authority, and not of the Church or churchmen. But even this he saw was a standby, a provisional thing, until all men and women, all people, should live together in harmony, all equal, and come together as the Israelites did in every jubilee year and hand back to all, to the people as a whole, all personal property.

'Next, Father John believed that the central thing in every man's life was the immediate dependence of the individual Christian upon God, a relation which needs no mediation of any priest, and to which the very sacraments of the Church are not essentially necessary. Indeed, he went so far as to assert that round the sacraments, which are but signs and symbols, a dreadful and harmful habit of superstition has grown up, later hardened by the closed minds of the so-called fathers of the Church into dogma and doctrine. And by these means, by making the sacraments the prerogative of the priesthood, to grant or withhold as their fallen natures dictated, power and dominion over the gates of heaven and hell were seized by the Church. Thus no one can go to heaven unless they have received the body and blood of Christ and only the anointed priest has the power to magic the bread and wine into the body and blood. Brethren, I tell you, following the teaching of our Father John, this doctrine of transubstantiation is a blasphemous folly, a deceit which despoils the people and leads them to commit idolatry. If sacrament there must be, then let it be the sacrament of sharing the good things of life, the bread and wine, in good fellowship, as we have just done in our Easter Communion, and remembering as we do so the teachings of Jesus and his example, as he bade us.

'Brethren, these doctrines of the sacraments as laid down by Rome, Avignon or wherever the Pope is these days, deny the true Church that is in all of us and especially when two or three are gathered together in His Name. That is the Church our Lord left us with, the Church John lived and breathed for. The true Church consists solely of the community of the righteous, and its only authority is the teaching of our Lord as left to us in the New Testament. The supreme authority, the only authority, is Holy Scripture and particularly the actual words of our Lord as recorded in the Gospels. Which is why John Wycliffe devoted so much of his life to translating and disseminating the Gospels in our own tongue. It is for these and like reasons that after his death his bones were dug up and burnt for a heretic, as if this mean, malicious act could in any way diminish the power of his thought.

'John's wisdom was not a homely stuff woven together on the loom of mere common sense, though there is much of that in it. It was far more, drawing together the threads left by his two great predecessors, Roger Bacon and William of Occam. The first found truth in what he could see, feel, touch, hear, smell and measure. The second showed how the teaching of the fathers and the schoolmen has dragged us away from experience to speculation, from the particular to the general, from fact to essence. John began to see how all this provided the foundations for the tyrannies that spoil us all. It behoves us to continue down the road these three have shown us.

'It is my belief – no, my certainty, grounded in experience as well as logic, that we can use their teaching as stepping-stones, as stairs to a height from which, looking back whence we have come, we shall see exposed the gigantic fallacy on which our philosophy and morality were built – namely the transformation of facts into essences, of historical into metaphysical conditions. The weakness and despondency of man, the inequality of power and wealth, injustice and suffering are attributed by the Church and its thinkers to some transcendental crime and guilt. Rebellion, disobedience against God, became the original sin that tainted us all, and the striving for gratification which is life was stained with the sin of concupiscence.

'This departure into metaphysical realms culminated in the deification of time: because everything in the empirical world is passing, man in his very essence becomes a finite being, and death is in the very essence of life. Madness preached, "All things pass away, therefore all things deserve to pass away! And this is justice itself, this law of Time, that it must devour its children."

'And again this madness pronounced as doctrine that only the higher values are eternal, and therefore real: faith and a love which does not ask and does not desire became the goals to which we should all aspire. And why? By these means the Church seeks to pacify, justify, compensate the underprivileged of the earth, and to protect those who made and left them underprivileged. These doctrines have enveloped the masters and the slaves, the rulers and the ruled, in an upsurge of repression which has caused the increasing degeneration of the life instincts and the decline of man.

'Traditional forms of reason, as exemplified in the real thought of Aristotle, the peripatetics and the empiricists of ancient times, are rejected, and experience of being-as-end-in-itself – as joy, *lust* (I use the Teutonic word, which combines desire with joy), and enjoyment were thrown out with them. To return to the path we have been led from, to descend on the other side of the mountain not into the Valley of the Shadow of Death but into the land of milk and honey, to come to ourselves in a world which is truly our own, we must struggle against the dominion of time, against the tyranny of becoming over being. As long as there is the uncomprehended and unconquered flux of time – senseless loss, the painful 'it was' that will never come again – being will continue to contain the seed of destruction that perverts good to evil and vice versa. Man comes to himself only when transcendence has been conquered, when eternity has become present in the here and now.

'Before I came here to speak to you I took a turn about our garden. The cherry tree is in blossom, our cherry tree, the only cherry tree in the whole of creation to be just as it is at this very moment. Next to it the lilac tree our brothers in Anatolia sent us is in bud, just about to open buds already white at the tips, and in its branches a bullfinch sang, its black cap burnished so blackness shone almost like the sun and its red breast glowed like fire. No other bullfinch in the world but this one graced this morning a lilac tree like ours.

'Consider the lilies of the field, how they grow; they toil not neither do they spin. At this time of Easter, of blossom on the cherry tree, of the scarlet and black bullfinch in the lilac tree, of birth and resurrection, let us remember that if all things pass, all things return; what goes round comes round; eternally turns the wheel of Being. All things die, all things blossom again, eternal is the year of being. All things break, all things are joined anew; eternally the house of Being builds itself anew. All things part, all things welcome each other again.

'Eternity, long since the ultimate consolation of an alienated existence, was made into an instrument of oppression by its relegation to a transcendental world – unreal reward for real suffering. Now, here, at Easter, eternity is reclaimed for the fair earth – as the eternal return of its children, of the water-lily and the rose, of the lover and the beloved . . . The earth has all too long been a madhouse. We must reverse the sense of guilt; we must learn anew to associate guilt not with the affirmation but the denial of life, not with rebellion but with the acceptance of the repressive ideal.

'It is no sad truth, but rather a grand and glorious one that this earth should be our home. Were it but to give us simple shelter, simple clothing, simple food it would be enough. Add the water-lily and the rose, the apple and the pear, it is a fit home for mortal or immortal man. Woman. Persons.'

'What did you think of that Ali?'

'Uplifting, though a touch confused.'

'It's not easy to turn back the tide of a thousand years in a few pithy paragraphs.'

'I can do it one sentence.'

'You can?'

'As the Old Man in the Mountain said, "Nothing is true, everything is permitted."'

'That is the black side of my discourse, the far side of the moon.'

'If you say so.'

Brother Peter paused by the pond and looked at me, his pale blue eyes suddenly sad, his posture briefly tired, perhaps from the strain of giving his sermon, perhaps because he had decided our separation was inevitable.

'There is a small college of people,' he said, 'who have taken these thoughts towards a dark conclusion. They live in the north but to avoid persecution move about.'

'The Brothers of the Free Spirit?'

'I believe that's what they call themselves.'

'Just where are they?'

'Try Macclesfield Forest.'

But before I left I prevailed upon him to seek out the coded details of Roger Bacon's last experiments with gunpowder, and thereby, I think, did more to save the empire of Vijayanagara from imminent destruction than any of the rest of us.

CHAPTER
THIRTY-TWO

*H*aving found all this talk of Occam and Wycliffe deeply confusing, not to say boring and irrelevant, but with my mind concentrated again by Ali's last statement regarding gunpowder, I attempted to bring him back to what was germane.

'But what,' I asked him, after a short silence had grown between us, 'of the Prince and Anish during this time? Were they still locked away in the Tower?'

'I'm glad you asked. For, like you, I am now tired of my own voice. And, anyway, we have reached a point in our story where it is not out of place to return to the Prince's correspondence with the Emperor.'

And he pushed a small pile of papers across the table. While I read, he slept.

Dear Cousin

We are still incarcerated, after several months, well, weeks anyway, in this monumental prison and, of course, I still have no way of knowing whether or not you have received my letters and, if you have, what steps you are able to take to arrange our release. I suppose, even though we have languished here for so long, it is unreasonable to expect an answer from you in less than twice the time it took for us to get here, so I must continue to be patient.

Materially speaking things have not been as bad here as they might have been. Anish and I were given three small rooms to share in the central block or keep of this castle, which is known as the Tower of London, though it is in fact many towers linked by walls, or, like the central block in which we are living, free-standing. Everything is made of stone – either blocks of pale grey limestone or flint cores bonded with mortar – and roofed in lead or slate. The floors also are slate or limestone. There is almost no decoration apart from occasional tapestry hangings and only one of our rooms has a fireplace. Yet in spite of the primitive nature of our surroundings we are pestered to show gratitude for the comforts we have – and indeed, I have to say, our guardians fare no better than we do.

The chief of these is Lord Scales, an old and irascible nobleman, who is governor of the Tower for the King. Occasionally he invites us to dine with him when he rails against the Duke of York and his affinity, and against the merchants of the city who, he claims, plot to starve him out by refusing the passage of food and other necessaries into the Tower. Occasionally he demands money from us for our keep, or a jewel, and either he is unaware of the true value of things or he is modest in his demands, for a pearl no bigger than a pigeon's egg keeps him happy for a fortnight or more.

He has kept us up with the news too. The Duke of York is in Hibernia or Erin, an island to the west of Ingerlond, and smaller, but not much smaller, claimed as a domain of the King of Ingerlond, though his power extends only down the east coast and not far inland, the rest of the island or Ireland being occupied by savages. It is believed that Warwick has joined York there, in a port called Waterford on the south-east coast, where it is feared they are planning a joint invasion, York across the sea from Ireland and Warwick from Calais.

In Calais the same stalemate as before persists. The Duke of Somerset is tied down by Warwick's army, and Warwick's men by Somerset. Neither can embark without exposing himself to attack from the other; neither is strong enough to risk an open battle.

Of Eddie March, who is the cause of all our present woes (really it was a mistake on my part to hire him as a guide and protector, Ali was right about that, as about so much else), we have heard nothing certain. Either he is in Waterford with Warwick or he has made his way back to Calais. More important, the whereabouts of

Ali and his companion, the Buddhist monk, remain a mystery and, perforce, Anish and I, Anish anyway, have been at some pains to mitigate the effects of his disappearance by learning Inglysshe. Oh, yes. That fakir who attached himself to us has disappeared too.

So, dear cousin, the time has passed slowly but not without some benefits for our country and people, which I hope we shall one day be able to bring back to you. In spite of cold wet weather for most of the time Anish and I have been able to make, piecemeal to avoid suspicion that we are spies, a thorough examination of these fortifications, and particularly of their efficacy or lack of it against gunpowder and ball. To these ends we have had several conversations with the Under Master Sergeant of Ordnance, Bardolph Earwicca.

The actual Master of Ordnance is, of course, a Norman of noble blood and therefore a fool, a young man called Guy Fitzosbern with no chin and a voice like a horse's, or should I say donkey? Certainly a donkey when he laughs, *eeee*-aw-aw-aw-aw. He knows nothing about his job except how to draw his salary.

Sergeant Bardolph, however, is a master gunner. Thick-set like most Saxons, his ruddy complexion is further enhanced by carbuncles and boils, which glow like so many red-hot cannon-balls. Like many Saxons he puts the word 'fucking' into his speech wherever he possibly can, for no purpose at all that we can understand. The word refers to the act of love-making, particularly those actions that lead to conception, and their use of it seems to imply they hold love-making in contempt.

I began by asking Bardolph if he did not think the walls of the Tower, especially the outer ones, somewhat thin, lacking in substance. They would surely soon be breached by well-directed cannon-fire, I suggested. Would it not have been sensible, as mastery of the techniques involved in the use of gunpowder developed, to have strengthened them, thickened them?

'Waste of fucking time, squire,' he said, having first sucked in his protuberant lips and then expelled the air thus taken in, with a noise like a fart. Meanwhile, I asked myself, did he mean waste of time that could be better spent in love-making? It soon became clear that he meant nothing of the sort. In fact he meant . . . nothing.

'You see, squire,' he went on, 'there ain't no fucking wall yet been built can withstand the force of powder, no matter how fucking thick it is.'

'How about thirty feet thick and made of solid rock?'

'That ain't a fucking wall. That's a fucking mountain. But even so, given time and loadsa powder, it'd go, it'd fucking go.'

'So how, dear friend,' I asked, or rather Anish did on my behalf, 'can a town or castle be protected against cannon-fire?'

'Simple, really, innit?'

By now we were standing between two towers on a battlement, scarcely wide enough to allow two armed men to pass each other.

'Come wiv me.'

And he took us into a big round room, occupying the whole area of the nearest tower, about thirty feet across. Much of it was filled with a cannon twelve feet long and the accoutrements that went with it, videlicet a ramrod with an end like a giant mop, an open barrel of water, another of gunpowder, and about twenty spheres of stone laboriously ground to an almost perfect roundness, each about two feet or more in diameter. There was also a shelf on which was placed a flint, a stone and a tinder-box together with a wick that had been soaked in solution of saltpetre and left to dry.

'All present and correct,' Sergeant Earwicca shouted, 'and ready to blow the balls off of anyone who dares a misdemeanour directed against His Majesty's person or property.'

I marvelled he had put so many words together without a 'fucking'.

'The art you see of protecting these 'ere walls against a gun, is to be sure we have a gun here, and six more to be precise, bigger'n any they can fucking bring against us.'

'I see,' I said. 'If I have it right, the aim is to cannon-ball the opposing cannon into silence before they can knock down your walls, and you are certain of being able to do this because this cannon is bigger than any that can normally be brought against you, and, because it is placed at a height, it has a greater range.'

The cannon in question, as I have already said, was uncommonly big, an iron tube hooped with brass at every foot or so of its length. It was mounted on a solid oak chassis, which in turn was laid on what I took to be a giant wheel laid in an horizontal plane. So, within the limits of the embrasure from which its snout protruded, the angle at which it fired could be altered both from side to side and up and down.

'For gen'lemen you got some fucking brains,' our friend remarked, and tapped the side of his huge fruit-like nose with his forefinger – a gesture I took to signify appreciation of our intelligence.

So there you have it, honoured cousin: the way to make sure our fortifications are not knocked down by the Bahmani artillery is to make sure we are defended by guns bigger and better than any they might bring against us. I imagine we could have worked that out for ourselves without traipsing across half the world. However, there might be something to be learnt about the casting of large cannon, and that is something Anish and I will endeavour to look into. And maybe, too, there are ways of refining the exact constituents of gunpowder to gain optimum efficacy.

I remain, dear Cousin,

Your devoted servant

Prince Harihara

CHAPTER

THIRTY-THREE

Dear Cousin

Five months we have been here, and we are now approaching the end of the six month of the year 1460, Christian reckoning. Without the advice of our *sadhus* I can't work out what that makes it according to our more complicated lunar reckonings, but it's about a year since we sailed from Gové, Anish says two months more than a year, so I'm sure you'll get a rough idea.

Effectively we remain prisoners. Though in tolerable comfort, there is no question of our being allowed out into the city which we can see from the walls, or indeed of trying to find our way home. Although not formally charged we are tainted with Yorkism, with collaborating with traitors and giving them succour, and Scales, when the drink takes him badly, making him bellicose and hostile, reminds us that he can get the paperwork done at what he calls the drop of a hat and our heads off quicker than you can say Jack Robinson.

'Here' is, of course, this gloomy fortress-palace-prison called the Tower of London, though I have to say that, with the arrival of what they call summer, it is less gloomy than it was. Summer? A brief period when the sun shines rather more than it did, and the temperature is such that we need to ask to have the fire lit in our rooms only towards dusk, which I have to say now comes late in the day, the night being only about six hours long. You would think that with this amount of daylight it would be even hotter than our country, but no. The sun remains perversely low in the sky, even at noon, and the days are only rarely as warm as the coldest in Vijayanagara. Moreover, the *weather* remains wholly unpredictable: a week of cold rain may still occur, followed by a few days of warm sunshine though with a sharp breeze from the east. Then come cloudy, sultry days, even warmer, culminating in a thunderstorm, heavy rain, almost as heavy as our monsoon at times, and sometimes, even now, the raindrops are frozen into what they call hail. Then back to blustery winds with frequent showers.

Nevertheless, the gardens here, which are quite extensive within the walls, are now pleasant for much of the time, with many tall rose bushes, lilies, peonies (though they are now over) and many flowering herbs, particularly thyme, rosemary (also now over, it flowered earlier than the rest), and sage, dried sacks of which you will remember traders have brought us from time to time from the Himalayan foothills. Incidentally, they charge far too much for them.

The fish-ponds, too, have lotus in them, would you believe it?, which they call water-lily, smaller than ours but just now coming into bloom with flowers very similar, eight or sixteen petals in a mandala. Here they are a rarity apparently and are merely admired for their beauty and not at all for their spiritual significance. The sight of them filled me with a sudden longing to be back home.

What else? Fork-tailed birds, exactly like the swallows that haunt our temples from the end of the monsoons through to the hot season, arrived here a month or so ago and built tiny cement-like nests up under the eaves of all the towers and battlements, hundreds of them, and have laid eggs and are rearing chicks. You know it has long been a puzzle amongst those of us who bother to think about such things as to where our swallows go to breed; well, here, I think we have the answer. For reasons best known to themselves, and to Devi-Parvati who rules all things living, they fly north.

That is not the received opinion in Ingerlond. Quizzing one of the gardeners on the subject, an old man with a red face, long white hair and with the knotted swollen finger joints that afflict most of the elderly in Ingerlond, he spluttered through broken teeth, 'Why, bless you, zurr, come Michaelmas they doos dive into the mud round ponds and sleeps out the winter in a state of intoxified slumber, waking only when they feels the regenerative power of the sun on their backs.'

There are also ravens here in the Tower, again similar to those that dwell in the cliffs and crags of our highest mountains. These are almost tame and the guards of the Tower rear the chicks, which were hatched not long after we were incarcerated, feeding them scraps of liver and other offal. There is a superstition that as long as the raven flourish in the Tower, for so long will Albion (which is another name for Ingerlond) likewise flourish.

Well, cousin, I am boring you with these snippets of natural history, but Anish and I have been so bored ourselves for most of the time that we have found ourselves pursuing such trivia. On now to weightier matters.

Our gaoler here, Lord Scales, who prefers to call himself our host, came to us this morning, in the very garden I have been talking about. He's an old man too, bearded like a leopard, also with a red face (Anish says the preponderance of red faces amongst the elderly here is the result of drinking alcohol in excess since childhood), a bluff manner and filthy temper. He caught up with us just as we were contemplating the movement of a long-legged fly across the surface of the pond. Anish was musing on this phenomenon, attempting to find in it an example of the ephemerality of even great events in the flow of time. The significance he found arose from the fact that the fly left no footprints on the surface.

'Here's a thing, then,' rasped Lord Scales. 'Here's a damned thing. Your Yorkist cronies from Calais landed at Sandwich late the day before yesterday, and they're already at Canterbury. That arsehole Bourchier, the Archbish, is backing them, they've already doubled their numbers up to twenty thousand, and they'll be knocking on our door in a day or two.'

'What's their purpose?' I asked.

'They *say* to restore good government to the kingdom. They *say* they honour the King who they *say* is the rightful king. But these folk never say what they mean.'

'And what do they mean?'

'They mean to kick the King out, and put Richard Plantagenet,

Duke of York – who, believe me, is an arrogant bastard – on the throne instead. But I'll stop them, see if I don't.'

'But if they have twenty thousand . . .'

He knew very well that I am well aware that he has only a couple of hundred garrisoned in the Tower.

'I've got me cannon, haven't I? You've seen them. I'll blast 'em to bits, soon as they set foot in the city.'

Anish piped up. 'Who leads them?' he asked.

'Richard Neville – son of a bitch who calls himself Earl of Warwick because he married old Warwick's daughter – Salisbury, who is his father, Lord Fauconberg his uncle, who also got his title between the sheets, and Eddie March. Crooks. A gang. Gangsters.'

'Not York himself, then?'

'No. Got more sense. He'll hang on in Ireland until he sees how it all turns out. Well, it'll turn out badly for them all. Mark my words.'

And he stumped away, huffing and puffing up the steep stairs no doubt to inspect his guns and make sure our friend Bardolph Earwicca had them in working order.

'Could turn out all right for us,' said Anish, 'if March, Warwick and the rest remember who we are. And Alderman Dawtrey bothers to tell them where we are.'

'Anyway,' said I, 'at least we'll see how well these pieces he's got up there work.'

At this moment the long-legged fly came too close to a water-lily or lotus pad on which a small frog sat. A flick of its tongue and the fly was gone.

'Tell me, Anish,' I asked, 'just what part does that frog play in your miniature cosmology? Shiva the Destroyer?'

'Too grand,' he replied. 'Let's just settle for Tataka, the man-eating demoness.'

Honoured cousin, things are definitely moving here, changing, so I shall not after all commit this letter to the Arab trader I had in mind who has now sailed, hoping to raise Tyre in the Levant in a month or so, but keep it by me and make entries as events unfold. I'll find means to send it on when the situation has clarified. Five days have passed since I put my pen aside, and we are now at the beginning of the month they call July, after Julius Caesar who apparently invented this calendar they use at much the same time as he was building this fortress we are in.

Ooof! Perhaps I should have waited. Lord Scales is having a wonderful time shooting off his pieces. The gunners load and lay them, he rushes up to each emplacement in turn, touches his saltpetre wick to the charge, watches the touch-hole fizz, then bang! off the thing goes, and he rushes on to the next, back out of the tower, down the steps on to the battlement, along it, which is quite dangerous since he could fall off into the yard, up the stairs to the next tower, bang! and on again. He has six pieces pointing out over the city, three to the north towards the part they call Smithfield and three to the west shooting across the low rise they call Tower Hill and into Billingsgate. For all the height these pieces are set at, and their size, he does not seem able to inflict damage at more than five hundred paces, which is a matter of considerable distress and grief to him as it leaves the bridge just, and only just, beyond his range. And it is over the bridge that Warwick's army is now passing, having been welcomed by the Lord Mayor and aldermen, including, I suppose, Alderman Dawtrey.

Warwick and the Yorkists are much favoured by the City merchants for several reasons. The King, or most say the Queen in the King's name, has taxed them heavily and has also accepted huge sums from the Hanse merchants, in exchange for privileges they have not had before. The Yorkists promise to turn all this round once they have the mad King in their power and meanwhile Warwick's ships, under flags of convenience rather than those of the Calais Pale, have taken Hanse ships on the high seas. So not only have the London merchants welcomed his army, they have even given him fourteen thousand gold coins, an enormous sum, with which to pay and feed his soldiers.

Naturally as a result, like bees to a hive, men flock to join his army. One of Lord Scales's staff has been stationed on the highest tower and has attempted to count how many have crossed the bridge. He makes it as many as forty thousand, a very considerable army indeed, though how many will remain once they have been fed and paid and the prospect of long marches and actual fighting comes closer, remains to be seen.

Meanwhile, the bombardment of the nearer streets continues for a couple of hours each day. After that there has to be a pause while more stone balls are brought up to the pieces, and barrels of powder. At one point we heard a brief altercation between Sergeant Earwicca and Lord Scales, which went some way towards explaining the failure of the cannon to throw their projectiles as far as the bridge.

'The fucking powder, yer honour, was mixed up in Epping where the charcoal comes from.'

'I know that, you fool, but where was the powder mixed?'

'And brought in barrels down the river Lee.'

'You blithering idiot, they don't mix powder in the village of Finsbury . . .'

And so on, the point being that after two hours laying and firing the guns both men were deaf.

Eventually they came to an understanding of each other. The three ingredients of the powder were mixed in Epping Forest and put into barrels there. Now the constituents weigh differently and the shaking and jolting of the transports, followed by a year or more just standing, had separated them so the charcoal powder, being the lightest, was at the top, then the sulphur and finally the saltpetre. Not completely separated, you understand, but enough to compromise the powder's performance.

Meanwhile, the roofs of the nearest houses are being shattered, and the upper rooms ruined. There have apparently been some deaths and mutilations, and a deputation came to the gates of the Tower to ask Lord Scales to desist. He went out on to the drawbridge to meet them and abused them roundly, saying, 'You scurvy miscreants, I'll blow the whole bloody city apart as long as you harbour a single Yorkist soldier among you. Now get the fuck out of it before I blast you to hell!' and his bowmen let loose a flight of arrows at their backs as they ran for it.

But one man who had had the sense to bring a buckler along with him, which quickly looked like the back of a porcupine with the arrows sticking out of it, yelled back, 'I'll fucking get you, Lord Scales, when you get out of here. One of your fucking cannon killed my daughter!' and so forth, before, walking backwards, he rejoined his friends at a safe distance, up on Tower Hill, just outside the main gate, where traitors are sometimes executed.

Our social life has been much improved by these new circumstances. A handful of lords, supporters of the Queen, who were in London, have, with their households, taken refuge with us. I won't bore you with their names, but they're an uncivilised lot. The women go about with low-cut bodices revealing their breasts almost to their nipples, and with gowns cut away in front so you can see their stockinged legs as high as the knee. All, men and women alike, wear copious amounts of jewellery, but a lot of it I have to say is fake or cheap, as garnets for rubies, feldspar for amethyst and topaz, and gold much alloyed with copper. The general effect reminds us more of temple dancers and actors at home, than of princes or ministers.

Anish and I derive much amusement from watching them and conversing with them (we are both now quite at home with the Inglysshe tongue). The women talk of nothing but the expense to which their husbands and fathers have been put to provide their clothes and ornaments, the men of their prowess in the hunt, the strength of their horses, the fleetness of their hounds, and their achievements in jousting – of which more later, if I have time.

Every morning Scales sends out spies, who return every evening with news of what the Yorkists are up to in the town. They have a great asset in an Italian priest called Coppini, sent by the Pope to bring the opposing sides to a peaceful settlement, but who preaches to the citizens in favour of York. The Pope apparently expects to gain from the Yorkists various rights disputed between the Crown and the Church, and urges the King to accede to the Yorkist demands. Meanwhile, all the Yorkist lords made a great public show in the churchyard of St Paul's of swearing fealty and loyalty to the mad King, insisting that their sole aim is to restore good government to the country.

It is now the sixth day of July and the Yorkists have been on Inglysshe soil for a fortnight. The King has made no move against them out of Coventry and people say he fears an invasion in the north by York himself and durst not move. So yesterday they began their move against him instead and ten thousand men under Lord Fauconberg marched north. Today Warwick and March left with a further twenty thousand or more, leaving Warwick's father, Lord Salisbury, here with two thousand men to contain us in the Tower and hold the city.

We were to have a joust in the gardens here today, for the younger men were getting bored and restless. When that happens they fight amongst themselves like puppies while serving-girls, even some of the ladies, go about in constant fear of rape. The lists were set up and the young nobles got into their amazingly complicated heavy armour. This is a crazy sport. They mount horses and charge at each other with heavy spears and try to dislodge each other from the saddle. It looks terrifying, and there's no doubt that inside their steel shells, like crocodiles or giant turtles, those who fall are badly shaken though apparently few are hurt seriously. But it began to rain heavily in the morning, the grass lawns were turned to quagmire, and the whole thing was cancelled.

Here I must finish as Anish tells me he has heard of a carvel due to sail on the tide to the Levant, and he believes he can bribe a kitchen boy who goes down to the markets every morning to take our letters with him. I've rambled on somewhat but, believe me, I hold at the front of my mind, at all times, the plight of Prince Jehani and the hope that one day we may yet come up with him. And both Anish and I do our best to forget that our heads remain on our necks solely at the whim of an irascible old drunk.

Your obedient and affectionate cousin

Prince Harihara

CHAPTER

THIRTY-FOUR

'*R*ain, Mah-Lo, even warm rain like this, still fills my body with aches and cramps, and my soul with a blank numbness.'

It was indeed raining, the steady warm rain we know will come every evening in June, following a distant rumbling and tumbling of thunder over the Ghats behind us. Because of it we had moved from the shade of the cardamom tree, but only as far as the shelter of a small free-standing kiosk in the middle of his courtyard. It had a tiled roof and upswung eaves that caught the water and made it run to the corners where it fell into channels cut into the granite flags. The rain itself splashed into the little pond, and thudded on the leaves of the ornamental shrubs. Like us, the birds that haunted Ali's garden huddled along the ledges beneath the eaves, eyed it all balefully and waited for it to stop. His grey Burmese, very sleek, prowled up and down the edge of the verandah like a caged black-phase leopard, or panther, clearly longing to make a dash for it to a sheltered patch of soil where it could do its business but desperately loath to get wet.

Ali went on, 'Look, Mah-Lo, how my finger joints are swollen. My knees appear no different from normal, I grant you, but believe me, they burn inside with terrible pains, and up here in the hollow of my thigh, it is like a sword-thrust. If it was not for the hashish you brought me yesterday I would be dead or mad . . .'

And he thrust a ball of the oily resin, as big as the egg of a quail, which he had been rolling between his palms, the warped left one on top of the sound *right, on to the charcoal glowing in the bowl of his* nargileh *before sucking on the mouthpiece as if his life depended on it. As well it might, for all I knew. His sanity anyway. The rich sweet vegetable smoke, cooled by the rosewater through which it had been bubbled, billowed around us. Breathing it in passively, I settled back to enjoy the mild euphoria it provoked, which somehow went well, as far as I was concerned, with the cosy drumming of the rain, the damp warmth, the early darkness of the cloud-filled sky, and presently the steady drone of my companion's old voice.*

That last letter of the Prince's has taken us on three months or so. We must retrace our steps in the sands of time, back to Easter, and the day after Peter gave his sermon, the day I set forth again on my short walk through Middle Ingerlond.

It started to rain even before I had got to the wicket gate and by the time I was through it it was pouring. I damn near turned back. I did turn back. And what did I see but my friend now of several months not waving me goodbye from the dry safety of the door-keeper's lodge, but stumbling down the gravel towards me. He took me by the elbow and steered me straight on, along the way I was about to go, up on to the main road that passed by the walls of Oxenford leaving them on the further side of the brown, swirling, pockmarked water. In his left hand he held a large soft leather bag with handles.

'Forgive me, Ali,' he cried, 'it was boorish of me to send you off like that. Let me come some of the way with you.'

We splashed on through puddles and over ruts, and presently the rain eased a little, the sun warmed our backs, which steamed gently, and a rainbow appeared over to the right, blessing the bleak prison-like dwellings of scholars and clerics with a brief promise of something better. I have to say I felt happy to be on the road: it was three months since I had set foot outside the Osney priory and, pleasant and welcoming though it had been, I was ready to see new faces and new places. As you know, dear Mah-Lo, my wandering life has, until now, but rarely allowed me to spend more than a month or so in one place, and I still get restless, even now when rest is all I need, rest for these aching bones. Which, let me say, are feeling a lot better now. This is good blow you brought me, much better than the local stuff.

★   ★   ★

'Genuine Moon-disc from the Mountains of the Moon,' I said. 'There was a boat came in yesterday from the Gulf.'

'The real thing, then.'

And his eyes went dreamy – possibly he was remembering the years he had spent in his youth amongst the Assassins of the Hindu Kush, at the feet of the fakirs who followed Hassan Ibn Sabbah and took bhang for inspiration. Then he took a deep puff, shook his head, grinned lopsidedly, and went on.

Presently we came to a parting of the ways, a crossroads in fact. One path led to a bridge and back to the city, another straight on to the north towards, the signs said, Banbury and Coventry, while the one to the right indicated Burford.

'The Burford road,' said Peter, setting down the leather bag he was carrying, 'for the north-west. Burford is an interesting place.'

I fully expected him to leave me now, having set me on the right road, but again he took my elbow, picked up the bag and went with me, looking up at me with almost childish mischief in his eyes.

'We are, you know, a preaching order, a mendicant order, and I have dallied too long in the comfort of the cloister. I feel ready to get out now, preach a bit, see a few new faces, pass on some of the fruits of a winter spent in contemplation and hard study. And watching you go, knowing I'd miss you, I thought, if then, why not now? And look . . .' he loosened the drawstring on the bag, which was black '. . . I've brought with me what I could lay my hands on in the moment I had of Roger's writings.'

He pulled up four small books of parchment, bound in leathered boards. He gave the pages a flick. The writing was minuscule.

'All in code,' he added, 'but I've cracked it.'

What followed was not what I intended. We spent far too long walking and talking, many weeks, in fact, in pleasant companionship, with a little hardship but not much. Though I tried to urge on him that my objective was a conventicle of the Brothers of the Free Spirit, which he himself had told me might be near a place called Macclesfield or Manchester, Brother Peter was in no hurry to be anywhere in particular. And, after all, Prince Jehani was Prince Harihara's brother not mine, and for as long as I believed Harihara to be in prison, there was little point in me trying to find Jehani.

We begged for food (neither of us had with us more than our staff and the clothes we stood up in) and always we got more than we needed. Occasionally Peter gave sermons on street corners, at market crosses, in churchyards or out in the countryside away from the reach of authority or law. His congregations rarely numbered more than a score or so, but equally he was never forced to resort to the expediencies of his mentor, the founder of his order, and preach to the birds. We slept in barns, lazar houses, and occasionally the beds of widows.

The countryside greened up, the ditches filled with flowers, and I soon forgot that the trees had been leafless. Apple trees blossomed, then pears, the meadows filled with small flowers called buttercups, which sheeted them with yellow, and the woods rang with birdsong, especially that of the two-noted cuckoo that lays its eggs in other birds' nests. In the gifts people brought us, soft sour cheeses and cream figured often, eggs, too, and fresh young roots and cresses. The duck eggs were especially good.

For the most part Peter preached a message that was not as brave or far-reaching as that he had been inspired with at Easter, but spoke straightforwardly of the blessings of poverty, sharing, owning things communally. He attacked the priesthood and the Normans for stealing from the working people and he condemned superstition, greed, luxurious living, indolence, warfare and so on, and he used, from memory, the Bible in Inglysshe as a text, the translation of John Wycliffe. He always eyed his listeners with a cunning eye, and tempered his message to those who were there: thus if he saw a constable or a reeve he praised the King and the secular law, if there was a poor priest he praised his poverty but if there was a rich one around, a canon or even an abbot, he came quickly to a conclusion and we moved on.

More interesting were the long talks we had as we covered the ground from one village to the next.

'Let us agree between ourselves,' he said, quite early on, and even though we were alone, walking through an oak forest whose boughs were laced with brilliant yellowish fresh green, which he had pointed out was not leaves but green flowers, he looked over his shoulder and into the holly thickets, to check there was no one in hearing, 'that God is a meaningless concept. We have no need of him . . .'

'Or her?'

'Indeed, of her either . . .' and here he rocked with laughter. 'What a wag you are, Ali, but quite right too. Why shouldn't we call God a woman? Since we're agreed she probably does not exist at all she might just as well be female!'

'You were saying we have no need of her . . .'

'Save perhaps as First Mover. Something must have kicked the whole thing going, but once started then cause and effect take over, and she could push off to whatever other universes she has an interest in. Granted that, it becomes fascinating, does it not, to speculate on how cause and effect might have put together a chain of being that resulted in so many diffuse and different species as we see around us? And perhaps to guess what amongst them were the first originals from which the rest came.'

'Speculation is free and harmless,' I said, but also looked around warily, 'though it may lead to the rack and the stake. So. Speculate.'

'I was rather hoping you would.'

'Why me?'

'Since you have so reduced all human learning to the two postulates of your sect's founder, "Nothing is true, everything is permitted," you have sloughed off far more of the baggage of learning with which civilisation has loaded us than I have, and you can thus prance about more freely than I. I mean metaphorically,' he added, glancing at my withered hand and scrawny shanks.

'All right,' I agreed, 'here goes.' But I remained mute for some minutes as we rambled on through acorns and beechmast beneath a canopy of layered green until, inspired by his brief absence behind a holly bush where he performed a natural function, I began.

'The first life . . .' Then I corrected myself. 'The first *animal* life must have begun with the simplest, most basic form, from which all the others developed.'

'And that is?'

'A sack. No. A tube! A tube that maintains itself by sucking in food at one end, absorbing what it needs, and expelling what it does not need at the other. When you think about it, all animal life, including men and women, are at bottom just that. The rest is added to make the basic tube work better. So I'd guess the very first animals were just that and nothing else.'

'So how did they change? Become so varied and different. And so many different types. Species. What,' he added, 'in terms of cause and effect, of action and reaction makes a new thing? What is the origin of species?'

I gave that a little thought. 'Look,' I said eventually, 'I have travelled a great deal, I have seen animals like wild dogs and rodents thriving in deserts; in Muscovy I have seen an elephant, frozen inside a block of ice, with long, long hair, while in Vijayanagara they have almost no hair at all. I have seen monkeys that climb trees and monkeys like the ones on the rock of Jebel Tariq that live in caves and run about on the ground and have a different stance and use their legs in a different way from that employed by the tree-dwellers. And so on. The world is different from one place to another. There are mountains and plains, valleys and peaks, hot places and cold, wet and dry, rocky deserts and luxuriant forests. And in each place the differences between the animals help them to suit the place where they live.'

'Ah, I see where you're going.' Peter could hardly contain his excitement. 'The first simple tubes would have to change as soon as their surroundings changed, as soon as the food they sucked in and shitted out was different . . . But how did these changes happen? What was the machinery? Why did they not simply die?'

We trudged on, in a melancholy mood now, fearing perhaps that we might, after all, have to return to that bearded old monster working like a potter for seven days and breathing life into the clay creatures he had created.

Presently, on that day, the heat began to bother us, Peter anyway, who was less used to it than I. We had come into a small glade where a storm had uprooted one of the forest giants and left a space open to the sky on which short green grass already grew. We sat with our backs to the trunk of the fallen hero and looked up into the beechen green above us.

A hundred tiny worms were visible, though they, too, were green, suspended on threads of gossamer from the leaves, and through them flitted a pair of the small red-breasted birds with sharp black beaks. They caught the little worms, which were yet more than a mouthful for them, and carried them away. In the short space that we watched each must have taken at least ten.

'What are they doing with them?' I asked. 'They cannot be eating them all themselves.'

And then I laughed, for one of these robins let go and limed my friend's bald pate.

'Bugger,' he said, and groping around beneath the tree-trunk found a dock-leaf with which he cleaned himself up, leaving a green smear where he could not see it. 'So, up there we have simple tubes that chew up leaves or blossom and pass tiny green droppings, and larger, more complicated ones that fly about, eat the smaller ones, and shit what they do not need having transformed the detritus into a black and white mess. Incidentally, their appetite is apparently ravenous because they are feeding the chicks nested in that hole where the tree has shed a branch. Is there a lesson to be learnt here? Basically they are the same, tubular shit-makers, but in accidents so different. Why?'

'The simple ones have only to chew leaves, and when a leaf is nearly gone they spin a thread to get to the next. But the birds need to fly if they are to catch the worms, so they have grown wings and so forth to carry them from worm to worm. At some time in the past they, too, were worms, no doubt, but perhaps their food supply became inadequate, so they changed.'

'So. What you are saying is that we are all, all the animals there are and fishes and birds, just tubular shit-makers who . . .' he searched for the word '. . . *adapted* to changing circumstances so they could continue their main function of shit-production?'

'And staying alive . . . at least long enough to reproduce their kind.'

'The whole process took more than seven days.'

'I'd say so.'

'So. Those worms, and you and I, each adapted to his surroundings, are simply destined to feed, shit and, once we have reproduced, die.'

'Yes,' I asserted. And I felt a strange excitement well up in me, as might afflict a man who stood silent upon a mountain-top and surveyed a whole new ocean of knowledge, shrouded as yet in impenetrable mist.

'A destiny that lacks the dignity of being made in God's own image.'

'What's dignity got to do with it?'

Peter stood up, gave me a hand, and we set off again, both of us ruminating like a couple of cows.

'If,' I brought forth after a time, 'there were no robins, then the worms would eat all the leaves and there would be no more trees. If there were no more trees there would be no more worms, and soon no possibility even of robins . . . There is a sort of balance here, an equipoise.'

'Ah, but if there were no worms then I grant you there would be no robins. But there would still be trees. Lots of them.'

CHAPTER

THIRTY-FIVE

After a week or so of gentle walking, sometimes in widening circles (at one point we reached the eastern bank of the river called Severn, but then turned back as we were now in what Peter called the Welsh Marches, and the Welsh on the other side spoke a language as barbarous as their behaviour), much talking and some preaching we came at last to Burford, which was a place of some interest. But first the approaches signalled a change. We had moved from the river plain into an undulating country, the hills not high but frequent and occasionally steep. Many brooks and rivulets ran through them. There was much forest, but also, especially in the valleys, water-meadows where huge mushroom-coloured kine lay and endlessly chewed on lush grass and king-cups. In the uplands it became more and more the case that commons and what had once been ploughed were enclosed in wicker fences and harboured sheep. The villages we passed through, and occasionally stayed in, were prosperous, many of the buildings, even those of the poorest, of a pleasant warm grey stone. When it wasn't raining women sat in the doorways spinning wool from distaffs on to spindles, gossiping in the sunshine, while indoors or in lean-to sheds their menfolk wove the yarn into cloth on primitive looms. At any rate they looked primitive compared to the ones the Arab nation uses, whether for cotton and silk in Moorish Spain or fine wools in Asia. Many of these people spoke not Inglysshe but a tongue Peter said was Flemish, from the Lowlands across the Channel. They had the art of weaving and spinning better than the Angles and Saxons, and had been encouraged to settle in Ingerlond.

'With sheep and cattle in the fields, what do these people do for bread, which is the staple of life?' I asked.

'They buy the raw wool from the lords and landowners, who enclosed the land and brought in these people—'

'Wait,' I interrupted. 'What of the peasants who lived here first? The Angles and Saxons?'

'Three things,' he replied, as we toiled up a hill steeper than most on a track hedged with a thorny shrub with bright green leaves sprouting; pinched off between thumb and forefinger they made a delightful savoury salad, which we nibbled at as we walked along. Hawthorn, it was called. 'First, the plague carried off most of them a hundred years ago. This left the lords with a problem – too much land, not enough labourers. Wages rose. Second, those who survived married into the families of the Flemish people, each happily absorbed into the other. Third, those who were dispossessed by enclosure, and would not marry to become spinners and weavers, took to lawlessness and the forests, which they call the Green Wood. There they live off the lords' venison, rabbits, hares and so forth, or hire themselves out to the lords as soldiers in these wars. I'm surprised we have not met any. In many ways they practise what I preach.'

But I was more interested in how the spinners and weavers worked.

'They buy the wool,' Peter replied, 'then spin and weave it. They take it to market where they sell it to merchants. There is a difference, a surplus, between what they pay for it and what they sell it for, and with this difference they buy the necessaries of life, including flour from other parts.'

But by now we had breasted the crest of the hill and were able to look down into a wide lush valley where there nestled a small town or large village. My curiosity about the wool trade was forgotten for a time.

'Burford,' said Peter.

On the way down we passed a small pit in the hillside from which two men were cutting a bluish-grey caked but powdery clay and loading it into a cart.

'Fuller's earth,' said Peter. 'With abundant running water one of the necessaries for a flourishing wool trade. The others are good pasture for sheep, and skilled craftsmen. The fuller's earth is used for cleaning the grease and fats out of the wool, which help keep the sheep waterproof and well.'

'They certainly need it,' I supplied, for it had come on to rain again. 'Why do they cultivate giant thistles? Surely they are no use to anyone except donkeys.'

Just below the fuller's earth pit there was a small plot filled with the tall spiky plants, as yet only in bud.

'They are not thistles but teasels. Once they have flowered they form hard, brittle seed-cases with bent almost barbed bristles. The weavers use these to tease up the nap on their cloth, which they then shear off leaving a fine almost silky finish, which is much valued by the richer sort.'

'It seems there is a conspiracy between man and . . .'

'And . . . God?'

'Nature. To make this a region in which cloth manufacture can flourish.'

'Not forgetting history, the past. Remember the plague.'

Burford was indeed a prosperous place, and newly so. A main street of commodious new houses, timber-framed and brick, leads down from the Oxenford road, which we crossed to a small river on whose bank stood a curious church. Curious, because though three hundred years old it was undergoing substantial refurbishment and rebuilding. A new and graceful steeple had already been erected on top of the massive square tower, while the nave and aisles were being laboriously raised to new galleries with new piers supporting the new roof. Yet most of the lower structure, the side-chapels and so forth, remained unaltered.

I put these anomalies to Peter. 'Surely,' I said, 'it would have made more sense to start afresh. That way they would have produced a building in a uniform style, harmonious and properly proportioned, instead of this mish-mash. I suspect, too, it would have been cheaper.'

In answer he took me by the elbow, always his practice when something conspiratorial, confidential or requiring persuasion was in the air, and led me into the nave. He pointed up to a niche crowning one of the older arches. There was a statuette, a crude and primitive representation of a woman riding a horse. He then conducted me round the capitals of the older side piers and pointed at equally crude representations of the act of procreation and so forth. Finally in the churchyard he construed what we had seen.

'This,' he said, 'is a temple, not a church. It is a temple not to God but to the goddess, the white lady who throughout these parts rode on a white horse, naked but for her golden hair and garlands of flowers, at the midsummer solstice. There are signs of her, and of the cult that still worships her, all over the place if you know where to look. At Banbury she has rings on her fingers and bells on her toes. In Coventry she is Godgifu. The rulers of the Church may try to hide all this by building over it, but they dare not wipe it out.'

'So why,' I asked, 'is this temple, disguised as a church, dedicated to a man, the prophet John the Baptist. I mean, why not to Mary, the mother of the prophet Jesus, whom your people call God and whose mother must therefore be a goddess?'

He looked at me with solemn but expressionless eyes. 'You probably do not know this,' he said, 'but the day on which St John is remembered, and his death especially, is the twenty-fifth of June, the summer solstice. But you will be aware that he was beheaded as the result of the dancing of a beautiful naked woman, was indeed a sacrifice to her. In a few weeks' time you will believe me when the solstice comes and we see the bonfires that will be lit throughout the land.'

He preached that evening and, as usual, carefully pitched his sermon to the small group who had turned out by the bridge across the river. Most were buxom, pink-cheeked women, done out in some finery for the occasion, though not ostentatious like the nobility but rather neat and clean in whites, greys, browns and blacks, all with starched caps sometimes tilted up like sails above their not inconsiderable gold necklaces and brooches.

He spoke of the virtues of hard work, of prosperity as a sign not only of hard work but of godly living, not only of godly living but of God having chosen them to be his handmaids. He went on to say how a person was not saved and numbered amongst the elect by good works, or by the sacraments, which were but toys for the simple-minded, but – and this is what 'elect' means – by being chosen. And how does one know one is chosen? First, by an inner certainty that it is so, and second, by the outer signs, the prosperity brought about by good works and hard-won skills. In all this he used as support and example the words, in Inglysshe, of St Paul, also from the Wycliffe Bible. This Paul seemed something of a philosopher in the way he teased at the problem of faith, the chosen, and the efficacy or irrelevance of good works.

This they all loved. The women smirked and smoothed down their aprons, the men puffed out their chests, cleared their throats, ahem!, and nodded meaningfully at their companions.

'What need have we of priests and Latin,' cried Peter, coming to his peroration, 'when we have the Holy Scriptures set forth for us in plain good Inglysshe to guide us? What need of churches when two or three gathered together in His Name have been promised that He will be with them? What need of confession and absolution when we have our own consciences to guide us?'

Finally he produced a story that he said he took from the Gospel of St Matthew, chapter twenty-five, in Wycliffe's version, the story of the talents, and how the master praised the men who made best use of these weighty pieces of gold he had left them with and condemned the man who merely buried his and gave it back.

One weaver, a tall, thin old man, dressed in some splendour in velvet and with a gold chain round his neck, was especially pleased with this and invited us to take supper in his home and bed there too. So prosperous was he that he even had a spare room. His establishment put me in mind of Alderman Roger Dawtrey's in London, though it was not on the same scale. Still, he and his large fair wife, who had a big bony nose and huge breasts, together with his three daughters and his two sons-in-law, gave us excellent entertainment and a royal meal.

Later, as the maidservant of the household climbed the stair ahead of us with a beeswax candle to light us to bed, I asked Peter, 'And what of our lady? Our white lady on her white horse?'

And he replied, 'Oh, I love her madly, but would she get us to a table laden with roast goose, plum duff and cream? She dwells with the shepherds and the few ploughmen left, in the Green Wood, and with the gypsies.'

That night, as Peter lay snoring on the other side of the big bolster that lay between us I got to thinking. These people are prosperous. They make money. But they are frugal with it. They live well, but without ostentatious display or wild extravagance. Yet they are not misers. What do they do with their talents, their surplus gold?

A nobleman whose peasants have produced a surplus of food sells it for cash to artisans and merchants who do not have land. With this spare

cash he indulges in conspicuous display, for that is what he values above
all else, his self-esteem and the esteem of others. He will buy labour and
materials to build ever larger castles and palaces, finer clothes, furniture,
gargantuan* feasts, and, if, as so often happens, he is threatened by
another nobleman, or he himself covets another nobleman's land, he
will buy those most expensive items of all, arms, armour and men, and
go to war.

And what will a peasant do who earns, either by hire or by selling
his produce, more gold than he needs? Why, he will frugally save it up,
bury it beneath the floors of his hut or hovel, against a day when the
harvest will fail or his master turns him off his land.

But these weavers and spinners? And likewise merchants and artisans?
Well, as a trader for others I have seen it with my own eyes, and I was
seeing it again here in Burford. They buy another loom, more distaffs
and spindles, and more wool. But they have no time of their own to
operate them, so they buy the time of others. But just as they made
more money from their own spinning and weaving than they needed,
so they will sell their cloth for more than the cost of the extra looms
and spinning tools and the time they had to buy, all added together, for
there would be no point in doing it if they didn't. And that results in
even more gold than they need. What to do with it? Why, the same
again. Until one man would own hundreds, maybe thousands of looms,
buy time from thousands of workers . . . and so on, and so on?

There'd be an end of it, of course. There would soon be more cloth
in the land, in the world, than people needed, and once every man had
three coats, one for best, one for daily use, and one in case, there'd be
an end of it. But would there? Would not the enterprising man not now
look around for other things to make and sell?

My mind began to swim, I felt mentally dizzy, as I tried to formulate
examples in my head of how it might work, inventing figures, mult-
iplying them, forgetting the number I'd first thought of. Soon I began to
sweat and moan at the enormity of it all. Peter woke up and, grumbling,
prodded me into telling him what was bothering me.

When I had done so, with examples and figures, he finally said, 'Ali,

---

* *Allow me one footnote as a warning to would-be pedants. OK, Rabelais came a hundred
years later, but Gargantua and Pantagruel were popular names for giants throughout the middle
ages − Enc Brit, 1911. J R.*

with your tale of tubes that suck in sustenance and push out shit you fathomed the distant past. Now, with your man going to market with twenty yards of linen, you have unravelled the future. So go to sleep.'

'Wool,' I said. 'Cloth. Twenty yards of cloth not linen.'

'Funny,' he said, 'I could have sworn you said linen.'

The next day we set off in a north-westerly direction with serious intent to get towards Macclesfield, or Manchester, but still keeping to the byways and smaller places. The next night, I recall, we were given shelter in a barn in a bed of what was left of last year's hay. I remember it because when we stopped on the outskirts and looked around us there was a moment of evening stillness. Then a blackbird opened its throat and sang from the top of a willow tree, and round him, through the evening mist, we could hear all the birds, for miles around, singing their hearts out. The place was called Adle's Trap.

By now the bushes whose leaves had provided such tasty salads, and which served often in that area to make hedges, had burst into profuse bloom, which arched down over us, thousands of small white flowers in clusters so they looked like spray tumbling over the crest of a wave, the green surf that thunders against our coast here in Malabar. I know the comparison sounds far-fetched, but it was further justified by the fact that the ditches below these hedges were now filled with even tinier clusters of white flowers growing up in plate-shaped circles so it looked like the swirling of the wave before.

The first flowers, the ones on the bushes, had a heady fragrance, slightly sweet but somehow animal as well. Mah-Lo, I don't think I shall embarrass you by telling you what it smelt like. But for a man, and for some women, too, I daresay, it's the most exciting odour in the world. No wonder these flowers that bloom in the month of May are called may, which is one of the names Parvati or Uma has in those parts.

All of which led me to think with some nostalgia, indeed a little longing, for all I was even then a quite old old man, of our Uma, and to wonder where she might be and how she was faring.

Next day we passed through one of many towns in Ingerlond called Stratford. Peter said it was famed in those parts for the quality of the gloves it produced, which brought it some prosperity but nothing on the scale of that of the weavers and spinners in the hills we had left behind us. We crossed a river called Avon – there are as many Avons as there are Stratfords – and admired the swans that were building a big nest downstream in the rushes, which grew beneath a slanting willow in the churchyard. Then we pressed on a further hour or so up the Coventry road to a hamlet called Snitterfield.

Here a peasant called Shagsper took us in, showing some faith in Peter's robe for he needed help and guidance of the sort he felt a Franciscan might provide. The midwife had gone into Stratford for the day and his wife was in labour and bleeding. Two or three women of the village, of the sort who make a profession of mourning and laying-out had already gathered at Shagsper's door anticipating the worst – or, from their point of view for they were like crows gathering about a corpse, the best.

Peter immediately made several infusions in which both fresh young raspberry leaves, willow-bark, valerian and rosemary figured, and, between her groans and screams, persuaded Mistress Shagsper to take them. Then he got his patient off her bed and on to the birthing stool, which her husband had been loath to do without the presence of the midwife. Presently she brought forth a thin-boned and wrinkled little boy. Peter hastily christened him John, thus ensuring that if he died he'd go straight to heaven.

However, the baby fed well from his mother's breasts, and the blue colour of his skin receded, became a healthier pink, and presently, lulled by his mother's singing, he went to sleep. 'Never harm, nor spell, nor charm, Come our lovely baby nigh,' she sang, probably making it up on the spot. 'Lulla, lulla lullaby.' Not the most moving or penetrating of lyrics, but it served.

As we left Snitterfield we passed two villagers trimming a hawthorn hedge where its branches had grown over the track enough to be a nuisance to passers-by. One was hacking at it with a small axe; the other trimmed it with a pruning knife.

'Oi rough-hews 'em,' said the first, as we passed.

'An' oi shapes their ends,' the second concluded.

'What philosophers these men are,' cried Peter.

'Whatever do you mean?'

'The irresistible forces of nature, as witnessed in the causes and effects that create species, rough-hew our destinies. And accumulated wealth employed reproductively shapes our ends. History in a mouthful.'

Chapter

Thirty-Six

The roads were filling up now. Every day we saw men in armour, often on horseback, heading towards Coventry, and three times a cannon-train: mules pulling these cumbersome weapons along roads too narrow for them or too rutted, or which crossed fords too deep. Since we knew that the King and court were in Coventry it was not difficult to guess what was happening. He, or, if he was as mad as people said, his affinity and connections, especially the Queen, were preparing for the arrival of the Yorkists, both those with the Duke himself, expected any day from Ireland, and those from Calais led by his cousin, the Earl of Warwick. I recalled that one of these was Eddie March and how Uma had bedded him with so much pleasure to both that they had nearly been caught by Lord Scales. Only my quick intervention with his horse had saved him. It seemed not impossible that if she was still alive she might have sought to join him again and, indeed, perhaps Prince Harihara and Anish might do the same since they had employed March as their guide in Ingerlond. With this in mind I was not entirely loath to postpone our trip into the north-west to search out the Brothers of the Free Spirit – at least, until I had news of my friends' and employer's whereabouts and fortunes. Moving towards the area where the King's army was collecting seemed as good a plan as any since, no doubt, the Yorkists would do the same if they wanted a battle.

There was lots of fresh food now, much of it the same or like the foods we Arabs eat, such as beans and later peas and many green-leafed salads but lacking the interest our spices and herbs give them, apart from mint and parsley. Indeed, the whole countryside would have been a sort of paradise if it were not for the crazy weather.

But what I remember most, and it would have pleased the Hindus of these parts, were the fields held in common by all the local community, often by riverbanks, where the grass grew thick and lush with hundreds of smaller herbs and flowers amongst it, and cows munched their way through it. Most families had a cow, and each village had common land all could share. The cows were not as big as ours, had smaller horns and dewlaps, but huge udders; throughout this Middle Ingerlond, cream and butter, cheese and milk were abundant.

What our Hindus would not have liked – and Prince Harihara and Anish must have been disgusted by if they had come across it – was the eager, even greedy way these people feasted off beef. The bullocks were separated from the heifers and mostly killed and eaten before they were two years old, often roasted over huge fires at fairs and festivals. It didn't bother me, and once I had the taste for this Inglysshe beef I sought it out whenever I smelt the rich odour of burning flesh drifting across a meadow filled with stalls, pedlars and the common folk. On account of the abundance of green, fresh grass, and water too, these animals never had to walk more than fifty or a hundred paces in a day, so their meat was tender and rich with fat.

The one thing they did not grow in Ingerlond was hemp, which grieved me. I would not touch their stronger beers or mead, an alcoholic drink made from honey. Although I now counted the Prophet's interdiction a useless superstition, the avoidance of strong drink was so deeply ingrained I could not even smell it without a slight feeling of nausea. But bhang or hashish I would have given my soul for, supposing I have one and anyone wants it.

The fairs were an excuse for rural sports, which were often both absurd and dangerous. Men shot arrows at bird carcasses whirled round on the ends of ropes in simulation of flight or at distant targets made up to look like the heads of Saracens. Although it was many decades since anyone had been on a crusade, which is what the Christians call a *jihad*, they were still remembered. Oddly enough, no one hit on my dark visage as a sign that I might be one. Or perhaps they weren't bothered whether I was or not. By and large the Inglysshe are tolerant and easy-going – the old Inglysshe, that is, not the Normans – so long as their bellies and tankards are full. The men also sat on greasy poles set across brooks and tried to knock each other off with bags filled with sand; they ran races wearing armour; they split wood with giant axes; they wrestled in a variety of styles. Often we saw broken limbs, bloodied noses, and bruised faces worn with pride by winners and losers alike.

All these were one man against the rest to find the best, but we also came across, and particularly on Midsummer Night's Eve, a contest between all the men of one village against those of another. The object was to get an inflated bladder into the centre or some other agreed point in the opposing village. Simple. Indeed, very simple, for there were no rules except against the carrying of actual weapons. Teams seemed to divide themselves into those who relied on brute force and those who expected to win through cunning. The first, having obtained the bladder or ball, simply bunched around the man carrying it and in a solid block attempted to push their way through all opposition to their goal. The second used decoys and fast running to jinx their way through, often drawing most of the opposition after a runner carrying a similar but not genuine bladder, while the real bladder was carried or kicked by byways and round the back. Because of the nature of the bladder it was possible to kick it over quite long distances, up to a hundred paces, to get it over the heads of opponents to men of one's own side. Kicked, it travelled further and straighter than when thrown. Men who had this kicking skill were especially valued and honoured by their team-mates.

My companion had a strange liking for this sport. When we watched it he would quickly identify himself with one of the participating villages, buy or borrow the favours their supporters wore, such as ribbons in special colours or scarves, then run about cheering their successes and groaning or even using uncouth language when they failed, and shouting catchphrases and snatches. He explained that before taking orders in his early twenties but while still a student at Oxenford, he had been an adept and turned out for the student hall where he lodged.

At the end of the day the losing village played host to both communities and round a giant bonfire plied each other with beer, or cider made from apples nine or ten months earlier and now unbearably tart on the tongue, no sweetness left, which they nevertheless consumed copiously since it made them drunk even more quickly than their beer. Meanwhile they danced, they danced to bagpipe, flute and drum, strange maze-like dances, or dances in which they banged sticks together. Many had bells attached by ribbons to their bodies. And suddenly, through this cacophony, prancing, grotesque capering, I heard and saw something quite different, the whirling sword dances of the Moors in Granada, and the circling arms and stamped feet of the Moorish women. This may have been illusion, though I later learnt that it was believed these dances were first brought to Ingerlond by John of Gaunt, great-grandfather of the present King, who had fought campaigns in Spain.

Towards midnight all who were still on their feet jumped through the flames, those who were not on their feet but awake copulated with the girls, but many just snored through a senseless stupor until dawn.

As I have said, Brother Peter was much taken with the bladder-game, which he called 'footie', and a fortnight or so later suddenly revealed what may have been his purpose all along in taking us south and east instead of north and west: there was annually held, round about the tenth day of July, a particularly watchable contest between two villages on the banks of the river Nene a mile south of a town called Northampton. These were Sandyford and Hardingstone, which was a further mile or so to the south. We arrived on the site late on the evening of the ninth, wet through after two days of continual rain, and almost immediately ran into a picket of armed men on horses guarding the ford.

'Ah,' said Peter, 'these will be constables placed here to ensure that no members of either team will break the prescribed bounds of the contest by crossing the river and thereby stealing a march on the others.'

'Maybe,' I said, looking down into the swirling, rushing water, 'but believe me, no one is going to cross here without a boat.'

For fordable though it may have been on an ordinary day, on this day, on account of the rain, it looked deep and fast-flowing.

We walked on through the gathering dusk and presently came to the road to the south, the highway. Between the river and the undulating plain it crossed a low rise.

'This will be a capital vantage-point from which to follow the course of tomorrow's contest,' Peter exclaimed with glee, and we followed it to the top.

A gang of twenty or so men, in half-armour and supervised by another horseman, was dragging a large cannon up the hill from the river to join four more that were already deployed across the crest. They protected the approach to the town, whose towers and spires loomed through the murk a mile or so behind us and on the other side of the river.

'No doubt,' Peter continued, 'these men belong to the Sandyford team and are here to defend the extremity of their territory.'

He seemed not to have noticed the cannon, or chose to ignore them. It was then that I noticed something abnormal about his appearance.

'Peter,' I said, 'do you realise you are wearing your spectacles? Normally you only have them on when you are reading.'

A moment later, while Peter was still fumbling with his lenses and peering about him with ever-increasing signs of surprise, the supervising horseman accused us of being Yorkist spies and ordered his men to tie us to a gnarled and lichened apple tree that grew on the top of the rise.

'You can jolly well stay there,' this unpleasant youth added, in the accents I had learnt to associate with the Norman tribe, 'until we've seen your beastly friends awff. Then we'll take you deown to the teown and find out what colour your insides are.'

On top of everything else it rained all night.

Chapter

Thirty-Seven

I woke, yes, woke, although I was tied upright, facing outwards, my wrists to Peter's wrists, my ankles to his, with the trunk of the tree between us. A bough of tiny immature apples bumped my forehead, a patch of piss was running down my inside leg, and the sound of a skylark shrilled in my ears. We were both intolerably stiff, aching in every joint and muscle, but as we stirred the sun rose over the plain to the east and a few moments of warm sunshine eased the pain.

Around us and below, the gunners were also stirring, lighting fires and cooking a breakfast in which, from the smell of it, bacon and black pudding played a considerable part, smells both of us found disgusting for a time though soon even in my Muslim soul and Peter's Franciscan one they wakened hunger. Presently a sergeant-gunner, a barrel of a man with long yellow hair, a huge moustache of the same colour and a week's growth of beard, dressed in brown studded leather, a mail skirt, a breastplate and rimless helmet took pity on us and made one of his crew give us some bread, which, of course, he had to hold for us.

From his side of the tree, Peter asked me what I could see of what was happening.

Since I was facing east and south I had to screw up my eyes against the sun, still low in the sky beneath a bank of black cloud. 'Well,' I said, 'the slope is uneven but gentle, and loses itself in a plain that is yet not completely flat. There is common land, pasturage, a couple of villages, one of which I suppose is Hardingstone, with fields about them. Beyond them is the forest. The road winds down the slope, between the villages, and loses itself amongst the trees.'

'Is there much in the way of activity?'

'Quite a lot. A hundred yards away the men are trying to adjust the position of the cannon under the direction of the bastard lordling who put us here. But they are having a lot of difficulty since during the night they have sunk almost to the axles of their small wheels in the clay. Our young friend is growing very bad-tempered about it.'

'I can hear him.'

'No doubt you can hear, too, a monotonous hammering noise, wood on wood. This is because many more men, armed and armoured are coming into the scene and are hammering stakes into the ground with sharpened points angled upwards, digging a ditch and throwing up a rampart, stretching three hundred paces or more on either side of the road, in a line at right-angles to it. That's about it. No. I'm wrong. Suddenly they are all excited and I can see why. Coming out of the forest, and heading up the gap between the villages is a long column of soldiers carrying lances on their shoulders, and here and there in the column groups of fifty or more men in heavy armour on big horses . . .'

'How far away?'

'A mile or so.'

'And you can see them in that much detail?'

'My one eye is better than your two.'

A moment of silence from my friend, possibly a touch of chagrin. I sought to mitigate any offence I might have given.

'And what can you see on your side?'

'Not a lot. A large camp of soldiers. Tents. The King's standard. No sign of footballers, though. But it's early yet.'

The morning wore on. More and more men came up from the river and formed up behind the stakes, many of them archers with those vicious longbows. There were horses, too, clad in plate armour and carrying armoured men. Whenever they got into a declivity or a marshy patch — there was one such over to my left where a stream meandered through fields to join the Nene, which was out of my view — the combined weight was too much and the horses sank to their knees, whinnied and neighed in distress and panic and threatened to seat those of the knights who had not already dismounted. But most were foot-soldiers, also in full armour and carrying billhooks with axe- or mattock-like blades, and heavy swords at their sides.

About mid-morning we heard trumpet calls and drum-beats and, Here we go, I thought, but, no, it was for a parley that they sounded. Out of the more distant ranks now serried in front of the forest to the south came twenty or so horsemen with a herald's trumpet in front, carrying big banners covered with the complicated devices all Europeans carry into battle as means of identification. Though how an ordinary soldier is meant to distinguish each from the other, to know friend from foe in the heat of battle, without a dictionary of heraldic devices as part of his battle-kit, defeats me. Probably defeats him too.

Our popinjay, now mounted since the ground on the rise was firmer than below, shaded his eyes and spoke to a couple of similarly mounted and armoured young men who had come up to join him. 'Oh, Christ, it's the godgang,' he exclaimed.

'Godgang, Justin? What's a fellow meant to make of that?'

'Bishops, dear Maurice. There's old Bourchier there, Archbish of Canterbury, can't mistake his white beard. Cousin of York's, ain't he?'

'Brother-in-law, sort of. And that's Salisbury with him,' the third chipped in.

'You're talking through your arse-hole, old chap. Salisbury's even longer in the tooth than the archbish.'

'God, Maurice, what a wanker you are. It's the Bishop of Salisbury not the earl. And that swarthy character with him must be Coppini. Pope's legate. Wop. Eyetie.'

'Question is, what are they up to?'

'I reckon they'll try to get to the King and say it's not him they're after but the Queen and all her people, and if he'll come quietly there won't be a battle.'

'Well, it might work. The old fool can't stand fighting. Nasty men bashing each other with axes. Gives him a headache.'

'Old Staffers won't let them through, though, will he?'

'Not a chance. With this hill in our favour and the cannon, we can't lose. Staffers is spoiling for a battle. Get them out of the way and we can get down to London and sort out poor old Scalesy. He's been locked up in the Tower since Christmas.'

'I say, though, those chaps do seem to have an awful lot of chaps with them. Must be getting on for twice our lot.'

'Don't worry, Maurice. We've got the cannon, right?'

'Sure, you're right. No need to worry then. I'd better be getting back to the headman.'

And the one called Maurice trotted off with a great jangling and clanging of armour, leaving our man and Justin behind.

'Who's Morrers with, then? And why is he wearing that black stick thing on his helmet?'

'Lord Grey of Ruthin. Local chap. Joined the King because he reckoned he'd get help in a land dispute with his neighbour. Don't trust them an inch. If Warwick offers him a better deal he'll change sides.'

'Still. We do have the cannon.'

'Oh, yes. We have the cannon.'

It began to rain again.

It was all over by four'o clock. Peter and I had a good view of it and what we couldn't see we pieced together later.

First, the bishops rode back at about one o'clock, and since there was no reaction we supposed rightly that they had failed in their mission. Then Peter started hollering and shouting, 'Kick it, you stupid bastard, pass, pass the ball. Oh, he's lost it, the silly fucker . . .' and a lot more of the same and I could feel his hands tugging at mine so he wrenched my back into the trunk of the apple tree then gave my shins a jolt as he tried to mime kicking with his feet. I truly thought the battle had started, that the Yorkists had somehow got behind the King's lines and were rampaging along the river bank behind us, but, no, it was the footballers. I have to tell you, Mah-Lo, many Inglysshemen, and some of their women too, take these games very seriously indeed.

Then: 'Oh, no, the bastards, what are they doing?'

'You tell me.'

'The King's rearguard are seeing them off. They've – I do not believe it – they've taken their ball from them . . . They're all going home! They can't believe it's all over . . . But it is, for now.'

And he went on shouting and swearing about it so I wasn't able to tell him what was happening in front.

First there was another blast of trumpet calls, then the Yorkists below began to move forward. The man called Justin and our popinjay trotted off through the rain, which was now coming down like rods or the lances of the advancing army. I could see them moving about the cannon, and even how they were blowing on the fuse, trying to get a spark going, and indeed there was a puff of smoke and a glimmer of a flame, but instead of a bang a sound like nothing so much as a loud fart. The ball almost rolled out of the muzzle, trundled a few yards down the slope before it stopped and sank into the mud a clear hundred yards in front of the Yorkists. They gave a great cheer and quickened their movement up the slope as fast as the mud and rain would let them. Which was not very fast.

Going uphill, through the mud, the horses could not make it, not with the weight of their own armour as well as their riders'. The knights dismounted, or slid off their high-pommelled saddles, and waded up the hill with their men. They were a strange sight, like giant mechanical dolls such as I've seen at Byzantium. On their helmets they had huge crests in the forms of animals' and monsters' heads, trees, eagles with spread wings, castles, ships, even, giving them two or three feet more in height over the rest. If they stumbled and fell it took four men to get them up again, yet few were hurt. A well-placed arrow might find the chain-mail in their crotches, or a joint in their armour, but otherwise their plate, rounded and pointed, never presenting a flat face, turned the missiles.

And, of course, when they finally got amongst the ranks of the enemy, if they ever did, they were ruthless executioners of everything that came their way, smashing all the common soldiers in their slighter armour, with huge blows from maces, axes, or broadswords four feet long, which inflicted terrible wounds, crushing skulls, slicing through shoulders into ribcages, causing blood to fountain up everywhere and severing arms thrown up in supplication.

Below me, the fight was even since the cannon were useless in the rain: the Yorkists had more men, but the King's side had that hill, which on account of the thick, greasy mud was even more of an advantage than ever.

It was a different story, however, on the eastern side of the field where the marsh and brook were. Here, the advance was held up by the waterlogged ground; here, too, the lords and knights had to get off their horses, which could carry them no longer, and wade with their men towards the rampart and the stakes. As they came they faced salvo after salvo of arrows from those wicked longbows and men began to fall. And right in the middle and at the front, with arrows bouncing off his shield, waving a huge sword and shouting at his men to follow him was an awesome figure of a man. Somehow I knew who he was, even at that distance. Something in the way he held himself, something about the way he flourished that sword made me certain I had seen him before: Eddie March? Maybe.

The cannons had failed but the longbows, the clinging mud and the rain were doing their work. It looked for a few minutes as if the Yorkists were not going to make it to the ramparts and certainly not over them, not for as long as the bowmen had arrows to shoot, but then it all went wrong for Stafford, Duke of Buckingham and the King.

The line between the bowmen facing March and the cannon just below me was held by a thousand or more wearing that black stick badge, Lord Grey of Ruthin's men. Hardly any arrows had been fired from this sector and as the first Yorkists, led by a lord in full armour, tramping and clanking up the hill, reached the rampart, Lord Grey's men leant over it and helped him across!

Well, that was that. Grey's men turned themselves round, save those who continued to help the Yorkists, who were soon flooding through the gap and fanning out to the left and the right on our side of the fortifications. The King's men realised they were beaten and ran for it round the ridge and back to the Nene.

Now it was Peter's turn to tell me what was happening.

'Oh, the poor buggers,' he exclaimed. 'They can't get across the ford – the river's too full and fast and the bridge is too narrow. They're cutting them up like – like – so many bushels of rye in July. Ugh! Blood everywhere. The river's running with blood. It's a shambles. I can see the Duke. Stafford. Duke of Buckingham. He's trying to rally them, make them turn and fight. Oh, no. He's down. Oh, the poor sod. His standard's down too. There's about six men hacking at him. He doesn't stand a chance. Oh, that's it. They've got his head off, stuck it on a lance. Jesus, there goes the King. Ducking and weaving like a chased fox, heading for the bridge. There's men of his letting him through. He'll get away. Yes, he will. Oh, no, he won't. He's run up against an archer. Drawing his bow at him. Ooops, that's it, the Yorkists have got him, they're taking him back to his tent . . . Well, at least they haven't cut his head off. Yet.'

At this moment a Yorkist knight came puffing up on to the crown of the hill and, seeing us and our predicament, assumed we must be enemies of the King and therefore friends of York, so cut us free.

He stood beside us as we rubbed our chafed wrists and ankles and, indeed, supported me for a minute or so, since my knees were buckling under me. We told him we hadn't eaten for twenty-four hours save a crust of bread, so he scouted about a bit and came back with bread and cheese and a canister of milk. Nice lad, for all that the surcoat over his breastplate was splashed with blood, not his own.

Now there was a sudden stillness over all the field for in the entrance of his tent stood King Henry, lean and gangly, pale, his head shaking and his fingers twining in and out in front of him as, no doubt, he considered, as best his fevered mind would allow, how to behave. Should he fall on his knees and beg for his life?

But no. It was the Yorkists who knelt, and such was the silence that even at that distance one felt one could hear the creak and clang of their jointed armour.

'Odd behaviour for the winners,' I muttered.

First they unbolted their visors and lifted off their plumed and absurdly crested helmets so when they now stood I could clearly discern the one I knew: Eddie March, yes, it was he, his light brown hair darkened with sweat, his face still red from the heat inside the helmet and the effort of fighting while shut inside a hundredweight or so of metal. The heraldic devices on his shield were similar to the ones on the King's banner: gold lions on red, quartered with silver lily flowers on blue. I wondered if there was some magic in this, or calculated insult, but forgot to ask about it until the reason for it became obvious.

On this occasion, before I could give the matter any thought, Warwick, dark, big, handsome, a man in his prime in contrast to Eddie, who was not yet eighteen, having made the obeisance due to the man who was still king, the Lord's Anointed, as they said, threw back his head and bellowed like a bull: 'So where's the fucking Queen, then? And the bastard they call the Prince of Wales?'

At this point Ali, whose speech had been getting slower and slower, yawned and fell silent. The rain had begun to ease as dusk gathered; the Burmese returned from the bushes and leapt into his lap. He tickled her under the chin.

I heard a doorlatch click and looked across the pool and into the verandah. His two wives, veiled in muslin but as lovely with rounded breasts and slim waists as their aunt, were coming towards us.

'Come back tomorrow, dear Mah-Lo,' said Ali, 'and we'll hear what had been happening to Uma.'

PART IV

CHAPTER

THIRTY-EIGHT

I create something of a stir as I walk through the countryside in my robes, for most people know and venerate the idol whose raiment I have assumed. 'Venerate' is not the right word, for she is more than a goddess, the mother of god, she is a familiar, a friend. There is a world of difference, I soon discover, between the way the dignitaries of the Church approach their icons and that pursued by the common sort. The former make obeisances, offer formal prayers, incense, magnificent jewellery, much of it real, and precious metals. Thus they hope to make these images remote and unapproachable, objects of awe, inspiring fear, even. Through these means the images become legitimators of their own authority and rule, justifications for the taxes and tithes they impose on the poor.

The latter, however, in spite of all this, endeavour to keep in their hearts the particularity of their most local image of the mother and therefore the particularity of the mother herself. The Virgin of Coventry is not the same as the Virgin of Nottingham or Walsingham: she is theirs alone, and no one else's, someone they recognise, can talk to and confide in, adore rather than worship, and who may be capricious, unreliable, but is part of their lives, is the reason why their crops grow, their wives are fertile and, when the time comes, their deaths repose in her arms.

And so, when they see her walking down the lanes, across the hills, on the banks of the river, through their fields and villages, wearing her high gold crown, her blue mantle, her black dress and the jewelled accoutrements of her goddesshood, they welcome her, with some solemnity, some awe, but mostly with a childlike desire to please her . . . and a childlike faith that she will sort out whatever problems are pressing them at this moment. In all this they share with the people of our own country a genuine religion unmediated by the contrivances of the bosses.

For my part I am, at this time, in a dazed and confused state of mind. Weeks of torture followed by months of deprivation of everything but life itself and the determination to live have left me weak in mind and body. I seem to float slowly but almost effortlessly across the ground, I hear a voice chanting in high, flute-like registers songs of love and gratitude to Parvati and hardly dare believe, it is so beautiful, that it is mine. The villagers strew cherry- and apple-blossom petals in my path and moan with pleasure when I solemnly sway and turn and let them see my golden slippers as I dance to their wailing pipes, drums and tambourines, or signal the way to heaven with my twisting arms.

They feed me too: on cream and cheeses as the meadows fill with grass again; on last year's honeycomb, on fish, on bread, butter, coddled eggs and, as the month turns, waxy beans from wool-lined pods then peas, and salads made from sorrel shoots and hawthorn buds. And they are not surprised when I refuse the flesh of newborn lambs, rabbits, hens or pigeons.

I never outstay my welcome – or, rather, I never stay in one place long enough for the magic to wear off, in case what are human and woman in me become more evident than the goddess. And while their faith remains I can perform miracles. Old women on their death-beds rise up . . . or, if they do not, they sink into sweet, easy sleep with soft smiles on their faces; a young child, who in all his seven years has never said a word but grunts and mews, says the Hail Mary before lapsing back into meaningless splutters – or so his grandma tells us all; a man who fell out of an apple tree at harvest time and has not walked since hops out of bed to get a better view of me as I pass; and a pony that was almost lame walks almost straight when I ride on her back.

And through all this I prosper. The flesh gathers in my breasts and buttocks again . . .

At this point Uma leant back in her chair and gave her breasts, beneath her bolero, flame-coloured today, a proud and joyful shake. I have to remind myself that the mature lady who is talking to us was once the winsome creature, still in that borderline country between late girl and full woman, she is telling us about.

. . . my skin regains its creamy fresh smoothness, the shadows of pain and loss that lay round my eyes recede. I revel in the return of spring and summer, the heaped-up snow of hawthorn smelling like the cunts of virgins just at the moment when they take their first cocks between their lips, the drifts of parsleys and chervils beneath them, Solomon's seal with its white waxy testicles dangling below its fleshy leaves, then later the dog-roses, honeysuckles, and tall stands of foxgloves, meadows sheeted with golden buttercups . . .

Why are you looking so bored? You have heard all this before from Ali? I am sure he cannot speak of it all with the knowledge I have, or bring to it the love I felt . . . these northern springs. We have the glory of our gardens, fields and forests, but they do not change in the same way with the turn of the year, it is not the same glory. Grander perhaps, but not the same. You were not bored? The imagery I employed to describe the hawthorn smell? Well. Well. Take me as you find me. Never mind. I'll push on. Where was I? Getting better . . .

Yes, indeed. By the middle of the year, when the villagers are partying beside their midsummer bonfires, when the hay is cut and the wheat beginning to yellow and the rye is five feet tall and, when the breezes breathe across it, shot with blue like watered silk, and behind every hedge and in every woodland clearing boys have their hands on young girls' breasts or under their bums, and the girls wind their thighs around the young boys' hips and cling to their necks with arms like the boughs of beech trees or poplars and the swallows and white-rumped martins swoop along the rain puddles skimming the water-skin for drink and gnats' eggs, I grow tired of my Virgin's garb, the adulation of the mostly old and feeble that goes with it, and the awed respect of the men I meet. And, anyway, I am bursting out of it as my body returns to its usual shape. It's time to seek a new persona. And maybe Eddie March as well.

I have been of two minds about where to head. Some days I have been pulled to the south by a longing for Eddie, on others I have headed north and west knowing that in that direction lay the place where Prince Harihara's lost brother might be found and to find him might well mean reunion with Ali and the rest. Anyway, I am somewhere towards the north-west of the country, not far I think from the borderlands between

Ingerlond and Gwalia, of which more later, when, in a fertile undulating plain of forest and farmland laced with small rivers, with a castle in the distance on a low hill called Malpas, I spy a young knight pricking down the winding track on the back of a very big orange-coloured gelding. And, to be frank, I feel a sudden urge to have this lad as a surrogate for Eddie. I also have at the back of my mind the thought that if I can get him to get his kit off and maybe take a nap, I might get myself a new disguise.

He's moving slowly, his horse barely ambling, and from the slight rise I am on I can see that shortly he will pass by a mill-pond with a grassy sward starred with daisies on its bank. The mill itself is a ruin, surrounded by willows and rushes and yellow flowers they call flags growing out of the mud around it. Such is the lawlessness of these times many such places set apart from villages, towns or castles have been plundered by wandering bands of robbers, the inmates killed, their gold stolen and often their dwellings fired. Certainly a melancholy that should have served as a warning hangs over the scene, in spite of the healthy-looking sedge and the singing birds.

Moving swiftly, despite flowering brambles and thickets of dogwood, I get to the sward ahead of him and quickly divest myself of my Virgin's robes, crown and all, so that when he comes on to the grass, there I am, sitting beneath a willow, entirely as nature made me, with my knees pulled up and my arms hooked round them, apparently watching the emerald and sapphire dragonflies cruising and copulating over the lotus pads, whose flowers are just on the point of bursting from their glans-shaped cases.

'Oh, shit,' he says, then, 'Holy Mary Mother of God.'

Come on, I think. You cannot be serious. But no, he is not, the statement was an oath not a guess as to my identity. He swung a leg over his pommel and dropped to the ground.

'You're going to disappear, aren't you?' he said. 'Or turn into a wicked old crone? They always do. In the stories.'

Now I can see him I feel a touch disappointed. He's no more than fourteen, and rather plump, with blond almost white hair and a haze of yellow on his upper lip.

'Who?' I ask, still sitting, looking up at him over my shoulder.

'The naked ladies' knights come across when they're out questing.'

'Are you a knight? Are you questing?'

'Not a knight. Chaps don't get to be knights until they've done some deed of derring-do. That's in the stories. In real life it's more a case of having forty quid a year and being called to be in Parliament.'

His voice still flukes up every now and then – not a promising sign.

A moment passes. I straighten my knees, lean back on my elbows, let him see my tits. 'I'm not going to disappear. I'm not going to change into anything. I'm not even going to bite. Not hard anyway.' And I shake my hair, now growing back and glossy black again. 'Do you think you could move your horse off a bit? It's attracting a rather nasty sort of fly.'

He looks at me, looks at his horse, whose tail is slashing the air behind him and whose withers shudder spasmodically to shift the brutes and, 'Come on, Dobs,' he says, and leads him away to the other side of the lawn where he loops the reins around an alder branch. As he comes back he's already unlacing his jerkin. I stand and give him a hand. Also a full view of what I have on offer.

'This really is real, isn't it?'

'You bet.' And I fumble the buckle of his belt, which is heavy with his scabbarded sword.

'I'm John Coombe of Annesbury,' he says. 'What's your name?'

'You can call me Uma.'

Well, it still is quite small, long, thin, pointed, yet somehow fresh and unused, which is nice, standing up and pinging, and, of course, he's all over me before he's properly in, but at his age he's no shrinking violet and we get where I want to go second time round, and third too. Then I suggest we have a swim in the mill-pond because it's a hot sultry day and by now we are both very sweaty and smeared with misdirected semen. I stay near the edge, squelching the mud between my toes, and give myself a bit of a wash, then I tell him I bet he can't swim to the other side, having it in mind that while he's taking me up on this I can filch his clothes and his horse.

Now, what happens next is something I do not have in mind. I have no idea how treacherous these mill-ponds can be. You see, he can't swim, which I have not properly understood, he's just been wading about pretending to, and being the very young man he is, this is not something he is going to admit. So he wades off towards the other side. A shout, a cry, a gasp, a podgy white arm flailing amongst the lotuses which, even while we've been there, have opened their sixteen petals to welcome the light of their lord the sun into their fragrant hearts, and he's gone.

Sorry.

Still. I had just taken him to heaven and back, introduced him to the goddess within, in a way he would never have managed with the local girls, and, since he was a gentleman, probably saved him from being hacked up by some grown man with an axe. Lots of people get a far worse deal out of life.

His clothes are not at all a bad fit, and his buttercup-coloured horse is quite happy to take me on board. Together, horse and I, we set off towards Malpas Castle. We have not gone far when, rounding a bend, we come upon what looks like a robbery.

CHAPTER

THIRTY-NINE

C learly this is to be a day of chance meetings. Well, every day is, is it not? But meetings of some significance are rarer. What is happening is this. Within a group of four or five people a thin, pale man with a straggly black moustache and a black felt hat with a large brim is pulling his way through a large leather sack with a drawstring, sorting the contents into two heaps – what he wants to keep and what he does not want to keep. On the keep side is a fair amount of good-quality jewellery and clothes made from expensive stuffs, such as velvet, fine cotton and silk, while on the other side go toiletries, wool, leather, gaberdine and so forth. He is watched by a pale, tired-looking woman, basically handsome but now in a real cow of a rage, dressed in crimson velvet riding gear with gold embroidery, and very fine soft-leather boots. Her blonde hair is pulled up but coming adrift from beneath a velvet cap with a feather. As I come on to the scene she has a riding crop with which she is attempting to slash the pale thin man, but a fat man, his companion, is contriving to hold her back. The final character in the scene is a small boy of about seven years old who is screaming his head off.

I know them all.

The pale man is John Clegger, the fat man is Will Bent, the woman is the Queen and the screaming child is her son, if not her husband's, Edward, Prince of Wales. How did I know who they were? Clearly you have not been paying attention. I came across them all in Coventry, on the day I was taken, and at my trial.

But I, of course, am not Uma the Witch, but John Coombe of Annesbury, and my horse, Dobs, is not only an unusual yellow in colour but very big. I think they are all more frightened of the horse than of me, although I have managed to get poor John Coombe's sword out of its scabbard and am waving it, as best I can, over them all. I manage to give Clegger a full knock with the flat of it over his ear, which nearly takes off his head and sends him sprawling into the ditch. Yet he gets out of it and is soon running and stumbling through the corn on the other side. Will Bent makes off on the other side.

Madam, of course, since she is a queen, has forgotten me, doesn't know me from Adam. Or Eve. She collects herself, as a queen should, gets back her breath, boxes her son's ear, which he correctly takes as a request to stop his row, and does so, apart from an irritating snivel. Then she draws herself to her full height and gives me a most severe look.

I get the message and get down off Dobs' back.

'Young man, your manners are despicable. Do you not know who I am? Of course you do.'

What am I meant to do? Bow? Fall on my knees? Knock my head on the ground?

I give her a nod and say, 'Glad to have been of service, ma'am,' before I begin to lead Dobs away. Then I stop, gather the reins in my hand, and grasp the pommel, which I can only just reach, as if intending to mount again.

'Stop. What is your name?'

'John Coombe,' I say, remembering.

'Master Coombe, you will take me to Denbigh. In Wales. It lies some thirty miles or so away to the west. I have friends there who will pay you well. Your horse looks big and strong. I will ride in front of you, my son will ride behind you. But first, please pick up the belongings of mine these ruffians, who were meant to be looking after me, were attempting to steal.'

I think about it for a moment. I have a maxim in life that has always, or almost always, stood me in good stead. You may, Mah-Lo, be able to guess what it is. Quite simply – say yes. Say yes to everything that comes along. I think my tale so far demonstrates how well I follow this maxim. So, although I have no reason to like this woman, or her brat of a son, I say yes. The prospect of payment helps, of course. I have already established that the total of

John Coombe's readily negotiable wealth is a sixpenny piece and two farthings.

'All right,' I say, 'but your son can pick up your things.'

She gives that some thought. Then: 'Edward? Do what the young man says.'

I manage to make a cushion from the less expensive of her clothes and strap it on Dobs' crupper. I then give Madam a bunk-up. She sits pertly, in the side-saddle position, and gets a good grip on Dobs' yellow mane. I get up behind her. Then I get off again because Edward can't climb up on his own. I hoist him on to Dobs' back behind the saddle. It's impossible now for me to get between them. I get down again, lift Edward down, pick up her sack, tie it behind the saddle, put Edward on top of it and get up again. We're off.

After five minutes she begins to talk.

'When we heard that vile bastard Warwick was on his way north, Buckingham said it would be best if the King went with him and the army while I and Edward went the other way. That way, if things went badly, they wouldn't get us all in the same net. Not that we expected any such thing. Not only are right and God on our side, we had six very big cannons. God tends to side with the big guns.' We jog on. 'So I went north to Eccleshall, and waited for news. Lord Lovell was the first with them and told us how a rainstorm had rendered the cannons useless, how our army had been beaten, Buckingham killed, and the King taken. So I took horse and, with my two stewards and my son, set off for Denbigh. At Malpas more news reached us. York, the most evil-minded sod of a bastard of the lot of them, was on his way from Ireland and would be made king. Those cretins Clegger and Bent decided to make the best of what now seemed a bad situation by robbing me. And you turned up.'

Not a word of thanks.

We jog . . . on and on.

I am apprehensive that she will penetrate my disguise. Of course she does. As soon as we have crossed the first brow of a hill and are descending on the further side, Dobs takes it into his head to break into a slow gallop or canter. I am thrown forward. To avoid falling over the horse's ears the Queen forces herself to lean backwards. I let go of the reins and clutch her waist, which is small but strong. Behind us the Prince screams again. Once we are on the

level, his mother turns her head a little and brings her cheek close
to mine.

'I think, mistress, we should change places.'

I assume my gruffest voice. 'Why should we do that?'

'Because you are a woman. I felt your breasts against my back. And
because you do not seem to be properly in control of this beast. Probably,
being of low birth, you do not have the art. Anyway, I am taller than you
and will be able to see better where we are going than you can with me
in front of you.'

So we go through the whole rigmarole again, including, of course,
getting the Prince down and up again.

We spend the night in a tiny Welsh inn, three rooms, of which only
one is made available to us.

Her Majesty allows me to share it with her and her son, only requiring
me to leave the room when she wants to pee in the bucket provided.

'A commoner,' she says, 'should not see her queen pissing.'

My lowly rank does not preclude her from asking me to pick up the
tab. Since Her Majesty has insisted that she and the lad should dine off
three brace of skylarks and a couple of quail grilled on skewers over
a charcoal fire with strawberries and cream to follow, and a breakfast
of hot milk, new-baked wheaten bread and half a dozen coddled
eggs, we are lucky that the woman who runs the place (she wears a
shawl and a tall conical black hat) professes herself satisfied, just, with
sixpence-halfpenny.

I thus learn two important lessons about the rich and powerful.
They become rich by never spending their own money. They become
powerful by having horses to ride and knowing how to do it.

On the evening of the second day we arrive at Denbigh Castle in
the principality of Gwalia or Wales. This is a wild and inhospitable
land, peopled with savages much like our mountain and forest tribes.
It lies along the western borders of Ingerlond. Denbigh itself is close to
Ingerlond and the country is not much different, though bleak, featureless
hills with impenetrable woodland in the valleys lie to the west. When
we arrive we find Denbigh, or Dinbych, as the Welsh say, to be a small
town nestling in the shade of a large castle. The outer wall was a mile
in circumference, enclosing the town, with a large, almost palatial keep
set in an inner area laid out to terraced gardens. It is occupied by a
Welshman, a sort of chieftain, called Owen ap Maredudd ap Tewdyr.

I think 'ap' must mean 'son of'.

Forgive me. I have to weep when I think of Owen.

Ah . . . Hah!

He was six feet tall, had broad shoulders, strong arms, oh, very strong, and legs like trees. His chest was deep and formed like a barrel or a bell. His hair was white, cut short, but with one black lock or streak in the middle. His brows were still for the most part black. His face was coppery red and his hands too, but his body white as snow. His mouth was broad, and small-toothed, his breath sweet like well-water or milk . . . All, in their way, marvels, for he was an old man, sixty years old.

Well, well. He welcomes us, he and his children and his children's children, for he is by family tradition and his own history a supporter of the King and Queen's cause. There are good reasons for this, which he tells me when I catechise him about it all.

We are in bed at the time. We spend a lot of time in bed after the Queen has gone to Scotland to raise a new army and I have been there long enough to feel I can express my resentment, well, jealousy, really, of the beautiful girl whose portrait hangs on the wall by the door.

'Ah, me,' he says, in that deep voice of his. Even when he speaks softly it resonates in my ear, which is pressed on the white hairs in the middle of his chest. 'She was the first love of my life. A king's daughter and the wife of a king.'

'Wife? You are not a king, are you?'

He laughs. 'Who knows what a king is? I am a king in everything but name. She was, look you, the daughter of the mad old King of France and after the big battle there, on St Crispin's Day – I was there, though I was only fifteen years old – the Inglysshe King married her, though she herself was a year younger than I.'

'Which king was that?'

'Henry, though Harry was what he liked to be called.'

I frown, trying to work it all out. He senses my puzzlement.

'That's right,' he says. 'The father of the present King.'

'So she, your lover, was his mother. The mother of the present King?'

'That's right too. But King Harry died when she was just twenty-one. Now I had been a page in the King's court, and was by then a squire in her service.'

'And you fell in love?'

'That's right. Of course, they didn't like it one bit. I even went to prison for her after the birth of our son Edmund but in the end they let it stand, let us live as man and wife, so long as we kept out of the way of things. You see, in some ways they were grateful to have the Queen off their hands. She was French, the old wars had started again, as the child king's mother she might have interfered, insisted on being part of the regency, messed up the war effort . . .'

'But instead you brought her here and lived happily ever after.'

He hears the envy in my voice.

'No. We remained in the south, in or near London, mostly at the palace of Waltham where I was master of her wardrobe. As a mother she continued to look after her son, the King, as well as the children we had together, so we had to stay down there.'

'There were more children?'

'Three more.'

'And then she died. In childbirth?'

'No. Of a long and painful illness. The one with claws. Like a crab's.'

'I can cure it. When was that?'

'Twenty . . . twenty-three years ago.'

I take heart from that hesitation. At least he isn't counting the days.

He sighs a little, then runs his hand through my hair while the other strengthens its clasp round my back, pushing my breasts into his midriff. He answers my questions before I have to ask them.

'You are every bit as lovely as she was. But in a very different way.'

Well, I can see that. The lady in the portrait is fair-skinned, though dark-haired. Later, on my own, I look into her hazel eyes, and kiss her rosebud lips. She was all right, you know? But different.

How does all this begin? You mean this passion shared with Owen ap Maredudd ap Tewdyr?

When we arrive, the Queen, the Prince and I, through the gates of that massive long wall, and ride Dobs up the gravel paths between rosebeds filled with blooms, and past ponds where carp drift in the summer heat, Owen is already there, beneath the keep's portcullis, with his family about him to welcome us. His son Edmund died some four years previously but his daughter-in-law is there with their son Henry, a three-year-old who never knew his father. This son is already an earl, the Earl of Richmond, a title granted his commoner father since his wife was the great granddaughter of John of Gaunt by his third wife. There was, therefore, a connection by blood to the royal family, as well as that by marriage through Katherine of Valois, Henry the Fifth's queen.

This little boy is a serious soul, whom I get to know well in the next few months. He plays most seriously and is advanced for his age in manner and speech. He also has a certain low cunning, playing off one grown-up against another. His grandfather, my Owen ap Tewdyr, which the English call Tudor, does not much like him, detecting a meanness of nature foreign to the old man's disposition, but says he will go far. Maybe. To go far in Ingerlond, if you are a man, requires only that you should be strong, violent by nature and cruel. This Henry so far displays none of these, save perhaps cruelty, but even then only when it serves his ends. But, as I said, he is cunning.

I'm sorry. You ask how it all begins between me and my Owen. Simple enough. A day soon dawns when it is decided the Queen should go to Scotland whose queen is an old friend and may help her to raise money and an army. While they are all seeing her off I nip upstairs, take off my man's clothes and get into his bed. Where, an hour or so later, he finds me.

There. That is quite enough for now. Much was happening in the south, which Ali knows far more about than I do. I'll leave him to take up the tale.

CHAPTER

FORTY

A ctually not. More letters from Prince Harihara to his illustrious cousin, written out in Chamberlain Anish's neat hand, were left out for my perusal.

Dear Cousin

We have been relieved at last, taken out of our palace/prison, and set free. Wonderful! Let me tell you how it happened while it is fresh in my mind. You will remember, if you ever got the letter, that we were still in the Tower, though London was in the hands of the Yorkists, that the main Yorkist army had marched north under Warwick, Fauconberg and March, leaving two thousand or so under Lord Salisbury, Warwick's father. For three weeks they laid siege to the Tower but without a great deal of effort, being prepared to starve us out. Meanwhile our host, the irascible Lord Scales, continued to hurl cannonballs amongst the houses his guns could reach, to the annoyance and discomfort of the burghers who owned and lived in them.

He boasted loudly that no fire was returned, because if it had been he would have cannonballed the guns aimed at him. But in this he had made one foolish miscalculation: all his guns were sited in the towers that overlooked the city from which he might expect any attack to come. Lord Salisbury, after a fortnight or so, perhaps during which he ascertained that this was indeed so, moved five large cannon across the bridge (the move necessitated the destruction of a row of shops) on to the south bank and thence downriver so they could fire across at the riverside walls from a mere two hundred paces and without any danger to themselves – the guns in the Tower were so securely emplaced they could not be easily or quickly moved.

A lesson for us here – again obvious in its way, but the sort of thing one does not think of until too late: one's guns need protection from the enemy's, but the protection should not be such as to render their redeployment difficult or impossible.

For three days they pounded the riverside walls, which soon began to tumble as they had not been designed to withstand any sort of punishment, and by the fourth day the south wall of the inner keep was exposed. We were now in some danger and certainly suffered severe discomfort from dust, falling masonry and noise. It was not long before the lords who, as I told you in my last, had come with their families for shelter from the Yorkists, now urged Lord Scales to surrender. Since, as I have said, we were also running short of food, this he felt constrained to do, and yesterday evening it was proposed between heralds chosen by each side that this morning there should be a formal handing over of the keys of the great gate. Our chief concern now is that Lord Salisbury will remember and recognise us from our brief sojourn in Calais nearly seven months ago and thus identify us as people sympathetic to the Yorkist cause.

At nightfall, after this had been arranged, Anish and I came upon Sergeant Bardolph Earwicca in the Tower Gardens, drunk and maudlin: his fear was that, having merely done his duty for the King and the King's man, by which he meant Lord Scales, he would now be out of a job, that another, more solidly inclined towards the Yorkists, would be given his place as Under-Master-Sergeant-of-Ordnance, and he would end up begging on the streets. Where, if his identity and previous occupation were revealed, he would probably be torn to pieces as the main instrument of the bombardment of the town. Anish, ever quick to see an opportunity, immediately promised him employment in Vijayanagara if he had no objection to travelling some distance. He had no objection for he had lost his wife and three children to the most recent outbreak of plague and was on his own, at which he became maudlin again and began to sob for the loss of the people he referred to as his 'fucking loved ones'.

That he was right to fear the citizens was vindicated, just at that very moment. We heard shouts of anger, the clash of weapons, a howl of rage. Then, over the battered ruins of the riverside fortification, was thrown a head. Ghastly and bleeding though it was, twisted into a grimace of fury and fear, we recognised the face and beard of Lord Scales. Advised of the hatred the people of London now bore him he had attempted to row himself in a skiff upriver to Westminster Abbey where he hoped to achieve sanctuary. Apparently, under certain complicated rules compounded by these people's superstitious beliefs regarding holy places, even convicted criminals can escape arrest by entering the chancel of a church. Once inside, their bodies are judged to be inviolate.

Anyway, sundry watermen of the Thames, men whose trade it is to ferry people and goods both across and up and down the stream, recognised him and guessed his plan. They dragged him from his tiny boat, took him to the steps of what is called the Traitors' Gate, for through it traitors are brought to the Tower by boat for execution, and there stabbed and beat him to death before chopping off his head.

I am not sorry he has gone, though I would not have wished him so harsh a departure.

Next day, the eighteenth of July, by their reckoning, Shiva knows what by ours, and we are back in Alderman Dawtrey's house on the corner of the street they call East Cheap. Now that Lord Scales has gone, the Yorkists here are in control and we are identified with the Yorkists, the vintner and his emotional wife are all over us, insisting we should stay until we can find lodgings of our own. They have also kept safe the few goods we had left unsold, and we still have a fair quantity of gold and jewellery hidden about us, so one way and another our fortunes are well mended.

But there is more than this to tell you. Yesterday, apparently, though no one told us and we were suffering for most of the time from the last hours of the bombardment of the Tower, the Yorkist army returned, having won a great victory over the

Queen's army at a town called Northampton, where they also took the King prisoner. The King has been lodged in the Bishop's Palace close to Baynard's Castle, which is where the Yorkists stay, a fortification close to Lud's Gate, now a palace. The King, who is frequently disturbed in his head, is quite content to be guided by the Yorkist lords.

All that now remains is for the Duke of York to return from Ireland and assume the reins of government in the name of the King, but in effect on his own account. The thing is, cousin, and I may have mentioned this before, these people have an irrational reverence for a crowned and anointed king, believing superstitiously that to do one harm is to invite the curse of their god. So, although this king is the grandson of a usurper who arranged, so everyone agrees, the death of *his* rightful king, nevertheless, this one, old before his time and subject to grievous fits of madness, is still reckoned to be touched with a sort of holiness, a sanctity.

Finally, a wonderful piece of good fortune: Ali ben Quatar Mayeen was with this Yorkist host, in the company of a Franciscan brother called Peter Marcus, an intelligent and open-minded person for an Ingerlonder. Ali still has with him the two *kurundam* crystals I entrusted to him. I'm not sure of what use they are since they are far too valuable to be sold or bartered, but no doubt their time will come. At all events it's good to have him with us again and he seems to be none the worse for his adventures.

The Buddhist monk who left Gové with us seems to have disappeared, as has the fakir. Well, they were just hangers-on, but I feel a certain responsibility for them and I don't like to think of them wandering about this barbarous island on their own.

News just in. These wars are not over yet. The Queen escaped after Northampton and is rumoured to be in Scotland raising an army. Even in Ingerlond she still has many adherents amongst the nobility. They fear to lose the huge gains in land, fortune and position they made under her protection, and also they fear the revenge of Yorkists whose families have suffered at their hands. No doubt we shall see more military activity and learn more from it.

The worst is that we have moved no nearer to finding my brother Jehani, though Brother Peter thinks he may have heard of a person answering his description. However, he advises caution in our attempt to find him. He is almost certainly in the company and under the protection of a secret group called the Brothers of the Free Spirit who are known to preach a free society and look towards a heavenly city on earth where all are free, well fed, equal and happy. Sounds like Vijayanagara. However, to hold to such beliefs is considered heresy and sedition and punishable by a protracted and painful death.

There is a ship in the port of London, chartered by the mercers and bound for Jezair, which the Ingerlonders call Alger, on the north coast of Africa. Alderman Dawtrey has arranged for the master to take this letter thus far. Well, it's a step in the right direction, and who knows?, it might get through to you.

Your affectionate cousin and servant

Prince Harihara Raya Kurteishi

Chapter

Forty-One

D ear Cousin

What joy, what bliss! Through what adventures and vicissitudes I suppose we shall never know your letter, sent to me in answer to the one I sent to you from Calais nine months ago, has reached me. It was handed to me this morning by the mate of a cog that had just come in with barrels of a drink they call sack from Jerez in Spain, now in the hands of the Christians but still trading with the Arab port of Motril south of Granada. It has done our hearts immense good to know that four months ago at any rate all was well with you and the City of Victory, that indeed your new Bedu cavalry have had some success over the squadrons of the Bahmani sultans. We are glad, too, to learn that the extensive building programme you had planned before we left is now in hand and going well, and that the dispute with medical practitioners over free public health care has been resolved. Enlightened self-interest usually works.

Since my first letter got through to you I must now assume that the later ones will do so too, so I shall not bore you with a recapitulation of these (though I shall ask Anish to provide a brief summary, just in case) but will instead bring you up to date with what has happened since I wrote to you a month after the summer solstice.

Well, the answer for the first couple of months is – not a lot.

The seventh, eighth and ninth months would undoubtedly, in this generally rainsoaked and wretched island, be the best for martial enterprises, since the sun achieves a certain warmth and, even after rain, dries the ground quite quickly. However, there is an abundance of new food in the land, first pulses and roots, then grain and fruit, and fodder for animals and the common people are loath to turn out for their lords and indeed many lords are loath to ask them to.

The reason is clear once you realise that these three months provide, in a sudden rich harvest, the food off which the whole nation will feed for the rest of the year, and what is left ungathered will rot in the fields, creating shortages in the coming winter. So although we received a steady trickle of news that the Queen was first in Scotland and then in the north of Ingerlond raising a large army, she made no move on us, and this perhaps because this army was a figment, an unborn entity, a series of promises which, now, in the month they call October, are about to be fulfilled.

Meanwhile, here in the south in London, not much has happened of importance either, until the last two weeks or so. The interim was filled with festivity and celebration on the part of Warwick, Fauconberg, Salisbury, March and the rest, much time spent in their absurd tournaments and even more in their absurd mode of hunting, which, as Ali warned us, really does consist of pursuing animals – yes, even foxes – across the countryside on horseback with dogs! When I suggested to these magnates that a more civilised way of proceeding would be to station themselves on the side of a valley with crossbows and have their followers drive previously corralled quarries in front of them within range of their engines, I was laughed at outright – even though I was prepared to use my crossbows to demonstrate what I meant! I know you disapprove of hunting of any sort but you must concede that my method is more civilised than that employed by these Inglysshe.

However, generally speaking we have been treated with courtesy by the Yorkists and allowed to rent a substantial dwelling in a street called Lombard Street (it takes its name from the Milanese merchants who have settled there), hire servants and so forth, and all with the money we can get from selling the precious stones we brought with us. Rubies and pearls are especially valued and sell for prices that would amaze you, especially the former. They have hardly seen true rubies before and cannot believe the brightness of their colour or their hardness. Indeed the King's crown was reputed to have one set in it, very large, which once belonged to the Black Prince, the great-great-grand-uncle of the present king. I was shown this 'ruby', a dull, brownish stone, almost certainly a garnet.

Where was I? Tournaments and hunting. And also a lot of dancing, something, would you believe?, the lords and ladies do together rather than watching trained professionals. The result is, as you would expect, a certain lewdness of behaviour that leads to worse, especially when it is compounded with the drinking of vast amounts of alcoholic beverages.

It has not all been pursuits of this sort. During this time the Yorkists, under Warwick, have consolidated their relationship with the City of London, giving the merchants more and more privileges and rights, restoring old ones taken by the Queen, and withdrawing those given, or rather sold, by her to the foreigners who trade here, especially the Germans of the Hanse.

But what of York? Well, nothing, not for three months. This great man, this magnate, this man who had ruled before as Protector during an earlier fit of madness suffered by the King and who, it was said, would be king himself, on whose behalf great men had stirred themselves and many small men have been slain or maimed, remained in Ireland. But a week ago he came at last and, with one throw of the dice, seems to have lost it all.

I have told you how much these superstitious people revere kingship, and what they call the Lord's Anointed. Well, Henry remains King Henry, and Richard Plantagenet remains merely Duke of York, however good his claim to be king. And duke he remains until he is anointed. Yet he came to London with trumpets before him, the sword of state unsheathed in front of him. This is a gigantic, ornamental affair of, again, mystical significance for these strange people. No one will deny, while barbarians exist, the necessity of swords, but to make a revered fetish out of such ugly things bespeaks psychopathology. Worst of all, banners were displayed with the lions and lily flowers that, undifferentiated with any other mark, are the King's alone.

Thereby he lost the support of half his followers or more, who, fearing the fires of everlasting torment, would no longer side with him. Indeed this whole business led to a near terminal falling out between York and Warwick . . .

At this point a page ended and I turned it over on to the pile of those I had already read. As I did so a splash of monsoon rain plopped on the corner furthest from me. I looked up. Ali had arrived by my side, was looking down at me with his one good eye gleaming in his destroyed face against a background of dragon eaves and purple sky. He was rubbing the swollen knuckles of his good hand against the cloth that covered his pigeon chest, while the claw of his left hand endeavoured to scrape bent nails through his ragged goatee beard.

'You've no idea,' he rasped, 'what October was like in Ingerlond.'

And he pulled up a cushioned chair and sat beside me, eye now almost sightless as it looked out across his garden, which seemed to burgeon even more beneath the evening downpour. He was high, high on bhang, I could smell it. He leant into the table between us and, taking a small hashish cake between his thumb and finger, popped it in his mouth. His eye glittered.

He turned over the page of Prince Harihara's dispatch that I had just read, swallowed, then wiped his mouth on the sleeve of his bad arm. Nodded to himself a little. 'Read it,' he said, 'aloud. I'd like to hear it all through again.' I picked up the next sheet and, returning to the Prince's account, did as he asked.

Warwick and his brother Thomas Neville were actually at our lodging in Lombard Street, buying pearls for his wife Anne. He had a jeweller with him who was picking out what he needed to make a coronet for the Countess, when a squire came banging through the doors demanding to see the Earl. York, he said, had arrived in Westminster, with a vast retinue, trumpeters and the offensive banners. Since it was known he had been at Abingdon, not far from Oxenford, only two nights earlier, he had not been expected before evening at the earliest.

Well, I was curious to know what this Duke of York, who had caused so much trouble, was like, so Anish and I, with Ali too, all bundled behind Warwick to Westminster Hall, at the other end of the track called Strand, a distance of a couple of miles or so, and got into Westminster Hall, where Parliament was met, just ahead of the Duke.

I think I told you in an earlier letter that I would explain what Parliament is when an appropriate time came, and this would seem to be it.

Parliament is a large gathering, first, of all of the lords and magnates of the realm, then of the knights of the shires, as they are called. These are landowners or -holders, often chosen by their neighbours, a certain number from each shire or county, and all having a fair amount of wealth, which expressed in terms of income is at least forty pounds a year. Such is the general poverty of the country compared with ours, the buying power of forty pounds is about the equivalent of what a good temple dancer might earn in Vijayanagara, or a holder of a market stall. Yet in Ingerlond it is thought of as a noteworthy fortune. Anyway, these people are gathered together usually once every year by the King to ratify whatever laws he wants to have passed, or taxes raised, and so on. It is rare that any objection is made to what the King wants since those who come have been summoned by the King himself and it all seems something of a waste of time. It dates back, I believe, to customs that were in force and meant something before the Norman invasion four hundred years ago, and was a sop to the Inglysshe sensibilities and traditions.

Anyway, Parliament usually assembles at Westminster, where the last but one Inglysshe king before the Normans had built a great hall and a big church, and was now in session, having been summoned under the seal of King Henry, once he had been brought down from Northampton. It had been summoned with the view of ratifying the Protectorship of York and the placement of Yorkist supporters in all the principal posts of government.

The hall has a throne at one end and many handsome windows down the sides. There is also a minstrels' gallery at the back above the large doors and it was there that we were allowed to sit with ambassadors from other lands. Trumpets sounded and in came York, his sword of state still carried in front of him, making his way through the crowd beneath us, straight up to the throne. He stood for a moment, turned, and put his hand on it. The gesture was clearly proprietorial and drew a sort of sigh and moan from all there.

This York, whom we were seeing at last and for the first time, was a big, proud man but already fifty years old or thereabouts, dark hair grizzled, broad-shouldered, large-chested with big hands and strong thighs. But his face was lined, even wrinkled, and his mouth wore an unchanging expression of dissatisfaction. One felt that here was a man capable of almost anything that would not injure his self-esteem to perform. And claiming the throne did not come under that heading.

Clearly he expected applause, acclamation. None came. After that first sigh, like wind through trees, there was silence, scarce broken by the jingle of a spur or a cough.

He took a deep breath. His eyes narrowed. 'Know ye all,' he announced, in a deep, resonant voice, 'I, as grandnephew of the usurped King Richard the Second and great grandson of Edward the Third, do challenge and claim the realm of Ingerlond. I propose to be crowned on All Hallows Day coming . . .'

'When?' I whispered to Ali.

'All Saints' Day, first of November, three weeks' time . . .'

He might have said more but at that moment a man in gold robes and a strange jewelled hat divided in two as if cloven with an axe, pushed up to York. This turned out to be his brother-in-law Thomas Bourchier, Archbishop of Canterbury.

'Don't you think, Richard, since we already have a king, and we have all, yourself included, made holy vows of allegiance to him, we should have a word with him first before we go through with this? See what he thinks about it?'

This drew a rustle of assent from Parliament.

'I know of no one in the realm who would not come more fitly to me than I to him,' said York. But he looked around and took in from the manner and expressions of those in front of him, that he had gone too far. 'Well, if that's what you want, take me to the King,' he added, and he marched out of the hall.

We followed as best we could but this time were left behind. But we were told of how King Henry, for once achieving some dignity, faced his cousin down, claiming he was king by right and law and the acclamation of the people, and reminding them all of their oaths of allegiance.

There seemed now to be no solution in sight. Henry was indeed king, though the grandson of a usurper, since he had been anointed, crowned. On the other side, York was descended from an older uncle of Richard than John of Gaunt, Duke of Lancaster, who was Henry's great-great-grandfather, though through that older uncle's daughter . . . It was all very complicated, as you see.

However, Warwick, who was astute and not as hotheaded as York, understood that the lords' and commons' feelings were with Henry, though not with his queen and government, and the upshot of it all, after a fortnight of wrangling, was that he was able to persuade York to accept for now the governance of the country as Protector but not as king, but with the provision that if Henry died first he, York, would succeed rather than Edward, Prince of Wales, the son of Queen Margaret and possibly of Henry too.

I realise now, dear cousin, that throughout these proceedings, which I have described to you, I have written of the lords and commons as if these were all the lords and commons. They were not. Many lords, many more than had been at the battle of Northampton, were in the north with the Queen and Prince, and most of the knights and common people of the north also sided with her. The Duke of Somerset, he whom we had met at Guisnes in the Pale of Calais, had returned to Exeter in the west and was raising an army too, and all her other supporters were now flocking to the north-east, to Northumberland on the Scottish borders, where she already had an army of twenty thousand. When she heard that her son had been disinherited she became mad with rage. And she is now moving south, encouraging her army to loot and sack all who live on land owned by the Yorkists.

Here in London Parliament has dispersed and most of York's potential army with it. It seems he has lost much support by aiming for the throne, and all fear the Queen. Only his most loyal friends, those who could never expect clemency from the Queen, remain. York says he will go north to fight her, but the opinion is that he will be lucky to raise an army half the size of hers.

Thus, through pride and overvaulting ambition, York has lost what he might have had and is like to lose much more. Some say, even his head.

Dear cousin, believe me, I shall keep you informed of the outcome as soon as it is known.

Your obedient and affectionate cousin,

Prince Harihara Raya Kurteishi

I drew breath at last and laid down the last page of Chamberlain Anish's neat, correct script.

'There,' I said. 'I must say I am all agog to hear what happened next.'

However, a gentle snore told me that Ali was less than eager and had at last succumbed to the blessed relief he sought from the pains and aches that came with the rain. I picked up the next page and began to read once more, silently, to myself.

CHAPTER

FORTY-TWO

D ear Cousin
A fortnight before the winter solstice we left London.
Having ascertained that the campaign would take place in
the north I decided that we might as well travel with the protection of the Yorkist army as near to Macclesfield Forest as possible
in an attempt to get to Jehani's hideout. Thus we would avoid
the dangers of highways now given over almost entirely to the
depredations of bands of brigands and outlaws.

The case was that, with these civil wars, lawlessness stalked
the countryside and, indeed, the smaller towns too. With two
monarchs in arms against each other, instead of doing their duty
and maintaining order and decency in their realm, lords and
lordlings were taking the opportunity to settle old feuds and
pursue rival claims for land by means of arms rather than recourse
to the law. At the best of times, though, recourse to the courts is
always a slow, protracted business in this country, relying not on
the wisdom of tried and disinterested judges but an endless parade
of lawyers loaded with piles of parchment, deeds, grants, reversals
and titles going back to the Conqueror and even beyond. The result
is, more often than not, that the disputed property is wasted in fees
before a court, also administered by lawyers, arrives at a decision.

A quicker settlement can be arrived at with a few discharges
from blunderbusses and beatings with clubs, and the consequence

is that if one is not directly robbed and murdered one may easily be caught up in the cross-fire between rival feuding parties.

So, on the ninth of the month they call the tenth, although it is actually the twelfth, we left by Lud's Gate, near the front of an army said to be ten thousand strong but known to be not much more than half that number, travelling at the speed of a team of oxen pulling a large cannon over bad roads. That is, at a slow walk. Need I say it was raining? But now it was a cold, penetrating rain driving in grey curtains across the rolling countryside, or drifting down out of a grey sky.

York rode at the head of this motley band with his son, a handsome young man of seventeen years, known as the Earl of Rutland, at his side, while the rear was under the command of Warwick's father, the Earl of Salisbury. Warwick himself, with other leading Yorkists remained in London, ostensibly to ensure that a steady train of supplies would be sent on behind the army, to raise further funds from the merchants (who had already contributed four hundred marks, a considerable sum) but in fact poised to return to Calais should matters not turn out as they wanted them to. The King, too, was kept in London with them, a figurehead symbolising the justness of their cause, though in fact a prisoner in the Tower, in the very rooms we had occupied for so many months.

Eddie March was the exception: he was sent into the borderlands between Wales and England where the Yorkists owned much land and where he was expected to recruit a large army, which would link up with York hopefully before they confronted the horde of Scots and Tynesiders the Queen had collected. These were now moving slowly south, looting, raping, burning as they came and thereby costing the Queen much willing and loyal support. Such was the booty, and the freedom they were given to make off with it, though, that her army steadily increased in size. All those bands of vagabonds and bandits I mentioned just now were happy to join her and thereby legitimise what they were already doing.

Our army, however, for all new recruits joined it daily out of fear of the looming presence of the Queen's and because many were tenants of York himself, remained much the same size or even diminished: the further we got from London the more the original drafts melted away and returned home.

At the solstice we came close to a town called Wakefield and at a distance from it of a mile or so to a huge grey castle, called Sandal Castle, set on a hill amongst woods and fields. This was the very midnight of the year, when, just as at the height of summer the sun dipped below the horizon for a mere five hours or so and the sky remained bright even after it had gone, now the reverse was true. Now it was up for barely five hours, remained low in the sky even at midday, often behind cloud, had no heat in it and left the nights long and impenetrably dark. Being that much further north it was worse than Calais. Though why this should be was beyond me to work out.

Sandal Castle, though huge, with a keep as big or bigger than that of the Tower, could still not accommodate an army of some six thousand. Nor had it been properly provisioned. Nevertheless it was a safe refuge and all York's captains urged him to keep his army within the walls or close up outside them until Eddie March could come to his aid – for aid he needed. The Queen's army now numbered twenty thousand at least. On their side the Queen's captains were desperate to bring him to a fight while they had such a huge advantage.

You will already have gathered from the scenes in London described in my last letter that this York was a wild, uncontrolled proud man, easily angered, and impatient. Desperate to be king in name as well as fact. Urged to remain within his castle's walls he threw some furniture about and shouted, 'Would you have me shut my gates for fear of a scold? Would you have all men call me a coward and a sot? For they certainly will if I give in to a witch whose only weapons are her nails and her tongue.' Which was irrational, considering that as well as her nails and her tongue she had three times as many men and cannon as he had.

Christmas came, the time when Christians celebrate the birth of Jesus. They do this, as indeed we had already seen in Calais twelve months before, by drinking themselves stupid over twelve days, and eating enormous amounts of meat, both of which stimulate the production of choleric humours especially in men sanguine by nature. The Queen played on this. She sent heralds into the castle who taunted York with being afraid of a woman. Meanwhile his victuallers reported that food was running out and, worse still, strong drink, and that the Queen's army lay across his supply lines.

Worse than that, all attempts failed at dealing with the human waste of six thousand men kept within walls. It was not something these Ingerlonders were good at. Quite simply, after seven days of shitting everywhere, there was shit everywhere, freezing and thawing out of doors, gently steaming in corners indoors. Yet, his only hope and best strategy was to stay put and hope March would soon come out of the west with reinforcements.

Then, on the night of the twenty-ninth, while most of the notables were in the castle hall chewing over the stringy carcasses of laying hens slaughtered for the table, there was a sudden clanging of feet from the passages, a timbered nail-studded door was thrown up and a guard of five men surged in with a mud-bespattered but armed knight in their midst wearing a surcoat with a white diagonal cross on a red ground, the arms of the Nevilles, appliquéd to it. Hauled to a spot on the floor just below where York was sitting, the following conversation took place.

'My name and style are Arnold Fiennes, knight, and I am of the affinity of Andrew Trollope—'

'He's an arrant traitor,' cried our noble duke. 'Fifteen months ago, at Ludlow, he defected. Bugger off.'

'Not so, Your Grace, he merely put himself in mind of his oath to King Henry. He is mindful now of that oath, and recognising that you are here in the King's name will side with you if tomorrow you will bring forth your power against the Queen.'

'How many men has the old bastard got?'

'Six thousand, Your Grace.'

'Bloody hell, that should do it.'

This Trollope – which, by the way, is a word signifying harlot, so is an odd name for a warrior – was an old man who, when he was only fifteen years old, had fought for King Harry at Agincourt and in many campaigns since; moreover, he had been captain of Calais for a time. This all led to his harbouring a grudge. He had done so much service for royal masters over so long a period he believed he should have been a lord many times over. But the Normans are so jealous of their blood they are reluctant to ennoble any who may be tainted with Inglyssheness, unless it be in the female line, and so plain Andrew he remained.

York was blinded by pride but not so Brother Peter, who did not think we should allow ourselves to be caught on the losing side. He was all for getting out of it while we were unscathed. At first light, an hour before dawn, he managed to talk us through. Wrapped in our cloaks we passed for burgesses of Wakefield going back to town with orders for food and so forth.

The track from the castle took us across an open stretch of land, known as Wakefield Green, kept in better times as grazing for the castle's cattle and sheep and even those of the common people. It took us down a gentle rise to a river with a bridge then up again, over a distance of half a mile or so, to a low, rounded ridge between two patches of woodland. The river was a brook only, almost dry and what water was in it frozen, easily crossed anywhere but yet an obstacle if one was in a hurry.

There was not a soul in sight as we left the castle by a sallyport a bribed sergeant had opened for us. Behind us the walls and dungeons of the castle rose up through the mist, impregnable and safe – it would take even cannon a week or so to breach them and great expense of powder. In front and around us the meadow was so whitened with frost, which crunched beneath our feet, it put me in mind of the way countrywomen at home spread washed sheets and so forth over bushes to dry.

In the woods the cackling crows rose from their roosts in the crowns of the trees and were answered by the jackdaws in the castle – it was as if the Queen's army had melted away in the night. But as soon as we breasted the ridge we saw this was not so.

Below, stretching back into the countryside, was a vast camp of tents and makeshift shelters made out of bent hazel branches with cloaks and blankets thrown across the hoops. The tents were round and in front of them standards drooped from poles and shields were hung on lances. Brother Peter, whose knowledge was encyclopædic, had just begun to identify these: 'Somerset,' he began, 'Northumberland, Exeter, Devon and Clifford . . .' when we were arrested and taken to the Queen's tent.

She was beautiful, yes, but with a hard meanness in her lips, a harsh voice, or a voice made harsh by constantly having to be heard in the company of proud men with few manners. Having heard we were from the castle she was all for taking our heads off there and then but first asked us if we knew the intentions of York.

'Madam,' I said, 'we are travellers in your country and as such have much to be grateful for. We have been received everywhere with kindness and we have been honoured with hospitality from both sides in this sad conflict. It would therefore be invidious of us to . . .'

Her anger appeared to deepen, although I was speaking with no more ceremony than a prince should. However, at that moment a bishop to whom Brother Peter had been whispering, intervened. 'This holy friar,' he said, 'has news that will interest us all. Even as we speak, York, believing Trollope will fight at his side today, is preparing to bring his power on to the field.'

The Queen then turned to her captains, Somerset and Northumberland. 'Sound drum and trumpet,' she cried. 'Let the men go to the positions we have already decided upon.'

What we were about to see, was the first of four battles that all took place within a quarter of a year of each other. It was the only one where it could be said of one side that a coherent plan had been formed in advance and was more or less adhered to, right from the ruse of persuading York to venture out by Trollope's apparent treachery. Each succeeding engagement was worse than the one before. This one was straightforward slaughter. I have already described to you the ground on which it was fought. As was the custom the Queen's army was divided into three. The central body was commanded by Somerset, with the Queen and her seven-year-old son at his side. Other lords led large bodies of men into the woods on either side of Wakefield Green, by devious routes so their presence was not detected by the Yorkists. Though a flurry of soaring crows might have given them cause to wonder if they had had the eyes of a simple ploughman amongst them. All they could see was a single line of men-at-arms, in full armour but most unmounted, along the low ridge in front of them.

They came down across the grass, and across the rivulet at the bottom. They formed up, all six thousand in a solid line six deep, with their cannon in front. And still the Queen did not move.

Presently three men, fully armed, with squires carrying their battle standards with them, rode out in front of the rest. The Queen's herald, standing near us, interpreted their armorial bearings. 'The royal arms, madam, and the royal arms with a difference. Must be York and his younger son Rutland. And the white saltire on red for a Neville – Salisbury, I suppose.'

'I'm not an idiot, Garter,' she said. 'I've got eyes in my head and, believe it or not, I know the royal arms when I see them.'

York now turned in his saddle drew his sword and waved it at the troops behind him. The cannon fired once, but firing uphill their shot fell short. They began to move forward, away from the rivulet and uphill.

'All right,' said the Queen, and her eyes were now alight with satisfaction. She was riding side-saddle, a newish fashion, especially designed for ladies, I suppose to protect their private parts from unnecessary chafing, and was dressed in hunting gear, a long crimson velvet gown, black boots. She had on a crown. 'Tell Somerset he can go for it.'

And a page trotted along the line with the message.

And over the top they went, about six thousand, no great numerical advantage, but with the slope in their favour, good ground hardened by the frost but not so hard or slippery as to be a hazard, the lords and knights horsed but scattered throughout the body to provide leadership and rallying points, reined in to a slow trot so the men-at-arms, for the most part in full armour but on foot, could keep up. And just as the two bodies of men clashed the two wings of the Queen's army, with archers in the front on York's right, where they were not protected by their shields held on their left sides, came streaming out of the woods.

York's men would have run. But they had nowhere to run to. Even the castle was cut off from them as Trollope's troops, having come round the back, had already got between them and it. Moreover, no one had thought to raise the drawbridge or lower the portcullis and there was no garrison save potboys and kitchen hands to hold it. It was very soon in Trollope's hands.

York was pulled from his horse and killed almost straight away. Rutland, accompanied by his standard-bearer who was also his tutor, got away and over the bridge across the main river into Wakefield where he was caught by Lord Clifford, who had chased Eddie March out of Alderman Dawtrey's house in London nearly a year earlier. Salisbury, old man though he was, got clear away but Trollope saw him go and sent a troop after him. They caught up with him ten miles away just as he was about to get into another castle – Pontefract, it was called.

The upshot was that next morning, the last day of 1460 by their reckoning, the Queen was presented by Clifford with three heads. 'Madam, your war is done,' he said.

Some say she went white, but not that I saw. She slapped York's cold dead cheek, then ordered them to put a paper crown on him. 'Stick it on a pike and put it above Micklegate Bar at York,' she said, and her voice rang out. 'Let York over-look York.'

Then she paused, her mouth worked, and she spat at it.

Later that day she went over the list of all who had been caught and ordered more executions, beginning what became routine on both sides, the summary murder of all nobles and gentry taken, with their families attainted, that is all their lands and titles forfeit. She pricked the names, marked up on parchment. 'Chop his head off! Get the kids too, if you can. I want to see that one die myself,' and so on. She even extended the lists to include those who took no side and no part: 'For as Jesus said: He that is not with me is against me.'

All this and the battle before it made me wonder: just what is it makes a man get inside so much steel casing, and lum-ber down a hill to strike and be struck until one or another falls to the ground to be skewered through the interstices of his armour? Or, worse than that, hacked at with mace and axe until the steel casing crushes him? Fear that if he doesn't his lands and life will be forfeit anyway? Maybe. The hope of ransom or loot from a vanquished foe? Loot, perhaps, but not much, for who takes valuables on to a battlefield? And no ransom, not while neither side is taking prisoners. I noted, too, though, a strange sort of camaraderie amongst many of the men, an eagerness to band together and, in their words, 'go for it', coupled with a fear of being thought cowardly or idle by their fellows. Drink too. Both sides drank huge amounts of beer and wine before the battle started. Finally . . . being Inglysshe helps.

Your affectionate and obedient cousin

Harihara Kurteishi, Prince of Vijayanagara

CHAPTER

FORTY-THREE

'*It's all about contrast, difference, is it not?*' Uma murmured. *For next day she was back with us again. Her gentle but knowing eyes were unfocused by the power of memory. She sighed. 'He was the best, you know.*'

Contrast and difference. Let's begin at the top and work down. His short white hair that I run my fingertips through and that strange black streak just long enough for me to wind once round my finger: my hair, almost back to its fullest length now, dark but hennaed to a red with occasional wires of bright gold in it and glossy, silky, fragrant. His chin and cheek, bristly with white above the coppery red, against mine, which has the bloom and colour of a ripe peach. His breath a touch sharp, like milk on the turn: mine like currants and honey. The squareness of his chin and the roundness of mine; the sinews and wrinkles in his neck – well, I have those now, but then . . . My shoulders creamy and smooth, rounded yet delicate: his twice as broad and white, with, I have to say, red spots to match the mole or two I have. My breasts like pomegranates, but soft and with large nipples that corrugate at his touch and even leak a sweet drop of ichor; his, massively wide and flat with nipples like pimples, which yet my tongue can raise so they feel hard as grain, and a mat of iron hair between. His arms like the roots of the banyan, strong and sturdy yet capable of grace in their slow yet greedy grasp; mine like the smooth branches of a tall aspen tree. My stomach a shallow dome with a whorled dent in the middle where Parvati pressed her thumb: his hard and six times ridged with muscle.

He has short, strong white toes that, even so, can grip a coin or feather while mine are long, with, when I can get the lacquer, painted nails. His ankles are finer than I would expect, which indicates nobility, but not as fine as mine, which put him in mind, he says, of things as fragile as glass. His calves are twin cords of muscle hazed with hair brindled grey and brown like a cat, and his knees, which he grumbles about at times, but nothing like as often as Ali does, are broad and strong, mine smooth like butter but as firm as apples. His thighs are pillars to support a temple, his buttocks like twin coconuts in a palm-tree; mine are like the mangoes he's never seen.

And our fingers, his short for the width of his big hands but strong with square ends, mine long and thin – what secret joys they find where thighs and torsos meet! His thumb runs down the crease and curves to cup the mound of bone, they part the wiry hair and probe the puckered lips; my thumb and forefinger ring the root of his prick while the other three roll his balls in their wrinkled sack. We play on each other as if on musical instruments smoothing the mucus between the pads on our fingers, teasing the tissue until his strengthens like timber and mine swells like a grape.

And now breath is taken by beauty, beauty of doing not seeing, of tasting and smelling and softly caressing. The longing now is nostalgia for a past that never yet happened, and I pull myself close to him, releasing his sex so I can hold his head and force my tongue and kisses on his neck and mouth, while he rolls us round and with one hand beneath me, in the small of my back, feeling out the cleft between my buttocks and with the other feeding his hungry pillar into me sends tides of hot joy up from my . . .

Well. Ali. You and I did it a couple of times, so you know what I'm on about, and you won't mind if I tell you that this Welsh chieftain knew what he was doing, was the best.

Summer drifts into autumn. Here the Welsh hills, which were a dull russet, slowly become lilac-coloured and then purple, spread with tiny bell-like flowers, so many millions of them it's like a purple blanket and springy and soft so that with care, avoiding the bigger branches that hug the ground, one can lie on it and lose oneself in the sweet but light fragrance of it, gazing up into a blue like aquamarine and watch where eagles soar with necks collared in gold. And beneath these low bushes yet another bush hides from the snows and wind that howl across here in winter, blowing fine powdery drifts, but now rich with small black berries, black that is until Owen names them: then you see how they're really blue, a deepest indigo.

These hills are cleft and riven with valleys so narrow near the crests you don't really see them until the hillside suddenly falls away beneath your feet to brown rock and water clear as crystal but brown, too, from the gravel beneath or grey and flat where the water has rounded boulders through the millennia, bubbling and gurgling from pool to pool. Deep in these declivities the air is still and the sun hot. With our ponies grazing on the ridge above us (they'll move and maybe neigh if anyone approaches), we can strip off our woollen cloaks and trousers and, on cropped thyme-scented grass beside the stream, make love again, and yet again, or just lie in each other's arms, backs against a sun-warmed lichened rock and watch the brown fish browse the moss beneath the surface.

At such times Owen feeds my head with tales of ancient Wales such as those of Pwyll, Prince of Dyfed, and Branwen, daughter of Llŷr and I tell him the tale of Rama and Sita. Then he sings the love-songs and laments of Dafydd ap Gwilym and Dafydd Nanmor, who, he says, is a living bard and may one day come himself to Dinbych to sing to us. And I teach him the lore of Parvati, the mother of us all, and Kali too with her necklace of skulls, whose avatars I sometimes am, and he calls her Rhiannon, who is both virgin mother and mare-headed eater of human flesh.

The frosts come, and then, as I hinted, the snow and gales sweep in out of the grey sea we sometimes glimpse from the higher hills. Wolves howl amongst the sheep-pens and one day early in December we ride out with great grey hounds, long-limbed so the snow is no problem for them, with massive necks as strong, I say, as Owen's. We take no wolves but drive them deeper and deeper and higher and higher into the mountains, seeing them always streaking ahead of us, loping and lolloping up almost vertical steeps, then silhouetted against the darkening sky, three of them, to howl their praise at the moon and defiance at us below, freezing in a shepherd's hut beside a black tarn. But there's wood stored there, and candles too, and the five of us, for Owen has brought three huntsmen with him, dine off biscuit and salt-dried mutton, before sleeping beneath the fleece of a bear.

Christmas comes, which Owen and his clan or tribe celebrate with some solemnity. Mah-Lo, you will have understood how in those climes far to the north of us and even of your own country, the steady decline of the sun towards the winter solstice is a matter of some significance. All people who live in those climes hope and trust that sooner or later it will be halted and when it is, when by fine calculation, based on careful observation of the sun in relation to tall stones set in circles like giant teeth on hill-tops for this very purpose, they can assert with certainty that the sun has risen at a point a little to the left of where it rose the day before and sets a little to the right, they declare that the goddess has conceived and borne a son, which they call Adonis or Adonaï.

On that day, out of the hills and woods came priests called druids, not Christian. Their leader bears mistletoe, and they enact certain rituals using drums made from oak, which simulate thunder. The leader carries the ancient sword shaped like a sickle and made of gold with which he cut the mistletoe and with which he now guards it.

He personates in flesh and blood the great god of the sky who has come down in the lightning flash to dwell among men in the mistletoe, the thunder-besom, that grows on the sacred oaks in the deepest valleys of Gwalia, by the side of black and fathomless tarns. The goddess whom he serves and marries is no other than the Queen of Heaven . . . for she, too, loves the solitude of the woods and the lonely hills, and sailing overhead on clear nights in the likeness of the silver moon, looks down with pleasure on her own fair image reflected on the calm, the burnished surface of the lake, Diana's mirror.

Here, in this country, we call them Shiva and Devi or Parvati.

Thus with due solemnity, and joy, too, the marriage of the gods is celebrated and the birth of the sun, the new year, and the hope of lambs born, barley and rye in the sheltered valleys and fleshy salmon flashing silver up the rivers and streams.

But that year, before the twelve days are done, news comes that fills me with foreboding, though Owen says it is good, of the Queen's great victory at Wakefield and the death of York and his son Rutland.

'A nest of vipers has been rooted out,' my lover cries in his deep voice, like an organ. 'Maybe we can now live in peace.'

But as winter deepens, the couriers who gallop up to his gates carry reports and commands as bad as winter itself and most especially bad are those carried by his son.

One day, when we are riding down a long winding valley, under the rowan trees, which still bear the odd berry, not all have been stripped by the birds Owen calls redwings, he comes. No snow now – as always happens on this island it lasted a week and then melted away – but frost again and the ice crackling in the puddles beneath the ponies' hoofs. A couple of red, fork-tailed kites circle in the updraught from a shepherd's croft, wondering if a quick drop on a dead sheep nearby is worth the risk from a mountain cat that's crouched under a boulder with an overhang nearby. And I'm riding in front (Owen is the only man I've ever met who'll let me do that), when I see a couple of men breaking away from the castle wall a mile away, and coming at a steady gallop up the track towards us. Both in half-armour, the one behind carrying a standard – presumably that of the one in front.

I rein in, let Owen come alongside. His broad forehead furrows and he pushes that black lock back. Of course it falls forward again.

'Shit,' he says.

And he lets out a quick sigh, his shoulders sink, and his hands, holding the reins, drop on to the pommel. I sense some life has leaked out of him and I feel ineffably sad. This man is old enough to be my grandfather, just; he is, well, an old man. As old men do he finds the bad moments, when they come, more and more difficult to cope with.

'What's the matter? Who are they?'

'It's my son. My younger son, Jasper.'

'You should be glad to see him.'

'Of course, yes. But he's been raising the Welsh and the men of the borders for the Queen. He can only be here for one reason.'

'He wants you to join him.'

'Just so.'

The two riders come up with us, wheel, a clatter of metal on metal and this Jasper, whom I haven't seen before, reaches out of the saddle to embrace his father and shake his hand. He looks a little like Owen but fairer, and I can see in his eyes those of Katherine of Valois, whose portrait I have already described to you.

'This is Uma,' Owen says. 'A princess from India.'

I am about to make a disclaimer but catch a look from him. He wants to scotch the rumour that in his dotage he has taken up with a gypsy.

Jasper touches the top rim of his helmet. 'Ma'am,' he says, which is nice, but that's all I get from him.

'I know why you're here,' says Owen, and it's a tired sort of growl.

'York's at Shrewsbury gathering an army out of the west of Ingerlond. He already has twenty thousand. When he has thirty and as soon as the roads dry out, he'll move on London. There's been a lot of rain in the south. If he gets there and links up with Warwick they'll have the beating of the Queen. Especially as they still have the King in their hands and can say they have his support.'

Well, even at the time I fidget at this and wonder, as no doubt you are too, but they're well into men's talk now as they turn their horses back down the track towards the castle.

'Where is the Queen?'

'After Wakefield she left her army at Hull while she went back north to Berwick-on-Tweed, which they say she'll give to Queen Mary of Scotland in return for more troops and funds. But even with these she and her captains doubt she has the beating of Warwick and York together.'

Again I frown but they ignore me. Owen rides on ten paces past a giant yew that spreads its ancient shade, wide as a banyan, over the dry needles and fallen berries beneath it. These berries are cherry red but small, and hide a poisonous black seed in a tiny but fleshy cup. You can squeeze the seed up and it brings with it a colourless ooze like the bead you get on the tip of a . . . Ah, well, it's a sad time I'm on my way to, I'm trying not to push on too quick from the happy times.

Owen rides on past the yew then turns to his son.

'So. She wants us to raise a power and get to London before York can.'

'That's it.'

At last I get a word in edgeways.

'But York, and his son, were killed at Wakefield and their heads placed on the gate at the city of York. That's what you told me.'

'He had another son. Older than Rutland.' It's Jasper who answers me. 'And though attainted he calls himself the new Duke of York. Duke and king too.'

'So,' says Owen. 'It's come to that at last.'

Candlemas. The day when the year in the north quickens. They take all the candles they will need in the church for the next twelve months and bless them, but really it's for the goddess whom they call St Bride.

In the cottages they make straw dolls of her and lay them in a bed and burn candles round her all night. But that Candlemas was ruled not by St Bride, or Parvati, Deva or Uma, for in the evening of the day following the night of Candlemas, in a town called Hereford, they take poor Owen out into the market square. Poor soul, he cannot believe they will execute him. He has led his men for the Queen in the King's name. Surely that queen whose life I saved is Kali incarnate, a true avatar, dragging the deaths of thousands in her train.

Owen's crime, apart from leading an army against this second York, at a battle a few miles north of Hereford, and losing it, is that he is the stepfather of King Henry. An eye for an eye, is what the obscene scriptures of both Christians and Muslims call for, and so it is a case of a father for a father.

Others taken with him, including two young lads, go first and one lad breaks free. The soldiers hack him to pieces, as if he is a steer in the shambles.

Owen turns to the headsman and says, 'I trust you will not handle me so roughly. You have an axe and a block.'

Then they tear off the collar of his red velvet doublet and placing his head on the block he says, 'This head was wont to lie in more than one queen's lap.'

Later, when they have gone, I take up his head and place it on the top step of the market cross and with three ladies of the town I gather up a hundred candles from the church and we place them on the steps around him. I wipe the blood from his face and kiss his cold lips. The air sparkles with frost, and the candles burn all night. As the late dawn streaks the sky with red I feel the presence of another behind me as I sit on the bottom step. The candles, now burnt low, gutter with the first breeze of morning and the smell of beeswax soured by heat drifts about us.

I look up and round and see a tall figure in full armour, blue steel enriched with gold inlay. Behind him two squires carry two shields. On one are blazoned silver flowers on lapis, quartered with golden lions on a field of blood. On the other there are three gold-leaf suns, freshly laid on gesso and burnished to a brightness that catches the light. I have heard the story of the battle at Mortimer's Cross. I have heard how three suns appeared in the sky above the man who would be king and both armies took it as a sign that God was on his side.

He lifts his visor. It's Eddie. Eddie March. Edward Plantagenet, King of England, Duke of York. Behind him, the great black stallion I once saved from a whipping strikes sparks from the cobbles and neighs like a trumpet.

CHAPTER

FORTY-FOUR

S *he sighed deeply, dabbed her eyes with a scrap of muslin.*
'I'll go for a little walk, if you don't mind. The rain has almost stopped.
Ali will tell you what, in the meantime, he had been up to . . .'

The day after the battle of Wakefield we found that, in the general business around us, we were ignored. Prince Harihara remained determined
to push on towards Macclesfield Forest, which now lay some fifty miles
south-west but, of course, with the destruction of York's army we no
longer had the protection a prudent traveller would want in those lawless
roads. The Queen herself was heading back to the north-east to recruit
more help and troops from the Scottish Queen, while her main army
celebrated its victory and showed no immediate will to move south or
north. Nevertheless, the Prince felt we should never be so near our goal
again and instructed me to find a guide who would take us those last
sixteen or seventeen leagues.

Brother Peter found a small Franciscan friary not far from the cathedral.
Its prior directed us to the home of a cobbler, whose sympathy with the
Brothers of the Free Spirit went beyond even that of the friars. Setting
aside his lasts, needles, leathers, hammers and other tools of his trade,
this worthy man cheerfully agreed to take us on. He declared himself
especially happy to, for his trade was scarce worth carrying on at that
time of year with the short days and the expense of good candles. No
doubt the sight of the Prince's gold played its part too. But what gave

the enterprise point and us great encouragement was that, on seeing our complexions, he asserted that he had heard some time ago that a man with just such a skin had been living with the brothers in Macclesfield Forest and was an object of some curiosity amongst the simpler people who lived thereabout.

How long ago?

Oh, three or four years ago, maybe more.

This shoe-mender's name was Edwin. Although by nature cheery he lived alone, had sober habits, was industrious and frugal. His father, a travelling mason, had worked on the rebuilding of the cathedral (still, twenty years later, in progress) married, then almost immediately died after falling from the clerestory, which they were modernising, when a piece of wooden scaffold broke. His mother's brother was a cobbler and to him Edwin was apprenticed when still a boy. He had never married, being much attached to his widowed mother, but studied alone and mastered the art of reading. He had read the gospels in a Wycliffite translation that was copied and passed underground, as it were, amongst the weavers of Wakefield, who were among his clients.

Here, and not for the first or last time, I felt a sudden sense of comradeship, of companionship. I mentioned this to Brother Peter.

'I call such people,' he said, 'the Johnson family.'

'Why?'

'It's a common, anonymous name, yet it suggests a sort of toughness, an independence, with a decent ordinariness too. Not all of them are Brothers and Sisters of the Free Spirit, but many are. They pay no respect to authority, whether secular or religious, but quietly, keeping themselves to themselves, go their own way.'

He meditated for a moment, then went on. 'A Johnson minds his own business, but he will help you when help is needed. He doesn't stand by while someone is drowning, or trapped under a fallen tree or piece of masonry. The Johnsons know good and evil are in conflict and the outcome is uncertain. But the conflict is not eternal since one or the other must win the final victory. The question is: Which side are you on?'

The last stage of our pilgrimage was wretched, crossing a low range of hills known as the Pennines. Being the first weeks of the year the weather was cold and wet, the days short, the nights interminably long. Wet and cold, we came down the western slopes of those hills into rain

driving out of the west and into a small town called Manchester. I can
remember hardly anything of the place except that whatever it is makes
joints swell and ache when rain comes took hold there. As I shivered in
the corner of a tavern where we stopped for the night Brother Peter and
Edwin argued with each other over whether the best footie players came
from the west or the east side of the Pennines. For two intelligent men,
one very learned, it seemed a stupid dispute to get into, but I was too
miserable to care.

We were now less than a day's walk from Macclesfield Forest, and
Prince Harihara was agitated at the prospect of arriving there, alternately
pacing about the public room with excitement lighting his eyes, or sitting
in the corner, morose and anxious over what the morrow would bring.
Anish, having made sure that we had dry bedding and had eaten and
drunk enough, sat beside me. 'Tomorrow,' he said, 'we should be
through. Mission accomplished. Whatever happens, we should be able
to turn south at last and head for home. How long will it take us, Ali?
Tell me, not as long as it took us to get here.'

He stretched out his still podgy hands to the fire, turned and beamed
at me. 'I can't wait to get back,' he added. 'Still, we've seen a lot. I
wouldn't have missed it for worlds. And all arising from that bundle of
parchment you brought with you from Calais to Vijayanagara.'

That stirred my interest. 'Do you have it about you?' I asked.

'It's upstairs in our room. I'll get it.'

He was back in a moment, undoing the red leather strings, folding
out the creaky parchment.

> As John the apostel hit syy with syght
> I syye that cyty of gret renoun
> Jerusalem so nwe and ryally dyght
> As hit was lyght fro the heven adoun
> The birgh was al of brende golde bryght
> As glemande glas burnist broun
> With gentyl gemmes anunder pyght
> Wyth banteles twelve of tiche tenoun
> Uch tabelment was a serlypes ston . . .

Ali must have noted the puzzlement on my face.

'For you, Mah-Lo, let me put it into a tongue you can understand,' he said.

As John to each of these jewels gave name
I reckon each stone from his narration.
Jasper was the name of the first gem
I saw adorning the base foundation;
It glimmered green on the lowest tier.
On the second step, sapphire was seen,
Then chalcedony, stainless and clear,
On the third step showed with pallid sheen,
The fourth was emerald with hue of green;
The sardonyx was the fifth stone
And the sixth was ruby, as it was seen
In the apocalyse, by the Apostle John . . .

Ali's eyes grew misty. 'I am remembering,' *he said,* 'the first time I read these words. In the courtyard, was it? Or the hall, in Vijayanagara. With the Prince. What a lot we saw and did following that day.' *He sighed.* 'In Manchester, opening out the pages, I said much the same to Anish after I had read the third verse.'

And John yet counted the chrysolite,
The seventh stone on the tiered plinth.
The eighth was beryl, clear and white,
And topaz inlaid with twin hues ninth;
The tenth, chrysoprase, firmly fixed,
And gentle jacinth the eleventh stone.
The purple and indigo amethyst
Cure of all woes, made the twelfth zone . . .

'You know, Anish,' I remarked, when I had read these verses, in that Mancunian inn, with the rain splashing outside, and a howl of cold wind in the chimney, 'I can't believe that a heavenly city, like the one described here, lies twelve miles away.'

Anish frowned, peered at the Teluga script, which appeared below the Inglysshe verses. 'There's no suggestion,' he said, 'that the place described here is in Ingerlond.'

I was nonplussed. 'Why are we here, then?' I asked at last.

Anish was puzzled. 'To find Jehani and bring him home.'

'And?'

'And to learn as much as we can about military matters from the most warlike people on earth so we may defend ourselves against the Bahmani sultans.'

I took a turn about that gloomy low-ceilinged room, partly hoping to ease the pain in my knees, partly to give myself time to think. I tripped over the stretched-out ankles of a drunk as I did so.

'Mind where yer at, yer silly bogger,' he growled.

Returned to where I had started, I stared down at Anish, who had now sat himself in a settle with the package on his knees.

'But not to discover the heavenly city made manifest on earth?' I asked.

'Why should citizens of Vijayanagara want to seek a heavenly city?'

He had a good point there, I conceded to myself, if not to him. Man comes to himself only when transcendence has been conquered – when eternity has become present in the here and now. Those had been Peter's words in his Easter sermon. At that moment he was dozing in the inglenook.

'So why did Jehani write out these English verses if not to point us in the direction of a city where we can shovel up precious stones by the sackful?'

Anish frowned, possibly put out by the slightly belligerent, not to say sarcastic, tone I was adopting. Perhaps the beer, of which I'd had a pint or three (I'm afraid by then I was quite addicted to the stuff), was talking. The landlord's own. Boddington, his name was. It was on the sign outside. Anish glanced down again at the part written in Teluga, the language of the Dravidian princes and their entourages, a closed book to me.

'He says he came upon them in a rather beautiful poem written by a man whose daughter died. She appeared to him in a dream and showed him this city, which the poem describes. It made Jehani feel homesick, made him long for Vijayanagara again.'

Brother Peter stirred, leant across him. 'The poet was a knight,' he said, 'but also a Brother of the Free Spirit, or at least a Lollard, and these verses are an adaptation of Wycliffe's translation of the last book of the Bible.'

Anish went on, with some reproof in his voice, 'I don't see why any sane man would want to shovel precious stones into a sack.'

'No?' said I.

'No. Precious stones should adorn dancers. Men and women. Even buildings and statues. As they do in Vijayanagara.'

'You forget. I am not a native of that city. I'm a traveller. And sometimes, for travellers, it is convenient to have precious stones in sacks.'

He had the grace to acknowledge then that we could not have come so far, had warm clothes to wear and the wherewithal to buy food and drink, and a more or less dry bed for almost every night, had we not, at my suggestion, brought a large number of jewels with us. In sacks.

At this point Prince Harihara, who had been watching us from a draughty corner near the door, his face in shadows, his dark eyes gleaming, called out: 'That's enough, Anish. And you, too, Ali. We'll discover all we need to know soon enough.'

And he asked Boddington for a candle to light our way to bed.

So. No heavenly city. No jewels beyond the dreams of avarice littering the streets. What did we find? First, a river called the Mersey, across which we took a ferry, then a forest, with a glade in its centre. At the ferry Edwin left us. It was dangerous, said the ferryman, for a poor man with no education to be found anywhere near where the Brothers of the Free Spirit had lived. Had lived? Gerald, the ferryman, looked grim but would not respond to our questions.

Forests, to be satisfactory, require management. So said a forester who appeared on the other side of the river and agreed to take us further. He was a big man, one of the biggest I have seen, with a red curly beard and a merry eye.

Old and rotting trees need to be taken out; rides created, which will also, in dry summers, act as fire-breaks; thickets allowed to grow for deer to shelter in and the roe deer especially, who are secretive, to have their young – some birds, too, prefer thickets to trees for their nests. Streams should be banked or encouraged, where the lie of the land suggests it, to form ponds and stocked with fish. Macclesfield Forest, like so much of the rest of Ingerlond, had been neglected for twenty years or more, due to the wars, both foreign and civil. Rides and paths were overgrown, brambles and briars had filled them, and the fallen trees had been left to rot. But in the heart of winter none of this was too much of a problem – the briars were reduced to coils of thorny stems, the grass was withered and the leaves dropped from the saplings as well as the giants so one could see one's way clear and, from the occasional rises, across extensive views. All this was explained by the forester as he led us to the centre.

It rained, but not as heavily as it had in Manchester the day before. More a gentle mist, a healing rain, the forester called it. Not only tall, he was well-built too, dressed in green, with a longbow, and a horn on his belt. Brother Peter teasingly called him Robin Hood, and had his head bitten off for his pains. The gear was pretty standard for a forester was the message we got. From the pommel of his saddle there swung a large axe, its blade sheathed in leather. It didn't seem unreasonable for a forester to carry an axe but Peter muttered something on the lines that if he wasn't Robin Hood then he must be the Green Giant, whose head was struck off with his own axe by Sir Gawain at the court of King Arthur.

At this point the forester reined in and pointed down from the low escarpment we had arrived on across a wide valley, an almost perfectly circular bowl, about a mile across. And even in winter it was evident that here things grew with a floridness, a burgeoning, a freshness and greenness different from the rest of the forest.

'Some call it the Garden of Eden,' he said, 'others the Garden of Earthly Delights. But most follow the Church and bishop and call it the Devil's Bowl. Fifty years ago, or thereabouts, a ball of fire dropped out of heaven. The earth shook. A fire raged through this part of the old forest for a week. And when the smoke cleared and the fire died down, there was this great hollow in the land like an upturned palm. All the people were terrified of it, and no one would go into it. Within a year or so, though, it began to green up again, first just mosses and heath, but then the trees came back and, of course, because the people were afraid of the area, all species that are hunted came into it and bred undisturbed, perhaps as they really did in paradise. There are deer, of course, and hares, wild boar, pheasants and partridge, orioles and magpies, and in the river that runs through it otters, beavers, trout, crayfish and, in early summer, salmon. And all are bigger and more handsome than any you will see elsewhere. And also a wider variety of plants – not just the forest ones but apple, pear and cherry, too, currants, raspberries and strawberries all took hold before the big forest trees like the oak, the ash, the beech could cover all with life-denying shade. And flowers, of course: aconites which you may find in bloom already on the forest floor, do not eat them they are poisonous, then celandines, wind-anemones, primroses, snowdrops, and violets, daffodils, Solomon's seal, borages, worts of all sorts, wild garlic and many, many more. It's a shame you cannot see it in May or June . . .' He pulled up and looked around at us. 'You will find the Brothers' dwellings as near to the centre as you can get.'

'And the Brothers?' cried Prince Harihara, his face pale with foreboding.

But the green man had already turned his horse's head and was making his way back down the outer slope of what we now realised was a rim, very like that of a shallow bowl. As he went, a shaft of sunlight broke through the clouds and a shower of raindrops as clear as stainless shards of chalcedony fell about his shoulders. Then he was gone.

CHAPTER

FORTY-FIVE

A bare half-mile down a track that had been wide and over-arched with beech, but was now encroached upon by holly and butcher's broom, took us to the centre. On the way red squirrels chattered from the boughs and dropped nut-casings on our heads. A red fox trotted by. We crossed a stream that ran between banks of red clay and a robin redbreast sang on a willow twig above it. I recalled aloud that red is the colour of death, but pushed the thought away when none of my companions found an answer.

When we arrived in it there was no doubting we were there. First a hedge or ring of holly, much of it heavy still with red berries, twenty yards or so across, enclosed a wide swathe of grass, a lawn cropped by deer and rabbits to less than an inch but even in January thick and lush. This in turn made a ring round a low fence of wicker hurdles many of which, untended, had fallen or been pushed down. Inside this circle there was a tiny village of about ten stone huts roofed with turf, though again most had been tumbled by malice or time. In the very middle a round hut stood, bigger than the rest, and apart from a hole or two in the roof where the turf had fallen through, more or less intact.

In the huts and the tiny passages between them we counted fifteen skeletons or cadavers, including eight who were young: babies, small children, older children. Skeletons? Not quite. Although the beasts of the forest had eaten out the hearts, lungs and livers, and the birds had attacked their eyes and smaller parts, the summer heat had dried what was left and patches of skin still clung to their heads, and hair too. Some had been decapitated but most had been stabbed with spears or slashed and hacked with swords or axes.

There was no sign to suggest that any had been other than naked. Four still held in their hands single roses, dried and withered now, no doubt cut before they were attacked or perhaps when they knew they were about to be attacked, to be offered to their assailants. These had been plucked from the gardens, overgrown now, of course, we found on the far side of the settlement.

The larger hut in the middle seemed to be a blank, a circular wall with no door or windows. We walked round it. Brother Peter mumbled and sighed, and stumbled on the dressed stones that lay in his way. Tears streamed down Anish's plump cheeks. Prince Harihara looked angry to the core of his being, his lips tight, his fists clenched, his complexion white, his eyes burning. I paused to consider how I felt. Well, I have seen such things too often since I was left for dead at the top of a well stuffed with the bodies of my parents and siblings. I felt numb. And my knees and knuckles hurt.

One thing I felt sure of. I knew the signs. When men kill for power, prestige, or out of greed or hunger, even for revenge or to punish, you feel there is an imperative there that is natural, even rational, that has come from something deep in our natures. It means something. Even for the victims. They know why they have died. But the cruellest, stupidest, meanest and most horrible murders, murders preceded by rape, living dismemberment, come from a hatred that has only one root and that innately meaningless and trivial, unnatural and irrational. Religion. These people, like my own people, had chosen the wrong god.

Why should this be? If you live a life that is mean and ignoble, impoverished and filled with crippling labour that enriches others not yourself, as long as there are masters and men, your only hope is to be rewarded in heaven. And if your neighbour's heaven is not your heaven, his god is not your god, then one of you must be wrong. And what is even worse is if he believes, as these people had, that there is no god at all . . . That is unthinkable, unacceptable. In his head lies the possibility that it might be you who has been deceived, so crush his head with all the venom . . .

'Ali, I know you're not feeling well, but could you give us a hand with this?'

The Prince – even then courteous, certain as ever of getting his way. 'This' was a large flat stone, somewhere between the shape of a square and an egg, one foot thick at the edges but nearly three feet thick in the centre and six feet high. It seemed likely it served as a door but its base had sunk into the turf and it took the four of us an hour to shift it.

'Does it have to be moved?' I grumbled, after the first twenty munutes of useless heaving and pushing.

'My brother is not out here so he may be inside.'

He was right.

The stone shifted at last. The hut breathed out – a musty, dry smell, faintly aromatic. The cold light flooded in, joined the sunbeam that was already there, thanks to the hole in the roof, a patch of almost lemon-yellow light on the curving, undressed stone. Four sparrows flew out, also through the hole in the roof, and a tabby cat, a queen, snarled and spat before launching herself up from the lap she had been sitting in.

There were seven of them, sitting in a circle, ankles crossed, hands, palms upturned, in front of them. None of them wore clothes though all, three women and four men, were dressed: in tiaras and necklaces, arm bangles and wrist bangles, girdles and anklets, made from twisted lead and copper, now tarnished with time, but still set with crystals, felspars, yellow, white, red or green. Some were opalescent like moonstones, others, like sun-stone, spangled. Each had a simple handleless tin cup in front of their feet. Presently Peter picked one up. There was a smear of dried-up purply black residue, a paste, in the bottom. He sniffed at it.

'A concoction of extracted and concentrated belladonna, aconite and hemlock,' he said. 'The dehydrating effect and spasmed muscles could account for the fact that they have remained upright in the positions they adopted before drinking it. Though they would have had to resist the onset of considerable if brief pain to remain as they are.'

But Prince Harihara did not hear him. He was on his knees in front of one of the figures, with his face in his hands, rocking sound-lessly to and fro. Although the skin of all these dead had withered and browned with time, this one was perceptibly darker than the rest. And although the faces of all shared the same rictus of death and the same effects of mummification by poison, heat, cold and dryness, the Prince could no doubt detect in the mask in front of him the physiognomy of his younger brother. Besides, as we had been warned to expect, his legs had been removed at the knee joints.

In the centre of this ghastly circle there had been placed the one object of monetary value to be found in the whole settlement: a gold bowl, very thin, embossed with a crude oak-leaf pattern. When we had left and had found it possible to talk of what we had seen, Anish offered the supposition that this was the Holy Grail, believed by many Christians to be hidden in these islands. But Peter said no. It was much older that Christianity, he said. Similar objects had been found in long barrows all over the country.

Anyway, this one had held water, now dried up, and two flowers, a lotus, or water-lily, and a rose. But they were withered too, dried up and dead. We rolled the stone back, leaving Jehani where he had chosen to be, then led the Prince away. He did not speak for forty-eight hours, but when he did he seemed himself again, though his mouth retained a melancholy downward twist at the corners for as long as I knew him.

Our mission now done, we headed south. Peter was anxious to return to Osney, the rest of us for London and a ship to take us east, back to the Orient. We had not gone far before we met up with a troop of men led by a knight who was marching on the command of his liege lord to Shrewsbury where the King was gathering an army. The King? Henry? No, Edward, son of the Duke of York, Edward the Fourth.

On the way Prince Harihara catechised Brother Peter about what we had seen, about what had happened to his brother and why.

Although he expected or at any rate hoped to be back in Vijayanagara as quickly as any letter, he wrote it all down for his cousin. In fact we were delayed further, as you shall hear, and the letter reached its destination a month ahead of us. Here it is.

CHAPTER

FORTY-SIX

Dear Cousin,
I have sad news to report. We found the body of Jehani, my brother and your cousin, in a hidden settlement. He had been dead for at least two years, possibly three, and was entombed with six of his friends. His place of rest was decent enough and reflected the life he had been leading and the beliefs he held so we felt it appropriate to leave him, undisturbed, where he was, simply sealing up the tomb again behind us.

Although nothing can be certain we have, with the aid of a wise man who knows about such things, pieced together a picture of Jehani's last months or even years.

It seems likely that apart from his death, and the earlier mutilation he had suffered, he had been happy and this must be our consolation, though it cannot wipe out the guilt I feel that it was my stupid jealousy that sent him on his travels in the first place. However, I must believe that the happiness he found here was at least as deep and ennobling as that I made him forsake in Vijayanagara.

He was in the company of a small group belonging to a sect called the Brothers of the Free Spirit. This sect exists in secret cells across the West, some of which have managed to find places in the wilderness where they can live undisturbed according to their beliefs and without interference from the authorities – for a time at least.

Ali tells me that the Assassins, whose founding father was Hassan Ibn Sabbah, the Old Man of the Mountain, and the Thuggees, too, share some of their characteristics, the difference being that the Assassins and Thuggees both pay an excessive and obsessive attention to the experience of death. The Brothers, however, see it as part of the natural order and as such to be welcomed when its arrival is timely.

I shall now summarise the main tenets of their faith, if that is the right word, expressed through praxis rather than dogma.

They hold all in common; there is no private property. Women are the equal of men. Where the climate is suitable or the time of year conducive, they go naked of clothes but not of personal ornament. They practise singing, dancing, story-telling and poetry, and they play on musical instruments. They eat simply and eschew animal flesh except at times of the year they hold holy. They use hallucinatory plants such as various mushrooms, hashish and other substances. They believe in a god, or a goddess, but it is the god or goddess within them they seek to discover, not an alien entity. They eschew all violence, even in self-defence. They do not tell others what to do and they do not expect others to tell them what to do. They condemn no activity or behaviour that brings pleasure and does not harm others. To avoid conflict, division into parties, power struggles and the like, they limit their numbers in any one group to twenty or so people. Out of these, seven or so of the older members form a council who take decisions for the whole group.

Such were the people Jehani lived amongst. My informant tells me that he may have lost his lower legs as a result of torture by crushing before he was taken in by these people. He may have been tortured because he was already identified as a Brother of the Free Spirit, or simply because he was a stranger with skin darker than those around him.

There is much we shall never know about him for certain, we can only guess.

He lived, in some comfort, with all a rational man could wish for, in a small settlement hidden in a forest, in a part of a forest where ordinary people were afraid to go since it had been the site, some fifty years earlier, of a meteoric impact. The Ingerlonders believe such occurrences come from the devil, who, in their cosmology, is the spirit of evil. However, hidden away though they were, it seems likely that the authorities became aware of their existence and most of the group were murdered by soldiers, probably sent by the Bishop, the spiritual authority in the area. The elders however, including Jehani, were able to seal, or have themselves sealed, within their largest building where they took their own lives by means of herbal poisons.

These are the facts as well as we know them. Much more could be said, but little that is worth saying and nothing that will bring him back. We are now on our way home.

Your affectionate and obedient, but grieving cousin

Prince Harihara

PART V

CHAPTER

FORTY-SEVEN

We arrived at Shrewsbury at the end of January to find that the new Duke of York, or King, as he preferred to be known, had left the day before, heading south to Hereford where, we gathered, he aimed to consolidate all the various divisions of his army, raised as it had been in the counties of the west as well as in the borders or Marches between Ingerlond and Wales. From Hereford he planned to move to the support of Warwick in London who now awaited the onslaught of the Queen following the battle of Wakefield.

But we were still five miles short of Hereford when we met his army heading north after all. Apparently, a few miles to the north and west this new king's scurriers, or spies, had discovered a large power of Welshmen who, it was thought, were heading for a crossroads at a hamlet called Mortimer's Cross where they would go east and south towards a point north of London where they would be a more than useful addition to the Queen's army. Since these scurriers were certain that York's army was double the numbers of that led by Owen and Jasper Tudor, it seemed sense to move forward and deal with them before they could add their numbers to the Queen's.

On the afternoon which was the eve of Candlemas, the day, as Uma has already told us, when Christians bless all the candles they will use in their churches during the next twelve months, the army drew up on the river Lugg and waited for the new Duke to make his dispositions. A mile or so away the vanguard of the Welsh could be seen moving tentatively towards us through the murky gloom.

It was at this point that the Duke, riding past us with an escort of knights and squires, with his standard, the royal arms, carried behind him, his visor up, turned his face towards us so we recognised him and he recognised us.

He was only eighteen years old. Irrationally we had expected him to be older. As indeed he might have been. His father, Richard of York, was fifty when he died at Wakefield.

It was Eddie. Our Eddie. Eddie March. Eddie, *Earl* of March.

'Good Lord,' he cried, reining in with a slight clatter of armour. 'It's the Oriental chappie. Prince Hurry-hurry. How are you, my dear fellow? And Ali too. My goodness, your quick thinking got me out of a scrape, what? Nearly a year ago, as I'm alive. Is the witch with you? That wonderful girl. What was her name? Uma. Of course. How could I forget? I say, I'm a touch busy right now, things to deal with and so forth, but Gervase here will look after you and bring you to my tent for a bite to eat and a glass or two when I'm through. What do you say? Fine, good. Dashed glad to see you again. À bientôt, then, what?'

Gervase was a squire of about fifteen years old, who did as he was told.

Eddie had changed. The deaths of his father and younger brother had aged him. You don't believe in death, not even when you've seen it and dished it out, until the first person close to you goes. Then you believe. And in his case the manner in which they had gone was a source of pain and hate: they had been betrayed by Trollope and others into fighting a battle they should never have fought. Then the insult to the dead, the abuse of their bodies. Older he certainly was, and bitter with a deadly, cunning bitterness, a thirst for revenge that quite overcrowed the jolly, whoring japer we had known in Calais and East Cheap.

And now, just a month after his father's death, he had his own army and the first chance to satisfy the thirst for revenge that burned like acid bile within him. Yet there was fear too.

At dusk we stood outside his tent and looked down over what would, in the morning, be the field of battle.

There was a bridge, the river Lugg, and Wigg Marsh, across the Worcester road. A local man, Sir Roger Croft of Croft Castle, stood beside us and pointed east. The crossroads were below us just south of the hamlet, two furlongs north of the bridge.

'My lord . . .'

'Sire.'

'Indeed, yes, Your Majesty. The marsh. The road crosses it. If they break that way . . .'

'Yes. We'll put the archers on that side, on the far side of the marsh. And the main body over the bridge, on the other side.'

'Your Majesty, if you do that, you cut off or make a bottle-neck of our retreat, should we need it.'

'There will be no retreat. And it's best if they know that.'

There were no cannon. At Candlemastide the roads were too deep in mud or snow to move them, the very air, even when it didn't rain, too moist for gunpowder.

They were in place by nightfall, and as the darkness closed in we could see the torches of the Welsh winding through Mortimer's Cross then spreading out. We could hear the jingle and clang of their armour, the neigh of their horses.

But with darkness came doubts. Eddie had twice the number of men, twice at least. But that was at dusk. How many at dawn? So many lords and knights, with their affinities, in his army: Lord Audley, Lord Grey de Wilton, Lord FitzWalter, Sir So-and-so of This, Baron That of So-and-so. And all, just like Trollope, had sworn their oath to Henry, if not when he ascended the throne then at some time after. How many, like Trollope, would return to that allegiance when the sun rose and the skylarks left their watery nests?

Once back in his tent all this weighed heavily and Eddie said, 'We need a sign. An irrefutable sign that we will win because God is on our side. Only that way can we be sure that chaps will realise that their oath to Henry was falsely sworn and that I am rightfully king.'

He turned to our prince. 'Hurry-hurry,' he said, 'you Oriental chaps have a reputation for magic and so forth. Could you conjure something up for us? An eclipse, perhaps. Put the sun out and say the sun is Henry?'

And that, dear Mah-Lo, is as far as I shall go tonight with the spinning of my yarn. It's a good place to stop is it not? Just on the eve of a battle whose outcome is in the balance. Scheherezade could not have done better.

I've had occasion, once or twice, *said Ali when, the next day, he took up the tale again,* to mention the fakir who attached himself to us right from the start. He came and went like a shadow, a not very familiar familiar. Tall, dark, a Mussulman god-man, he was, I sometimes thought, my other self, my similar, my brother, the ghost of the man I might have been had I not been mutilated as a child in the way you see before you. Indeed, at times I was none too sure in just what dimension he existed, for it seemed to me that none saw him or were aware of his presence but I. He was often there, a flicker in the corner of my eye who was gone when I turned; a presence between the sun and a wall that faded with the light whose rays it interrupted.

It's a trick fakirs perfect, often by the simplest of means. Appear in a locked room? Simple. Hide there before the room is locked. Manifest in a crowd? Easier still. Arrive in disguise and when there is a distraction, throw it off. They have garments that look coarse and poor through cunning weaving and painting but made of silk so fine they can be crushed and balled away.

They can swallow almost anything so their bodies provide hiding-places that walk with them; they can get their fists up their rectums and leave there a king's globe, cross and all.

They also know substances with strange qualities, unlikely powers, that can turn metals into ashes; they can make a rope stand on end with no apparent means of support and encourage a small boy to climb it. Lying on the ground they make six people each put a finger under them and, lo, they rise into the air and none of the six feels the weight. They work with mirrors. And . . . they understand how the track of light can be concentrated and bent by passing it through cunningly shaped lumps of glass.

I had seen him quite frequently on the way from Macclesfield Forest. Once walking towards us through the rain up an unusually straight track (unusual, that is, for Ingerlond where all but the Roman roads wind like corkscrews), climbing a hill. But he crossed the ditch when he was still a couple of hundred paces from us and strode away into the mist that came down over the moor. On another occasion he sat opposite us in a tavern, went out as if to take a piss, and never came back. Three times he walked just beside and behind me for an hour or two, then was gone.

Peter insisted that he was a figment of my imagination, that he had heard of such manifestations appearing to people suffering from extreme physical exhaustion and mental distress. Christians even identify this presence with the risen Jesus.

Considering what we had all been through, my response was to ask him, 'Why then, Peter, are we not all suffering the same hallucinations since we have all suffered in similar ways?'

At all events, having heard this plea from the youth we still thought of as Eddie, the fakir came up behind me and whispered in my ear, 'Do you still have the *kurundams* in your bag?'

'Yes, indeed I do.'

'Let's have a look at them then.'

I pulled them out and laid them carefully on a table, beside the candles that lit the tent. The others were still in the doorway, watching the torches of the Welsh, drinking wine and eating pork. Two good reasons why I was already hanging back behind them.

Have I described these precious stones, these crystals before? Well, I will do so again, but in more detail. They were six inches long, shaped a little like a weaver's shuttle – that is, pointed at both ends and about one and a half inches in diameter at the thickest point in the middle. They were multi-faceted but basically hexagonal, the points at each end being six-sided pyramids. They were perfect, unflawed rubies and even in the dim candlelight on a simple small black oak table, they gathered the light and glowed with it.

'We shall,' said the fakir, 'need the brightest mirrors that can be found. Not polished steel or silver, but glass ones, the backs coated with an amalgam of mercury. Such mirrors are made in Nuremburg and Venice but can be found in the houses of the wealthy almost anywhere in the known world.'

By now those who had remained in the doorway of the tent had turned back in and were listening to us.

'It would help too, if we had someone with a proper knowledge of the science of optics.'

And, of course, Peter cleared his throat. 'I am not myself an adept,' he said, 'but I have here,' and he tapped the bag he had been carrying since Easter, 'the investigations the great Roger Bacon made on the subject.'

Eddie turned to Sir Roger Croft. 'Get us a couple of mirrors, of the sort the chappie wants, there's a good fellow.'

'I know where I can lay hands on a pair,' said the knight. 'There's a cloth manufacturer in Hereford who trades with the Arnolfini family in Bruges. They sent over a pair as wedding presents when his son got married.'

'While we are waiting,' the fakir went on, 'we could initiate some simple experiments as precursors,' and he picked up one of the *kurundams*, held it point first towards one of the candles and moved it further and nearer. Presently we all gasped. From the pyramidal point furthest from the candle a narrow beam of bright light, not red as one would expect but green, appeared, and with almost no spreading at all linked the stone to a tiny spot of light six feet away on the canvas wall of the tent. Which began to smoulder.

'Light amplified by stimulated emission through a ruby,' said Peter, with awe.

The fakir frowned, as if the Friar had got something slightly wrong.

It took some doing, but it worked. It had never been done before. There was no possibility of a rehearsal or a trial. At sunrise the next morning it would have to work. And Nature, too, would have to co-operate. A river, a low hill to the east, which was behind us, they were given. What was not given, but could reasonably be expected, was a mist. At that time of year, on nights when there was no wind, there was almost always a mist, a fog even. And if there should not be, or if it was not of the substance the fakir wanted then fires burning green wood and wet dead leaves would be lit on the other side of the rise, to create a false mist. These, too, were prepared but in the event not needed.

But all this was as nothing compared to the calculations and brain-racking that the fakir and Brother Peter put into the application of the theories of optics Bacon had adumbrated in code, based on but taking far further the discoveries of his Arab predecessor Abū Yūsuf Ya' Qū' Ibn Ishāq ul-Kindī. Worse still was calculating the exact point at which the rising sun would be at the right height to make the projection they desired.

All was done in time, but only just. The mirrors, which were small, scarcely eighteen inches across within their carved and gilded frames, but very bright, were placed on scaffolding made from lances and ashpoles found in a nearby farm. The *kurundams* were mounted in front of them and tilted to what the fakir and Peter calculated would be the correct angles.

'Why three suns?' asked Prince Harihara.

'To represent the Trinity. The Three in One, the One in Three we are stupid enough to insist represents the godhead,' Brother Peter replied.

'How,' asked Eddie, 'will the sun shine on two mirrors at once, filling both with its light at the same time?'

This gave one or two who were there a moment's doubt – we could see it in their faces.

'By the same means,' said the fakir, with weary patience inflecting his words, 'that it casts a shadow from your body at the same times as it casts one from mine.'

'Ah. Yes. Of course. I see.'

But I doubted that he did.

It worked, all right. It worked. There was a mist. It hung in the tree-tops, grey like a wolf's pelt in the pre-dawn light. It became rosy then golden and . . . began to shift. But then the sun, a red disc beneath a bank of cloud, rose above it and the illusion was there, there for perhaps two minutes, but long enough.

The sun's rays hit the mirrors, were reflected back into the *kurundams*, which projected them as beams that spread enough to form red circles of light on the mist, just below the sun itself, giving an illusion of three suns not one. The army cheered, they'd been told to. Two lords, who had been about to lead their men across to the other side, reined in their horses and rather bashfully waited Eddie's command to charge. It came as the two lower suns faded. Pausing only to announce that from henceforth the sun in its glory, this sun of York, would be his personal badge and that he wanted a shield with the three suns on it prepared immediately, Eddie touched spurs to Genêt's flanks and trotted across the bridge to lead his men to victory.

The fakir looked around, touched fingertips to the bottom hem of his turban in the Allaha Ismahrlahdik. 'Light amplified by stimulated emission through *radiation*,' he said, over his shoulder, as he walked off down the reverse slope, away from the battle. We did not see him again.

'And that was the battle at which Owen Tudor and his son were taken?' I asked.

'That's right.'

'And Eddie had their heads chopped off that evening.'

'That, too, is right.'

'I should not think that endeared him to Uma.'

'Well. We shall see what she has to say about that.'

CHAPTER

FORTY-EIGHT

*T*he day's monsoon was over when we gathered again to hear Ali's account *of the last great battle, the one that finished the war. Uma and her two children arrived a few minutes later than she had promised, which irritated Ali a little. However, generally speaking he was now in a much better mood although the atmosphere was still humid, almost like a Turkish bath. The sun shone, the stones and flower-beds exhaled steam, the birds sang and flitted through it, the flowers opened, and the garden was filled with the most wonderful overpowering scents. The Burmese cat slept, stretched out in the shade.*

'I am sorry,' said Uma, as she handed her twins to their ayla, who took them into the shady back rooms to play, 'but they insisted I should buy them sherbets on the way.'

She took a seat next to Ali, and occasionally took his clawed left hand on to her knee and stroked it, but added little to his tale. Like me, she was there to listen.

Already a fortnight before the battle of the Three Suns in Splendour, the Queen's army had begun its march from the north. However, these huge armies of thirty, fifty thousand men, particularly if they have cannon with them, can only move a few miles in a day. Fifteen at the most, often as little as ten. It takes a lot of organising, too, to make sure that all are fed on the way and the usual practice, wherever the roads will allow it, is to split up into three columns moving by different routes, but always in touch with each other and ready to pull in together if their scurriers discover a large force of the enemy.

Feeding was not much of a problem once they were across the river Trent, which is taken as the natural border between north and south Ingerlond, and this war was in some ways becoming a conflict between north and south. At all events, once across it the Queen unleashed the hounds of war upon the land, famine, sword and fire, urging her men to loot and destroy, burn, pillage and rape their way forward: these were the lands whose men had filled the ranks of York at the battle of Northampton. But what she saved in money she lost in time, for her progress became even slower as her men became more preoccupied with destruction and theft: many it was said attempted to carry quite large items such as chests, plate and tools with them.

And, of course, it was the coldest time of year, the days only just beginning to lengthen, and each day time was needed to find food, light fires, cook, find warm lodging for the night, rape the women and slaughter the children.

Nevertheless, she was at St Alban's by the seventeenth of February. Warwick had already marched out with his army from London to confront her, and a battle followed, at first fought mainly in the streets. However, as the Queen's army took the upper hand, Warwick pulled back to defensive positions across the London roads with cannon and anti-cavalry devices in front of him, and a group of five hundred Burgundians armed with flaming arrows and handguns. But, of course, it began to snow heavily and yet again the cannon and guns failed those who had put their trust in them. More effective was a unit of crossbowmen, some of whose weapons were very large, capable of firing a bolt into a compact group of men that would transfix three or four on it before losing momentum.

Worse than the snow for Warwick was treachery. Ah! Treachery. One of the best captains of the time was a Sir Henry Lovelace. He had been a Yorkist, was captured at Wakefield, but escaped execution by swearing henceforth to fight for the Queen. The night before St Alban's he came into the Yorkist camp and swore to return to the Yorkist fold. However, he held back his troops until he saw how the Queen's army was gaining the upper hand when, instead of coming to Warwick's rescue, he reverted to the Queen and, just as Lord Grey had at Northampton, left a gap in Warwick's lines, through which the Queen's

men streamed. Warwick now realised that the battle was lost, sounded
the retreat, and managed to get clear with four thousand men.

King Henry, whom Warwick had brought with him to add credence
to his cause, was found beneath an oak tree, mumbling madly. However,
he seemed pleased to be reunited with his queen and putative son.

Next day, the heads of the nobler prisoners were lopped off in the
market-place, including those of the two lords whose duty had been to
protect the King. The Queen asked her son, 'Fair son, what death shall
these two knights die?'

'Let them have their heads taken off,' the eight-year-old replied, and
stayed to see it done.

It's very likely they lost their lives for carrying out their commission
too well. The Queen would have been happy to see the King, her
husband, chopped up in the battle, thereby leaving the way clear for
her monstrous son to rule with her as regent.

The way to London was now clear for her, but uncharacteristically she
hesitated, or her captains did on her behalf. The city, though vulnerable,
was for the most part Yorkist, having been taxed and bullied by the
Queen for far too long. It could defend itself against a siege, could cause
endless trouble if it let the army in but then refused to accommodate
it properly. Then news came that Warwick had met up with Eddie at
Abingdon and that was enough. A convoy of money and provisions
the Mayor had put together for the relief of the Queen's army at
St Alban's was seized by the citizens and disappeared. Negotiations
continued for a few days but, beset with massive desertions from her
starving northerners, the Queen withdrew first to Dunstable, a further
ten miles or so north-west, and finally to the north.

Having won a battle at Mortimer's Cross, and lost another at St
Alban's, the Yorkists, led by Eddie and Warwick, entered London in
triumph on the twenty-seventh of February.

Meanwhile, our purpose was to get home as quickly as possible, and
that meant finding a boat that would take us as far as the Mediterranean
and into Arab lands and civilisation. This we had decided on in preference
to making the trip back across France and north Italy to Venice – Prince
Harihara was in something of a depression about his brother and had
now developed a hate for this cold wet land we were in – well, we all
had: the joys of its spring and summer now seemed a long way off, and
somehow unlikely to return. He longed for his own country and was

ready to risk drowning on the seas for the sake of getting home a few weeks earlier.

I recall how, one night, just before we reached Oxenford where we left Brother Peter, the Prince in his melancholy speculated about the world we live on, with these distances in mind. We were in yet another hostelry at the time.

'You know,' he said, 'no one knows just how far away India and Vijayanagara are.'

Anish waited, not wishing to show by his expression what he thought of his master's sanity. I was less constrained. I was going through a bad time with the onset of these pains.

'Of course they bloody do,' I said, using an Inglysshe expression I had picked up. 'Give or take five hundred miles or so.'

But Brother Peter looked up from the soup he was eating, eyes shining with interest.

'We all know,' the Prince went on, 'that the world is round. A sphere, a globe. Right?'

We all nodded. Flat-earthers went out two thousand years ago – old Aristotle and his friends had seen to that.

'We don't know what the circumference of this globe is at its greatest girth, but we do know that the distance will be less according to how close to or distant we are from the part where the girth is greater.'

Anish was looking puzzled now. Brother Peter, who had often speculated along these lines, as indeed had Roger Bacon in his coded writings, now came to his rescue by picking up an apple. 'Look,' he said, 'if we are here,' and he poked it with his finger then picked up a knife and with the point made a tiny cross, 'and Vijayanagara is there,' he marked it on the other side, 'then it does not much matter if one goes east to get to Vijayanagara or west . . .'

'But,' said Prince Harihara, 'if it were *here* . . .' and he took the apple out of Peter's hand and marked it with a third cross just to the left of the first one, 'then everyone's been going the wrong way round. For all we know we're just, say, a week's sailing from home, if we go west rather than east.'

At this point another customer intruded, a small man with a beard whose tarred gaberdine suggested a seafaring man. He leant over us, took the apple. 'We're not fucking daft, you know. Not the way you are.'

'Who are we?' asked Peter, laying a restraining hand on Prince

Harihara's sleeve. The Prince was clearly annoyed to lose his apple and the centre of attention.

'Fucking sailors, of course. The fucking wind, four days out of five, blows from the fucking west, don't it? Even if you left on an east wind you'd be back home in a week on a fucking westerly. Like it or not . . .' and he took a noisy crunch out of the apple, which was sweet and crisp though it still smelt of the hay it had been laid up in.

'But,' said Brother Peter, in his gentle way, 'I have heard how if one goes further south, to the south of Spain, or better still the north-west coast of Africa, one finds almost constant winds blowing from the north-east. Los Alisios, they call them.'

'All right for fucking dagos and darkies,' said jolly Jack Tar, 'not much bloody use for us.'

The next day we said farewell to Peter at the gate of his friary. First, he gave us the pages of Bacon's writing to do with gunpowder and the casting of cannon. 'His secrets are in better hands with you. If this lot,' he meant the Inglysshe, 'get hold of them, then the Prime Mover alone knows what will happen to us all . . .'

'What was the main gist of these disclosures?' I asked, as quietly and politely as I could.

'Ah, dear Mah-Lo, I do sometimes wonder about your occasional curiosity, your willingness to be bored by me day after day. Is it really just generosity to an old man, or do you have another agendum?' Ali sipped his lemonade. 'Well, I'll tell you. There were three important things only. First, the best proportions in which to mix the ingredients. They are as follows. Split it into one hundred parts. Seventy-five should be saltpetre, fifteen charcoal, and ten sulphur. Not the sixty-six, twenty-three, eleven split now in general use. The second is more clever. To avoid the separation of the three constituents by shaking and settling, the art is to mix them thoroughly, then wet them to a paste, then let the paste dry out. The three parts will remain in granules, each granule containing all the ingredients in exactly the same distribution as they were. Three, a method for extracting saltpetre from rotting vegetation. There were other hints of smaller importance, which I won't bother you with, but I can say that in recent skirmishes with Bahmani troops, the artillery in the pay of the Vijayanagarans has outshot theirs by a hundred paces or more. No, that is all I am saying. You must let us bring our story to a conclusion. Then you may ask questions.'

Uma smiled sweetly at her hands, spread like a cup in her lap, and Ali went on.

As I say, perhaps the saddest moment on the trip for me was parting with Brother Peter, whose company I had shared now for more than a year. I tried to persuade him to stay with us, to come back to the lost city of paradise with us, heaven on earth, the City of Victory, Vijayanagara.

'Ali, I would like to, but however beautiful and wonderful it is, however gloriously content the inhabitants are, I would always be a stranger.'

'Peter, I have been a stranger wherever I am, all my life. It's no bad thing.'

'Precisely. You are used to it. But I am used to these two cloisters, my library, my fish-pond, my cat. I am used to the English countryside through which each summer I make my peregrinations and preach, using what I have thought out during the winter months. It's a routine, but sufficiently interesting not to be dull. I am too old to change it.'

We embraced, then he pulled back.

'I shall miss you, Ali. I have learnt much from you. Not least that across the world, amongst Muhammadans, Buddhists, Hindus, whatever, as well as Christians, there are people like us who have moved on to a more mature, wiser, more solemn religion based on being not becoming, living not dying, joy not pain. It is wonderful that this community exists, each . . .' he searched for the word '. . . atom in it separated from the rest, there are so few of us, but reaching out and touching, so one day we may envelop the world, which will become a better place as a result. Damn it, I'm sermonising.' And he embraced me again. 'Ali, thank you.'

He pulled the bell-rope that hung against the wall beside the outer double door. We heard the jangle distantly behind the walls.

'Be off with you now.'

I walked back to my friends, who had already crossed the rebuilt bridge. I turned once. Peter was still at the door, a familiar, short, dumpy figure. He waved, then reached up and gave the rope a second yank, more impatient than the first. The bend in the road and river took us out of sight.

Ali wiped a tear from his eye.

'The Bishop's men were waiting for him. They burnt him a month later, a week or so before we left.'

For a moment his garden seemed to hold its breath. Then the cat stirred, a bird flew across an angle from one eave to the other. The fountain began to tinkle again. Ali sighed, drew in a second breath and went on.

The first thing we did, once we got to London, was scout along the south bank to the east looking for a vessel that might take us to the north coast of Africa or, anyway, into the Mediterranean. Since we were now down to three people with little baggage this proved to be no great problem – we found a caravel taking on cloth and ingots of copper, preparing to sail in a day or two.

Very little problem? Baggage? That put the Prince instantly in mind of what he had forgotten for nine months – his damned crossbows. Anish and he had the first serious falling-out I had seen between them as they argued about whether or not the infernal engines had been left at Alderman Dawtrey's house or had gone with them to the Tower. It scarcely mattered: they were in neither place now. We spent a week looking for them, eventually tracing them to Clerkenwell Fields, outside the walls, where the army was camped, and there we found a group of soldiers being taught their management by a Genoese mercenary. There was no question of them being released: they had already proved their worth when the cannon failed at St Alban's.

What soon became clear was that Prince Harihara had no intention of leaving without them. We went to Baynard's Castle for an audience of Eddie, the King, already a changed man, not exactly haughty but busy, and the best we could get out of him was that Prince Harihara could have them all back just as soon as the Queen had been beaten, once and for all, scotched like a snake, stamped on like the poisonous spider she was. The army was to begin its move north in a day or two.

'That's all very well,' said the Prince, once we were well clear of Baynard's Castle and walking back down Thames Street, 'but supposing she wins? We're going north with them and that's final.'

Well, we did what we could to persuade him to write them off, but he'd have none of it. They were the nucleus of a unique collection, he said. Anish and I threatened to stay behind while he went after them, but when he said that he'd give what was left of our store of jewels, even the *kurundams*, to get them back, we thought it wisest to fall in with his wishes.

Which is why and how we got to be on the field of the most terrible battle I have ever seen. But, first, Uma must bring us up to date with what had been happening to her.

CHAPTER

FORTY-NINE

I was, you remember, at the cross in Market Square, Hereford, mourning my lost love, my poor dead love.

Eddie recognises me, of course, as readily as I recognise him.

'Let the dead bury the dead,' he says, and holds out a gauntleted hand towards me.

I look down at Owen's head. It's grey now, like lead, drained. The eyes are slits of white between almost closed lids. The hair seems thinner than I remember it when he lay on my breasts and I ran my fingers through it. The cold and the stiffness of death have twisted his lips into an obscene rictus. This is not Owen Tudor. This is a thing. Let them do with it whatever they want — it's not mine any longer. I blow out the last candle-flames, stand and suddenly feel the cold. I have a shawl which I pull round my shoulders — it's useless and I begin to shiver like an aspen leaf in a breeze.

I follow him a step or two, then turn and go the opposite way. One of the three women who helped me with the candles falls in with me and takes me to her house. Her name is Gwynnedd. She is the widow of a knight who died in an earlier battle. For safety and comfort she has chosen to dwell in town rather than out in the Marches where his small manor house had been in effect a fort.

She makes me eat some old bread warmed in hot milk and puts me in her bed. When she sees I will not sleep she comes and sits beside me.

'Why did you help me,' I ask, 'with the candles? And the other ladies too?'

Gwynnedd pauses, reaches out to a chest covered with an embroidered cloth, picks up a needlework ring and begins to sew as she speaks.

'Owen ap Maredudd ap Tewdyr was the Wizard. The King. The King of all Britain and the high priest of the old religion. He carried the most royal blood of any in these islands. He was descended in the direct line from the King of the first of our race, he who came with the bronze celt, the war-axe of our tribe, copper and gold. His name was Brutus and he was the grandson of Aeneas, the son of Priam of Troy, who founded the Roman race. Empires are in our blood.'

'Are you yourself of that blood, then?'

'Yes. A cousin.'

I look more closely at this woman, whom I had taken to be nothing out of the ordinary. Gwynnedd is of middling height, and at her age – in her late forties, I suppose – would not instantly attract attention, her face being lined with pain and grief lines, her breasts slack, her hips broad. But there is fire, passion there, and dignity too, the compact strength women have when there is not much left to do but hold on and help those who still must struggle with the tricks life, and men, play on us.

'And why are you so ready to help me? What you have done might well bring danger to you.'

'You are the Marry Gyp. We knew of you before you came. We have heard of your journeys round Coventry and your trials, even of your miracles, the stories of which are already much exaggerated.'

Here she gives a shy little smile, the conspiratorial smile small girls share when they know more than they are meant to know.

'Still, you are the Marry Gyp, and you have been Owen's lover. That is enough. But we hope, too, you might have been impregnated by him. If that is so then perhaps your child might take the place of that dull grandson of his and become the leader of the British nation, the peoples who live west of the Severn and the Dee.'

But here, as I explain to her, I have to disappoint her. Until now I have done those things women do to ensure conception cannot take place. The blood on my petticoats is not Owen's from where I had wiped my hands of it, as might be supposed, but menses just beginning to flow.

'Well, never mind. We already know, from casting runes, that you will make it possible that Owen's blood will flow in a line of monarchs. That much is certain. If you choose the destiny the goddess has prepared for you.'

I think this all through for a bit. Then with determination swing my legs off the bed.

'I'd better get back to Eddie, then, if I'm to have a say in how things turn out. You must help me.'

When I turned away, showing that I would not follow him, he walked on. I knew therefore that I must not pursue him. He must find me. For that to happen I must put myself in his way, but by such means as will make him think it is he who is the hunter.

This is not difficult to arrange. It is known Eddie will go as quick as may be to London, or rather St Alban's, to support Warwick, and that his first stop on the way will be Gloucester where more newly recruited troops wait to join him. There are two roads between Hereford and Gloucester, one by Ross-on-Wye and one by Ledbury. His army will split, and all we have to do is be sure we know which of the two he will take. Gwynnedd soon discovers he is going by Ross-on-Wye. She lends me a pony and her man to show me the way – I would say to look after me too, but he is fifty years old and can scarcely walk, though he can ride. Any man younger and fitter has already been pressed into the army.

We reach the forested hill that overlooks the river Wye above Ross, and I hide in a thicket where the old man ties me to a silver birch tree that grows amongst the brambles. Eddie, as befits a king, is riding at almost the front of his troops and we hear them clattering, thumping, trudging up the other side, the squeal of the cannon wheels and the carts not far behind. The old man lets the squadron of twenty knights in front of the King go past, then bursts out of the wood. Almost one of Eddie's minders chops his head off there and then, but stays his hand long enough.

'My mistress,' he screams, 'she is in the thicket. Even now three ruffians are raping her. Help, help!' and so forth.

Well, Eddie may be a king, but he's still a teenager. Spurs to Genêt's flanks, a leap over the ditch, his sword out, he almost gallops past me, but a low bough nudges the gold circle he now wears round his unvisored helmet, and he reins in for a moment.

'Help, help!' I call, and he hacks through the undergrowth and finds me. He looks down at me.

'So, Mistress Uma, you are not so proud now.'

'My lord, I never was,' I reply, letting him see my bosom, which I have left exposed as if my gown has been ripped from it, one breast bleeding a little from the bramble I have dragged across it. 'I was grieving.'

'Do you still grieve?'

'For Owen Tudor, no.'

'For whom, then?'

'For the death of chivalry that has left me thus bound in front of a youth who should know better.'

Well, he laughs at that. He knows it's trickery, but he remembers the ship from Calais to Dover and thence to London; he remembers the nights in Alderman Dawtrey's loft, and as his bodyguard rides up he leaps down and unties me, remarking that, with a little ingenuity, which he knows I have, I should have been able to free myself.

'Not, my lord, with those two ruffians molesting me.'

'Your servant said three,' and he laughs again.

That night, at Gloucester, we return again to what Lord Clifford and Lord Scales interrupted so annoyingly a year and a month ago.

I delight him. Oh, yes, I delight him. Were I a man and the memory of my dead lover so fresh in my mind I doubt I could so deceive him, but for a woman, as any whore will tell you, it is not a problem, and before long he is mine again.

My curiosity overcame me.

'Lady Uma,' I asked, 'just what means did you use to so ensnare a prince?'

She looked me coolly in the eye. 'Mah-Lo, those Ingerlonders know nothing of the many and varied delights that a woman can bring to a man in bed. All I had to do was suck his cock and stick my finger up his bum. And the one thing I was sure of, and it was part of my plan, was that once I was out of his life he would not wive until he had found a woman who would do as much.'

'And did he?'

'Of course. I do not need to be told these things, I know them. He married me in secret when I threatened to withhold these and other subtler delights. Once he's convinced himself I'm not coming back he'll do it again. I suspect she will be, or may already be, a certain Elizabeth Woodville, a widow of wonderful

beauty by their standards having hair like Welsh white gold. Since she is a commoner, and her family were slighted by both Eddie and Warwick when we were all in Calais, and she was widowed at St Alban's where her husband was killed fighting for the Queen, she will be trouble. Bad trouble.'

She said all this with a gleeful certainty.

'How can you be so sure?' Ali asked.

'Never mind.'

'And meanwhile you married him?'

'Why do you sound so incredulous?'

Once we reach London he installs me in Baynard's Castle, the large fortified house in the corner between the river and the west walls of the city, which his family have used for three decades and where he now lives like a prince, receiving embassies as if he is already crowned, remitting taxes and borrowing money instead from the burgesses, withdrawing privileges from their foreign rivals, and so on. He summons Parliament and they proclaim him King Richard the Second's rightful heir, declaring the three Henrys descended from John of Gaunt, Duke of Lancaster, all to be usurpers.

They want to crown him there and then, but this he refuses, though he goes to Westminster Abbey and sits on the throne while the regalia of kingship are carried before him. He will not take on the full panoply of monarchy until, he says, the death and desecration of his father are avenged.

I am known only to his intimates and soon I tire of being thus kept secret. I withdraw my favours, refuse to delight him with my tricks. He asks what I want. I tell him I desire to be acknowledged, I want to be his queen. He says he durst not do this until his enemies are vanquished for to do so would cost him the support of some of the most powerful magnates, the Earl of Warwick himself, perhaps. This, I say, I can understand, but for my own satisfaction, and safety too perhaps, he must marry me in secret.

But where? And who will perform the ceremony?

The answer is obvious. I have by then a couple of maids and I send one to Brother Abraham in the churches of St Benet Sherehog and St Pancras, and after a little to-ing and fro-ing it is all arranged. Brother Abraham unites us according to Christian and more ancient rites, on the holiest, most sacred spot in that city. We return to Baynard's Castle and there I remove the tampon of natural sponge, soaked in oil and vinegar . . .

'The children, twins, who are even now playing with their ayla in the back rooms while we converse here?'

'Yes, Mah-Lo. They were born in Egypt on our way home, as Ali will tell you.'

'So when King Edward dies, one of them should be King of Ingerlond.'

'It is not a destiny I would wish on anyone. But perhaps when those distant savages at the end of the world have civilised themselves, it will be an option their descendants might care to look at. Now, let me hurry on to the close of their story, for soon I must take them home.'

I go north with Eddie and the army. It is clear that before long there will be a battle. He fears for my safety, and it is almost the only sign he gives of having any doubt of the outcome. He leaves me in Pontefract Castle where I make an ally of a child of eight or nine, and I think I should tell you about him. For he, with Elizabeth Woodville, is a likely tool. Because of these two I am sure it will be the Tudors who will reign before long in Ingerlond.

Eddie has two younger brothers. He fears leaving them too far behind him: so many have changed sides during these wars, it must have crossed his mind that anyone back in London, hearing perhaps the Queen had gained a victory or even a lying rumour to that effect, might seek favour with her by having them murdered. They are left with me at Pontefract. One is twelve years old, a light-headed, chancy lad, easily swayed, called George. Forget him. It is the other whom I make my slave, who will revenge me for the death of Owen.

He is a twisted, warped boy, in mind as well as in body. He has one leg longer than the other, and something of a hunch on his back. I surmise that a lot of the time, maybe all the time, he is in pain. Such afflictions fester in a lad's soul. But he is also physically strong for his age.

On the day before the battle I meet them, during a brief warm sunny spell, in the castle garden.

George goes off on his own, tossing a ball and catching it in a cup, which seems to please him. The younger sits on a bench and I sit beside him. Presently I notice a bag hanging from his belt. It squirms and flicks, as if something is alive and kicking inside it.

'What have you got there?' I ask.

'A baby rabbit,' he replies. 'My dog caught it this morning. They are so stupid when they are young – it thought my dog wanted to play with it and it would not run away.'

Petrified, I think, but do not say so. 'What are you going to do with it?'

'Pull its legs off. Maybe first its ears.'

'You won't kill it first.'

'No. Why should I?'

I shrug. He senses a dare in the air.

He pulls out the rabbit and does exactly what he has boasted he will do. He takes an ear in each of his fists, and yanks them in opposite directions, each held in his small fist. The rabbit screams. What the boy is doing requires a great deal of effort. At last one ear comes away in his hand. He fears the coney will escape. So now he takes its hind legs and yanks them apart. I suspect he shows some interest in the beast's genitalia. Soon he has it in several pieces, some of which, the larger ones, still flap as if there were life in them.

'This is no worse than the things the public executioner does to traitors,' he says.

'You look askance, Mah-Lo. Have I upset you? Remember, I am Kali as well as Parvati.'

And suddenly this normally beautiful woman used the finger and thumb of each hand to pull down the corners of her eyes and stretch her mouth into a hideous grimace. Then she stuck out her tongue as broad and flat as she could make it and waggled it furiously. I flinched, she laughed, and all was back to normal.

'So,' I say to him, when he has kicked away the bloody remains, 'your big brother is king. Would you like to be king?'

He looks at me, all eyes, and plays with the ring on his little finger. 'Of course. When Eddie dies I shall be king.'

'Even if George is still alive?'

'I . . . doubt he will be.'

'You will be king even if Eddie has children by whomever becomes his queen?'

He shrugs.

'I will be king,' he says.

A cloud is over the sun now and suddenly the air is chill. I stand. 'What is your name?' I ask.

'Richard,' he says.

I feel his power in my diaphragm, little boy though he still is. I look at the bloody remains of the rabbit. 'An omen,' I say, and ruffle his hair, thinking, the Inglysshe will surely put Owen's grandson on the throne once they've had enough of this monster.

'Don't do that!' he commands. Then he repeats: 'Yes. I will be king.'

CHAPTER

FIFTY

D ear Cousin
    Owing to circumstances beyond our control, we were
    taken back to the north of Ingerlond, to a small place
called Towton where we witnessed . . .

*'Hang on a minute, why does he say that? Why does he say "Owing to
circumstances beyond our control"?'*
'He could not admit he was in pursuit of his beloved crossbows.'
'Why not?'
*'We've been into this. The Emperor has a Buddhist monk whom he consults
on all spiritual matters. As a result he does not approve of Harihara's hobby. He
expects his relations to follow his example . . .'*

. . . where we witnessed the horror of a full battle between large
armies. In order that we may learn as much as we can from this
experience it is my intent to record here a full account of this
terrible affair.

Both hosts were huge. The Queen's army numbered perhaps
fifty thousand and was led by the Duke of Suffolk, though
many great magnates and lords had also brought their powers.
Men had been recruited from right across the north of England.
King Edward's force was smaller, perhaps forty thousand men. In
all, this equals about one in fifty of the entire population. Both

sides had cavalry in large numbers, men-at-arms and archers. King Edward's also had a small contingent of crossbowmen, some of whose weapons were of the highest order. And both sides fielded cannon and men with handguns called ribaudkins.

The Queen's army was based in York, the largest city in the north of the country, where she remained with her evil son and mad husband. King Edward advanced up the road from London. Some twenty-four miles or so south of York the London road has to cross a small but militarily important river called the Aire at a settlement called Ferrybridge. The bridge was destroyed by a large force led by Lord Clifford, whose father had been killed by Edward's father, and who had himself killed Edward's brother after the battle of Wakefield.

The Yorkists attempted to build a floating bridge but were attacked by the Queen's men. There was fierce fighting and Edward showed his generalship to good effect. Remember, he was only eighteen, the age of Alexander when he won his first victories. He poured reinforcements into the battle for the bridge when a less determined commander might have given up, and sent a flanking wing to the west to the next crossing upriver at a place called Castleford. Faced with this threat Clifford withdrew into a marsh. The fighting here was fierce. Exhausted, Clifford briefly removed the lower part of his helmet for greater ease and comfort and was struck by an arrow. He died later in great agony, which pleased King Edward.

This all happened on the twenty-eighth day of March in terrible snowstorms and bitter cold.

The Queen's advance guard now fell back and met up with the main army, which had reached Tadcaster, some ten miles south-west of York. A mile or so south of Tadcaster they took up a defensive position. Near the village of Towton the Tadcaster–Ferrybridge road winds along higher ground but keeps a more or less constant north–south direction. To the west of it the land drops in a horseshoe declivity to a meadow, several hundred paces wide, and on the west side to the winding river known as Cock Beck. The banks of the beck ('beck' means narrow river) are wooded, quite deeply in places. The more southerly of these woods fills an ox-bow of the river and is called Castle Hill Wood;

the more northerly, where the valley narrows and its sides become steeper, Renshaw Wood.

These woods played an important part in the battle. Somerset hid several thousand men in Castle Hill Wood from which they emerged to attack the Yorkist left flank and rear at a crucial time, nearly winning the battle for the Queen. Renshaw Wood, and the ravine it filled, initially protected his left and rear, but eventually became a trap where thousands were slaughtered.

Dear cousin, do not imagine there is anything grand in the landscape I have described. The hills are low, at most a hundred feet above the plain, and, except down to Renshaw Wood, not steep; they are turfed, support sheep; there are no outcrops of rock; the trees are small, rarely more than forty feet high and mostly as little as fifteen or twenty but with thickets of thorny brambles on their edges.

Edward could possibly have joined battle on that late afternoon, but five thousand of his men, under the ailing Duke of Norfolk, were a day's march away and he decided to wait through the night.

This brought us to the day the Christians call Palm Sunday, which commemorates Jesus's triumphal entry into Jerusalem five days before he was crucified. This year it fell on the twenty-ninth of March. Usually, I am told, one can expect reasonably clement weather by this time of year, a week past the equinox, with small yellow trumpet-shaped flowers blooming in fields and hedgerows, and some trees beginning to green up. There was little sign of that this year, and although the grass was green and lush, it was bitterly cold with a severe snowstorm blowing in from the south-east through most of the day.

The armies were positioned just within lethal arrow-shot of each other, that is, about two hundred and fifty paces. Shortly after daylight was established, but with driving snow and poor visibility, Lord Fauconberg on King Edward's left, facing north, ordered his archers forward and commanded them to let loose one flight of arrows. I have already described to you the power and deadliness of these missiles. At a distance curved, well-visored helmets and breastplates will turn them, but chain-mail or unvisored helmets are no protection. At close quarters they will pierce steel plate. On this occasion, this one flight of perhaps five thousand arrows caused the Queen's archers great distress, and they loosed off salvo after salvo in return, shooting at will, until their quivers were almost empty.

However, because of the driving snow, their arrows fell short by forty yards and because they were blinded by the snow they could not see that this was so. Lord Fauconberg now ordered his archers forward and at ever closer quarters they loosed off their arrows into the Queen's army, replenishing their stock from the arrows of their enemies, which strewed the grass. Lord Northumberland, commanding for the Queen in that area, now ordered his men-at-arms to attack rather than remain at the mercy of this hail of arrows. Fauconberg's archers fell back through the ranks of the men-at-arms, and hand-to-hand fighting was now joined.

In spite of the initial success of Lord Fauconberg's archers the Queen's army, by sheer weight of numbers, began to get the better of what was essentially an even battle. It was extremely savage. Both sides had sworn to kill all nobles and gentlemen they might take – this had already become common practice. But Edward had also issued an order that no commoners who surrendered or fell wounded should be spared either. There was a sense that these wars had gone on long enough and should be ended on that day.

Men fought until they fell wounded. Or merely fell. This was the common fate of every loser in what was basically a series of single or almost single combats, one against one, two against one, two against two: the combinations constantly shifted and gave the impression that at the point of contact a large body of men fought a large body of men. But essentially they were single combats. This gave the advantage to the side that could field the most men who were fit, had good arms and armour, who believed in the profit they would gain by winning, who had the requisite skills to a high degree. Now, these wars had been going on for some years and themselves followed a hundred years of fighting against the French. Both armies therefore had a large nucleus of professional, trained combatants who, over a series of engagements, had put together the arms they used most effectively and the armour that fitted them.

They were encased in armour from head to foot, from rounded, visored helmets to steel-plated boots. Many did not carry shields for a shield is cumbersome, leaves one side unprotected, and occupies a hand that might otherwise join its brother to wield a sword five feet long and a foot wide at the quills, or a double-headed axe, or a mace with spikes or chain and ball, or a pike with blade, point and hook.

There were men on horseback too, but the horses tired easily under such a weight of armour, over rough ground, and were vulnerable to archers. The commander of a company of men-at-arms, whom he had probably recruited himself, remained mounted so he and his standard could be seen, and he might have mounted men around him, squires and relations who would not only protect him but serve as messengers to and from the overall commander of that part of the field. For the rest, the cavalry rarely charged in formation: stalwart infantry, if holding ground protected by stakes or firmly held pikes, could always turn them. However, the cavalry came into its own in the pursuit of a beaten enemy, to charge in surprise the flank of a body of men-at-arms already pressed from the front, and so forth.

We should bear all this in mind when we consider how to cope with the Bahmani cavalry. Well-trained and -armed infantry may be a better solution than attempting to counter horsemen with horsemen.

Back to the mêlée. Few men-at-arms were killed outright in hand-to-hand fighting – the armour saw to that – but any man-at-arms who was beaten to the ground by the force and weight of blows on his armour, or slipping in the snow and blood, was in mortal danger. His fate now depended on the success or failure of his companions. If they were winning, moving forward pace by pace, they might pass over him and the ranks behind would bring him succour, quite often simply a matter of getting him to his feet and pushing him back into the fight. If, however, his side was slipping back he would soon find himself amongst his enemies, whose first instinct would be to continue to batter him with their heaviest blows, denting his armour and crushing his body inside it. A few yards on, men would risk the time taken to loosen his armour in his groin or armpit and stab him with a dagger, or thrust one through his slitted visor. Once dead he was stripped of his armour and anything of value he might have on his person, either there and then or when the battle was over, and thrown into a gravepit along with hundreds, thousands of others.

You will understand from this process that all men-at-arms going into a battle knew they faced one of two fates depending on whether their side or the other gave ground first. To give ground was to invite defeat and death. Fear of losing was a motive as great or greater for fighting with the utmost savagery as a desire to win. Once a sense grew within a body of men that ground was being lost and that therefore a fall meant almost certain death, the desire to turn and run, ahead of one's fellows, became overwhelming. But before that happened you fought like a mad devil to forestall it.

However, two other factors delayed this catastrophic moment. First, reputation. To be known as one of the first to flee was a terrible dishonour, leading to possible punishment, and certain ostracism for a lifetime, a loss of livelihood in the army and even out of it, the scorn of men and women alike for ever. And there was not much point in fleeing unless one was the first to do so . . .

The second reason for not running lay in the nature of these cases of armour. Once inside them, and especially once inside the visored helmet, one became an automaton, a thing without conscience, pity or restraint, a machine fighting machines whose faces one could not see. Once the battle madness had taken hold, one did not stop but went on, kill, kill, kill until either one was killed or there were none left in front to fight.

This is very different of course from the way our Dravidians behave on a battlefield. In scant armour and with physiques better adapted to running than wielding huge and heavy weapons, with families who depend on them to till the rich land behind them, they find it too easy to retreat.

So, this is the sort of fighting that was taking place along the seam of blood between the two armies, terror, triumph and above all desperation, sewing them together.

Two separate movements of the Queen's troops now had an accidental but profound effect on the outcome . . .

Eddie. He was in the centre and as he saw the Queen's army marching in a huge solid phalanx towards him he must have felt a moment of doubt, of fear. Until the old Duke of Norfolk came up, his was the smaller army. The Queen's army had won the

last two major engagements at Wakefield and St Alban's, and at
Northampton the numbers had been two to one in favour of the
Yorkists. Anyway, young man as he was, he pushed up his visor
so it looked like a giant beak over his head, and hacked along the
line in the rapidly shrinking gap between the armies. Fine snow
was swirling about him, beginning to settle on the grass.

'My lords,' he shouted, above the jangle of his armour and the
thud of Genêt's hooves, 'you're here because you want me to be
your king. You're here because for sixty years Albion has been
ruled by cruel usurpers. I am the heir. I am the Plantagenet. Fight
for me today to lift this curse from the soil of Albion, and if you
do not believe my cause is right then for God's sake go . . .'

It had an effect. The front ranks, mostly filled with nobles, gave
a cheer and pressed forward. At that moment Genêt stumbled a
little, perhaps hit in the buttock by a Lancastrian arrow, Eddie
heaved on the reins, got him upright but still thrashing about,
turning and twisting. He drew his sword, slipped to the ground
and handed the reins to the ostler who followed him.

'Come on lads,' he shouted, 'today your king fights on the
ground beside you, and I will live or die with you. May I rot
in hell if you see me rehorsed to flee the field. When I ride again
it will be through the gates of York . . .' And he gave his sword
a sort of flourish and, pulling down his visor, turned to face the
Queen's army, that was now only fifty paces away and all bellowing
'Henry, King Henry!'

'Where were you in all this?' I asked.

*'On the Yorkist right, hanging a little back but half way up the slope
towards the road that ran along the hill, we had the cannon just above
and ahead of us. It was a good place to see what was happening . . .'*

'Ah, the cannon. What happened with them?'

*'Usual story. Filthy weather, driving snow, the buggers didn't work.
But they had some effect.'*

'How was that then?'

*'The Queen's left were coming in across the slope which was difficult
anyway, and all the time they were looking up the hill into the muzzles
of the guns. They could see how they were lined up, how another fifty,
forty, twenty, ten yards would bring them into their line of fire. They*

hung back. Who wouldn't. It was the beginning, the seed of the end for the Queen's army.'

'How so?'

'Hang on a bit and I'll tell you.' He cleared his throat. 'Fucking, excuse my Inglysshe, fucking monsoon always leaves me full of phlegm . . .

'For the next three hours or more,' he went on, 'it was just simply the foulest sort of fighting I've ever seen . . .'

'I'm sorry, but could you explain why you were there?' I asked.

'I told you. We were there to get back the Prince's crossbows.'

'But why in that part of the field?'

'Because that's where the crossbows had ended up. They were still in their cases . . . the troop with them had got lost and arrived up the road from Ferrybridge just before the battle started. The Prince spotted their arrival and took us all over to them. He offered the Genoese Sergeant in charge a handful of rubies, almost the last we had, if he'd keep them in their cases. Can I go on now?'

'Of course.' Ali returned to the papers in front of him.

Soon inside every armour casing along that seam there was blood, crushed bones, urine, faeces, fear and intolerable pain. For all the din of clashing metal, the shouts and war-cries of those behind, the only audible sounds within all those shells of metal will often have been the howls of pain of those who wore them, until it would be almost a relief to go down. Imagine the darkness inside, the slit to peer through, or a sieve of tiny holes, the confusion of shapes outside, the weight, the shock as an axe or mace thudded into you, even the cold. It was close to freezing, the temperature when water turns to ice and metal burns almost as badly as when it is hot. And then the panic when your knees begin to go, or the sudden stab of fear when a blow sends you flat on your back as helpless as an upturned beetle.

We saw some pretty foul things you know. Two men hauling at the leg armour of a fallen knight and it comes away taking the leg with it, they up-end the boot of metal and tip out blood and shit. The helmet off another reveals he's drowned in his own vomit. Remember, on both sides no prisoners, no ransoms, so any extra you get from owning a body is what you can find on it, a ring or two mashed in with the finger bones, a holy medal on a gold chain crushed between steel and ribs.

Between the fallen bodies in their twisted cages of scrap metal the black soil, glistening with tiny crystals of snow, was churned up with blood so one's boots stuck and squelched in it. Bit by bit, very slowly, perhaps at the rate of a yard every quarter of an hour, it became clear the Yorkists were losing ground. You see, they did have fewer men on the ground, and as the front men of both lines fell, the Queen's were replaced more quickly, and there was a greater press of men behind, pushing them on. But all the time the Yorkists knew that if only they held on five thousand more would be joining them along the road that ran along the ridge to their right, at least before nightfall, if not earlier. Maybe the Queen's generals knew this too, because just when all seemed in the balance they launched an attack led by the Duke of Somerset, he who had held the castle of Guisnes in the Calais Pale when we first arrived, on the Yorkists' left, coming out of the wood that lay in the oxbow of Cock Beck.

The first thing Edward did was commit his reserve to shore up his left. Much to his chagrin they were driven off and pursued up the beck in a southerly direction by the Queen's reserve cavalry, neither group being seen again. Many thought Edward was now lost but he so encouraged his men, fought with them so bravely, and was so skilful at bringing in fresh troops under their lords at points where they were needed, that his line held.

Moreover, at this point he behaved like a true general – the young Alexander could not have done better. He knew that the funda-mental thing was to keep his line straight. Any bulge or indenta-tion would cause a weakness. The powers on his left were dropping back to face Somerset on their flank so somehow he must bring up his right to straighten the line. The Queen's army was already weakest on that side, because of the slope and the threat of the cannon – if he could only push them back another fifty yards, his line would hold.

He was on Genêt again, all that 'not mounting until he was in York' was flannel, of course, and he knew it was important enough to make sure it was got right. In short, he came galloping over to us, in person, reined in with a spatter of snow and mud that splattered Ali in his good eye, and looked down at me.

'Hurry-Hurry,' he cried, 'now's your chance to do a chap a favour and pay me back for all the kindnesses I've shown you.' He hurried on, perhaps forestalling any crude calculation we might want to make. 'Be a good chap and get those crossbows out, and let my men have a crack at those bastards over there.'

I did not like to admit that I had already paid the sergeant to keep the crossbows cased. These were not crude things to be used in a battle, they were elegant, crafted, works of art made to grace the formality and style of a properly organised hunt, but Eddie muttered something about guts for garters and having our balls off, and anyway the men who had been carrying them were readier to obey their putative king than the darky cove who kept getting in the way.

It took ten minutes or more to get them uncased, the right bolts assigned to the right engines, and all pointing in the right direction, during which the Queen's power in front of us, perhaps heartened by the success on the further flank, or guessing at last that the cannons were not firing today, were pushing harder than before.

There was a problem: the line of Yorkists, some five hundred of them, between the crossbows and the enemy. Eddie got in amongst them, got some to lie down, others to run for it before he himself, still riding Genêt, got out of the way. By now I had got into the spirit of the thing: I stood at the end of the line of crossbows, my previous collection of bird-shooters and crocodile killers, drew my scimitar, held it above my head, and at a nod from Eddie brought it down.

Some bows clicked, some clanged. Some bolts whistled, some screamed. A lord leading the enemy took a tiny bolt right through the slitted visor and in the eye. The largest bolt, fired from the monster that had to be mounted on a man's back, took two Yorkists from behind and skewered them to the two Lancastrians in front of them. After that they fired at will until the enemy broke, scattered and scampered down the hill.

Ali looked up from the Prince's manuscript. 'But not,' he said, 'before one of them had managed to trip Eddie, and threaten his life with a broadsword. The distance was not great and I was by his side in no time with my little stiletto fumbled out from under my furs, cape and loin-cloth. Trained by the followers of The Old Man of the Mountains I knew exactly what to do with it, even without the aid of hashish, and I fiddled the point between his third and fourth ribs. Eddie rewarded me later with a farmstead in Thorney Hill in Hampshire, but since it was reputed to be on poor soil and with few inhabitants I never bothered even to visit it.'

And screwing up his good eye he went back to what he had been reading.

Thus, by these events on both wings, the whole battle was skewed from an east–west line to one that ran from north-east to south-west with the ridge and the road in Yorkist hands. When, a little later, Norfolk's men arrived along the road from the south they found themselves on the Queen's army's flank and cut off their retreat to Tadcaster and York by the road. The only way to go when they broke was into the Renshaw Wood and the ravine and these created a terrible bottle-neck.

The river was no longer a brook but a torrent, fast-flowing and filling the floor of the ravine, as the snow of two days, which never settled properly but ran off as soon as it hit the grass, poured into it.

Trapped in the trees, thickets and water and soon by those who tripped and fell and could not get up again, men were slaughtered in their thousands, many falling at the hands of their own people who slew them from behind in their desperation to get clear. The water ran red with blood and indeed the mightier river Wharfe, into which the Cock Beck emptied, ran with blood all through the next day.

The sum of all those fighting that day was reckoned at ninety thousand. All in all twenty-eight thousand men were butchered and maybe half as many again were wounded and died later. We were told it was the biggest battle ever fought in Ingerlond, never as many killed. And I doubt if these numbers will ever be equalled on Inglysshe soil.

And for what? For religion, to impose one set of beliefs on another – the most common cause for such killing fields? No. So one nation could conquer and take over the land of another – the second most common cause? No. For booty, loot, gold, slaves, to take back to one's homeland? No. But simply so that one man could be king rather than another, to rule in the same way and under the same laws. For two men to fight for such a prize is not a wonder, but that they should be capable of getting a nation into arms, father against son, brother against brother, for so feeble a reason, is indeed a wonder. Whatever else can explain this phenomenon one factor must be present. These Inglysshe, or at any rate a great many of them, enjoy fighting. It's as simple as that.

Silence spread around us. Then there was a sudden flurry down by the pool. Ali's cat had caught a small frog. Hobbling and swinging about after her, Ali shouted and swore at her, hit out at her with his stick until she dropped it and leapt into the cardamom tree, snarling and spitting back at him. The frog now sat frozen with terror on a coping stone below. Ali picked it up, held it gently in the palm of his hand. Struggling to get his breath back he said:

'She looks all right . . .'

And he took it back to the edge of the pool. It leapt, plop, back into the water. Ali lifted his cat down and soon they were friends again, she purring in his lap.

'Is that the end of the story?' I asked.

'Not quite,' Uma murmured. 'You see I too was there at the end. What happened was that that younger brother of Eddie's, Richard, bribed an ostler and got a pony which he rode to the battlefield. I followed him. It was dusk when I found him. He was going through the wood searching out the Queen's men who still lived inside their boxes of iron. When he found one who did he fiddled the point of his poniard through the man's visor, searching for an eye and when he found it he rammed it home. This is a boy of eight, you know? A boy who will be king until Owen Tudor's grandson kicks him out.'

'There was a coronation too, before we left,' Ali added. 'In the middle of June. Gross business. Very barbaric. Long ceremony in Westminster Abbey with wailing monks and braying brass, endless business with anointing oil, a big jewelled crown, sceptres, globes, whatall. And afterwards absurdly huge feasts with barrels of wine and beer, lewd dancing, wild extravagance in clothes and jewellery, much of it sold by us, and mass executions carried out in public. In the middle of all this Eddie made our Prince a knight, for his help with the crossbows. A Knight of the Garter. Big deal. You had to buckle a strip of velvet just below the knee and wear a star made out of cheap little diamonds. It's meant to be the highest order he could receive, but the Prince now keeps the doings in a box with a few other oddments he picked up in Ingerlond, as souvenirs. After that we came home.'

It was time to go. Ali was tired. The sun was already beginning its swift fall into the Arabian Sea. Uma was anxious to get her children to bed. But I knew I would not be back and I wanted the last ends of the story tidied up.

'You got back safely?'

'Clearly.'

'And with the military expertise the Prince had gone for?'

'Oh yes. I suppose so. It didn't interest me greatly. But Bardolph Earwicca is now the Emperor's master of ordnance, and we also brought back four other youngsters, a knight, a couple of men-at-arms, and an archer, who professed *themselves at a loose end now the wars were over and were anxious to travel. They have settled in well and are retraining the army.'*

'Anish?'

'He's all right. Still Prince Harihara's Chamberlain as far as I know.'

There was a silence for a moment or two, which I broke.

'And you Ali. What did you bring back? Apart from a pension which seems adequate.'

'A more certain conviction than ever, maybe, that the Old Man of the Mountain had it right: Nothing is true. Everything is possible. Nothing matters. No. That's not all.'

He stood and turned away, but he could not disguise the slight break in his voice.

'From the best friend I ever had I learnt a better way of looking at things: that it is no sad truth that this should be our home. Were it but to give us simple shelter, simple clothing, simple food, adding the lotus and the rose, the apple and the cherry, it would be a fit home for mortal or immortal man.'

Later that evening I went down to the quay just as the sun was making its swift descent into the ocean. I would be leaving Mangalore and the Malabar coast in the morning aboard a Chinese trading junk on which I had booked a passage, taking my Dravidian wife with me. We would be heading south, round Sri Lanka and back to civilisation. But at that moment, looking west, the offing was barred by a blank bank of clouds, and the tranquil waterway leading to the uttermost ends of the earth flowed sombre under an overcast sky — it seemed to lead into the heart of an immense darkness.

POSTSCRIPT

A year later Mah-Lo presented himself and his account of Ali ben Quatar Mayeen's adventures to the court of the Ming Emperor Chêng-Hwa in his capital Cambaluc. In his preamble he said that while the Vijayanagaran empire's army had recently undergone a radical transformation the reforms were all made with defence rather than expansion in mind. The defences of fortresses had been improved to withstand sieges supported by gunpowder; they had their own way of making gunpowder which was better than anyone's apart from the Chinese; they were training heavy infantry to withstand cavalry. It was Mah-Lo's opinion that with these improvements they would be able to withstand Muslim invasions for the foreseeable future but they presented no threat to Chinese expansion or trade.

Looking further afield, to the other side of the world, it was his conclusion that none of the European kingdoms need be considered an immediate danger to the Chinese apart possibly from the Portuguese. And even the Portuguese, it seemed, were more interested in building up a maritime trading empire based on enclaves of merchants rather than military domination.

However, in the long term, he had no doubt that eventually the Inglysshe could become a problem. If Ali was right in his depiction of this island race, once their internal disputes were settled Mah-Lo feared they could well become a problem for the whole world. Their history, particularly the Norman Conquest and its aftermath, had developed a set of contradictory characteristics which gave them an edge over all the other peoples he had encountered in all his wanderings.

'They are,' he told us, 'a nation of individuals who yet can combine and behave with ferocious bravery under leaders they respect; they are skilful and ruthless traders with few natural assets of their own to exploit; they are foolhardy sea-farers; they are inordinately arrogant; they are ruthless, unforgiving, cruel enemies. Unfettered by morals or a common religion they take an empirical, pragmatic view of life, adapting their beliefs to circumstances, though always favouring an approach which leaves each individual the captain of his own soul.

'Ali once heard an Ingerlonder say: "I do not tell others how to live and I do not expect others to tell me."'

Mah-Lo continued: 'They enjoy and even live for camaraderie, the company of their fellows, physical prowess, hedonistic if simple enjoyment shared with others, strong drink and rough, speedily concluded sex. They have an incredible capacity to suffer pain for a short term, and will face death willingly. But they will not put up with pain or toil as a life-choice. They hate boredom.

'They will cheerfully accept individuals of other creeds and races as individuals, especially if they take a personal liking to them, while continuing to despise all foreigners in general.

'They are mad,' Mah-Lo concluded. 'One day they will conquer the world.'

There was a moment's silence, then the Grand Chamberlain made a dismissive gesture with his long-nailed fingers.

'But not China,' he said.

'No,' Mah-Lo agreed. 'Probably not China.'